DAWN OF WAR: ASCENSION

FOLLOWING THE CATASTROPHIC losses during the Tartarus campaign, Captain Gabriel Angelos journeys to the planet of Rahe's Paradise in a desperate attempt to recruit new warriors into the Blood Ravens Space Marines.

However, once there, he discovers an archeological dig that could challenge all he thought he knew about the origins of the Blood Ravens. Under scrutiny from the Adepta Sororitas and under attack from his old nemesis, the eldar Farseer Macha, Gabriel is unwittingly threatening the resurrection of something ancient and terrible from both his and the eldar's past!

As the fleets clash above the planet's surface and all-out war is unleashed around them, Angelos and his allies must discover the secrets of the past, and it is a revelation that could destroy them all.

Pulse-pounding action and adventure, based on the smash hit game from THQ, this is destruction on a planetary scale!

A WARHAMMER 40,000 NOVEL

DAWN OF WAR: ASCENSION

C S Goto

For Ckrius - If you think it can't get any worse, you're completely wrong.

Based on characters created by: Lucien Soulban, Jay Wilson, Raphael van Lierop, Josh Mosquiera.

A BLACK LIBRARY PUBLICATION

First published in Great Britain in 2005 by
BL Publishing,
Games Workshop Ltd.,
Willow Road, Nottingham, NG7 2WS, UK.

10 9 8 7 6 5 4 3 2 1

Cover illustration by Neil Roberts.

A CIP record for this book is available from the British Library.

ISBN 13: 978-1-84416-285-7
ISBN 10: 1-84416-285-0

Distributed in the US by Simon & Schuster
1230 Avenue of the Americas, New York, NY 10020, US.

Printed and bound in Great Britain by
Bookmarque, Surrey, UK.

See the Black Library on the Internet at
www.blacklibrary.com

Find out more about Games Workshop
and the world of Warhammer 40,000 at
www.games-workshop.com

IT IS THE 41st millennium. For more than a hundred centuries the Emperor has sat immobile on the Golden Throne of Earth. He is the master of mankind by the will of the gods, and master of a million worlds by the might of his inexhaustible armies. He is a rotting carcass writhing invisibly with power from the Dark Age of Technology. He is the Carrion Lord of the Imperium for whom a thousand souls are sacrificed every day, so that he may never truly die.

YET EVEN IN his deathless state, the Emperor continues his eternal vigilance. Mighty battlefleets cross the daemon-infested miasma of the warp, the only route between distant stars, their way lit by the Astronomican, the psychic manifestation of the Emperor's will. Vast armies give battle in his name on uncounted worlds. Greatest amongst his soldiers are the Adeptus Astartes, the Space Marines, bio-engineered super-warriors. Their comrades in arms are legion: the Imperial Guard and countless planetary defence forces, the ever-vigilant Inquisition and the tech-priests of the Adeptus Mechanicus to name only a few. But for all their multitudes, they are barely enough to hold off the ever-present threat from aliens, heretics, mutants – and worse.

TO BE A man in such times is to be one amongst untold billions. It is to live in the cruellest and most bloody regime imaginable. These are the tales of those times. Forget the power of technology and science, for so much has been forgotten, never to be re-learned. Forget the promise of progress and understanding, for in the grim dark future there is only war. There is no peace amongst the stars, only an eternity of carnage and slaughter, and the laughter of thirsting gods.

PROLOGUE

BEGINNINGS SWIRL INTO *the forgotten past, like ideas fad-ing into the inconstant oceans of memory. They swim, free-floating on the cusp of the empyrean, flickering in and out of reality, as though prodding at the consciousness of a submerged mind. Without warning – or with warn-ings so subtle that they pass as mere comets' tails or clouds of burning gas – an old beginning can push itself out of forgetfulness and cast itself into the glare of a new sun, dragging itself out of the oceans of darkness and into the light once again.*

There are but few whose thoughts sense the eddies and dances of moments gone by, and fewer still whose souls sail the very brink of the abyss from which the ghosts of beginnings and ends emerge into our world. And those few are both the best and the worst of us, for there is nothing hidden to them in the great expanse of time. But even the greatest of them is not always free to choose the sea-lanes on which their visions might sail.

The future is no different from the past. It is nothing more than a beginning yet to come, and it curdles in the endless ocean of time, riddling the depths of the invisible realms with immaterial phantasms. It is the idea of a current and the suggestion of a storm; it is the gathering cloud that persuades a sailor to drop anchor, to head for land, or to brace for the coming of hell. But not every wisp of vapour births a maelstrom, and not every sailor looks up to heaven.

The future grows from myriad beginnings, but each of those beginnings also have a beginning of their own – an infinity of regressions back to The Beginning, before which an origin was not even a word and the future was an unbounded explosion of light. It was not a moment or an event, but a tear in the very fabric of our universe, through which the empyrean and the material realm could spill and mingle. Before the tear, there was nothing but darkness or perhaps nothing but light, and from it was born reality itself.

The Old Ones told of a time after The Beginning when an Ancient Enemy emerged from the hearts of a thousand suns, feeding on light, drinking the very life of the galaxy. These glittering beings were born entirely into the material realm, and they were its undisputed lords – commanding the very stars themselves. But mastering the materium and conquering the galaxy were not the same thing, and the Old Ones confronted this Ancient Foe by surfing the tides of the immaterium, drawing ineffable power from realms incomprehensible to the star gods, realms swimming with the unformed and raw powers of daemons and gods.

I have heard legends that this was the time when daemons first dragged themselves into existence, clawing their way through the rift between realms, salivating at the scent of life on the other side. And I have also heard that eldar more ancient even than Asurmen himself were born into this time, fed by curdling eddies of power where the Old Ones stirred the material and immaterial together with a giant, warp-stone jewelled spear. Thus the Old Ones stood against them at the dawn of war itself. Despite the machinations of the Ancient Enemy, the tear in the galaxy was never sealed, and from it continues to pour the echoes and promises of our eternity. From it seeps hope and damnation together.

Buried in the deepest vaults of the Black Library, hidden from the eyes of the young races and the foolish hearts of our time, lie the tomes of the most ancient of the eldar, the very first volumes to be taken into the care of the Harlequins, older than the mysterious library itself. There are rumours that these timeless texts may even bear the imprints of the Old Ones themselves. I have seen them, and they are exquisite.

The Black Library itself lies veiled in the lashes of the webways that riddle the great tear, surfing the empyrean tides as a glorious galleon in the light-streaked darkness. If the Ancient Enemy were to return to complete their Great Work, then the tear would be sown up, the Library would blink out of existence and the sons of Asuryan would be cut off from their life source forever. We would cease to be;

cease to ever have been as the universe was severed from its own memories. The Eye of Isha would dim, closing for all eternity. The legacy of the Old Ones would vanish.

For the Ancient Foe have no souls, and thus nothing to fear by severing reality in two – draining the life force from the substance of life.

For the Ancient Foe have only life, and an insatiable thirst for death.

For the Ancient Foe were turned back only by the blinding brilliance of Isha's gaze, and, were that gaze ever to fade, there would be nothing to stand before them.

Thus the gaze of Isha is cast over the universe, sprinkling it with moments of light, ever vigilant for the first stirrings of ancient endings.

And it is to the farseer that we turn for visions of time beyond and around our own; it is they who pilot our craftworlds through the treacherous tides and webs of fate, casting their eternal souls to skim the fringes of the ineffable abyss. They are the navigators of our souls, seeing the past and future blended into our present, seeing ancient origins swimming into our destinies together with the daemons who continue to claw their way into our realm.

But I have seen the treachery of our ways: even the farseers cannot see everything or everywhen, and if they could it would drive them into madness. Visions of paradise and hell are inseparable: the great tear brings both glory and annihilation – it is the birthplace of war and victory. With the eldar, our daemons were also born into reality, and even I cannot see whether it was wise to pay this price to arrest the advance of the Ancient Foe. Even the present is unclear – visions of elsewhen are doubly treacherous.

From *The Treachery of Vision* by Eldrad
Ulthran, Ulthwé

CHAPTER ONE
VISIONS

IN THE GLITTERING darkness of her sanctum, deeply enshrouded in the immensity of the Biel-Tan craftworld, Farseer Macha was sitting in concentration. The stones scattered into the air, spiralling and spinning like tiny planets in a vacuum. Each glinted with a pregnant light, shimmering gently as though pulsing with energy, and casting kaleidoscopic reflections through the shadowy chamber. The fragments of light danced delicately over Macha's inhumanly elegant features as she gazed intently at the shifting patterns.

The eldar farseer was kneeling quietly, her long white hair falling in loose cascades over the skin of her exposed shoulders. It rippled slightly, as though caught in a breeze from another realm. She was wrapped in a translucent, emerald-green cloak, fastened by a silver clasp just below her super-sternal notch. Its delicate, diaphanous fabric seemed to shift like the air itself, caressing the immaculate pale skin that was concealed beneath it.

As she watched, the rune-stones swirled in the air before her, etching patterns of light into the darkness, spyring and gyring to and fro like birds of prey circling their quarry. Her glittering green eyes flicked and tracked the movements, but her body remained absolutely motionless.

The configuration of the stones shifted and swam, as each hovered and flew above the glistening, circular wraithbone tablet that was set into the floor in the centre of the chamber, just a breath away from the farseer's knees. Their movements defined a rough sphere, as though their paths were bounded by an invisible orb; they swept into curves and arcs, skating the perimeter before being turned back by some mysterious gravity.

Macha's eyes narrowed as the flight of the stones accelerated, bringing her concentration into sharper focus to prevent the runes from escaping the curved pocket of space-time in which they raced. A fizzing, whirring whine began to build as the stones rushed against the banal, material resistance of the atmosphere in the chamber, and the scent of heat started to waft into the air. Trails of deep green smoke were left in the wake of the stones, like lines of vapour behind aircraft. After a few seconds, the invisible, floating sphere became a dull cloud of dirty green, shot through by the burning flashes of the runes.

An instant later and there was peace. The runes fell into stillness, as though they had suddenly run out of energy. The smoke began to dissipate into wisps that snaked up and away from the stones, spreading silent tendrils across the smooth blackness of the low ceiling. For a moment, the rune-stones lay in the air, as though supported on tiny, hidden platforms. But suddenly they fell, dropping straight down and clattering against the polished surface of the wraithbone tablet below, bouncing and skidding until finally coming to rest.

Without moving her body, Macha lowered her profoundly inhuman eyes to gaze upon the pattern defined by the fallen stones. Each lay in its own reflection on the water-like wraithbone while the intricate and ancient runes etched into their surfaces glowed with understated power. Macha stared at them, letting her long eyelashes touch together, blurring the faint lights into muffled stars. Then her eyes closed completely and her vision exploded into light.

WHITE. PURE WHITE. Resolving into javelins and streaks of brightness, like torrential rain. Blinding light, like an exploding star, ripping through space. An inferno, rippling like water, gushing and flooding, crashing and cascading over a craft. An eldar cruiser. A wraithship. The *Eternal Star* was afloat in the surge, with waves of fire smashing against its shimmering hull. It bucked and heaved, fluttering wildly like a great oil-drenched bird, bleeding energy in terrible swirls of blue.

Despite herself, Macha flinched at the uncontrolled violence pouring through her mind. She pressed her eyelids together more tightly, sending fine creases jousting across the smooth skin of her perfect face.

Tiny specks of darkness flashed through the wash of brightness, darting and flicking like a school of fish. A flock of birds, twisting and diving through the hail and the driving rain. The miniature black moments seemed to conduct the searing white energy around them, like small magnets dragging the flows into curves and pulling them into new pathways that punched straight into the fleeing shapes of other vessels. The escapees were fleet, but they were no match for the specks of night that zipped along in pursuit. The little white and green ships danced and spiralled with exquisite grace, defining sweeps of beauty in amongst the waves of destruction and ruin, but it seemed that they were reduced to slow motion as the shoals of darkness ripped at them with threads of lightning. The prey were Shadowhunters – eldar escort ships…

The farseer strained her vision, struggling to contain the carnage that raged in her mind. She could feel the despair flowing out of the images, and it was exciting an anger deep in her soul, which fed the violence of the imagery still further. Even though it clouded the echoes and reflections of time, it was not always possible to keep the personality of a seer out of her visions, especially when the images were so emotive. Eldar emotions could be the ruin of the universe, if only in the minds of their farseers.

There had to be more detail. She could not tell who the attackers were – she had never seen such vessels before. And she could not tell when the attack was taking place – was it the past or the future that she saw?

With an abrupt anti-flash of darkness, a swirling vortex whirled up in front of the star, seemingly sucking the light into itself and drawing the life out of the sun. The ghoulish shadow spun and shimmered with an eerie black light, somehow more brilliant than the star that it appeared to consume. For an instant, the spectral shade seemed to resolve itself into the suggestion of an iridescent humanoid figure, eclipsing the sun with its radiance. Then it blurred back into motion and was gone.

Another image pierced Macha's thoughts, pressing in from behind her and making her mind's eye spin to confront it.

On the fringes of the torrent of light there were other ships. Bulky and ugly, like those of the mon'keigh. Slow and cumbersome, with repulsive angles and crude explosive weapons. They were bobbing in the waves of energy, like ships about to be lost to the sea. Their weapons flared with desperate abandon, shredding the space with torpedoes, shells, and fragments of death. Streaming out of the larger vessels were lines of smaller ships, not much bigger than the Shadowhunters, but much slower. They swam through the quagmire of energy and battle, heading for the *Eternal Star*.

'IT WAS LSATHRANIL's Shield,' said Macha, meeting the gaze of the exarch with such passionate certainty that he could not doubt her. The light in her chambers flickered imperceptibly, echoing her own intensity.

'You're quite sure, farseer?' asked Laeresh, deciding that it might be prudent to doubt her a little; Macha was a passionate female, and she always wore the fierce mask of certainty. 'It would not do to be mistaken in this.'

'Quite sure, Laeresh. The planet is unmistakable, and the light is definitive.'

The warrior considered her for a moment, studying her exquisite features and searching them for the tiniest flickers of doubt. He was sure that she could not be right all the time. None of the seers could see everything, and none had perfectly crisp vision – there was always room for a slip, or for personal interest to breathe clouds across the vista.

Laeresh himself had been a seer once, during one of his previous stops along the winding Path of the Eldar, so he knew the racks of doubt that plagued the sensitive mind. He had not withstood them well, and he had marvelled at Macha's mastery of her thoughts even then, when she was little more than a youthful seer, still searching for her place and role on the craft-world of Biel-Tan.

Whilst Macha had finally found her calling on the Path of the Seer, plunging her destiny into the wild oceans of her people's souls, Laeresh had found his certainty in the hilt of a reaper launcher; abandoning the Seer Way he had fixed his soul into the hands of Kaela Mensha Khaine, the Bloody-Handed God. He joined the ranks of the Dark Reapers, one of the most sinister and lethal of all the temples of Aspect Warriors, finally losing himself in the craze and passion of battle – finding his soul reflected in the slick sheen of the blood that pooled around his feet.

He regretted nothing and could remember little of his life before becoming the temple's exarch. Such was the price of his ascension. But he could remember Macha: he could remember her face when it was younger and fresher than it was now. If anything, she had grown more beautiful as the pain and terror of her visions had gradually carved themselves into the depths of her emerald eyes. Every time he looked at her, he ached with half-disremembered, half-buried emotions. It made him doubt his own judgment. It made him resent her certainty.

The Reaper exarch gazed at the farseer for another moment, as though calculating his decision. 'If you are so certain,' he said, tilting his head inquiringly, 'then we must take this to the Court of the Young King. Biel-Tan must prepare for war.'

'I NEVER SAID that it was the future,' replied Macha flatly, as though the question itself had missed the point. To an outsider, she might have seemed to be chiding a slow student. 'I could only see where the battle was raging, not when. It may have been the past that I saw.'

Despite her almost whispered tone, the farseer's voice echoed repeatedly around the great reception hall; in this elaborate ceremonial chamber, Macha's ineffable majesty was at its most dramatic. The sound swept round the elevated throne in the centre and reflected back on itself, bouncing up into the vaulted reaches of the ceiling. It was as though there was more to her voice than the audible noise, and the small congregation of eldar arrayed before her shifted uneasily, aware that the farseer lived in a space that was a mystery to them.

Although Laeresh had requested an audience with the Court of the Young King on behalf of Macha, the traditions of the craftworld dictated that the Court would honour this request by visiting the ritual

throne chamber of the farseer herself. Laeresh
enjoyed the Court's discomfort in this glorious space.

Most eldar craftworlds were governed by a Seer
Council, headed by the farseer, but Biel-Tan had
been an exception for millennia. Alongside the
seers, Biel-Tan was ruled by a military council comprised of the exarchs from the biggest Aspect
Temples on the craftworld. The balance of power
between these councils was delicate, and the exarchs
resented any and all appeals to traditions that
implied their subordination to the Seer Council. In
practice, most of the political decisions were made
behind the closed doors of the Young King's Court,
whilst the exarchs begrudgingly acknowledged their
need for the advice and guidance of Macha and her
seers.

'Then what do you propose that we do, farseer?'
asked Uldreth, the exarch of the Dire Avengers. His
tone was harsh and his voice scraped through the air
as though dragging itself over rough metal. It was a
challenge, not a question.

'We must unleash the Bahzhakhain. We must dispatch the Swordwind to Lsathranil's Shield,' intoned
Laeresh urgently. He was standing on the throne
pedestal itself at Macha's right shoulder, his deep
purple cloak hanging like a shroud around his glistening black armour.

'I did not ask you, Reaper,' responded Uldreth,
almost spitting on the polished floor. He kept his
eyes fixed on Macha, not even turning his face to
address Laeresh; his immaculate blue armour shone
and its emerald edging seemed to glow with suppressed fires.

The other exarchs arrayed on the floor offered no response. It was not clear whether they were ignoring Laeresh or whether they were ignoring Uldreth, but they made no attempt to intervene in the obvious tension between the two great warriors.

'We cannot afford to take the risk, Uldreth Avenger. If the vision is of the future, then we must act now,' pressed Laeresh, ignoring the manner of the Dire Avenger and appealing to his deep-seated concern for the survival of the ancient and precarious eldar race, a concern common to all eldar, even if only at the most subconscious level.

'Can you tell us nothing of time, farseer?' asked Uldreth, his voice still bitter, albeit tinged with hints of resignation. 'Are there really no clues about whether this battle lies in the future or the past?'

'I have said,' stated Macha simply. 'The vision raged as though in the present, but such is the way with visions that are seen in the present. I could see nothing of time, except that it continued to pass as it does now.'

Macha could see the frustration on Uldreth's face. His eyes narrowed slightly, as though the uncertainty afflicted him with physical pain. Finally, he shot a glance towards Laeresh. 'And you, Reaper, what role is there in this for you?'

'I will accompany the farseer, Uldreth Avenger,' replied Laeresh, nodding a slight and stiff bow, affecting deference where it was due but unfelt.

'Will you, now?' hissed Uldreth, his eyes narrowing still further, until they were little more than slits. 'I see that you think this matter decided already? Well, it is not – Farseer, what of the other seers on the council? Do they share your visions?'

Macha had expected this question, and she had already given it a great deal of thought. If she were honest, she had to admit that it was unusual for no aspects of her vision to be shared by the others. It was not uncommon for the seers of the council to experience the same visions at similar times, or, at least, to be struck by different versions of the same vision – the same vision from differing standpoints. But, in this case, not a single seer had even glimpsed the light-riddled battle of Lsathranil's Shield – not even Taldeer, who was usually so in tune. Her mind was growing increasingly unsettled, as though the vision had seeped its way into her own soul and become part of her. She had seen her ancient Wraithship, *Eternal Star*, in the midst of the battle, and there was more to her role in the vision than forgotten pasts or a sentimental attachment to her ship.

'They do not.' The answer was simple and direct, and Macha held her gaze firmly as she spoke. 'This is my vision. Mine alone.'

For a moment, Uldreth held her gaze, peering into her bright eyes as though searching for some hidden truth. When he broke contact, he flashed his own green eyes at Laeresh and then turned to leave. He spun on his heel, whisking his blue cloak into a whirl, and then strode towards the great staircase that led up to the Triclopic Gates at the entrance to the farseer's throne hall. The other exarchs bowed abruptly to Macha and then hurried off in Uldreth's wake. One of them, the sparkling golden form of the Fire Dragon exarch, Draconir, paused momentarily and nodded to Laeresh.

* * *

SECURE IN THE depths of the venerable battle barge, *Litany of Fury*, the young neophyte's eyes bulged, but he did not cry out. His body could not even twitch, since his limbs were bound to the great, ceremonial tablet with adamantium hoops and a heavy strap ringed his chest. Beneath the restraints, Ckrius's muscles spasmed and knotted, his body attempting to thrash against the violence being done to it.

There was already a long scar running down the boy's chest, where his sternum had been cracked open and a second heart inserted into the cavity below. There were a couple of tributary incisions slipping out of the scar, where the small, tubular ossmodula organ and the little, spherical biscopea had been implanted at the same time as the extra heart.

These zygotes were usually implanted when the neophyte was much younger than Ckrius – perhaps as young as ten years old. It took time for them to stabilise, and for the young human bodies to accept the new organs. The ossmodula and biscopea implants were developmental, flooding the body with hormones to encourage rapid growth and strengthening of the skeleton and its musculature – an older neophyte may not respond well to such traumatic processes. But time was not a luxury that the beleaguered Blood Ravens Space Marines could enjoy; they needed new initiates as quickly as possible, and the surgical processes were being accelerated beyond the point of caution or good sense.

A thin jet of blood was spraying out of another slit in Ckrius's chest, and the neophyte's eyes seemed fixed on the crimson shower. There was barely controlled horror in his face as he flickered on the edge of consciousness, waiting for shock to dull the searing pain. But a complicated web of intravenous drips supplied him with a constant flow of stimulants, ensuring that he would not drift into unconsciousness or even be able to sublimate the memories afterwards. These horrific procedures would stick with him forever, always present behind his eyelids if ever he tried to close them for sleep or dreams. He was becoming a Space Marine, and it was important that he should never forget what that meant.

The mechanical, skeletal, metal arms that augmented the surgical dexterity of the Blood Ravens apothecary twitched and clicked as they worked the instruments inside Ckrius's flesh. Meanwhile, the apothecary's real arms were braced against the neophyte's shoulders. The spray of blood had erupted as one of the main blood vessels exiting the primary heart had been severed, and now the apothecary was carefully inserting the tiny haemastamen organ into the line of the vessel. It was designed to monitor and control the make-up of the Marine's blood, particularly to ensure that the other implants would receive rich enough sustenance for proper development and maintenance.

Before reconnecting the severed blood vessel, the mechanical, chittering arms of the apothecary tugged the incision in Ckrius's chest a little wider, making him moan and gasp. Another thin metal arm appeared from under the apothecary's black smock, carrying a dark, fleshy organ of about the size and shape of a small fruit. The arm pushed the Larraman's organ through the opening in the neophyte's flesh, while another of the many arms quickly stitched it into place – setting it next to the primary heart like an extra valve in the severed blood vessel, and then connecting the artery again on the other side of it.

With smooth slithering motions, the various metal arms and instruments withdrew from the violated body and slipped back into place under the apothecary's smock as he simply turned and left, leaving the gaping wound on Ckrius's chest open to the air with blood pouring out of it. The neophyte's head strained against the restraints that were looped over his forehead, as he watched the apothecary vanish. Up until that point, he had wanted nothing more than for his torturer to leave him in peace, but now that the oddly augmented figure was leaving him half-finished, his mind welled up with panic that he would simply bleed to death on the tablet.

In fact, he might bleed to death there and then. Many neophytes did not make it past this, the fifth phase of the transformation into a Space Marine. The apothecary had deliberately left the egregious wound open. One of three things would now happen: Ckrius would bleed to death; Ckrius's Larraman's organ would eventually kick in and stem the blood flow, but his immune system would be too weakened by all the body-trauma and he would die of an infection – nothing would be done to prevent this; or the haemastamen organ would already be working to provide the Larraman's organ with the enriched blood necessary to help it heal the wound quickly enough to prevent either infection or too much blood loss. Then he might survive.

The only way Ckrius would still be alive in an hour's time would be if his genetic make-up was an almost exact match with the Blood Ravens' gene-seed. If not, one or other of the implants would fail, or would be inefficient, and he would die. The apothecary would let him die: if the zygotes did not take root, then the neophyte was basically worthless to the Chapter.

STANDING IN THE shadows at the edge of the Implantation Chamber, Captain Gabriel Angelos watched the ritual surgery taking place. Every time he saw it done, it seemed like only yesterday that it had been him lying on that ancient tablet. The myriad scars that adorned his body flared with pain at the memory, sending sparks of agony rampaging around his brain. Part of him wondered whether this reaction had been hard-wired into his brain during the course of hypnotherapy which accompanied the surgery and then continued for much of the rest of a Marine's life – it wouldn't have surprised him. Then again, the implantation process was not something that could easily be forgotten.

Clouds of smoke billowed around the room from the burners that had been lit at each corner of the operation tablet. The smoke was slightly toxic – enough to cause lethal infections in any untreated wounds, and enough to choke a normal human being. Gabriel and Sergeant Tanthius who accompanied him breathed easily, their multi-lungs working naturally to filter out the more unpleasant effects of the gas. Ckrius had to make do with his old lungs for now.

The ceremonial conditions of the implantation process were deliberately unhygienic. Purity was an entirely ritualised concept in this context, as the bank of masked Chapter priests ensconced in prayer at the far side of the chamber showed. The neophyte had to survive the various surgeries, but he had to survive them himself: the apothecary would administer the transformation, but would offer no medical care. A Space Marine should have to rely on nobody, and if he required a sterilised atmosphere and shiny new surgical instruments, then he was not of the right stuff. The Implantation Chamber was a haven for death and disease – its carefully controlled air supply was rich with some of the most deadly viruses and bacteria ever to have plagued the galaxy.

The unusual air-conditioning also acted as a defensive precaution – this was one of the most secure locations in the Blood Ravens' realm. At the back of the chamber were a pair of massive, heavy, adamantium doors, bolted and encrusted with purity seals. Sprinkled around the frame of the great doors were a series of automatic defence cannons that tracked and whirred constantly, drawing tabs on anything and anyone that moved into the room. An ancient, runic script had been inscribed in a giant arc around the super-armoured portal, but there were few who could decipher its meaning. And at the apex of the arch was a shimmering, blood red, stylised raven.

Behind those doors was kept part of the Chapter's supply of gene-seed. This was the most heavily guarded place in the entire battle barge – even more secure than the magnificent armouries of the Blood Ravens. Without a home world of their own, the

Blood Ravens had no central planetary Fortress Monastery in which to hide their genetic treasure. Instead, the reservoir was divided amongst the Chapter's magnificent battle barges, including the epic fortress of the *Omnis Arcanum*, buried deep in their impregnable hulls and encased in concentric spheres of armoured shields. Even if the unthinkable were to happen, and a battle barge was destroyed, the gene-chamber would survive, tumbling invisibly through space until its heavily encrypted signal was picked up by another Blood Ravens vessel. It could survive for centuries, even millennia without external power. Like their brother Chapters, the Blood Ravens took no risks with their gene-seed, for without it they were doomed.

'Do you think he will survive?' asked Tanthius, his concern etched clearly into his wide, open features. The veteran sergeant had discovered Ckrius himself, during the terrible battles of the Tartarus campaign, which had cost the Blood Ravens so dearly. The youth had made an impression on the wizened old Terminator, despite his jaded professionalism, and Tanthius felt some responsibility for the safety of his young charge.

'We will see,' replied Gabriel. That was all he could say: only time would tell. 'He is strong, Tanthius,' he added, as though consoling his old friend.

A hiss of decompression made the two Marines turn. The doors to the Implantation Chamber slid open and a sheet of light cut into the deep, smoky shadows. For a moment the huge green tank on the far side of the chamber was lit up, as though held in a spotlight. Inside it, Gabriel could see the vague, ill-formed shape of a man; it was a growing-tank, in which the apothecary was already preparing the black carapace for Ckrius, should he survive long enough to need it. The insertion of the carapace under the skin of the neophyte was the last phase in his transformation – once it was complete, he would become an initiate Marine, finally able to bond with the ancient power-armour that characterised all Space Marines.

Then the tank fell into shadow as a heavy figure strode into the light-flooded doorway. The Marine bowed deeply on the threshold, paying his respects to the sacred site into which he was about to enter, and then he stepped inside, letting the doors hiss shut behind him, extinguishing the light altogether.

'How is he doing, captain?' asked Librarian Ikarus, staring straight at the bound figure of Ckrius on the tablet, without looking over at Gabriel.

'Ikarus,' nodded Gabriel in greeting. 'It is still too early to tell.'

'His suffering is great,' whispered the librarian, a wave of pain seeming to wash over his own face. 'I can feel his anguish – he radiates it as a star gives off heat.'

'I am sure that it was this way with us, too,' said Tanthius, almost to himself. He was watching the boy's muscles tense and bulge as he fought against the panic and the agony.

It was not usual for three such high-ranking Blood Ravens to be present during these rituals, but these were unusual times for them. Gabriel's Third Company had been severely tested on Tartarus, and he had lost many Marines in the battles against the orks, the traitorous Alpha Legion, and the manipulative, xenos eldar of Biel-Tan. And from the whole population, they had found only one warrior with the character and constitution of a hero. Only Ckrius had seemed a likely neophyte, but even he was older than they would have liked, and there was no guarantee that he would be a genetic match with the Blood Ravens' seed.

Although the Blood Ravens could claim a magnificent victory at the end of the Tartarus campaign, it was tinged with a profound sense of loss. Great Marines had fallen, including Gabriel's oldest friend, Librarian Akios Isador. And in return, the Chapter had taken Ckrius, an Imperial Guardsman who had fought the orks with glorious abandon, standing side by side with the Marines until the very end. But they had taken only Ckrius, and he could not replace the numbers that had been lost. The Third Company stood perilously close to their own extinction.

Thus, Gabriel, Tanthius and Ikarus maintained their vigil in the Implantation Chamber, watching every change in the condition of their neophyte, muttering silent prayers to the Emperor of Man that he might survive the vastly accelerated process that he was being forced to suffer.

THE FOUR EXARCHS stood facing one another, with their retinues fanned out behind them, resplendent in the glorious colours of their temples. The Courtroom of the Young King was one of the most elevated spaces on Biel-Tan, lifted like a majestic dome out of the peaks of the craftworld. Its vast curving walls aspired to a distant apex, all but invisible from the polished wraithbone floor. The dome was almost transparent, and the brilliance of the stars outside pierced its substance with heavenly patterns that swam and trailed with the steady, interstellar motion of the immense craft. The bonesingers who had fashioned the grand hall from wraithbone drawn directly from the warp were the finest in the long and noble history of the Biel-Tan. The walls glinted and glistened in accord with the mood of the occasion, and the patterns of stars outside seemed to form and reform into ancient eldar runes, spelling out the glorious heritage of the sons of Asuryan. The hall was big enough to hold a thousand eldar warriors, but today there were only a dozen.

The Court had been comprised of the same four exarchs for centuries. They were the keepers of the largest Aspect Temples on Biel-Tan, and between them they determined all the military affairs of the craftworld. They were each warriors to the core; each the absolute personifications of their Aspects; each had abandoned the Path of the Eldar, having lost themselves in the service of Kaela Mensha Khaine himself – never again to leave the bloody road of the warrior. But they were not all the same – the Aspects each had personalities of their own, as though aping the moods of Khaine.

As usual, Uldreth spoke first, planting his ornate diresword between his feet. He was the youngest of the four, and the most afflicted by the extremes of passion that plagued his race. The others had mellowed slightly as the long years had passed, although none might be considered cold. The Court of the Young King had a reputation amongst the other peripatetic craftworlds of the eldar for being bellicose and aggressive, and this was not just because of the Dire Avenger in their midst.

'The farseer is confused and her vision is vague,' began Uldreth, turning his face from one exarch to the next. 'And the Reaper is not to be trusted. We should not risk Biel-Tan on the whim of a maniac and a fool.'

'You will not speak in this way of our farseer, Uldreth, Dire Avenger,' intoned Draconir, his voice calm and low. 'She has led us to safety and to victory many times before now, and it is not the place of this court to challenge her. We are here to decide how to respond to her visions, that is all. As for Laeresh of the Dark Reapers – his role in this is as yet unclear. It does not become this council to speak so cheaply of another exarch. The Reapers have always been amongst us, and we must not do them any further dishonour.'

'Yet, there is a reason that their Aspect finds no place in this Court, Draconir, Fire Dragon–' began Xoulun, flashing her black eyes like miniature anti-stars.

'–we are all aware of the composition of this chamber, Xoulun, Scorpion Queen, and we need no reminders of its rationale. The Dark Reapers are not here, and Laeresh's voice is not heard in this hall. This is the precaution that we have taken for millennia, and nothing further needs to be said about it now.' Draconir returned the Striking Scorpion's glare, casting the reflected fires of his golden eyes into the fathomless black of hers.

'The Fire Dragon is right,' said Azamaia, shaking her glorious, golden hair as she spoke, bringing everyone's attention back to her. 'The only matter that we need to discuss is the question of whether we should unleash the Bahzhakhain against Lsathranil's Shield. If it was the future that the farseer saw, then we must act quickly–'

'–if it was the future, then the choice is already made,' spat Uldreth, cutting the Howling Banshee off in mid sentence. He hated the way that this court kowtowed to Macha, as though she were some kind of goddess. She was no Eldrad Ulthran, and she had made mistakes before. It was not that long ago that she had summoned forth the Avatar of Khaine and sent it to its doom on the backwater world of Tartarus. That whole affair had been a disaster for Biel-Tan, costing the craftworld many fine warriors, and all for nothing. The mon'keigh had ruined the Avatar and unleashed a hideous daemon from the warp. Macha had not foreseen that – her visions had been 'clouded' by something or someone that she could not or would not explain. In the meantime, the birth pains of the Avatar had drained all the life force from the Young King himself, leaving Biel-Tan without its premier warrior lord. Had the Court forgotten this so soon?

'We are Biel-Tan!' asserted Uldreth forcefully. 'We are not Ulthwé, and we have no need to sneak about in the shadows of the galaxy hiding from our fate, led by the vague ramblings of farseers and witches.'

'Hold your tongue, Avenger!' snapped Draconir, rising to the bait, as he always did. Behind him, his honour guard bristled with readiness, always prepared to fight. They were treading the Path of the Warrior, and fighting was always at the forefront of their minds. The eldar were an obsessive species, and theirs was a special kind of decadence, an indulgence in the arts of death at every available opportunity.

'This bickering will not help us, friends,' said Azamaia, stepping into the space between the two males and keeping them apart. 'We must keep our minds focussed on bigger questions for now. The chance will come later for you to resolve your differences here. That time is not now.'

'She is right,' agreed Xoulun, reluctantly holding out her arm across Uldreth's chest. 'Now is not the time for this. We must decide about Lsathranil's Shield.'

'I do not believe in Farseer Macha,' stated Uldreth, standing down and letting his voice sound calm and reasonable, despite the green flames still dancing in his eyes. 'She has been wrong before, and she may be wrong now. We would be taking a tremendous risk to take Biel-Tan so close to Lsathranil's Shield, since it is now buried deep within the territory of the mon'keigh. I cannot condone this action without greater certainty than Macha can offer us. We must fight the battles that present themselves to us, not go chasing around the galaxy looking for those that may not even concern us.'

'That does not sound like the reasoning of a Biel-Tan warrior,' mumbled Draconir under his breath.

'Uldreth is right about the risk, Draconir,' said Azamaia, acting as the intermediary and pretending not to hear the murmured insult. 'We can ill-afford a costly war if it is unnecessary. What is the use of a farseer if she cannot prevent us from reliving the mistakes and disasters of our past? If it is the past in

Macha's vision, we would be fools to drag it into our future by our own actions.'

'If it is not the past, then we risk everything – that too should be a lesson from our history,' countered Draconir, aware that he was not going to win this debate.

'I agree with Uldreth,' announced Xoulun predictably. 'Biel-Tan has other battles to fight at the moment. The foul, green-skinned orks are infesting the system of Lorn, once a splendorous exodite colony. There are also signs of mon'keigh in the sector. The extermination of these vermin and the re-establishment of an eldar colony is a much more fitting task for the Swordwind. Taldeer and the other seers on the council have foreseen great victories for us.'

'Are we really so vain that we must act only where our victories have already been assured?' asked Draconir, already knowing the answer. 'Sometimes the right battle is the one whose outcome lies obscured beyond the battle itself.'

'If you really believe those honourable sentiments, Draconir, Fire Dragon, then you are really agreeing with me that we should not base our actions on the visions of a seer, not even on those of our venerable farseer. We should act according to our will and do what we believe to be right. We are warriors, for Khaine's sake! Biel-Tan no longer has any need for the archaic institutions of our forefathers. The Seer Council has no place in my craftworld.' Uldreth was enthused with passion.

'You go too far, Dire Avenger–' began Draconir, shocked by the audacity of the other exarch.

'–let us devise a test,' interrupted Uldreth, his mind racing only fractionally ahead of his words. 'If Macha and Laeresh are correct and this vision is of the future, then it should not matter what decision is reached by this Court: the battle will occur anyway. If, on the other hand, we decide to pursue the vision, then we will make it happen through the efforts of our own wills – which will prove nothing about the vision other than that we believed it. So, I propose that we decide to ignore Macha's vision. If we end up fighting for Lsathranil's Shield, thenceforth I will bow to your greater wisdom, Draconir of the Fire Dragons.'

'THEY WILL DO nothing. Uldreth carried the Court, as usual,' said Draconir, bowing deeply at the pedestal in front of Macha's throne. 'I am sorry.'

As the Fire Dragon exarch spoke, Laeresh turned violently away from Macha's shoulder and stormed away towards the stairs that led up to the Triclopic Gates and out of the chamber.

'Laeresh!' called Macha, with more affection than anger. 'They must reach their own decisions. That is their function.'

The Dark Reaper paused at the foot of the great staircase, leaving his back to the farseer and Draconir. They could see the rage in his shoulders as his purple cloak rippled. He did not turn.

'I never said that it was the future, Laeresh–'

'–but we cannot run the risk, Macha,' said Laeresh. He did not snap round suddenly, but turned very slowly and whispered his words with aspirated force.

'I agree with Laeresh, farseer,' confirmed Draconir, stooped on one knee before her. 'If there is uncertainty about this, then we must assume the worst. I do not think that the Court really appreciates the significance of Lsathranil's Shield. Even if your vision were of the past, farseer, there must be some significance to the fact that you have had it now?'

'Perhaps, exarch. But there is not always a simple reason behind the appearance of ghosts from the past. Or for those from the future, come to that. If I were confident about this, then I would have told the Court.'

'I do not think that Uldreth's decision was entirely rational, farseer. There was a passionate quality to his voice. There is something else informing his thinking on this. He distrusts you and your visions. Even had you been certain of the timing, I suspect that he would have refused to act.' Draconir said.

'He is passionate. It is the curse of our people that the best of us are also the most passionate. They believe in things, and through their belief they make them true. Uldreth believes in his sword – that is his way.'

'I also believe in my sword, farseer,' confessed Draconir.

'Yes, but not only in your sword – that is why you have come to me now. It is the fixation that causes the problems. Eldar souls are powerful beings, intimately connected to immaterial realms beyond our own. Our beliefs have repercussions. They produce ripples and echoes in the empyrean. If too many of us believe the same thing, we sometimes have the power to make it real. Or if the most powerful of us believe something passionately enough, he might create the echoes of it in the unseen realms. This is the curse of the eldar.'

'Do you not believe in your visions, farseer?' asked Draconir, still on one knee.

'Yes, I believe in them. I see them, and they are real. I have no doubts about them. Everything I see is real. But it has taken me many centuries to learn about the difference between reality and inevitability. Time and space are interrelated in infinitely complex ways, and space is not delimited by our material realm. I can believe in my visions without ever expecting to see them occur, without ever desiring to see their truth realised. I can believe without passion.'

'I believe in your visions, Macha,' stated Laeresh, striding back to the throne. He had seen the passion in her eyes when she had first described the vision to him. He knew that she was not as free of the 'curse' as she purported to be.

'I know you do,' smiled Macha faintly, looking up at her old friend and seeing the fierce certainty in his eyes. He knew her well, and, even if he could no longer remember the details, the knowledge was lodged somewhere in his subconscious.

'I also believe in you, farseer. But Uldreth's belief is of a different nature from ours. He is searching for...' Draconir searched for the right word, but could not find it. 'He is distrustful of everything except his sword.'

'I can understand this distrust,' confessed Laeresh. 'I too feel it. This is the way of Khaine.'

'But your distrust is general, Laeresh. As is yours,' said Macha, waving Draconir to his feet. 'For Uldreth, his distrust must be focussed on someone or something in particular. He is an Avenger, and his nature is to search for vengeance. He is never stronger than when he feels wronged, and his soul craves that feeling at all times.'

'That is as may be, but why must he focus his ire against you, farseer? He shows poor judgement in his choice of enemies.' Draconir was genuinely confused.

Macha shook her head and sighed. The past was a complicated place for her, but for the exarchs it was simple. They could remember precious little of their lives before their ascensions. Their personal histories were nothing more than wisps of cloud to them, lingering in the unused recesses of their minds. She didn't know whether this was a deliberate consequence of the ritual transformation, or whether it was simply a side effect of the psychic changes affected during the soul's dedication to Khaine. She knew, as the keepers of the Aspect Temples had known since time immemorial, that the exarchs were war personified, with the hindrances of their personalities stripped away like inhibitors from a powerful engine. In an ugly, alien tome stolen from the mon'keigh, she had once read that the Imperium of Man also aspired to the creation of warriors who lived in the eternal present, with their lives stripped away by drugs, augmetics and conditioning.

But Macha also knew that the personalities of the eldar warriors did not disappear completely, even though their consciousness of their identities vanished. There were residues hardwired into the neurological and psychic structures of their brains, and ghosts that danced across the surface of their souls. They may never be able to articulate these things, but Macha could see them clearly. Besides, she had known Uldreth and Laeresh for centuries, since before either of them had become exarchs – although neither of them might remember much of that now.

'I'm sure that he has his reasons,' said Macha, unsure about what to reveal of Uldreth's past. Some things were best left in the past, without deliberately creating new echoes. Beginnings had a tendency to resurface from time to time of their own accord, and she was certain that the histories of Uldreth and Laeresh would come back to haunt them soon. She had foreseen it.

'I cannot come with you, Macha,' said Draconir, with honest resignation in his voice. 'I am part of the Court and thus subject to its pronouncements. There is nothing I can do.'

'The Dark Reapers will accompany you to Lsathranil's Shield, farseer,' said Laeresh, dropping to one knee before her throne and punching his fist against his chest. 'We are not so bound as the Fire Dragons.'

Macha nodded sadly. A long time ago she had warned the Young King's Court about the Reapers, and part of her wondered whether it had all been about this moment.

THE SHACKLED NEOPHYTE had finally been permitted to lose consciousness. The bleeding had stopped, and the pool of blood that had gathered around him had eventually drained away through the matrix of grooves and channels cut into the surface of the tablet beneath him. It would be collected into a reservoir under the adamantium table; it would certainly be needed again before the end of this process.

'He's still alive?' asked Gabriel, striding into the Implantation Chamber as the doors slid open. He peered at the prone figure of Ckrius.

Tanthius nodded deliberately from the shadows; he had not left the room since the surgery. 'Yes, still alive.'

'He is a genetic match?'

'So it seems,' said Tanthius.

'Perhaps we should return to Tartarus and do another sweep?' wondered Gabriel out loud. He knew that it was impossible – the planet was ruined and most of the population had been infected by tainted blood that ran under the surface like subterranean rivers. In truth, Gabriel knew that he was taking a risk even with Ckrius. The Blood Ravens could not afford to introduce any residual taint into their Chapter, even in the blood of just one of their initiates. But they did not have the luxury of choice, and they had to take what they could get, within reason. Ckrius would make a fine Marine, if he survived long enough.

In their long and glorious history, the Blood Ravens had never managed to find a planet to act as their home world. Terrible fates had befallen most of those that they had set their eyes upon. In the most recent past, just before the Tartarus campaign, Gabriel had led his Third Company back to Cyrene, the planet on which he himself had been born. It had been used as a recruitment planet for generations, and it was the closest thing to a home that Gabriel had ever had, although he could remember very little of it now. Except the screams. His memories of that once green and verdant world were now flooded with pain and the contorted agony of the people as they fell beneath the righteous fury of the Blood Ravens themselves.

When he closed his eyes, he could see nothing except the tortured hell of Cyrene as the Exterminatus finally consumed all the living tissue on the planet's surface. Not only had Cyrene been unsuitable for recruitment on that visit, but it had been riddled with corruption, taint, mutation and heresy. Gabriel had not had any choice – he could not suffer those abominations to live. From orbit, he had killed the entire planet.

It was a terrible irony that he could remember so little of the beauty of that planet from his boyhood, but that he could still feel its loss so intensely. The hypnotherapy that he had undergone as he became a Space Marine had overwritten certain memories of his youth, leaving his mind tuned perfectly to the present. But the process could not obliterate his past completely, and his emotions continued to tug at his mind when he thought of what he had done to his own home planet. It was a curse of the Blood Ravens that they could not forget anything that they did as Marines; their minds were finely tuned to encourage their academic tendencies, which was why they had such a reputation for scholarship and knowledge. Gabriel had heard that it had something to do with a slight mutation in their catalepsean node. Whatever the reason, he could not forget the hell that he had unleashed on Cyrene, but the visions of the heaven that he had destroyed were gone forever.

The pattern had not escaped Gabriel's notice: first Cyrene and now Tartarus – the Blood Ravens seemed to find their recruits amongst the damned. Or, perhaps, damnation followed the Blood Ravens to these planets. Either way, there was cause for concern about the Chapter, and Gabriel needed to do some more research. There was a cavernous hole in its ancient history, and not even the great Father Librarians had been able to fill it – the Blood Ravens were hiding something from themselves, buried deep in their past, and now it seemed to be haunting them.

'We are coming up on the Trontiux system, sergeant. You will be needed for the landing party,' said Gabriel, turning to face Tanthius.

'Very well, captain,' he answered, nodding to acknowledge his duty, although it was clear that he did not want to leave Ckrius alone.

'He is about to start his hypnotherapy, Tanthius. There is nothing that you can do here. The apothecaries will drill the catalepsean node into his skull, but that is a simple procedure compared to what he has just gone through. There is little risk. He will be fine…' Gabriel trailed off. 'Although, he may be a different Ckrius when you see him again.'

Tanthius nodded and strode out of the room, leaving Gabriel alone with the boy. Trontiux III was another planet from which the Third Company had drawn recruits before, and they were hoping that there would be a new generation of warriors waiting to prove their worth in the Blood Trials. After this, the battle barge would make its way to Lorn V and then Rahe's Paradise – a backwater world on the fringes of the segmentum. These too had provided recruits before, although not on the scale of Trontiux III.

Gabriel gazed down at Ckrius, his heart swelling with a mixture of pride and pity. The boy was being transformed into the most Emperor-blessed form in the galaxy – he was joining the Adeptus Astartes. He was becoming a Space Marine of the Blood Ravens Chapter. He was being given the opportunity to serve the Undying Emperor in the most glorious ways imaginable. He was to be bathed in the pristine light of the Astronomicon, and guided by its imperial grace. There was nothing more magnificent, beautiful or terrible than a Space Marine.

But just for a moment, looking down at the broken, scarred body, Gabriel wondered what the cost of ascension would be for Ckrius, and whether he would ever understand, or even remember, what he was giving up. One thing was certain, he would be a different person tomorrow.

CHAPTER TWO
WRAITHBONE

THE FOUNDATIONS OF the monastery-outpost on Rahe's Paradise were heavy and deep, plunging down into the rock substructure of the planet's crust. Although the edifice was only an outpost, with a minimal detachment of Marines, it was still the largest building on the planet, and it needed every centimetre of its foundations, especially when it fired its huge air-defence cannons. Its jet-black, ornamented and armoured gothic walls towered over the rocky desert, dwarfing the outcroppings and boulders that peppered the sands.

Father Librarian Jonas Urelie had been based at the outpost for decades. He was old, even by the extended standards of the Blood Ravens, and he was not discontent with the slower pace of life on the backwater planet. In many ways it was an important post, being both the furthest reach of the Blood

Ravens' realm and an important source of fresh warriors for the Chapter. After Cyrene and perhaps Trontiux III, Rahe's Paradise was the closest thing that the Blood Ravens had to a home; the locals were not technologically advanced, but they were an intelligent and passionate people showing excellent psychic potentials, which suited the librarian-rich Chapter.

Most of the planet was violently inhospitable for human life, with vast, scorching deserts fading into permafrost around the poles. What little life there was on the planet was concentrated into the hoop of massive mountains and volcanoes that swept around the crust, forming a perfect, diagonal ring that could be seen from orbit. The foothills were lush testaments to the fertile alluvial soils that the volcanoes spewed from time to time, and they received all of the scarce precipitation of the world, as the water vapour was forced higher into the atmosphere, riding up through the jagged passes of the mountains.

Life in the shadows of the mountains was manageable, although competition for the scarce food resources was intense. As a consequence, the various peoples of the range were fiercely xenophobic, distrusting anyone from outside of their groups, perhaps fearing for the security of their storehouses. Hence, the children grew up with weapons in their hands, always ready to defend their homes from the threats of others, or from the claws of the various wild beasts that also competed for food in the same restricted spaces. Life was hard in the mountains, but compared with life in the desert it was a veritable paradise.

One of the early Blood Ravens missionaries, the legendary Chaplain Elizur, had remarked to a local that this was a harsh place to live, and the local, perhaps not understanding exactly what the huge, god-like warrior had said, had thrown his arms wide to indicate the lush vegetation of the foothills and said: 'No, this is my paradise.' The local chieftain had been called Rahe. The scene is portrayed in a fresco in the great entrance hall of the monastery-outpost, beneath calligraphy in High Gothic: Rahe's Paradise, Raised out of Hell. The name had stuck, and the irony of it had been noted by many subsequent visitors.

It had been to the surprise of many that Jonas had specifically requested the posting; he had been a great warrior in his time, and his brethren could not imagine him fading away in the dark. Rahe's Paradise was certainly no humiliation – it was a worthy post for an aging Space Marine librarian – but there was little combat to be had, except for occasional ork raids and not infrequent civil wars. However, Jonas had harboured a desire to visit Rahe's Paradise for a long time: it had something more important than war buried beneath its sands.

Since arriving, he had started excavating under the flagstones in the lowest level of the monastery, digging down into the foundations. At first he had tentatively lifted a few slabs and had dug carefully in small, controlled areas, not wanting to cause too much disruption and not confident that there would be anything to find. His explorations were not entirely official. But after only a few weeks it had become clear that there was even more down there than he had ever hoped.

Over the years, Jonas had lifted nearly all of the stones out of the cellars, even transferring the dungeons into one of the monastery's towers, which he reinforced with the stone taken from the floors. There was not much need for them on Rahe's Paradise, but it would have been unthinkable for a Blood Ravens outpost to be without detention facilities. Occasionally, local warlords might take a step too far in their competition with their neighbours, and then the Blood Ravens would step in. But, in general, the Marines left the local population to their own devices, only imposing their presence when it was time for the Blood Trials once again. At those times, the warring groups would pause and the finest warriors from all sides would congregate in the ancient amphitheatre, cut into the volatile volcano, Krax-7, which loomed up behind the imposing shape of the monastery. And during the trials themselves, the animosity between the contestants only made them fight harder.

Most of the ground that had once been the floor of the lowest level of the monastery was now an elaborate dig, roofed in by what was once the ceiling of the dungeons and cellars. Gradually bringing in more machinery, Jonas had cut down through the sand and rock, shifting tonnes of debris and effectively lowering the base level of the building by nearly ten metres. The excavation had become so deep that he had felt it wise to buttress the great walls of the monastery to prevent his digging from weakening their massive structure.

Eventually, the site had become too extensive for him to manage on his own, and he had sent out a request to the Order of the Lost Rosetta, an Order Dialogous of the Adeptus Sororitas, ostensibly affiliated with the Ecclesiarchy. Sister Superior Meritia had answered the call.

The Blood Ravens had an ancient agreement with the Ecclesiarchy that Sisters of the Lost Rosetta would be seconded to them on request, for the purpose of mutually beneficial historical research. In fact, the Blood Ravens were one of the few Chapters of Space Marines that maintained better than cursory relations with the Ecclesiarchy. Most Chapters kept the priests at arm's length, disapproving of all the dogma and the rituals that subordinated everyone absolutely to the God-Emperor. The Adeptus Astartes had a much more complicated relationship with the Emperor – he was simultaneously both more and less than a god: he was not exactly the ineffable, untouchable, pristine figure at the centre of Ecclesiarchal law, but rather he was a father and a hero – the historical founder of the Space Marines, friend and battle-brother to the great primarchs. In many ways, the Emperor was the first and greatest of the primarchs themselves, and the Adeptus Astartes were living incarnations of his will – angels of death, born of the Emperor himself. They had no objections to the Ecclesiarchy preaching absolute obedience to everyone else in the galaxy, but they themselves required no reminders of the debt or duty they owed, and they were certain that they owed nothing to the bureaucrats and priests of the Ecclesiarchy.

However, the Blood Ravens were serious about scholarship, and to that extent they had something in common with certain parts of the Ecclesiarchy. As long as questions of dogma could be subordinated to questions of history, things tended to progress smoothly, more or less. It was to their mutual advantage to suspend their grievances and, more importantly, it was to the benefit of the Emperor and to the history of his glorious Imperium. Everyone could agree that such glory was a good thing. At the most fundamental level, that was the commonality that kept much of the sprawling Imperium together, despite the variances and differences between its myriad and multitudinous parts.

Between them, Jonas and Meritia had uncovered dozens of Adeptus Astartes artefacts from the dig. To their mutual fascination, many of them dated from before the recorded date of the arrival of the Blood Ravens on the planet, from before the construction of the monastery-outpost itself, or even the now legendary Blood Trials that were conducted by the missionary-chaplains Elizur and Shedeur. Even more incredibly, they had discovered the suggestions of the remains of another fortress that had been built on exactly the same site before the construction of the current monastery. The archaeological evidence suggested that the previous structure was at least co-extensive with the present buildings, and that it had been home to a considerable number of Marines.

Jonas had heard rumours about lost Blood Ravens fortress monasteries before, when he had been still a young librarian, little more than a scout, and he had always thought that they might hold the secrets of the lost period in his Chapter's history. However, when he came to Rahe's Paradise he never really believed that he would discover something like this.

'Meritia,' said Jonas quietly, sweeping his hand across a slab of engraved rock and sending up little clouds of dust. 'Meritia, have you seen this?'

The Sister was kneeling to the ground inspecting the cracked remains of what had once been an auto-reactive shoulder plate – its red sheen suggested that it was from a long dead Blood Raven, but the Chapter markings had weathered away, so she could not be sure. She rose to her feet and turned to face Jonas, letting her ragged grey hair flop over her face. She was not an old woman; her hair was prematurely grey. It had been shimmering and black when she had first arrived on Rahe's Paradise, but she had awoken one morning after a restless night of violent dreams to find her hair glittering and grey.

'What is it?' she asked softly as she strode over towards him. She always felt as though she should whisper on site – it was like being in a librarium.

Jonas dug his fingertips down into the sand next to the tablet, feeling along its length for a crack. With a slight nod of satisfaction, he found some leverage with his index finger and drove it underneath the stone. With a faint grimace of effort, the librarian prised the slab of rock off the ground; it pivoted along the far edge, as though hinged, and cascades of sand fell away, revealing the full extent of the object. The tablet was nearly two metres long, perhaps a metre wide, and at least ten centimetres thick.

As she approached, Meritia shook her head in amusement: Jonas hadn't even noticed that he had just lifted more with the index finger of one hand than most men could have done with the strength of their entire bodies. It was remarkable, in fact, how quickly the excavation had been able to proceed because of Jonas's considerable abilities. Space Marines and their librarians were not designed with archaeology in mind, but, in the hallowed halls of the Lost Rosetta Convent, there were whispers of admiration about the military efficiency with which the Blood Ravens executed their scholarship. Between the two of them, Jonas and Meritia had made more progress on this dig than an entire team of Ecclesiarchal researchers could have done.

The dirty, red sand fell easily off the stone lid as Jonas tilted it, revealing curving patterns of engraving beneath. For a moment, Jonas cast his eyes over the cursive inscriptions, taking instant and careful note of the patterns that he recognised and those that he didn't. Most of the intricate detailing was already familiar to the librarian from other finds that they had discovered in the site; it was ornamentation that would have been familiar to any Blood Raven – swirls of High Gothic and stylised imagery of wings. However, the designs on the artefacts uncovered in this dig had a different quality from those found elsewhere in the galaxy. The images were broadly the same, but there were some subtle differences – different angles of curvature, extra strokes added to the wing-shapes, and some slightly altered characters in the script, a more archaic form of High Gothic. If anything, these designs were simply more beautiful than those Jonas was used to – less purely functional – and these artefacts were older than anything the Blood Ravens had ever come across before.

Meritia gasped, and Jonas snapped his attention away from the carvings on the stone and followed her line of sight down into the small chamber that he had uncovered beneath it. The stone slab had evidently been some kind of lid on a long, slender casket. It had been well sealed, and not a single grain of sand had found its way inside. Laying in the centre of the uncovered space was a shimmering black tablet, nearly a metre in length and perhaps half a metre wide. It seemed to contain a universe of miniature stars, glittering and winking in a complicated darkness.

Entranced, Meritia could find no words. She had never seen anything like it before; it just seemed to draw her in, capturing her eyes and her mind in an eternal instant. She had read about such materials, and had heard accounts from other Sisters who had been fortunate enough to glimpse it, but she had never dared hope that she would come so close to it herself. Legends told that it was fashioned out of the very fabric of the warp itself, rendered material by the impossibly ancient technologies of the eldar. And the warp contained no time – it was utterly timeless. This manifest fragment might be older than the galaxy itself. Her mind seemed unable or reluctant to grasp what she was seeing.

'Is that wraithbone?' asked Meritia, still staring at the object with wide, brown eyes. It seemed to thrill as she spoke its name, drawing her down to it. With aching trepidation, she stooped to look at it more closely, crouched under the lid that was still propped delicately against Jonas's finger.

The librarian closed his fingers around the edge of the heavy stone slab and lifted it clear of the exposed interior of the casket, placing it carefully onto the ground with one hand. Then he knelt softly on the sand next to Meritia and stared at the tablet. 'Yes,' he said simply. 'It is wraithbone.' Jonas had had dealings with the eldar before, and this was not the first time that he had come across their mysterious material.

As they watched, the surface of the glistening tablet started to shift and stir. Little marks began to appear, like gashes through the fabric of space itself, revealing glimpses of something unspeakable beyond. But the marks stretched and swirled, swimming into different configurations before finally settling into a distinct pattern.

'Those are eldar runes,' said Meritia, squinting slightly with concentration as she tried to decipher their meaning.

'Yes, but ancient ones – different from any I have seen before,' replied Jonas, unable to work out what they said.

There was a long pause while the two scholars knelt at the side of the grave, gazing silently at the entombed alien object that they had unearthed in the remains of an ancient fortress.

'We should take it to the librarium,' suggested Jonas eventually, breaking the spell. 'Perhaps we will be able to translate it there.'

Meritia nodded absent-mindedly, her thoughts lofty and distant, but then she voiced the question that was also niggling at the back of the Blood Raven's mind. 'Jonas. What is it doing here?'

THE ROAR OF the engine sunk into a deep purr as the shining, red bike crested the volcano and stopped. Streams of lava ran through grooves on either side of it, rolling laboriously down into the desert beyond the edge of the foothills. The deep red sun had just broken the horizon over the sand, and its first rays burst into crimson brilliance against the armoured panels of the Blood Ravens scout-bike, bathing the flows of molten rock in a more general haze of red. After a couple of seconds, half a dozen other bikes pulled up alongside the first, flanking it dramatically against the sunrise.

Behind them, a great column of sulphurous smoke filled the sky, and a steady rain of molten rock filled the air with streaks of fire, splattering the ground all around. The volcano, Krax-9, had erupted during the night, and Sergeant Caleb's squad had been dispatched to investigate.

The monastery-outpost on Rahe's Paradise hosted two scout squads. They were on the point of graduating from the Tenth Company into one of the main combat Companies of the Chapter: it was tradition that one would go on to join the Third Company – led by the Chapter's Commander of the Watch – and one the Seventh, each of which was famous for its explorative functions and hence required some extra training for its scouts. This extra training was received on Rahe's Paradise partly because two scout squads was considered to be a suitable defensive force for such a small and relatively peaceful outpost and partly because the terrain was harsh and the people just bellicose enough to keep young scouts on their toes. The occasional raid by pirates or even by the foul green-skinned orks was simply a bonus.

There was also usually a single squad of Assault Marines stationed at the monastery itself, in case the

Chapter had any need to flex its muscles on the planet or in the most inaccessible regions of the mountains. The Assault squad was seconded on a rotational basis – one being supplied by each Blood Ravens' company in turn for a period of no more than two years at a time. It was in the interest of the entire Chapter that the outpost should be maintained, but none of them could afford the loss of an entire squad on a permanent basis. Sergeant Ulyus had departed with his squad from the Second Company nearly a month ago, and Jonas was still waiting for the replacements to arrive from the Third Company – reports from Captain Angelos suggested that they had been delayed by unexpected complications on Tartarus.

Caleb scanned the glorious sunrise for a few moments, training his eyes into the red glare of the local star as fragments of falling lava sizzled against his armour. In the past, pirates and rogue traders had taken advantage of the signal disruption caused by massive eruptions to plunge down into the desert undetected. It was no secret that Rahe's Paradise was under the protection of the Blood Ravens, but it was also no secret that the Marines maintained only a minimal presence there. From time to time, the more unsavoury characters in the Imperium thought that it would be worthwhile to test their luck. Caleb was there to make sure that their luck ran out as soon as they emerged from the morning heat-haze that was already sheening over the desert.

The light was more intense than it seemed; the deep red hue belying the strength of the star and bathing everything in a warm, bloody atmosphere.

Caleb squinted, waiting for his occulobe implant to filter out the obfuscatory glare. The small, slug-like organ at the base of his brain had been working inconsistently recently, but the repair facilities on Rahe's Paradise were not sufficient to deal with zygote maintenance, so Caleb was waiting for the arrival of the Third Company's apothecary. In the mean time, his vision was occasionally glitchy, and he was contemplating simply having the implant removed. Just a few moments earlier, on the early morning ride, Caleb had seen a sudden burst of bright light that almost blinded him. It seemed to have been a hallucination or an occulobular malfunction; none of the other scouts in his squad had seen anything.

'There,' said Caleb, pointing out into the desert with his gauntlet.

A black speck seemed to blink and flicker on the horizon, silhouetted against the bloodied sun. After a few seconds of staring into the light, Caleb could see that the speck was actually a constellation of even smaller figures.

'Pirates?' asked Abraim, staring alongside his sergeant.

'Perhaps,' replied Caleb thoughtfully, watching the tiny flecks move and dance against the morning sun. 'Certainly too fast to be orks.'

An instant later, and the specks disappeared.

THE ELDAR RANGER inspected the landing site quickly, checking to ensure that his team had not left any traces. He knew that they would not have done – they knew their jobs better than anyone – but their team had not survived for as long as it had by being careless. Confidence and complacency were much more comfortable bedfellows than urgency and discipline. Confident though he was, Flaetriu knew that his life and his soul rested upon his diligence; he checked the site carefully.

The elegantly curving shape of the Vampire Raider was now fully submerged under the sand. Although its twin dorsal fins protruded out of the desert, they were virtually invisible. A light-gravitic shield clung to the shiny surface of the fins, refracting and bending the surrounding light around them so that they were visible only as slight distortions in the already heat-distorted scene. The technology was a variation on that used in the cameleoline cloaks worn by the rangers themselves. One of the clumsy mon'keigh would walk straight into them before he saw them.

Flaetriu pulled the hood of his cloak down over his face and tightened the scarf that covered his mouth. The heat change caused by the sunrise was whipping up eddies of wind, sending sheets of sand scraping against the faces of the eldar rangers. The team's cloaks were fluttering in the cycling breeze as they settled into a dull orange colour, roughly matching the hue of the desert under the red sun.

The eight immaculately camouflaged rangers climbed into their desert-pattern jetbikes, and Flaetriu checked the line. His team were flickering in and out of visibility, but their long shadows stretched out on the sand before them, as the sun continued to rise at their backs. A couple of kilometres in front of them were the first undulations of the foothills, beyond which towered the massive mountain range that ringed the planet. A huge plume of smoke pushed up into the sky above the glowing peak of a jagged volcano, and thin rivers of lava coursed down its sides in an intricate lattice.

Even from this distance, Flaetriu could clearly see the squadron of blood red mon'keigh warriors bestride their cumbersome, bi-wheeled vehicles, staring out into the desert towards his rangers. He smiled underneath his scarf, certain that the primitive humans had no idea what was about to happen to them.

Let's go, he said, without a sound, whispering the command directly into the minds of his team.

A bank of jetbikes flashed forward from each side of him, accelerating to maximum speed almost instantaneously and virtually without sound. Flaetriu sat for a moment, watching the dust trails of his team disperse in the morning wind, enjoying the heat of the sun on his back. Then he smiled again and kicked his own bike into motion. Following the Path of the Outcast wasn't always melancholy: he was going to enjoy this.

ON REFLECTION, IT was strange that the four of them had chosen such different paths. At one time, they had all been together, bonded by a commonality of purpose and even by friendship, but then something had changed in each of them and their worlds had pulled them apart. Not one of them had been content with the cycling way of the eldar, and each had plunged their souls into specific paths, grasping hold of their fates with both hands in a manner both horrifying and inspiring to the rest of their kin.

They were the best and the worst of their people – magnificent and terrible. Each of them had given up their chances of a normal life on Biel-Tan, and each had condemned themselves to lives of power and agony. In their own ways, each had found the truth of the eldar soul, and they lived with a suppressed contempt for their fellow eldar, who also called themselves sons of Asuryan.

For Flaetriu the choice had been agonising. He had already spent a cycle as a seer, and had served for a time in the Aspect Temple of the Dire Avengers, but in neither path did he find his soul at ease. After centuries of life, he still felt as though he was not yet fully alive.

It was not that he disliked his fellow eldar, he simply could not understand their contentedness. They were all committed to a way of life that had been deliberately constructed to prevent them from becoming themselves, and they thought that they were happy.

In the ancient and long misremembered past, at the time of the Fall, it is said that the one who is now known only as Asurmen led the eldar into exile aboard the great craftworlds. It was he who founded the first of the Aspect Shrines, the Shrine of Asur, in the discipline of which the Asurya would cleanse their souls of the passions and savagery that had brought doom to their race.

Asurmen taught that there was a way for the eldar to harness their nature into weapons that could be used to protect their people, rather than to ruin themselves. The way of an Aspect Warrior was to channel the violence in an eldar's soul into service, transforming self-indulgence into acts of worship for Kaela Mensha Khaine, the bloody-handed god. War became a way of purging the eldar nature without encouraging the warriors to be consumed by the thirst for violence itself.

In the centuries and millennia that followed, the Asurya took the Path of the Warrior to all the craft-worlds, founding first the Temple of the Dire Avengers. After time, other temples were created, reflecting the multitudinous aspects of the terrible thirst in eldar souls. In mirror images of the warrior path, other paths were established within eldar society, including the Path of the Seer. Each path permitted the controlled and disciplined expression of part of the nature of the eldar, such that their souls might never again fall into the decadence that had led to their Fall. In this way was born the Path of the Eldar – a winding road of self-discipline and self-reproach. Every craftworld eldar would spend a cycle following each of the eldar ways, taming her passions and controlling her myriad nature. In this way the eldar race hoped to escape its daemons.

Of course, the way is not clear to everyone, and the souls of a few are so passionate that they cannot easily be tamed. Such rare individuals may return to the same path over and over again – perhaps flitting between different Aspect Temples until finally meeting their deaths. Even more exceptionally, some become trapped by their own essential tendencies, never able to leave their paths – doomed to fight for all time in the guise of an exarch, becoming the living incarnations of Kaela Mensha Khaine himself, both admired and abhorred by their fellow warriors and by all eldar. Such had been the fate of Laeresh and Uldreth. In her own way, this had also been the fate of Macha. But Flaetriu had been adamant that this would not be his destiny.

Flaetriu had seen the manner in which choices had changed his friends. Laeresh and Uldreth, in particular, had drifted apart, losing contact with their own memories and settling into a bitterness that they could not even explain to themselves. Even Macha had changed, although her movements were subtle and beyond the comprehension of a normal mind. She forgot nothing and found memories lurking in her mind that she had never seen before – memories that may not have been hers, and may not have been of things gone by in the past at all. The forgetfulness of the exarchs and the knowledge of the farseer transformed them all – each withdrew from their kin, vanishing deeply into their paths where non-travellers could not see.

There had been no call in Flaetriu's mind – he felt no compulsion to immerse himself utterly in one way or another. If anything, there was a general disillusionment with the entire eldar way and a faint sickness at the prospect of a life cycling through various distractions. He was an eldar, and he could see no point in his long life if he had to spend it denying his nature. These were dangerous thoughts, he knew, and they had led eldar into darkness and damnation before.

But Flaetriu was no traitor and, despite his misgivings, he loved his people and the craftworld of Biel-Tan. When his friends had begun to vanish into themselves, he had found nothing left to keep him there. Not wanting his dangerous ideas to endanger others, nor desiring his psychic presence to alert daemons to their location, he had taken his weapons and left the glorious sanctuary of Biel-Tan, setting himself adrift into the vastness of space, finding himself on the Path of the Outcast before he had given it any conscious thought.

Since then, Flaetriu had found other eldar of likemind and they had formed themselves into a ranger team, patrolling the wake of Biel-Tan and eliminating anything that strayed too close to the vast craftworld. It was a peripatetic, indulgent and liberated life that brought peace to his heart. He was loyal to his race and to himself.

Most of the Biel-Tan eldar didn't even know that the rangers existed, but Macha knew. She had always had a special bond with Flaetriu – indeed, the four friends had always been very close. Macha knew that his loyalty to Biel-Tan was beyond question, and she could rely on him to act when the Court of the Young King might be reluctant. They had fought together many times before, including during the debacle with the mon'keigh on Tartarus. Unlike many of the eldar, Macha understood that the Path of the Outcast was as essential to the eldar way as any of the other paths.

'THE REPORT STATES that one of the scout patrols has come under attack, captain,' reported Sergeant Corallis, his face creased with urgency. The veteran Marine, who still served as a scout for the Third Company, had completed his training on Rahe's Paradise decades before, yet he was still surprised at the way that the news of the attack had affected him.

'You're certain that they were eldar?' asked Ikarus, taking careful note of the emotion in Corallis's expression.

'Yes. Caleb was very clear. Five or six eldar warriors in camouflage gear ambushed them while they were investigating a volcanic eruption on the edge of the mountains,' said Corallis, nodding for emphasis.

'IT'S THE BIEL-TAN farseer again,' said Gabriel. His back was facing the assembled command squad and he was staring out into space through a giant view screen that dominated the wall. As he spoke, the others turned to face him, but he did not turn.

'You cannot be sure of that, Gabriel,' said Prathios calmly.

Nobody knew better than the chaplain how disturbed Gabriel had been by the events with the eldar on Tartarus, especially since they followed so closely on the heels of such trauma on Cyrene. The Blood Ravens captain was amongst the finest warriors that the Chapter had ever produced, but there was still a part of him that was merely a man. And that part could not hide from its conscience. The conscience could not be surgically removed during the Implantation Process, and they was no zygote that could completely cripple it – not even hypnotherapy could deprive a man of his humanity. That was why Chaplain Prathios was there, after all.

'Prathios is right, captain,' agreed Tanthius, eying his captain with concern. 'Eldar raids are not uncommon in that region. We have seen them before.'

'Not like this,' countered Gabriel, turning at last. 'This is an invasion.'

The other Marines stared at their captain. They knew better than to doubt him, but they also knew that there was no way that he could know anything about this 'invasion.' He was not a librarian, and he had no sanctioned gifts of foresight. However, he did have uncannily acute senses, and the eyebrows of the Inquisition had been raised in his direction before, particularly since Cyrene.

'You can't know that,' said Ikarus bluntly, speaking what was in all of their minds as the only librarian amongst them. 'Caleb saw five or six warriors, not an invasion force. Even a vanguard force would have been larger than that, and the main force would have appeared on the Monastery's long range sensors – the web-portal that used to be on Rahe's Paradise was destroyed centuries ago.'

'I know it's an invasion,' repeated Gabriel without anger, his blue eyes brilliant and certain. It was just a statement of fact. 'It is an invasion, and that farseer is behind it. Don't ask me how I know, I just know.'

'What do you propose that we should do, captain?' asked Tanthius, cutting to the chase. For him this was the most important question; he would follow his captain into the Eye of Terror itself if he asked him to, and he would not ask why. Gabriel had been his battle-brother for as long as he could remember, and not once had the great captain led him wrong. If he said that this was an invasion, then it was an invasion, and at the end of the day Tanthius didn't care how he knew.

Gabriel paused for a moment as he formulated an answer. The battle barge, *Litany of Fury*, in whose conference chamber they now stood, was on its way to

the Trontiux system, where it would fall into an orbit
around the third planet so that a small detachment
of Marines, including himself, Tanthius and Chaplain Prathios, could descend to the planet's surface
and conduct the Blood Trials. After Trontiux III, the
Litany of Fury would head for the Lorn system, before
finally heading for Rahe's Paradise. Even as they
spoke, guardsman Ckrius was being rapidly transformed into an initiate down in the *Litany*'s
apothecarion, and the Third Company had to ensure
that he was the first of a new batch, not just a single,
isolated neophyte.

The Third were not the only Company who found
their home on the *Litany*. The Ninth was also based
within its revered and venerated halls, under the
command of Captain Ulantus. It was a Reserve Company, comprised mostly of Devastator squads, and it
was at about three-quarter strength. Ulantus was a
straightforward and direct man; he would not enter-
tain Gabriel's fantasies, even though, as a Battle
Company commander, Gabriel was technically the
ranking officer on the *Litany*.

'The *Litany* will continue to Trontiux III – we cannot afford to miss this opportunity to run the Blood
Trials there… Captain Ulantus can oversee the trials
in my place. I will take the *Ravenous Spirit* to Rahe's
Paradise, immediately,' said Gabriel eventually, confident that his plan was sound.

'I do not approve of this plan, captain,' hissed
Ikarus heavily. 'We have no reason to assume that the
five eldar on Rahe's Paradise are anything more than
pirate-raiders. Sergeant Caleb and Father Librarian
Jonas will be able to dispatch them – that is why they

are there, after all. In only a few weeks, the *Litany of Fury* itself will arrive and we can deal with any residual problems then, if necessary. I am sure that Captain Ulantus would agree with me.'

'I'm sure he would, Ikarus,' replied Gabriel dryly. 'But Ulanus is not Commander of the Watch and neither is he captain of the *Ravenous Spirit*. Neither, for that matter, are you, librarian.'

Chaplain Prathios had already lowered himself into one of the chairs that ringed the perimeter of the room, surrounding the depression in which it was expected that speakers would stand to address the chamber. He watched his old friend's eyes narrow with bitterness as he spoke to the librarian, and a wave of concern washed into his mind. Ikarus was newly elevated to the command squad, following the recent fall of Isador on Tartarus, and the two Marines did not yet know each other very well. Gabriel and Isador had been like brothers, and nobody should ever have had to step into his shoes so quickly – especially after the terrible way in which he met his end.

Prathios had watched Gabriel in prayer on many occasions over the last few weeks, and even he could see Isador's tainted and ruined face plaguing the captain's already tortured mind: there was certainly little room for Ikarus in Gabriel's affections at the moment. Not for the first time in the last few months, Prathios found himself concerned for the balance of his captain's mind.

Ikarus bit his tongue and nodded in silence, shifting his shoulders into a slight bow. He had voiced his opinion, in accordance with his duty, but Gabriel was right that his viewpoint was ultimately irrelevant if the captain chose to ignore him. This was not a democracy, and Gabriel was not just any captain – he was the Chapter's Commander of the Watch, charged with safeguarding the boundaries of the realm against incursions and threats. If he saw a threat to Rahe's Paradise, then he should act; Ikarus could and should do nothing to stop him.

'I will explain this course of events to Ulantus,' said Gabriel, striding over to the reinforced metal doorway, which hissed open as he approached. 'I realise that many of you have duties to perform during the Blood Trials or misgivings about my choice,' he continued, without staring back at Ikarus. 'So I will not oblige you to accompany me to Rahe's Paradise. However, I would ask that you assemble a force large enough to man the strike cruiser, *Ravenous Spirit*, and have it ready to embark immediately.' Then he was gone.

The rest of his command squad exchanged glances: a mixture of resignation, confusion, and determination flooded around the conference room. Then, without a word, they bowed to each other and left to make the necessary preparations.

CHAPTER THREE
CLANDESTINATION

THE GLITTERING, ELEGANT form of the *Eternal Star* glinted in the opening of the webway, fluttering like a giant, weightless bird of prey. It was caught in the immense shade of Biel-Tan itself, which dominated the system like a colossus, drawing all eyes to it as though trapping them with some mysterious gravity.

A faint, black light spilled out of the portal that led into the webway, sheening across the entrance like a thin film of oil, making it visible only as a slight distortion in the light cast by the stars beyond. It was not properly in the material realm, and its presence there was more suggestive than substantial. If travellers could really see what lay beyond the portal, none might dare enter it.

The *Eternal Star* seemed to flex its wings, rippling with semi-visible energies as it closed on the portal, drawing away from the gravity of the gargantuan craftworld behind it. Standing on the control deck and gazing out into the portal, Macha's mind was a labyrinth of hesitations.

'I never said that it was the future,' she muttered, as much to herself as to anyone else. When there were so many thoughts echoing around inside her head, it often helped Macha to vocalise one of them just to give it some immediacy.

Without shifting the view on the screen, Macha could see in her mind the image of a sleek form slipping out of one of the huge docking bays in the underside of the craftworld. The vessel just seemed to drop silently out of the bottom of Biel-Tan, as though it had suddenly been born into the galaxy then and there, and then it accelerated towards the *Eternal Star* with smooth and effortless ease. Macha held the image in her mind for a couple of seconds and then shook her head, still uncertain that this was the right course of action: the Court had decided not to act on her vision, but to commit the Swordwind to the increasingly volatile situation on Lorn V – that was their choice, and it was not her place to challenge such decisions, only to guide them.

Yet something had convinced her that this was an exceptional circumstance. It had not been the faith of Draconir or even the personal bitterness of Laeresh; something in her soul told her that she had to go to Lsathranil's Shield, although she could not tell what it was. For some undecipherable reason, her vision of that world was clouded and hazy.

The Reaper's Blade *is in position*. From the command deck of his Void Dragon cruiser, Laeresh's voice eased its way directly into Macha's head and broke her chain of thought, resolving her confusion with its single-minded clarity.

The *Reaper's Blade* was a beautiful ship, almost invisible against the darkness of space because it was immaculately black from prow to stern. It was unique amongst the vessels of the Biel-Tan fleet since it did not bear the emblem of the craftworld – the seeing eye set into a triangle of power. Instead, the runic symbol of the Dark Reapers was emblazoned in shimmering silver into the star-sails that projected out of the middle of the hull on both sides, like wings. No eldar could command that ship, except for the exarch of the Aspect Temple himself – not even the Court of the Young King could order it into battle, and Laeresh was taking great pleasure in ignoring Uldreth's requests that the *Reaper's Blade* should accompany the fleet to Lorn.

The Dark Reapers occupied an unusual position in the society of Biel-Tan. Unlike the other major Aspect Temples, they were not represented in the Court of the Young King. Instead, they were a semi-autonomous force on the craftworld, which placed them on the periphery of Biel-Tan society and caused some eldar to view them with suspicion. This marginal status was reinforced by the low numbers of eldar who joined the temple during their cycle on the Path of the Warrior, which meant that the temple was always one of the smallest and most mysterious on the craftworld.

Legend had it that the Dark Reapers found their origins on the lost craftworld of Altansar, which once partnered Ulthwé as a guardian of the Eye of Terror. Many millennia ago, the Eye expanded and Altansar was caught in its grip. For centuries, the doomed craftworld battled the daemonic forces of the massive warp storm as it was slowly pulled in. But, after half a millennium of fierce resistance, Altansar finally succumbed and plunged into the Eye, never to be seen or heard of again. From the millions of eldar who perished, their emerged only one survivor, the Phoenix Lord Maugan Ra, the Harvester of Souls.

Maugan Ra was the first of the Dark Reapers, wielding the first Reaper Cannon – the Maugetar. His armour was blackened and tortured by the rapacious currents of the Eye, and in that terrible visage he dedicated himself to wreaking vengeance on those who had brought destruction to his temple. With no home left to defend, Maugan Ra adopted the maxim that remains etched into the wraithbone shrines in Dark Reaper temples to this day: war is my master, death my mistress. He had no lord other than death itself. Although Asurmen was the first of the Phoenix Lords and his Dire Avengers are the most numerous of all Aspect Warriors, there was never a warrior that more perfectly enshrined the nature of Kaela Mensha Khaine, the Bloody-Handed God, than Maugan Ra. Perhaps this is why his temple is still viewed with such dread.

The temples of the Dark Reapers are doomed to stay on the edge of craftworld society, since the craftworld on which they were born was destroyed long ago – the Reapers find their home in battle, and nowhere else. This means that none can claim dominion over them, and they answer to none other than their own exarch, aspiring always to rediscover the ancient armour of Maugan Ra and the lost craftworld of Altansar.

Hold there, replied Macha at last, her mind wandering in search of a sign that they were on the right path.

Uldreth had made it very clear that he did not approve of her departure, but there was little that he could do to stop her. She was the craftworld's primary farseer, head of the Seer Council. However, even the seers of the Council were concerned by her actions – Farseer Taldeer had foreseen a more pressing crisis on Lorn V, and her vision had been shared by a number of others. They were certain that the situation there was unfolding in Biel-Tan's future, and that they had to act now. Macha could not help but think that it was strange that she had not also seen that vision, and part of her was struggling to connect it with her own. Her intuition told her that there had to be a connection, no matter how or why it was hidden to her now. It was very unusual for the minds of the council members to be completely out of synchronisation. However, if there was a connection, it remained invisible to Macha.

'Things have come too far to stop now,' she muttered to herself, shaking her head slightly and sighing. Part of her knew that things had come this far because of the antipathy between Laeresh and Uldreth – they drove each other to the extremes of forbearance, and it was dangerous. Laeresh was out there now in the *Reaper's Blade*, and Macha could feel his smug sense of satisfaction even from the control deck of the *Eternal Star* – she was fully aware that the Reaper was doing this only partly because he had faith in her vision. He was passionate beyond good sense. For a moment she lamented the way eldar passions could escalate events so quickly. 'I did not say that it was the future.'

Just under the surface of her consciousness, Macha knew that this situation was partly her fault – although neither Uldreth nor Laeresh could remember that.

The Hand of Asuryan will guide you. It was Draconir's mind, projected from somewhere in the interior of the craftworld itself.

Macha nodded at the unexpected thought from Biel-Tan.

Follow my lead, she suggested, directing her thoughts to the sleek cruiser that flanked her own.

Very good, farseer, replied Laeresh. There was an edge of eagerness in his mind.

With a sudden but smooth movement, apparently thrusting its shimmering wings back into a dart, the *Eternal Star* flicked forward into the slick sheen that filmed across the portal, and it vanished.

'Yes,' said Laeresh, smiling, as the *Reaper's Blade* shot into the webway in the farseer's wake.

GABRIEL'S FACE TWITCHED and contorted with painful concentration as his head flooded with images and memories. His eyes flicked back and forth, as though they were scanning across scenes etched into the back of his eye-lids, and beads of sweat rolled down his scarred forehead, running into streams as they hit the service studs just above his left eyebrow.

While final preparations were made for the departure of the *Ravenous Spirit*, Captain Angelos was kneeling in prayer in the Third Company's chapel, aboard the *Litany of Fury*. The heavy, gothic spire pierced out of the top of the massive battle barge, like a ritualistic gun-turret, sparkling with armaments and ornaments to the Emperor's undying glory. It was the preserve of Chaplain Prathios, who administered to the spiritual needs of the Company in the sanctity of the chapel's towering spaces.

Standing in the deep shadows behind the altar, a faint light flickering across his face, Prathios was watching the tortured figure of his captain suffer on the steps before the image of the Emperor.

It was not unusual for his Marines to suffer some minor trauma after completion of some of their most grotesque duties; it seemed to be an affliction of the sensitive minds of the Blood Ravens. The same process of genetic selection that led to the perpetuation of great numbers of librarians and scholars in the Chapter also guaranteed that all the Marines would be of unusually sensitive dispositions, even after all the hypnotherapy and psyche-conditioning. Prathios knew of some of the rumours whispered about them in the halls of other Chapters, but he was a chaplain of the Emperor and had more elevated voices to listen to than the malicious whispers of the ignorant.

When he thought back over all the things that Gabriel had been through over the last year or so, Prathios was not surprised that his soul was tortured. Despite all of the modifications and implants, despite the infernos of battle and the perpetual horrors of war, there was still a human soul hidden beneath that super-armoured shell. Immaculate duty, honour and courage could not shield his mind from everything. Every soul had a breaking point, and Prathios prayed to the Emperor every day that Gabriel's trials had not pushed him beyond his. But his behaviour had changed since Cyrene, and the incident with Isador on Tartarus had been hard on him; he had spent a lot of time in the chapel, alone with his nightmares. And now he seemed to have fixated on the eldar farseer, as though she were responsible for all the problems that currently beset the Chapter. If he were honest with himself, Prathios was concerned about his captain's state of mind, and he knew that he was not the only one who had noticed Gabriel's odd behaviour.

The captain's lips were working soundlessly, as he muttered prayers and litanies of purity, combating the vicious images that stabbed at his mind with the force of his faith. The muscles in his neck bunched and knotted against the physical pain that seemed to seep through from his waking dreams.

'Gabriel, you must rest. There is no need for us to depart so soon,' said Prathios, breaking the fevered silence with his deep voice.

'There is need,' said Gabriel, slowly and deliberately, keeping his eyes closed.

Prathios said nothing for a moment, watching his captain fall back into prayer. 'Your men will follow you, Gabriel. I will follow you. But you must give us more reason than your faith. You are a Blood Raven – we do not act without reason. Knowledge is our power–'

'–there is no need to lecture me on my obligations or my nature, chaplain,' interrupted Gabriel, his eyes flashing open suddenly. 'And it does not become you, of all people, to denigrate my faith. The

Emperor's light guides the Blood Ravens, just as it does the rest of the Adeptus Astartes. We have no less and we need no more than that.'

The chaplain nodded, taken aback slightly by his captain's sudden venom, but acknowledging that he was right. There was nothing more glorious than opening one's soul to the guidance of the Imperial light, although the sacred Astronomican remained invisible to most servants of the Emperor, radiating through the echoing minds of astropaths and sanctioned psykers. As a chaplain, Prathios had seen glimpses of its pulsating brightness, and he was always conscious of it as a beacon in the deepest subconscious parts of his mind. But he would never claim to have seen it clearly or unambiguously in the glare of his mind's eye. Ever since Cyrene, however, he had seen Gabriel blinded by visions of its radiance, and the Blood Ravens captain had no sanctioned psychic potentials.

'You are right, captain,' confessed Prathios, stepping forward into the flickering light and bowing slightly to Gabriel. 'It is not my place to question the wisdom of your decisions. But I know that you will forgive me my concern for you and for our Chapter. I am your chaplain, after all.'

'I know, Prathios, and there is no need for talk of forgiveness,' said Gabriel gently, rising from his knees and smiling faintly at his old friend. 'We have known each other a long time, and I have been grateful for your counsel on many occasions before now. You are a wiser man than I will ever be, but I must simply ask you to trust me now.'

'Trust is not something for which you must ask, Gabriel,' replied Prathios, staring into the captain's bright blue eyes and nodding his assurance. 'Where it is deserved, it is given freely and without question.'

'Do not abandon your questions, chaplain. I am sure that we will have need for them before this affair is over. Your trust I accept gratefully, but I would never ask you to stop questioning my actions. As you said, we are Blood Ravens: to question is our nature.'

The sound of an immense weight shifting made the two Marines stop and turn, casting their eyes back down the aisle of the chapel towards the huge ornamental doors that led out into the uppermost levels of the *Litany of Fury*. The ancient stone tablets that served as doors swung inwards slowly, letting a sheet of light stream in from the brightly lit corridor beyond, stretching down the aisle towards the two old friends. Silhouetted in the doorway, with his massive arms outstretched to each side, holding open the giant stones, stood the impressive figure of Tanthius. Except for his helmet, he was already sealed into his ancient suit of Terminator armour.

Tanthius gave the doors a final push, forcing them to open fully and fold back against the interior walls of the magnificent chapel with a resounding crash, flooding the cavernous space with light. He bowed sharply before he spoke.

'My apologies for the interruption, captain. The *Ravenous Spirit* is now ready for departure. We have a full complement of Marines and the servitors inform me that the service crew is also at adequate strength. The *Litany*'s apothecarion will not release Ckrius into our care, so he will stay aboard the battle barge under the watchful gaze of the apothecary. In case we or Father Librarian Urelie have need of maintenance services, Techmarine Ephraim has volunteered to join us temporarily from the Ninth Company. I understand that Captain Ulantus has approved this.'

'I am not sure that he approves of it, Tanthius, but he has agreed that it would be unreasonable of him to cause a Battle Company to depart into a combat zone without any technical support,' nodded Gabriel, smiling to himself at the futile protestations that been levelled by Ulantus when he had made the request. 'Ephraim is a fine Marine, and he will be an asset to us.'

The Terminator Marine offered no response – none was required. He simply nodded his understanding. 'We await your convenience, captain.'

THE SCROLL WAS one of the oldest artefacts that they had unearthed below the monastery. Its material was akin to paper, but somehow it had survived the passage of millennia in a small, vacuum-sealed, adamantium tube. It contained a mixture of images and passages of text, inscribed by hand in some form of ink that had neither faded nor dulled over time. The reds and blacks of the lines were vibrant and brilliant, as though only penned on that very day. The illuminations were breathtaking.

As far as Meritia could tell, the scroll was titled, 'The Sky Angel Steals the Light,' and it contained a folk-story of some kind. A myth perhaps. It had been written in an old and primitive version of High Gothic, hardly recognisable to modern eyes, but it was clearly the product of a culture under the influence of the Imperium of Man. The fact that she had found it in the ruins of an ancient fortress monastery

led her to believe that the story had some relevance
to the Blood Ravens – an implicit connection being
the angel in the title and the winged insignia that
punctuated the text in the place of section breaks. It
was not identical with the emblem of the Blood
Ravens, but it was similar.

The Adeptus Astartes did not usually enlist scribes
to record folklore or legends, and certainly not in
such elaborate or ostentatiously artistic forms, so the
scroll was intriguing for reasons other than merely its
content.

The oddly cursive curl of the script was similar to
that found on the casket in which they had uncovered the wraithbone tablet, which made Meritia
think that the scroll and tablet were probably con-
temporaneous with each other. But the wraithbone
tablet was covered in the impossible beauty of
eldar runes, and this scroll was definitely the product of human artistry – its undeniable beauty
being clumsy in comparison with the xenos artefact.

After Jonas had carried the tablet to the librarium,
the two of them had spent some time trying to decipher its markings, but they had not made much
progress. The runes were unconventionally shaped,
and they seemed to swim and shift as the scholars
tried to read them. After many hours, they had not
got much further than the title, and they were not
even sure that they had got that right: Ishandruir –
The Ascension. It was going to take quite some time
to translate the rest, but their only urgency stemmed
from their own excitement about the find. There was
no real hurry.

Returning to her little chamber for the night, Meritia had pulled out the scroll as a form of light relief. Its odd High Gothic was relatively simple to read, and the story that it told was interesting enough. As far as she could work out, it had something to do with a giant bird who could change shape into that of a man – the Sky Angel. Through a long and protracted process of trickery and deception, the Sky Angel stole a star from the evil gods who sought to keep the system in darkness. He tried to steal it for himself, but he dropped it as he fled through space, and it burst into life, flooding the local planets with light and giving them life. She was not really sure what happened to the Sky Angel after that, since the focus of the story then seemed to shift to the surface of one of the planets, where the gods remained fuming with wrath, which spewed out of the ground like lava from volcanoes.

As she read, the vox-unit in the corner of her chamber whistled delicately. In the still night air, the sound seemed unnecessarily shrill and loud, and Meritia glared at the little machine with irritation. The powerful amplifier arrays of the outpost-monastery were essential for the maintenance of communication with the rest of the sector, but they did mean that any sense of seclusion that Meritia might have enjoyed in her own chamber was entirely false. For some reason, the Blood Ravens Techmarines and even a detachment from the Adeptus Mechanicus had never been able to establish a reliable astropathic station on Rahe's Paradise. Two astropaths had been sent to the planet over the years, but both had been wracked with nightmares and agony. One had hanged himself in his cell. So the outpost relied on the slow, primitive vox technology even more than it might otherwise have done.

There was a loud hiss of static, and then a voice crackled with sibilance.

'...ister Meritia. This is Sister Ptolemea... en route to... e's Paradise... two days. Please acknowledge.'

Meritia just stared at the machine with mounting displeasure. Not only had it interrupted her studies, but it was now also the bearer of such troublesome news. She knew Ptolemea – she was also of the Order of the Lost Rosetta, although the two of them had never been close. She was young and ambitious, and Meritia was not sure why she should be on her way to Rahe's Paradise. This was not the kind of posting that someone like Ptolemea would request.

'Acknowledged,' she said simply, not bothering to repeat her message and not caring whether it was swamped in the rush of whining feedback that suddenly filled the echoing stone room.

There was no reply, and Meritia chose to interpret that as a good sign.

Part of the reason that she had answered the Blood Ravens' call for scholarly aid on Rahe's Paradise was that she had wanted to escape the internal politics of the Ecclesiarchy. There were so many agendas competing for resources in those hallowed halls, and factions were constantly at each other's throats, determined to discredit their hypotheses and research programmes. From time to time, there were even charges of heresy thrown about, when one powerful group of scholars realised that another was working on a competing project. For obvious reasons, charges of heresy within the Ecclesiarchy were taken even more seriously than such charges in other branches of the sprawling Administratum – and heresy was always the most serious of charges. The Adeptus Sororitas were in a unique and complicated position when such dramas began to unfold, since they were technically part of the Ecclesiarchy itself, but they could also be enlisted into the service of the Ordo Hereticus whenever there was need. It was more often the case that the militant orders of the Sisters of Battle would be seconded by the Inquisition for services outside the confines of the Ecclesiarchy, but from time to time the inquisitors of the Ordo Hereticus had need for the special talents of the non-militant orders, such as that of the Lost Rosetta, particularly when charges of doctrinal heresy were levelled at curators, scholars or priests.

Meritia was something of an idealist, and she sincerely believed that scholarship should be free of politics. Of course, she was aware that certain types of knowledge could be dangerous, but she was confident in the ability of scholars to draw a line between the discovery of dangerous information and the internalisation of any taint that it might contain. She was opposed, for example, to the puritans in her order who insisted that the Lost Rosetta should have no contact with alien artefacts, lest their own sacred purity be contaminated by the foul taint of the xenos creatures. She had seen Ordo Hereticus inquisitors summoned to investigate her own Sisters when it was discovered that they were analysing a lost eldar tract or an intercepted data-stream from a tau fleet.

Being on her own on Rahe's Paradise was supposed to free her from such considerations, although she was aware that her willingness to leave the order's convent would be seen as suspicious in itself by some, and that her association with the Adeptus Astartes might not be looked upon too favourably by the authorities in the Ecclesiarchy itself. Nonetheless, she thought that she would at least be out of sight for a while and thus free to indulge her scholarly nature. She had also been confident that, whatever their doctrinal differences, the Ecclesiarchy could never openly claim that association with a Space Marine Chapter would corrupt one of the Sisters Sororitas.

The imminent arrival of Ptolemea was a harsh wake-up call, and Meritia's mind raced with various explanations for the dispatch of the younger Sister. She was especially concerned since no word had been sent ahead of her by the order's Sister Superiors or by any agents of the Ecclesiarchy. It seemed that her arrival was supposed to be a surprise and, given that, Meritia wondered under whose authority the ambitious woman was really coming. She had certainly made no requests for additional researchers herself.

Finally turning her face away from the little vox-unit in the corner, Meritia inspected herself in the mirror that dominated the back of the main door to her chamber. It was there mainly to reflect the daylight onto her desk in the hours before sunset, since her slit-window was inadequate to the task of providing sufficient reading light, and for some reason artificial light was damaging to some of the older texts. Indeed, some of the most interesting tracts remained utterly invisible until exposed to natural light.

She stared at her grey hair, narrowing her eyes slightly in persistent disbelief. She could still remember the first morning when she had caught her own reflection in that mirror and had gasped in shock at the transformation. When she had arrived on Rahe's Paradise, her hair had been long and dark. One morning, without any apparent reason, it was shimmering and grey. She still had no idea what had happened to it, but now she was more concerned about what Ptolemea would think of the sudden, inexplicable transformation.

THE ENGINES ROARED and poured flames down into the desert as the Thunderhawk slowly descended, blasting a wide crater into the sand as its retro-burners flared. The crimson gunship shone like a second star against the red of the rising sun. It landed with a surprisingly delicate touch, and then there was a slight delay before the hatch cracked open and lowered itself into a disembarkation ramp.

Without hesitation or ceremony, Gabriel strode down the ramp, taking in the chilled morning air, the desert, and the black, towering shape of the Blood Ravens' outpost-monastery. He paused momentarily at the bottom of the ramp and turned to survey the horizon. Scans from the *Ravenous Spirit* in orbit had not revealed the presence of any alien craft or personnel on the surface, but Gabriel knew better than to trust that even the Imperium's finest technology could outsmart that of the eldar. He swept his eyes over the desert, satisfying himself that there was nothing there.

At the head of a line of scouts, Father Librarian Jonas Urelie stood next to Sergeant Caleb waiting for Gabriel to acknowledge them. The sand whipped around them like a heavy, red mist, but touches of gold in their armour burst with reflected light. Except for their helmets, they were in full, formal battle armour. They had not had much notice of the captain's arrival, otherwise they would have organised a more ostentatious reception – for now, the military honour of an armoured Blood Ravens librarian and scout squadron would have to suffice. Jonas was slightly concerned that Sister Meritia had declined his invitation to welcome the great captain, but he understood that it was short notice.

As Gabriel looked around, the rest of the command squad strode down the ramp behind him, fanning out into a wide formation at his back. They were fully armed and armoured, with their weapons held ready. Tanthius planted his massive feet immediately and started to track his storm bolter across the terrain. They were taking no chances.

'Father librarian,' began Gabriel, finally striding over to the older Marine and grasping his arm in greeting. 'We received news of your recent encounter with the eldar, and we are here ahead of the *Litany of Fury* to bolster your defences.'

'Captain Angelos,' replied Jonas, meeting his sparkling gaze. 'You are most welcome here, but we have seen nothing further of the eldar since they attacked Caleb's squad.' The veteran librarian tilted his head to indicate the scout sergeant on his left. 'As you can see, we are not under attack.'

'I will receive your report on the eldar shortly,' said Gabriel, sharply shifting his attention to Caleb before turning it back to Jonas. 'It is good to see you, old friend,' he said, smiling suddenly.

'It has been a long time, Gabriel,' replied Jonas, pleased that the formality had been dropped. 'We have much to discuss. Rahe's Paradise has turned out to be even more interesting than I had anticipated.'

'Father Jonas,' interjected Corallis, stepping up to Gabriel's shoulder. 'It is an honour to be back on Rahe's Paradise again.'

'Ah, young Corallis, the honour is mine,' replied Jonas, nodding his head in a show of mock respect. 'Although, you are no longer so young, I see.'

Corallis smiled and nodded in return. It was a long time since he had been stationed on Rahe's Paradise as a trainee scout, but Jonas had been in charge even then. The two had been through a lot together, and the old librarian was proud of the younger Marine's achievements. He was right, however, that the veteran sergeant was no longer a young man: much of his abdomen and right side had been destroyed by an eldar Warp Spider on Tartarus, and he was now riddled with bionics, even more than the average Marine. To recognise his valour on that cursed planet, Gabriel had elevated him into the command squad, making him a veteran sergeant despite the fact that he had been in a scout squadron only a year earlier. It was fitting that the Commander of the Watch should have an expert scout close at hand.

'Sergeant,' said Gabriel, interrupting the reunion without ill will. 'Take four bikes and run reconnaissance around the surrounding terrain. I assume that you can remember your way around.'

'Of course, captain,' replied Corallis, nodding sharply and turning to head back up into the Thunderhawk.

'Corallis,' called Gabriel after him. 'Take Ikarus with you.'

The sergeant paused to acknowledge the order, and then jogged up into the gunship, inside which the bikes were braced into the deck. Ikarus, who had heard Gabriel shout the order to Corallis, strode up the ramp behind him.

'He is a fine Marine, father,' said Gabriel, turning back to Jonas.

'Yes,' replied Jonas, watching Corallis disappear into the ship. 'He always was.'

There was a moment of silence, and then Jonas spoke again. 'Will you be conducting the Blood Trials before the *Litany of Fury* arrives, captain?'

Gabriel considered the question. 'Perhaps it would be wise to make a start, father. We may not have much time.'

Jonas inspected Gabriel's eyes again, searching for some clue about the urgency. It seemed clear to Jonas that the eldar were gone – there had been raiders on Rahe's Paradise before. Indeed, he had heard one rogue trader refer to the place as Raider's Paradise. He wondered what Gabriel knew that he did not. He simply nodded.

'Tanthius, organise a defensive deployment around the monastery,' said Gabriel, looking back over his shoulder at the magnificent, towering form of the Terminator. 'The rest of us will move inside. The monastery is clearly the strong-point in this area.'

As he spoke, a thunderous growl echoed down the ramp of the Thunderhawk as four blood-red bikes emerged into the morning sun. They paused for a moment at the top of the ramp, and then Corallis gunned his engine, pulling the front wheel up as his bike shot forward down the ramp. As he hit the sand he threw the bike to one side and roared out into the desert, his ad hoc squadron in close pursuit.

IN THE FAINT blue light of the sanctum of the Dire Avengers' temple, Uldreth paced restlessly around the holographic image that was projected in the centre of the octagonal chamber. The three dimensional picture was intricate and complicated, laced with the glowing tracks of spacecraft and trace lines of weapons discharge. The vectors were plotted in wisps of green as luminous blue darts flickered and flashed through the image.

The exarch shot occasional glances at the shifting scene, taking in all the details in a fraction of a second. His mind had become so accustomed to strategic layouts that they no longer seemed to require any conscious interpretation. Despite the fact that the complicated image was actually a composite of two separate theatres, Uldreth could see the potentials and realities of each instantly, while an inner voice continued to rail against the reckless abandon of Macha and Laeresh.

One of the projections showed the farseer's wraithship as a burning wing of brilliance, fluttering like a mythical bird on the cusp of an impossibly black abyss. Another cruiser, presumably the *Reaper's Blade*, flickered on the edge of the image, dark and foreboding in deepest purple. The intent of the two ships was clear from their formation; they were about to enter the webway portal, at which point they would finally blink off Uldreth's chart.

The second scene, overlaid and interlaced with the first, showed a clutch of cruisers setting forth in the opposite direction, taking the vanguard of the Biel-Tan Swordwind to the Lorn system. The youthful farseer, Taldeer, was in the command ship. In painful and sorrowful tones, she had spoken to the exarchs of the Court about an unfathomable foe hidden in the depths of Lorn V. The other seers had also glimpsed shadows moving across the once glittering system, and the decision to despatch the Swordwind had been unanimous in the Seer Council – Macha had not been there to oppose it, and Uldreth was not convinced that she would have opposed it even had she still been there to do so.

The Court of the Young King had not been so united. The old Fire Dragon, Draconir, had objected to the ease with which Uldreth had offered his support to Taldeer, whilst denying it to Macha, the craftworld's most senior farseer. He had complained that the ramshackle army of orks on Lorn V was hardly a threat worthy of the Bahzhakhain, and certainly did not constitute a dark, unfathomable, or mysterious foe. The force of orks was dangerous, certainly, and its presence on an old exodite world was an insult that could not be suffered for long, but it did seem that the green-skin-hating mon'keigh were already on route to Lorn, and it seemed sensible to let the two fumbling, parasitic races kill each other for now. The Swordwind could always be sent later, to deal with the survivors, after it had followed the advice of its principal farseer in Lsathranil's Shield.

Uldreth stopped pacing suddenly and glared at the intermixed trails of fluorescent colour, as though willing them into new patterns, although he was unsure about which fleet he wanted to stop. It was too late to do much about either, but Uldreth was angry with himself for his post facto indecision. He hated that he could not control Macha, and he hated that the cursed Dark Reaper could accompany her without fear of retribution from the Court. He knew that Laeresh would be loving this. At the same time, Uldreth could not suppress the suspicion that Macha might be right. At an unconscious level, Uldreth knew that he could and should trust the farseer, and he was not sure what prevented him from doing so. It was just a feeling, but it was complicated by invisible, subconscious currents that he could neither see nor understand.

As he glared at the racing images, Uldreth raged inside at his desire to call back the *Eternal Star*. He raged even more at the niggling certainty that he should really send out the order to arrest the Swordwind before it was irrevocably committed to the assault on Lorn. Instead, he just stared at the holographics with his green eyes burning until the *Eternal Star* blinked into the webway portal, and the Swordwind's cruisers streaked off the scope, accelerating into javelins of light.

CHAPTER FOUR
CAMELEOLINE

'I HAD BEEN led to believe that Librarian Akios Isador would be here,' said Ptolemea, as the desert wind whipped her long, red headscarf around her pale face. Her skin was porcelain-white, tinged with the faintest hints of blue, as though her veins ran a little too close to the surface. It gave her an air of elegance and fragility, belied by the harsh near-blackness of her stark eyes. Unlike the other Sisters of her order, Ptolemea had no cloak to hide her body, and no shoulder bag in which to store her trappings. Instead, she wore a crimson and asphalt body glove that clung to her figure like a second skin. It was scarred and well worn, and was studded with pockets and holsters, in which she presumably stored the equipment that she would need as a field agent of the Order of the Lost Rosetta. It appeared to Jonas that the straps around her thighs were as likely to hold weapons as styluses.

'Isador did not land with the Third Company, Sister,' answered Jonas, intrigued to know why Ptolemea might be so interested in the deceased librarian. 'I understand that he was killed in battle shortly before Captain Angelos brought his men here.'

'Indeed,' replied Ptolemea without visible emotion, looking past Jonas at the cloaked figure of Meritia.

'Perhaps I may be able to offer my own services in his place,' continued Jonas. 'Or there is Ikarus Yuiron, who is part of the honourable captain's landing party. Was there a particular issue that you wished to discuss with him?'

'I am sure that there is more than enough expertise here,' answered Ptolemea vaguely, turning her attention back to the old Blood Raven without speaking a word to her Sister.

'Yes, indeed, Sister. And I must say that it is an unexpected honour to have you here. Had you informed us of your arrival, I could have arranged a more appropriate reception for you and your escorts.' Jonas gestured casually towards the women standing on the landing ramp behind Ptolemea. The four of them were in the shimmering power armour of the Order of Golden Light, one of the smallest of the militant Order Minoris of the Adeptus Sororitas; they occasionally accompanied the non-militant Lost Rosetta on expeditions to the less hospitable parts of the galaxy. In fact, the two orders were related historically, each splitting from the now defunct Order of Lost Light after a virulent purity sweep by the Witch Hunters of the Ordo Hereticus found its particular mix of scholarship and martial prowess threatening to the stability of the Imperium.

The Sisters of Battle held their weapons braced across their chests as they scanned the sand-fogged air for signs of danger. For a moment Jonas wondered why the Ecclesiarchy would have organised such an escort for Ptolemea on a research trip to Rahe's Paradise – it hardly counted as a high-risk environment.

'I made several attempts to contact Sister Superior Meritia whilst in transit,' replied Ptolemea, looking past Jonas once again. 'It would seem that my attempts were not successful.'

'It is not unusual for vessels to experience communication disruption in this region of the segmentum, Sister. But I regret that we were unable to arrange a proper welcome for you,' replied Jonas, conscious that Meritia had not yet greeted her Sister. 'As you may be aware,' he continued, looking back over his shoulder in an attempt to include Meritia in the conversation, 'we have found some interesting artefacts recently. One of them is truly fascinating, and your arrival is most fortuitous in this regard – we have been having some problems translating the script, but I am sure that we will be able to work it out between the three of us.'

'Perhaps,' said Ptolemea, disappointing Jonas with her apparent lack of interest. She was still looking at Meritia. 'Although I have to confess that translation has never been my forte, father. I would be happy to try.'

There was a pause as the strong desert wind blew a cloud of sand across the group, dragging Ptolemea's headscarf off her head and sending it fluttering off into the sky like a blood-red bird. She let it go without the faintest reaction.

'Sister Senioris,' began Ptolemea at last, bowing her immaculately shaven head towards Meritia, 'it has been a long time. The last time I saw you, I believe that your hair was black. Time passes quickly, it seems.'

'Yes, Sister Ptolemea, although faster for some than for others,' replied Meritia carefully, her muddled grey hair tangling in the wind.

'Nonetheless, it passes for us all,' enjoined Jonas with slightly forced joviality. The tension between the two women was obvious. 'That is why we are all here, after all – to study the passage of time. Come, Sister Ptolemea, I am sure that you are eager to see the librarium?'

'Yes, indeed, father,' said Ptolemea, breaking eye contact with Meritia once again. 'Is Captain Angelos also there in the Blood Ravens' monastery?'

'He is indisposed at present, Sister. But I am sure that he will want to welcome you himself at a more convenient time for you both.' With that, Jonas turned and strode back towards the walls of the out-post.

For a few seconds, Meritia hesitated, apparently unsure about whether to accompany the Space Marine or to wait for the Adeptus Sororitas, but then she fell into step next to Jonas, leaving Ptolemea to organise her Sisters of Battle.

THE ETERNAL STAR slid out of the portal like a sleek fish through water, easing itself into real space with graceful certainty. It slipped rapidly through the void, decelerating quickly, as though unable to sustain its previous speed in the thickness of the material realm, even in the perfect vacuum of deep space. Reality itself exerted its own particular friction on the wraithship, making it glow faintly with a new heat.

After a couple of seconds, the *Reaper's Blade* shot out of the shimmering, oily black of the portal, flashing past the *Eternal Star* in a blaze of energy before its engines were cut and it began to slow down. The Void Dragon was a very different vessel from the wraithship, very much a product of the materium; it may have fallen behind in the labyrinthine webways that had brought the two ancient cruisers to the fringe of Lsathranil's Shield, but in material space its engines could be counted amongst the most powerful in the Biel-Tan fleet. The myriad souls collected into the Reaper's spirit pool were happiest in the heavy void of deep space.

Ensconced in her throne-room in the heart of the *Eternal Star*, Macha felt the phase shift that always accompanied a ship's movement out of the webway. It was like suddenly plunging into a wall of water, as though the air around her was abruptly rendered into something thicker and more viscous than it had been before. She gasped audibly, drawing in the relatively treacly air, before her lungs and her mind re-accustomed themselves to normal space once again.

As the farseer sat in silence, motionless, the runes that she had previously laid carefully onto the glossy, circular wraithbone tablet in the middle of her chamber began to twitch, jitter and hiss, like shards of ice on a hotplate. A fine steam wafted into the air, making the atmosphere even thicker and more oppressive, filling the room with a sickly sweet fragrance. Macha's eyes snapped open and she stared at the suddenly animated stones, confused by their unbidden movement.

A moment later and they were a dizzying blur of motion, spinning into a tight vortex above the polished wraithbone. Macha looked on in consternation, unsure why the runes were suddenly spiralling of their accord. They were moving faster and with more energy than she had ever seen before. Reaching out her long, elegant arm, already resplendent in the white and emerald psycho-plastic armour of the Biel-Tan, she touched her finger into the miniature storm that raged before her.

It had taken her decades of patience and diligence to bring her set of runes into perfect synchronicity with her own particular psychic signatures, and the abrupt sense of alienation that slapped her as the stones repelled her touch was akin to horror. She stared in confused disbelief at the singed and smoking tips of her fingers as she withdrew them sharply from the runic maelstrom.

With an explosion of emerald light, the stones seemed to detonate, spraying themselves into shrapnel and jagged shards that ricocheted around the polished, wraithbone walls of her inner sanctum. A hail of razor-sharp projectiles, like the tiny shuriken used in eldar firearms, lashed into Macha's body, lacerating the psychic shields and armoured plates with microscopic ease. Before she could rise to her feet or even let out a cry, Macha slumped forwards onto the circular tablet, unconscious and bleeding from thousands of tiny incisions.

* * *

THE HUGE WOODEN table was set up against the wall at the far end of the librarium, directly beneath the soaring arch of stained glass that reached up into the shadows of the distant, vaulted ceiling. Light streamed through the window in great shafts of colour, perforating the cool air with massive javelins of warmth. The rest of the cavernous space was riddled with book stacks, aspiring towards the far-off reaches of the ceiling, each one filled with heavy, bound tomes, many of which were concerned exclusively with the long history of the Blood Ravens on Rahe's Paradise.

Jonas stepped to the side of the table to let Ptolemea get a better view of the shimmering black tablet that had been carefully laid on top of it. It was resting on a scarlet, deep-pile, velvet cloth, embossed in each corner with the golden wings of ravens. Set onto the surface of the dark, reflective wooden table directly in the full glare of the light that flooded in through the stained glass, the wraithbone tablet seemed to shine with vibrancy and energy, as though it harboured a life of its own.

Standing in the shadows behind Ptolemea, Meritia could not help but gasp at the beauty of the object that they had found in the foundations of the monastery. It had an indescribable radiance that left her breathless every time she looked at it.

'It is wraithbone?' asked Ptolemea professionally, leaning her face closer to the tablet as she spoke. 'And it is inscribed with eldar runes.' She paused, peering closely at the swimming, cursive strokes that shifted through the alien material. 'Very old eldar runes, from the look of them. I suspect that there are eldar today who would not be able to read this.' Another pause as she straightened up again. 'Very interesting,' she concluded. 'Where did you find it?'

'It was sealed in a stone casket under this very room,' replied Jonas, watching the young Sister for signs of excitement. 'The casket appears to have been decorated with ancient versions of both eldar and Gothic scripts.'

Ptolemea seemed almost bored by the remarkable discovery. She nodded distractedly and then turned away from the librarian, scanning the hundreds of book-stacks and the shadows in the hall behind her. 'Do you suppose that Captain Angelos will be joining us?' she asked.

'He is on his way, Sister,' said Jonas, sharing a glance with Meritia while Ptolemea faced back into the librarium. Meritia met his gaze for a moment, but then lowered her eyes back to the tablet on the table.

Just as Jonas spoke, the double doors at the other side of the librarium were pushed open and a blast of cold air swept through the hall, unsettling years of dust into brightly lit strips of colour, held in apparent suspension by the shafts of light from the window.

Gabriel strode along the central aisle towards the three scholars, letting the heavy doors swing closed behind him. As he walked, he seemed to be floodlit by the beams of brilliance from the stained glass, and his highly polished armour glinted with tiny, multi-coloured stars. Ptolemea's eyes widened as the captain advanced towards her.

'Sister Ptolemea,' he said as he approached the younger Sister of the Lost Rosetta. 'My apologies for being unable to welcome you earlier. You honour the Blood Ravens with your unexpected presence.'

For a brief moment Ptolemea said nothing. 'Thank you, captain. I assure you that I had no intention of taking you by surprise. I made several attempts to contact Sister Senioris Meritia whilst in transit, and I had been under the impression that Librarian Isador Akios might have alerted you to my visit.' As she spoke those last words, she watched Gabriel's eyes intently. 'However, it seems that I was mistaken on both counts, for different reasons.'

Gabriel stiffened slightly at the mention of Isador's name. He returned Ptolemea's inquiring gaze, searching for a motive. 'I was not aware that Isador had been in contact with your order, Sister,' he said, suddenly cautious. Isador had been less than stable towards the end, and, for a moment, Gabriel wondered whether this Sister had been sent to investigate him. No matter what Isador's crimes, he was still a Blood Raven, and his memory should be properly honoured.

'As you are no doubt aware by now, Brother Isador was killed in combat on Tartarus, just before the Third Company made its way to Rahe's Paradise. If there is a debt owed to you by Isador, then it will be my duty to honour it.' Gabriel bowed slightly, without taking his eyes off the woman in front of him.

'There is no debt, captain,' replied Ptolemea, returning the courtesy of a bow with a swift nod.

'Father Jonas,' began Gabriel, letting his eyes linger on Ptolemea just a little longer than necessary. 'What is this artefact that you seem so excited about?'

As he spoke, Gabriel walked past Ptolemea and approached the huge table under the coloured window. Jonas and Meritia approached and flanked him on both sides, leaving Ptolemea standing on her own behind them.

'It appears to be a piece of eldar wraithbone, inscribed with ancient runes that are beyond our understanding at present,' answered Jonas, noting with satisfaction the glint of awe that flashed in the captain's eyes as he looked at the breathtaking artefact.

'I have seen eldar tablets before, Jonas, but this is exquisite.'

'Yes, we believe that it may be one of the oldest eldar artefacts that we have encountered on a terrestrial dig,' explained Meritia.

'How long will it take to translate its content?' asked Gabriel, his eyes held transfixed by the complicated darkness in the tablet.

'We're not yet sure. But there are three of us now, so we would hope to make some progress soon,' said Jonas with a hint of optimism in his voice.

'Sister Ptolemea and I will certainly do our best to assist with this,' agreed Meritia, glancing back over her shoulder towards the younger woman.

Both Jonas and Gabriel noticed that there was no response from Ptolemea to this invitation, but they knew better than to ask about the internal affairs of the Sisterhood. Whatever issues existed between Meritia and Ptolemea, they were of no concern to the Blood Ravens, so long as the two Adeptus Sororitas performed their duties, and neither Jonas nor Gabriel had ever had any reason to doubt the honour of battle Sisters before.

'What was it doing in the foundations of the monastery, Jonas?' asked Gabriel, raising a question of equal importance to that of what the inscription said.

'Our working hypothesis is that the tablet must have been an artefact captured by the Blood Ravens during a campaign and then brought back to this facility for analysis,' replied Jonas, acknowledging the importance of the question with a grave nod.

'That is obviously nonsense, father,' snapped Ptolemea from behind them. 'I may have only just arrived, but it seems to me that this tablet was no spoil of war. You said that it was found in a casket bearing eldar and Gothic scripts? In what way would that be consistent with an artefact stolen during a battle elsewhere?'

Gabriel, Jonas and Meritia paused as they leant over the glistening wraithbone tablet, and then they slowly turned to face Ptolemea.

'She's right, Jonas,' said Gabriel. 'There must be some other explanation.'

THE SHOTS SEEMED to come out of nowhere, like a torrent of hail from a cloudless sky. Tiny projectiles rattled against the fuel tank on Corallis's bike, riddling its armour with microscopic explosions that threatened to ignite the liquid inside. Instinctively, the sergeant hit the rear brakes, skidding the back wheel into an arc and kicking up a mist of red sand. Then he opened the throttle and the bike powered out of the cloud, roaring back towards the forest-fringe on the foothills. As the machine ploughed forward, fountains of sand sprayed up from the thick tread of the huge rear tire. Immediately, he hit the brakes again and slid the bike back through 180 degrees, bringing it round to face in his original direction once again.

Shifting like shadows in the maelstrom of sand that now filled the air, Corallis could see the flickering images of several slim figures. They were clearly using some form of reactive camouflage, but, whatever it was, it was having problems adapting rapidly enough to deal with the wafting clouds of desert kicked up by the bikes. Whoever they were, they were moving faster than anyone local to Rahe's Paradise could ever move.

To honour the battle-brothers of his scout squadron who could not yet wear helmets, Corallis never wore the combat helmet to which he was now entitled. However, on this sortie he was grateful for the dark visor that swept across his eyes, shielding them from the harsh red light of the sun and from the constant barrage of sand. Out of the corner of his eye, he could see the rest of his reconnaissance team snapping their weapons back and forth, searching for their invisible foes. Ikarus was already off his bike, standing in the middle of a swirling dust-daemon with his force staff radiating flames like a beacon as he stared into the murky clouds.

Another rattle of shots ricocheted off the front of his bike, and Corallis squeezed off a volley of bolter shells from the twin-linked mount in response – he was not exactly sure where to fire, but was unwilling to let his elusive enemies feel too complacent about their camouflage.

A searing flash of blue lightning suddenly cracked out of Ikarus's staff, spiking through the red, gusting air. The jagged line of power sizzled energetically for a few seconds and then dissipated, apparently failing to root itself in a living target.

Meanwhile, the other two Marines in the recon-team were circling the fray on their bikes, keeping a constant mist of red sand spraying up from their fat wheels. Their bolters were unholstered and they unleashed the occasional experimental shot into the mire whenever they saw the flickering movement of faltering camouflage. Their circumambulations gave off an aura of confidence that pleased Corallis; they knew that Corallis and Ikarus could deal with whatever was hiding in the cloud. All the two of them had to do was prevent anything from escaping.

Corallis stared into the mist, straining his eyes behind the darkness of his visor, struggling to filter out the dizzying eddies of sand. Ikarus was probably only twenty metres away, but the sergeant could only just see his majestic form through the fog, and it was blazing with energy.

After a few seconds, Corallis realised that he was no longer under attack. Not a single shot had hit him since he had blindly returned fire with the bike's bolters. He was relatively sure that he hadn't hit anything, and for a moment he wondered whether the enemy had fled. But then he saw Ikarus stagger, as though something had struck his leg. A lance of energy jabbed out of the librarian's staff in response, but it punched into the ground next to his feet, spraying red sand where there should have been the blood of his assailant.

As he punched the accelerator on his bike, Corallis saw Ikarus fall onto one knee, the armoured plates of his left leg shattering under a silent and precise bombardment. The librarian jammed his staff into the ground to maintain his balance, and traces of blue fire coruscated along its length.

Corallis couldn't hear what was happening over the roar of his bike's engine, but in the second that it took him to close the gap he could see the speed with which the attack was taking place. Sheets of energy flashed out from Ikarus's staff, sizzling through the sand in concentric shock waves. Here and there the waves would ripple, as though breaking around invisible objects in the haze, and Ikarus followed through with great spikes of crackling flame at those points of interference. But he seemed to hit nothing.

Vaulting from his bike with his bolter drawn, Corallis attempted to trace the movement of the camouflaged enemy, rattling off shells in half-calculated, half-hopeful directions. More than anything, he wanted to draw some of the enemy fire to give Ikarus chance to recover. But whoever they were, they were not biting his bait.

Without any visible attack, Ikarus staggered back, pivoting on his knee as though some force had smashed into his right arm. Corallis could hear the librarian's roar of defiance as he struggled to hold onto his staff, which spat and dripped with power despite the assault, but the sergeant could still not see the source of the attack. Whoever it was, it was clear that their target was Ikarus.

The two other bikes came charging into the fray, skidding through the sand and coming to rest on either side of the beleaguered librarian, flanking him with their mechanical bulk and firepower. Without pausing, they opened up with their twin-linked bolters, perforating the desert clouds in both directions with long tirades of fire.

A stuttering movement made Corallis turn. About thirty metres to the east, he could see a humanoid figure flick into visibility, a long, dull orange cloak fluttering in the wind behind it and a scarf wrapped loosely around its face. There was a flesh wound on one of its legs, and it was limping. Although the sand storm blurred the image, this was the best shot that Corallis had glimpsed all afternoon. Almost instantaneously, the sergeant tracked his bolter across and squeezed off two rounds.

Ikarus had also sensed the movement, and a wave of psychic energy smashed into the eldar's chest just as the bolter shells punched into the side of his head. The ranger's incinerated and decapitated body dropped into a crumpled heap on the sand.

After the exertion, Ikarus slumped forward, using both hands to support his weight on his staff. Corallis kept his bolter ready, unconvinced that there could have been only one. If the assailants really were eldar, it would be unprecedented for them to be alone. Even eldar pirates travelled in packs, and the long, cameleoline cloak worn by the dead one was not the kind of thing that he would expect pirates to wear.

As he scanned the haze, Corallis heard Ikarus yell once again. Turning quickly, he saw the librarian lifted off his feet, thrown back between the two

Blood Ravens' bikes by an invisible blast. Before he hit the ground, another force seemed to strike at his side, spinning him in the air and severing his right arm in an abrupt fountain of blood. Ikarus crashed to the ground as the two bikes and Corallis opened up with their bolters, riddling the desert with explosive shells, strafing their fire across the vista in sweeping arcs.

Then everything was silent. The Blood Ravens held their fire, although there was no evidence that their fury had hit anything. There was no movement in the desert as the clouds of sand began to settle back down to the ground. Ikarus lay motionless in the blood-stained sand, with his severed arm still clutching his force staff nearly ten metres away from him. When Corallis stooped down over the librarian, he saw that his armour was riddled with tiny holes, across his chest plates and helmet. All of the librarian's major organs, including his brain, had been lacerated and pulverised.

THE BLOOD RAVENS had been recruiting from Rahe's Paradise for a long time before they finally set up a permanent base, and the sweeping, circular amphitheatre in which they conducted the Blood Trials was built centuries before the monastery-outpost. Its stone structure had survived more or less intact since it was first erected, until one of the local volcanoes, Krax-7, had erupted and spilt molten rock up against its north face, swamping the thick, curving wall in a lava-flow, making it look as though the edifice had been carved into the side of the volcano itself. An earthquake had then cracked straight through the arena, leaving a deep jagged ravine cut across the wide floor. The chasm dropped through the thin tectonic plate down into the liquid magma beneath, and thick sulphurous gases poured out of the rift continuously. The ravine had never closed again, and the river of molten rock had simply been incorporated into the trials that were hosted within the amphitheatre.

Gabriel stood on the centre-stone of the great arch through which the crowd of aspirant warriors poured into the arena. His armour glittered in the red sun, glowing with life and tinted with gold. On either side of him rose the daunting statues of two of the first Blood Ravens chaplains to come to Rahe's Paradise, Elizur and Shedeur, resplendent in their ornate death masks, each brandishing their staffs of office – the sacred Crozius Arcanum. The statues were nearly twice the height of Gabriel, and he was proud to stand between them, staring out into the volcanic mountains as the sun started to sink behind them.

Behind Gabriel, inside the amphitheatre, standing on a stone pedestal at the opposite end of the arena, lit by a conical beam of red sunlight that shone through the arch below Gabriel's feet, Prathios held his own Crozius into the air for the assembled crowd to see, and silence fell. He was bedecked in full battle armour, complete with his own ceremonial death mask – the contorted and tortured face of a beast, half man and half bird. The sudden silence made Gabriel turn away from the mountainscape outside and look back at the scene, casting his own long shadow across the crowd towards his chaplain. For as long as there were

Marines like Prathios, he reflected, the future of the Blood Ravens would be secure.

The arena was full of warriors already, pressed in next to each other like cattle in a corral. Their clothes were poor, worn, and ripped, and Gabriel could hardly identify their various political and familial allegiances from their ragged attire. However, although they were all pressed in so intimately, there was no jostling and no antagonism – these were men who would not hesitate to kill each other if they met outside this amphitheatre, and their restraint spoke eloquently of their awe for the Blood Ravens. Despite their ragged and ramshackle appearance, Gabriel was pleased to see the glints of finely honed and immaculately polished blades throughout the throng. These were warriors, after all, and they seemed to have their priorities right.

As the Blood Ravens captain stared down into the crowd, with the blood-red sun at his back, the bursts of light from the well-kept blades of the aspirants seemed to flicker and flash like tiny explosions in the throng. He saw them as starbursts of light, surging with bloody colours, and for a moment he was transfixed.

Then the lights began to blur together, pulsing as though driven from a common source, casting a haze of red over the scene and taunting Gabriel's senses with dizziness. He reached out a hand to steady himself against the statue of Elizur, shifting his weight against the heavy stone monument in an attempt to prevent himself from falling forward into the arena. As his hand punched into the image of the great chaplain, it seemed to fall through the carved rock, plunging into the material as though it were little more than a viscous liquid. As Gabriel slumped over to the side, his body crashed into the statue, which now seemed cold and hard.

Without his helmet, Gabriel's head smacked into the rock and then scraped down it as he slid to the ground. Even in his half-conscious state, he could feel the tear of pain as the skin on the side of his face was grazed and ripped by the impact and abrasion. Blood ran down his cheek and neck, and he could taste its metallic tang in his mouth.

For some reason, Gabriel's Larraman's organ did not seem to activate and blood continued to gush out of the wound on the side of his face as he lay on top of the arch between the feet of Elizur and Shedeur. It felt as though his eyes were filling with blood, and the scene within the auditorium below was cast into a deep red hue, as though viewed through a bloodied lens. Just at the edge of his awareness, Gabriel thought that he saw Prathios glance up towards him as he addressed the crowd, explaining to them that most of them would die over the course of the next few days. Even more vaguely, Gabriel was aware that a number of faces in the arena had turned towards him. They did not point or cry out. They drew no attention to him, and their faces seemed awash with compassion.

As he struggled to bring the faces into focus, one of them spiralled up out of the crowd towards him – its clear green eyes and braided blonde hair fixing themselves into Gabriel's mind. At the same time, a choir of voices started to chant into his ears, beginning with a single, soaring note of silver purity. The music began to swirl in sweeps of stereo as it grew louder and more voices joined the first, making Gabriel's mind spin in his head and bringing the gut-wrenches of nausea. For a moment, he thought that the aspirants were singing, but he quickly realised that these voices were from somewhere else entirely.

After a few seconds the voices reached a sickly crescendo, always verging on cacophony and then finally succumbing to it. Together with the music, the spiralling face of the blonde boy span faster and faster until its flesh started to contort and twist, finally ripping and being torn from a rapidly disintegrating skull. As the head collapsed into sprays of pulp, the whole amphitheatre seemed to be screwed into a giant spiral, curdling the entire scene as though it were painted on a vortex of oil.

Gabriel couldn't move. He just lay at the feet of the chaplains and closed his eyes, waiting for the confusion to pass; he had suffered from visions before – scenes of hell and chaos afflicting the people of Cyrene – the imploring face of Isador as he died at the end of Gabriel's own blade. But closing his eyes brought no respite, and the heinous choir seemed to sing with increased vigour in the sudden darkness, bringing a sickly red light into his thoughts with each glorious note. For a moment, Gabriel reached out for the choristers, realising that they were a beacon of sorts, that there was something pure, silver, and pristine hidden beyond the nausea. But then he lost consciousness altogether.

SLEEP HAD BEEN the neophyte's only solace, and now the Blood Ravens were about to take that away from him too. Ckrius had been pushed rapidly through the first five phases of the implantation process – a process that would normally have taken several years. During the process, he had experienced precious few moments of sleep, in which pain, surgery and transformation could be forgotten, but they had kept him relatively sane. Of course, the apothecary was not overly concerned about Ckrius's sanity or his state of mind during the first five phases – strength of mind was essential, but sanity was a relative concept and not necessarily an asset to a Space Marine. In any case, phase six would begin the process of eradicating any significant personality flaws. After its initial implantation, the catalepsean node would deprive Ckrius of sleep, thus preventing his brain from launching its automatic defences of his personality whilst a programme of hypnotherapy fashioned him into a Marine. Later on, the implant would enable him to regulate his own circadian rhythms by isolating different sections of his brain and letting each sleep in turn – at no stage in the future would Ckrius dream in the way that he did before. He would become able to sleep while he was still awake.

Over the course of recent centuries, there had been some whispered rumours that the phase six zygote had suffered a slight mutation in the Blood Ravens. In response, the librarian fathers of the Chapter had made some slight alterations to the long-term programme of hypnotherapy that all Marines continued to receive, even after they completed their ascensions into the Adeptus Astartes. It was hypothesised that the Blood Ravens' catalepsean node continued to interfere with the ability of Marines to sleep normally even after the implant was fully embedded and control of its functions should have become voluntary. The result appeared to be that some Blood Ravens never had any dreams of any kind, and the Chapter's leaders were concerned about the effects that this might have on their Marines' states of mind. Nonetheless, the zygote continued to be implanted in every initiate because, without it, it would be impossible to conduct the intravenous hypnotherapy required to alter the nervous systems of neophytes to sustain the other implants. And, in the final analysis, the Chapter maintained its faith that the node functioned as it should.

Standing in the observation gallery of the Implantation Chamber, Captain Ulantus was struck with a mixture of surprise and admiration for the youth: after all, he was still alive. If he had to be honest, Ulantus had thought that Gabriel had made a mistake to try and put someone so old through the process, no matter how much need there was for new initiates. It was dangerous for the boy and potentially a tremendous waste of resources for the Chapter. However, not for the first time, Gabriel had proven Ulantus wrong – although he would never admit it in public.

The apothecary's mechanical, skeletal, metal arms were twitching away feverishly under the adamantium slab on which the wide-eyed Ckrius was strapped. The piercing sound of drilling cut through the chamber as the device started to cut up through a hole in the table into the occipital bone in the back of Ckrius's skull. The horror on the neophyte's face was absolute as his body struggled and knotted against his restraints, desperate to yank his head away from this egregious invasion. His eyes bulged in unspeakable, reflexive panic, as though this were the worst of all the tortuous procedures that he had endured.

Ulantus watched the boy's face with something approaching sympathy; he had once been the man lying on that tablet with a shrouded, augmetic, inhuman-human drilling into his head, and he knew the horror of it. However, he also knew that if Ckrius survived this phase, he would do so by convincing himself that it was the worst thing that he would ever have to endure. His mind would be screaming that he just had to hang on for a few more minutes, then he would be able to sleep and prepare for the next implant, which couldn't be as bad as this one. Hence, Ulantus knew that Ckrius would only survive because he was ignorant: there would be no sleep and the procedures still to come made this one seem like nothing. In the captain's eyes there was sympathy, pity and disgust in equal measures, but his heart was burning with pride that all Blood Ravens had made it through this terrible ordeal. If he survived, Ckrius would also learn to despise the weak-minded optimism that got him through this day: hating who he once was would help him to forget it. If he didn't, he'd be dead.

The high-pitched whining of the drill abruptly changed into a crunch and then it growled as the bit sunk into something moist and soft, before accelerating into a shrill whir as resistance to its motion vanished. Ulantus saw a wet deposit fall under the table and then watched the apothecary's mechanical arms twitch with renewed motion as it manoeuvred the tiny implant into place.

Despite his well-practiced scepticism about Gabriel, Ulantus found himself hoping that the young neophyte would pull through. He had been less than impressed when the Commander of the Watch had decided to take his strike cruiser off to the other side of the segmentum on what appeared to be a whim, leaving Ulantus and the Ninth Company to complete the recruitment sweep of the Trontiux and then Lorn systems, as well as leaving Ckrius in his hands. But Ulantus took to responsibility well, which was why he had been made captain at such a young age, and it hadn't taken him long to adopt Ckrius as his own. It had only been a matter of hours after the *Ravenous Spirit* had departed that he had made his way down to the *Litany of Fury*'s Implantation Chamber to check on the boy's progress.

As he watched, the heavy doors to the chamber slid open with a hiss of decompression, letting a beam of light into the dimness inside and sucking a jet of noxious gas out into the corridor beyond.

'Captain, I thought that I might find you here,' bowed Sergeant Saulh.

'Sergeant – you were right. What news?' asked Ulantus, stiffening his posture into an affectation of formality.

'News from the Lorn system, captain. It seems that the local regiment of guardsmen is under attack by a horde of orks,' reported Saulh.

Captain Ulantus nodded his head. 'Understood,' he said. 'Have they requested our aid?'

'No captain. They have made no such request,' replied Saulh. 'The report suggests that they are confident that they should be able to bring the situation under control by themselves.'

'Very well. Tell them that we will be there presently, but that we will first continue to the Trontiux system as planned. In the absence of Captain Angelos and the Third Company, the *Litany of Fury* is not in a position to split its forces at the moment. Tell the guardsmen of Lorn V to keep us appraised of the situation there.'

With that the sergeant nodded and withdrew from the chamber, leaving Ulantus with his thoughts. Trust Gabriel to be off gallivanting around Rahe's Paradise when the green-skins decided to invade Lorn. He shook his head and sighed audibly. Casting his eyes over at Ckrius once again, he turned and strode out of the chamber, heading for the command deck.

JUST ON THE edge of hearing, Gabriel could sense voices speaking in hushed tones. His eyes were closed and his head was throbbing with a numbed, dull pain. As he lay there, memories started seeping back into his mind. He could remember organising the Blood Trial ceremony with Prathios. He could remember climbing up onto the apex of the great arch to watch the long procession of warriors making their way into the amphitheatre, and he could remember standing proudly between the magnificent figures of Elizur and Shedeur. Then things became a bit hazy. There were some images of a blonde haired man with green eyes, who may have been one of the aspirants. There had been an abrasive blow against his head, and he remembered the sensation of heavy bleeding down his face, which explained the pain now. But the details were vague.

Opening his eyes, Gabriel saw the familiar shape of Prathios standing in the doorway to his cell in the monastery. He was talking to somebody in the corridor outside, saying something about Cyrene and psychological traumas. From where he was lying, he couldn't see to whom the chaplain was talking.

'Prathios,' he said experimentally. 'What happened?'

Gabriel reached his hand up to his face and pressed his fingers against the side of his head, where the fresh wound should have been. His fingers quested across his skin for a few seconds, searching for dried blood or even fresh scar tissue, but there was nothing. His skin was laced with scars, but they were the old marks that he had earned over the course of long service with the Blood Ravens. Nothing new.

The chaplain nodded quietly to the invisible figure in the hallway and then turned into the room to face Gabriel. He walked slowly over to his old friend.

'Gabriel, you fell.' Prathios's face was lined with concern.

'Fell?'

'Yes, while I was opening the trials. You staggered and then fell. By the time I reached you, you were already unconscious,' said Prathios softly, watching his captain's eyes carefully.

Returning the chaplain's gaze with an even stare, Gabriel swung his legs over the side of the recuperation tablet on which he was lying. For a moment he thought that he saw his friend searching his soul.

'I banged my head,' he said, his hand still resting on the side of his face. 'It was bleeding.'

'No, captain, there was no blood,' replied Prathios, holding Gabriel's eyes for a little longer. 'There was no sign of damage when I got to you. And Techmarine Ephraim ran some checks on your armour when we got you back here – nothing.'

'I can see what you are thinking, chaplain,' said Gabriel, his eyes hardening. 'But this was no attack of conscience. It was not the inferno of Cyrene that filled my head, as it was on Tartarus. But there was blood. The air itself was weeping blood.' The images were flickering back through his mind as his spoke.

Prathios nodded gravely. As the Third Company chaplain, Gabriel's visions put Prathios in a delicate position. He was well aware that a Space Marine captain should not have such visions, indeed that they may be signs of a taint. However, he could see reasons behind his old friend's episodes, and Gabriel had never permitted them to lead him astray. If anything, his visions of the choir of the Astronomican on Tartarus had inspired him to heroics of legendary proportions. In Prathios's mind, the captain was not suffering any daemonic or psychic taint, but rather was afflicted by some kind of psychosis. The Exterminatus of Cyrene, Gabriel's homeworld, had been a heavy burden for the captain to bear – it had been launched at his command. And then on Tartarus, the sole other survivor of Cyrene, Gabriel's life-long friend and battle-brother Isador had succumbed to Chaos, and Gabriel had been forced to kill him himself. No matter how augmented, disciplined and even superhuman the Adeptus Astartes might be, the human mind could only take so much.

As he stared at the fierce and defiant face of his captain, Prathios could not help but wonder whether the Third Company's inexplicable dash to Rahe's Paradise was not in itself evidence that Gabriel was too close to the edge.

CHAPTER FIVE
PHANTASMS

EVEN FROM THE very edge of the system, where the webway portal spilt the sleek eldar cruisers back into real space, Laeresh could sense the presence of the mon'keigh. They were like a stench in the psychic wash that swept through his mind. The warp signatures in the region of Lsathranil's Shield had always been unusual, but Laeresh was not expecting to find the ugly dissonance of humans already mixed into the streams of consciousness that flowed through the apparent vacuum of space. It was as though an animal had died and fallen into the current upstream, filling his senses with atrophy and poisoned decay. His long, elegant face grimaced slightly in revulsion, even before the *Blade*'s long-range scanners confirmed the presence of an Imperium strike cruiser in orbit around the fourth planet.

In an involuntary reflex, Laeresh's upper lip curled back into a snarl. 'Cleanse the stars,' he muttered, half to himself. 'War is my master, death my mistress,' he whispered, and the *Reaper's Blade* surged forward towards the offending planet as though responding directly to his words.

Wait. It was a familiar but weak and hesitant echo of a thought, prodding at the edge of his consciousness as though trying to find a way in. Laeresh squinted, shutting the voice out and filling his thoughts with purpose: war is my master. The putrid stench of the mon'keigh could not be suffered around Lsathranil's Shield: death is my mistress.

The *Reaper's Blade* streaked away from the inconstant form of the *Eternal Star*, leaving it glowing on the cusp of the webway portal. After a few seconds, Laeresh registered the fact that Macha's wraithship was not following his lead, but his thoughts were already in the heat of the battle to come and he dismissed her absence as a strategic mistake rather than a significant communication. The *Blade* was more than a match for any of the cumbersome, ugly vessels of the Imperium – he didn't need the wraithship's support to deal with a single strike cruiser.

Wait. The echo came again, persistent and pressing, albeit still weak and feeble. The thought had a familiar quality that Laeresh refused to recognise, shutting it out as his Void Dragon cruiser flashed through the edges of the system, heading in towards the fourth planet.

As the *Reaper's Blade* closed, its frontal pulsar lances erupted with power, sending a volley of high-energy laser bolts searing through the vacuum towards the mon'keigh vessel. In tight formation, a clutch of Phantom torpedoes flashed along in the wake of the energy discharge.

The two vessels were still too far apart for a proper engagement, but long distance strikes were what the Dark Reapers were famous for, and the Void Dragon had been specially adapted to match the tactics of the Aspect Temple: the lance blasts would soften up the enemy's shields before the torpedoes impacted. It was a deep space vessel, capable of supporting the Dark Reapers for years or even decades at a time, if the exarch chose not to take it back to the Biel-Tan craftworld straight away. In fact, it was one of the very few Dragon-class cruisers that contained its own Aspect shrine, so that the warriors on board could be spiritually self-sufficient for longer periods. The spirit pool of the *Reaper's Blade* contained only the souls of deceased Dark Reapers, making it a ritually pure vessel for the exarch and his glorious army – like a miniature recreation of craftworld Altansar, for which the Void Dragon continued to search the deepest reaches of space. The refusal of the Dark Reapers to blend their souls with those of the other Biel-Tan eldar in the craftworld's infinity circuit excited both resentment and relief from the other members of the Court of the Young King. Nobody knew what effect their vengeful souls would have on the balance of that circuit, especially since there were now thousands of them in the *Reaper's Blade* itself, stored up over the centuries in the hope that they might one day be released into the craftworld of Altansar once again.

Wait. The echo was louder this time and more urgent, as though the source was drawing nearer or recovering its strength.

The volley of lance fire streaked towards the Imperium's vessel, which was beginning to pitch around to face the charging form of the *Reaper's Blade* and to bring its own frontal batteries into play. Laeresh also assumed that the mon'keigh would be unimaginative enough to place their thickest armour on the prow of their cruisers, so he reasoned that the apparently aggressive move was actually a defensive manoeuvre. Despite himself, he nodded slightly, surprised that the clumsy fools had even noticed that they were under attack: he was certain that their primitive sensors could not detect the Phantom torpedoes, and he was fairly sure that they would have great difficulty resolving the continuously shifting signature of the *Reaper's Blade* into a constant, definite image. Of course, even the mon'keigh would be able to see a volley of blindingly bright laser bolts heading straight for them, eventually.

Wait! The thought was insistent and powerful, activating something primeval deep in Laeresh's mind. His aggression subsided for a moment, and the *Reaper's Blade* slowed down, falling behind the dark, speeding flecks of the torpedoes.

As the Void Dragon slowed it was suddenly overtaken by a blur of light, swooping past it like a majestic bird. The *Eternal Star* drew itself up in front of the *Reaper's Blade*, blocking the route of the Dark Reapers' cruiser. As it did so, the lance bolts smashed into the prow of the distant, ugly Imperium vessel in orbit around the fourth planet. A second later, and the Phantom torpedoes ploughed into the cruiser behind them, detonating on impact and sending out concentric rings of shock waves into the surrounding space and the upper levels of the planet's atmosphere. With only a fraction of a delay, a burst of fire erupted from the Imperium's vessel as a flurry of torpedoes were sent chasing through space towards the eldar cruisers.

Laeresh watched the exchange taking place on the view screen in front of him, cursing Macha under his breath for thwarting his attack. He watched the slow little signals of the torpedoes heading for the *Eternal Star*, and he shook his head in dismay. By the time those pathetic rockets reached the wraithship, it could be on the other side of the planet, and the Void Dragon could be half way out of the star system. Why would Macha seek to prevent the Dark Reapers from ending this battle at long range, where the mon'keigh's weapons would be ineffective?

Laeresh, wait, came Macha's thoughts, firm and resolute.

I await your leisure, farseer, replied Laeresh, his thoughts full of repressed bitterness.

No, Laeresh, you await direction. Her mind seemed thin and tremulous, as though speaking whilst labouring for breath. *There is more to this battle than an Astartes cruiser, Laeresh*... Her thoughts faded into silence before starting up again, fainter than before. *Follow me*.

With that, the exquisite form of the *Eternal Star* seemed to flick its wings and sweep back out towards the edge of the system. For a few seconds, Laeresh stood on his command deck staring fixedly at the amplified image of the mon'keigh cruiser on the view screen before him. The little torpedoes were visible on the screen now, like small points of light or insects crawling over the *Blade*'s sensors. He shook his head again in resentment, and another flurry of Phantom torpedoes streaked out of the Void Dragon's prow, tearing invisibly through the distance between it and the mon'keigh.

As the *Reaper's Blade* banked and set off in pursuit of the *Eternal Star*, Laeresh laughed inwardly at the thought that his rockets would hit the enemy cruiser before the mon'keigh's weapons had even reached his launch location. What's more, the ignorant, myopic humans would probably not even know that they were still under attack, or notice that their foe had already left the system.

HUGE TREES LEANED their great branches together far overhead, until the tips of their broad foliage touched, closing off the sky with a blanket of translucent green. Below the canopy, Ptolemea could hear the chattering of birds and the howls of animals that she could not recognise. Rain fell heavily, but in patches, forcing its way between the interwoven leaves above and falling as sheets through the cracks. The constant drumming of water filled Ptolemea's ears until the screeches of unseen animals cut through it, punctuating the deep and indecipherable language of the jungle. She narrowed her eyes in concentration, as though trying to understand what was being said.

As she stared up into the canopy, watching the torrent of bulbous raindrops grow larger as they fell towards her nearly-black eyes, something hissed through the moist air by her ear, sizzling against the falling rain.

Turning, Ptolemea saw a rush of animals come charging out of the undergrowth, trampling the plants beneath hooves and ripping them into shreds with claws and talons. It was a stampede, like an immense ocean wave rumbling towards her. There was no way that she could stand against the tide and, frantically, she scanned the immediate terrain for some cover or high ground. But there was nothing. She checked behind her, hoping to find the glorious figures of four golden battle-sisters with their weapons primed. Nothing.

In an action that would haunt her for the rest of her life, Ptolemea slumped to the ground, pulling her head down to her knees, and closed her eyes. She muttered a silent prayer to the Undying Emperor, repeating it over and over again as though the words themselves would flood out into the space around her and shield her body from the bestial rampage.

A warm wind crashed into her body, rolling her over onto her back and ripping at the already worn fabric of her body-glove. Despite her hands clasped over her head, her crimson headscarf was torn from her and was whipped up into the jungle canopy in an instant.

And then there was a moment of calm. Opening her eyes, Ptolemea looked around and found that the animals had all vanished, although the jungle around her now lay in trampled ruins.

Crawling back to her feet, another projectile hissed past her ear. There was a pause and then another flurry of shots, zipping through the rain and leaving a faint trail of steam in their wake, like miniature contrails.

Emerging from around the edge of the sudden clearing of ruined foliage, Ptolemea saw a single, slender, humanoid figure leap and roll as it hit the ground. It didn't stand up again. A second figure burst out of the tree line, this one jogging backwards with a firearm unleashing a hail of projectiles back into the jungle from which it had just emerged. Then a third and a fourth, each hurrying in retreat across the clearing, firing constant tirades into the deep shadows of the jungle. After a few seconds, the makeshift glade was full of retreating eldar warriors, each filthy with combat, their green and white armour scratched and beaten with the scars of conflict. They didn't even seem to notice Ptolemea behind them.

The orderly retreat was on the point of breaking. Flecks of fire and shards of death slid out of the jungle shade, slicing into the eldar as they returned fire desperately. But they were falling. Not a single warrior had yet made it past Ptolemea, and she was standing in the middle of the trampled clearing. The eldar were being cut to pieces as they retreated. Limbs were being severed by whatever projectiles were searing out of the jungle in pursuit of them, sending the eldar stumbling to the ground, where they continued to return fire until they were lacerated beyond any hope of recovery by concentrated volleys of fire from the hidden depths of the jungle.

Soon, there were just two eldar left in the glade – a beautiful female, shimmering with an intense psychic radiance that seemed to repel all attacks, and a robust warrior clad in horrifying black armour. They stood directly between Ptolemea and the invisible assailants in the jungle beyond. As she watched them, Ptolemea saw an immense crack of power lash out of the trees, like a sheet of lightning. It came racing through the clearing in an instant, exploding into an immense white fireball against the coruscating shield projected by the eldar witch. Ptolemea strained her eyes to see through the flames to the source of the power and thought that she saw something black and glittering in the jungle. Then the huge fireball expanded even further, engulfing Ptolemea herself in an icy coldness that simply erased her senses.

'Ptolemea!'

A familiar voice jabbed at her consciousness, prodding her back into wakefulness and making her mind swim against the raging currents of icy, white fire that seemed to engulf her.

'Ptolemea!' repeated Meritia, shaking the younger woman by her shoulders. But still she did not open her eyes. Her already pale skin was bone-white and frosty but beaded with sweat. She was quite motionless, but her face was rent with angst, as though a terrible turmoil was raging inside, and perspiration coursed around the curve of her perfectly hairless head.

'Ptolemea, you must wake up,' insisted Meritia, pressing her voice firmly against the apparently prematurely rigamortised body. When she still got no response, she slapped the woman across her face, leaving a red palm-print clearly visible against the porcelain pallor. There was an urgency about the

Sister Senioris that spoke of deep understanding and empathy.

'No!' screamed Ptolemea as her eyes snapped open and she flung herself bolt upright on the sleeping-tablet. Her wide pupils contracted rapidly in the sudden light but then dilated again in panic as she looked frantically around the small cell in the Blood Ravens' outpost, which comprised her living quarters whilst on Rahe's Paradise. After a few seconds of uncomprehending and hysterical searching, her wide, wild eyes calmed and she lowered her head back down to the thick, bound book that served as her pillow.

Meritia nodded in silent companionship and then turned away, her cloak sweeping round behind her as she strode directly out of the little chamber, leaving the younger Sister alone with her thoughts.

Watching the Sister Senioris vanish out of the cell without a word, Ptolemea's mind raced with fears. The residue of her nightmare coated the inside of her head, leaving her thoughts muddled and sullied in the darkness. It was unlike any dream she had ever had – more like a vision, and that in itself was a horrifying thought. She was no stranger to the work of the Ordo Hereticus, and she knew what fate awaited those who experienced unsanctioned visions. She had seen such fates administered before, occasionally as a result of her own investigations.

Involuntarily, she laughed out loud, feeling her chuckle slip thickly into a hacking cough, making her sit up again to ease the pressure on her chest. The irony of being sent to investigate possibly heretical visions in a Space Marine captain and then to experience such visions herself did not escape her, and for a moment the irony overtook the terror in her mind. But only for a moment.

In fact, she had suffered a slight hallucination on the journey to Rahe's Paradise, just as her gunship had been released into the system from the *Incisive Light*, the Ordo Hereticus cruiser that had brought her most of the way from her order's convent on Bethle II. She had dismissed it as a side effect of the warp jump from which the *Incisive Light* had just emerged, but it now seemed possible that it had represented the birth pains of whatever afflicted her now.

And what had the vision been about? Although she had listened to the inchoate ramblings of heretics before, spouting the incoherent and delirious details of their blasphemous visions, she had never had to organise such visions into words herself. The words were always given to her by the foul witches, and then she simply had to interpret the language and reach some kind of judgement. Understanding had always been a linguistic exercise for her, and now she found that there were no words for her experience. As her mind tumbled and reached for phrases that would bring shape and form to her memories of the nightmare, she realised that every description that she could formulate made her sound like a witch: animals and aliens on a strange world being attacked by an unidentifiable force that struck her with brilliant, icy flames. Her reason rebelled: was it the case that people would always sound like witches when they tried to describe genuinely new experiences? After all, she was no witch.

Am I a witch? She was suddenly unsure.

I am no witch! She was fierce with resolve.

But the content and the fact of the vision were not the only shocks. As her mind started to function properly again, Ptolemea ran the events that occurred after she had regained consciousness back through her brain. There was something else: Meritia had acted very strangely too, as though she understood what was happening to her. There had been a look of resigned solidarity in her eyes when she nodded to say goodbye. What did the Sister Senioris know about her dreams? Was she somehow implicated in their occurrence or form? If not, could Ptolemea dare broach the subject of unsanctioned visions with a Sister Senioris of the Order of the Lost Rosetta? Ptolemea shook her head in agonising frustration as she realised that she would not have hesitated to turn Meritia in to the Ordo Hereticus had the elder Sister come to her with such a story.

SERGEANT KOHATH STARED down at the rusty, red planet of Rahe's Paradise, watching its giant diagonal ring of mountains and volcanoes slowly rotate. Most of the senior Marines from the Third Company had accompanied Captain Angelos down to the surface, leaving Kohath to hold the fort. The Blood Ravens' serfs who served as the bulk of the crew on the command deck of the *Ravenous Spirit* were poring over their control panels, which were clucking and chattering irritably.

'Well?' prompted Kohath, waiting for a definitive answer. 'Can you see anything?'

There was no reply, as the serfs continued to concentrate on their machines, none of them daring to give a response before they were absolutely sure. Knowledge was valued by all Blood Ravens; ignorance and foolishness were not tolerated lightly, especially not amongst the Chapter's own pledge workers.

The instruments had registered a slight interference signal on the edge of the system, but it had vanished almost the moment that it had appeared. The serfs were feverishly checking to verify whether it had been the ghostly signature of another vessel or whether it had been merely a blip in the ship's machine spirit. The local system was notorious as a hide-out for pirate-raiders, and the Blood Ravens could not afford to be seen to tolerate their presence, especially while there was a fully armed strike cruiser in orbit around the main habitable planet. In addition, Captain Angelos had made it very clear to Kohath that he should keep a constant watch for eldar infiltrations into the system. He seemed to believe that there was an imminent threat of invasion by the mysterious aliens, although nobody seemed entirely sure why. Father Librarian Jonas Urelie had certainly been surprised by this view when Kohath had checked in with him a short time earlier.

'There's nothing, sergeant,' said Reuben finally, glancing up from the glowing green screen over which he was hunched. 'It must have been a glitch.'

'Very well,' nodded Kohath, apparently satisfied by the eventual confidence of his serf. Nonetheless, he clicked the view screen to shift its orientation, bringing the scene behind the *Ravenous Spirit* into relief.

In the far distance, he could make out the slow per-
ambulations of the outer planets as they came into
alignment, eclipsing each other in a faint ring of
light. For a moment, he thought that he saw a tiny
glimmer, little more than a fleck of light dancing
around the farthest planet, where it would normally
have been hidden in the glare of the planet's
reflected light. Then it was gone. It was probably a
moon or even an asteroid orbiting the distant world
– the outer reaches of the system were peppered with
space debris.

As he watched, the little glittering speck reappeared
and then disappeared again, blinking like an incon-
sistent and far-off beacon. Clicking the controls,
Kohath enhanced the view and then strained his eyes
into the darkness, a quiet, suspicious voice in his
soul making him ill at ease. No matter what the *Ravenous Spirit*'s instruments said, there was something
not quite right about the faint, flickering light, but it
was just slightly too far away for Kohath to see it
properly. The thought that this could be a deliberately strategic placement prodded its way into the
sergeant's military mind.

'Bring the prow around,' said Kohath slowly, still
staring out into the blackness. He couldn't see anything unusual, but many battles were won on the
basis of sound human intuition, no matter how
insistent the Inquisition was that this was usually
folly bordering on heresy. If there was anything that
Kohath had learnt during his long years of service
with the Blood Ravens, it was that war was always the
most likely outcome – it was peace that should strike
the soul with suspicion and dread.

In the silent blackness at the edge of the system, the flicker of light shifted almost imperceptibly into a burst. It was the merest phase shift, just a slight alteration in the colour spectrum.

'There,' murmured Kohath, as though his suspicions had been confirmed. 'Target torpedoes on–'

A stream of light-bolts flashed into view and the view screen collapsed into a blanket of white. Instantly, a series of explosions shook the command deck. Some kind of laser fire sunk into the armoured shielding, but it was followed by a cluster of impacts from ballistics that Kohath did not see. The ghostly rockets punched into the softened armour and detonated, sending plates of adamantium splintering off into space.

The command deck bucked and rocked, sending any unsecured serfs and equipment careening across the floor, colliding and crashing into the instruments. Only Kohath stood immovable, even as a crate skidded and bounced off his armoured leg, ricocheting off and crunching into the workstation next to Reuben. The terminal exploded, spraying glass and metal shards up into the face of the serf that clung to it for stability. The serf threw himself back away from the unit, clutching at his head and screaming as mists of smoke hissed out of the cracked station. As he fell onto his back, his hands dropped away from his face exposing his ruined skull. His left eye was impaled by a spike of green glass and the right side of his face was completely missing, spilling his pulverised brain out onto the deck.

'Return fire,' said Kohath firmly, still standing in front of the main view screen, unmoving amidst the commotion around him.

'We still have no target identified, sergeant,' insisted Reuben, looking up desperately from his terminal.

'That's the target!' stated Kohath, finally losing his calm as he pointed at the starburst on the view screen, which had just flickered back into life. Whatever it was that was firing on them, he would not permit anything to attack the Blood Ravens without at least trying to fight back. If he had to incinerate the entire outer system, it would be done. Nobody and nothing could take a free shot at the *Ravenous Spirit*, not on his watch.

There was an audible hiss as the volley of torpedoes roared out of the frontal batteries and rocketed out towards the outlying planets. Kohath watched the progress of the missiles on the view screen as they diminished into distant invisibility, then he saw the even more distant flickering target burst into a streak of light and vanish.

Turning away from the viewer in disappointed disgust, Kohath surveyed the destruction on the command deck.

'Clear that body away and put those fires out,' he snapped, repulsed by the mess that disgraced the spirit of his venerable cruiser. 'Reuben,' he began, using the serf's name in an attempt to inspire him to greater effort; Kohath always tried to learn the names of a few serfs in the crew for this purpose. 'Track that vessel–'

Before he could finish his order, another cluster of explosions wracked the *Ravenous Spirit*, this time even throwing Kohath to the deck. When he climbed back to his feet, in amongst the flames that suddenly filled the chamber, he looked over to Reuben and

saw the serf's head rammed into the screen of his terminal with blood oozing out over the jagged glass
that framed it. The rest of his body had already
slouched back into his seat, where it was bathed in
fire.

'FARSEER,' CALLED LAERESH in greeting as the doors to
her chambers in the heart of the *Eternal Star* slid
open and he swept through into the shadowy interior. His frustration about the abortive battle with the
mon'keigh had abated and now his voice was tense
with concern for Macha.

In the half-light of the farseer's sanctum, Laeresh
could see the shimmering field of sha'iel that coruscated around her body as she lay on a shining black,
circular, wraithbone counter that had risen up out of
the floor in the centre of the room. Her body was
covered in a thin, white shroud, and underneath it
Laeresh could see thousands of tiny wounds speck-
ling her pale skin. She wasn't moving and her eyes
were closed, but the interlacing pulses of energy
seemed to both emanate from her and be feeding her
with vitality at the same time, as though existing in
multiple realms simultaneously. Laeresh had no
intellectual tools with which to understand what was
happening to Macha, but his intuition told him that
the field of sha'iel was a good sign – it meant that she
was alive, and that she was recovering.

Standing in a line behind the farseer were three of
the warlocks from her retinue, each clad in robes of
the deepest emerald – a colour that was darker than
black, which cast no reflected light whatsoever. Their
heads were bowed and a faintly audible chant was

seeping out from under their hoods, gently filling the chamber with an electric peace. The one in the middle, Druinir, looked up and acknowledged Laeresh with unblinking, sparkling, fathomless eyes.

Having burst into her chamber so vigorously, Laeresh now found himself at a loss, not really knowing what to do; acting without thinking was becoming his motif. As soon as the *Reaper's Blade* had taken up its position on the far side of the fourth planet of Lsathranil's Shield, he had rushed across to the *Eternal Star* to check on the farseer, gripped by a sudden panic that he had brought her across the galaxy only to watch her die within moments of emerging from the webway. He cursed himself for the recklessness with which he had charged into battle, and his mind taunted him with the voice of Uldreth the Avenger, accusing him of abandoning Biel-Tan's farseer at the first promise of combat.

Shutting out the jibes of his subconscious, Laeresh knelt down by the side of the wraithbone tablet and bowed his head, hoping that his strength might somehow be transferred into Macha's body, or that she might at least feel his presence. He had only the faintest understanding of the nature of farseers, but he had absolute faith that she would draw on him when she needed him most. He was no warlock, but he freely offered whatever he could.

Laeresh. The thought was weak and almost trembling, as though it had travelled a long way.

Farseer, replied Laeresh with an abrupt eagerness that seemed clumsy and loud. *Farseer, what happened?* he continued, more softly.

The runes rebelled, Laeresh.

What do you mean? asked Laeresh, raising his head and inspecting the multitude of lacerations that covered Macha's body.

There was blood coursing through the webway, began Macha. *It was drowning our souls in the blood of our own kin, crashing like a tidal wave against the defences of our craftworld. Biel-Tan itself was crushed under the liquid weight of its own dead as every eldar was suddenly drained of his life and flung from the bloody hand of Khaine.*

I don't understand, farseer, thought Laeresh, confused by the ghastly image.

Neither do I, Laeresh, but I am certain that there is more to Lsathranil's Shield than the mon'keigh. We cannot afford to be rash here. There are forces at work that I do not properly recognise.

I am sorry, farseer, replied Laeresh, accepting the advice as a reprimand and wincing inwardly as the voice of Uldreth returned to taunt him once again.

We need to get down onto the planet's surface, directed Macha.

What about the mon'keigh? They are already on the surface, farseer.

There was a long pause and for a brief, panicked moment Laeresh feared that Macha had died.

I cannot see them, she confessed, finally. *The planet has no present, and even its past teeters on the edge of an abyss. The mon'keigh are there, but I am blind to their presence and their role in the planet's fate, since the planet itself seems devoid of destiny. Lsathranil's Shield is cracked.*

* * *

THE AFTERNOON SUN was still bright through the stained glass, filling the librarium with coloured beams of light as Jonas sat at the great wooden table, deep in thought. The mysterious wraithbone tablet was laid out in front of him, and an inexplicable sheen shimmered across its surface as the runes glowed and shifted before his eyes. Every time he thought that the text had settled and he started the work of translating it, something or things deep inside the warp-spawned material would blink and swim, sending the lines of script spiralling into a vortex before they finally settled into an entirely new configuration.

After several cycles in this way, Jonas had realised that there were actually only a set number of patterns and that there was some kind of psychic mechanism at work that triggered the transition from one to the next. In a moment of clarity, he realised that the tablet was effectively turning the page for him, paced for the eyes of an eldar who would doubtlessly be able to read each page before the next appeared. Unfortunately, Jonas could not read the ancient alien script so quickly, and he had to labour over each rune in turn, waiting for the shuffle-cycle to complete itself before he could move onto the next as the first page reappeared.

Between them, Jonas and Meritia had finally deciphered the first rune, which appeared to act as a title for the whole text: *Ishandruir – The Ascension*. For the last few hours, Jonas had been working on the first cluster of runes by himself, struggling even to trace their unsettled shapes into a likeness that he could recognise. He had searched through dozens of tomes in the librarium, leafing through a collection of texts that had been supplied to him by the Order of the Lost Rosetta years before – hence the Blood Ravens' librarian assumed that he had inquisitorial sanction for these dangerous volumes, which contained within their illuminated pages the ruminations of researchers, priests and inquisitors on the nature of the eldar tongue. The Inquisition had been known to arrest scholars for the possession of much less perilous books than these, and it was a mark of the respect that the Ordo Hereticus had for the scholarship of the Blood Ravens that they were prepared to look the other way in this case, in the name of furthering truth and knowledge for the Emperor. However, Jonas occasionally wondered whether the Sisters of the Lost Rosetta seconded to Rahe's Paradise actually served a double function, not only to help with the research, but also to keep an eye on the research being done; in the back of his mind he was always vaguely conscious of the order's twin allegiances to the Ecclesiarchy and the Ordo Hereticus.

He had struggled for hours over the very first rune of the main body of the text. It was an archaic and complicated shape of sweeps and curls, run through with decorative strikes and other strokes that seemed intrinsic to the character's meaning. There was a bold triangle at its centre that seemed to glow with a sickly green. It had taken Jonas long enough just to work out which marks were integral to the rune and which were merely illuminations. Finally, he had found a rune in the forbidden *Obscurus Analects of Xenoartefacts*, inscribed by the notorious Inquisitor Ichtyus Drumall, who claimed to have spent three years in the underworld of craftworld Saim-Hann, attempting to incite a civil war amongst the bellicose gangs of that monstrous vessel. Within moments of his alleged escape, he had been seized by agents of the Ordo Hereticus, his analects removed from his possession, and his soul had been ritually purged until it was finally liberated from the irrevocably tainted form of his flesh.

The rune appeared to be an ancient variation of Jain'zar, which had been translated by Ichtyus Drumall as 'storm of silence,' but that interpretation seemed almost wholly inappropriate in the current context. The position of the character suggested that it should be the grammatical subject, and Jonas originally thought that it could be a reference to some kind of mythical figure in eldar folklore that bore the name Jain'zar. The tablet was ancient beyond reckoning, and it was entirely possible that the rune had subsequently appropriated the meaning gleaned by Drumall after this original figure had passed from the memories of the eldar. However, as he worked his way through the rest of that first rune cluster, Jonas realised that the rune was actually a variant of the markings seen on some eldar warriors that the Imperium called banshees, because of the way that they howled in the face of battle. Indeed, rendering the complicated rune as 'banshee' seemed to make sense, although it was still not clear what the sentence actually meant: The Banshee's call shall wake the dead, when dark portents wax nigh – heed them as the counsel of a seer, or a father.

Closing the heavy covers of the *Obscurus Analects*, Jonas pushed himself back in his seat, rolling his neck to loosen the tense muscles of his shoulders. Space Marines were not built to remain hunched over a desk for hours on end – his augmetic body needed to move. Through the window, high up in the atmosphere, Jonas saw a sheet of blue light suddenly flare and then vanish, like an aurora.

With his hands massaging the base of his neck, the father librarian gazed back down at the tablet that lay next to the old, forbidden book on the wooden table. He shook his head, partly to work his cervical vertebrae and partly because of his mystification concerning the meaning of the ancient runic script. He didn't know a great deal about the so-called eldar banshees, and he wasn't sure where he would be able to look to find out more. Perhaps the Ordo Xenos would have more information, but it would not be appropriate or safe to send off a request to them. Without that knowledge, however, it was almost impossible for Jonas to understand what was meant by the 'banshee's call' or what the 'dark portents' might be. Whatever they were, the author of the tablet seemed most insistent that they were extremely important and should not be ignored.

Sighing deeply, Jonas pushed his chair back and stood up, turning to survey the vast collection of book-stacks that filled the cavernous librarium. There had to be something there that would help him, even if he had to go through each volume in turn. He was in no hurry – research always took time, and it wasn't as though the banshee was calling right then.

THE LOW AFTERNOON sun rushed into the amphitheatre through the great arch, filling the circular arena with red light and dazzling any who dared to look out of the ancient stadium's only exit. Any aspirant who even thought of looking out of that arch was not wanted in the trials in any case. Fewer and fewer of the hundreds of warriors that had collected during the first congregation on the previous day would walk out through that arch each evening, until there were only a handful left. Of those, perhaps three or four would discover that there was, in fact, another exit from the amphitheatre, through a series of tunnels and valves in Krax-7 itself, which led into the heart of the Blood Ravens' monastery-outpost. Only those few, who would never dream of staring out into the blinding, bloody light of the local star, only they would eventually reach beyond it aboard the *Ravenous Spirit*, en route to the *Litany of Fury*, where their real trials would begin.

In full armour, Gabriel and Prathios stood side by side on the raised platform opposite the great arch, bathed in the blood-red light. They surveyed the combat that raged in all quarters of the arena with calm and dignified detachment, watching the eclectic mixture of techniques and styles during this first phase of the Blood Trials. This day was a free for all, designed principally to reduce the numbers of aspirants to a more manageable level. Prathios had explained the rules to all of them the day before: they were to arrive at dawn and they were not to leave until sunset; if any of them tried to leave while light still poured through the great arch, he would kill them himself. There was no gate or force field keeping them penned in, but so far not a single warrior had tried to escape the carnage through the wide-open archway.

In fact, Prathios had said nothing about what would be expected of the aspirants once they were within the confines of the amphitheatre. He had simply instructed them that they should not leave until sundown. Dawn had been seven hours earlier, and neither Prathios nor Gabriel had yet spoken a word to the battling warriors before them. All that Prathios had said on the previous day was that the aspirants should understand that very few of them, if any, would have what it took to be considered for the process of ascension into a Space Marine. That was the seed that he had implanted in their minds, and on this first day of the trials he could witness what potentials that seed contained.

Nothing had been said about combat, and, for the first thirty minutes or so after the dawn, nothing had happened. The aspirants had just stood there, bolt upright and proud, staring expectantly at Prathios and Gabriel. But when the two Blood Ravens said nothing, a murmured discontent gradually started to spread throughout the crowd. One or two of the bolder ones called up to the pedestal, voicing their impatience and wanting to know when the trials would start. Such actions seemed to germinate the seed as other warriors realised that the sole purpose of the trials was to reduce their numbers. As a hugely muscled, white-skinned man yelled up at Prathios, a blond-haired youth with dazzling green eyes sprang forward and drove a long-bladed dagger straight through his neck, transforming his angry cry into a gurgling death-rattle.

There had been an elongated moment of silence and shock as the huge man collapsed to the ground with blood pouring out of his ruptured arteries. He had died instantly – one down. Then, finally, after a few seconds of faltering comprehension, a burst of clarity erupted in the mind of another warrior – Prathios could identify the precise moment from the look of excitement that suddenly dawned on the man's face. The short, bearded man swung his axe in a powerful arc straight into the stomach of the taller man standing next to him. It was an utterly arbitrary act – there was no particular reason why the short man should particularly hate the man next to him, he was simply the nearest person. Without pausing, the little man yanked his axe head out of the body and brought it round in a back swing towards the man on the other side of him.

And that was how it started. Since that moment, there had been nothing but combat and bloodshed for the entire day, some of it arbitrary and some of it political, spilling over from the animosities between the gangs and groupings from outside the arena. The numbers were finally being reduced.

Ad hoc groups and alliances had formed as some of the warriors realised that they would stand a better chance of survival if they stuck together. But such alliances quickly collapsed as the fighters realised that they had no real friends in the arena, only competitors; some were stabbed in the back by those whose backs they were defending. More often, the groups collapsed because better groups became possible and people defected, as the warriors began to get a sense of who the best fighters were and tried to team up with them. A strong group was already developing around the boy with the braided blond hair, who had made the first kill, and the squat, bearded man, who had made the second. This was how the first day of the trials usually developed.

Gabriel could not remember his own Blood Trial, but Prathios had told him many times of the legends about him. It was said that he grasped the significance of the first day instantly, and that he arrived in the auditorium already set on his path – and what a glorious path that turned out to be. His intuitive decisiveness had set him apart from his brethren then – and it continued to raise eyebrows and provoke attention even now.

It was rumoured that Gabriel had been one of the last of the aspirants to show up for the Blood Trials on Cyrene. When he had arrived in the arena, it was already bursting with warriors, each of whom was standing proudly and waiting for direction from the Blood Ravens chaplain. Gabriel had not even broken his stride, walking in through the great arch of the amphitheatre on Cyrene, which was even more majestic than the one on Rahe's Paradise, drawing his sword and taking off the head of the first aspirant he came to, before breaking into a charge and hacking his way through the crowd towards the chaplain's pedestal. By the time the young Gabriel had reached Prathios's feet, he had already killed nearly a hundred of his fellow aspirants. Within minutes, a second figure emerged from the chaos and the two of them instantly struck an alliance, fighting side by side until the ground grew swampy with blood. On that day, Prathios had been forced to call a halt to the killing within an hour of dawn, fearing that there would be too few warriors left to guarantee that any of them would survive the traumas of the Implantation Chamber. As it turned out, only Gabriel and his ally, Isador Akios, eventually became Blood Ravens.

Today's trials were not quite as dramatic as the one in the legend, and Gabriel suspected that even the one from the legend had not been as dramatic as it was subsequently made to sound. But there were enough strong warriors on Rahe's Paradise to make Gabriel and Prathios confident that they would find some suitable neophytes from amongst them. In particular, the boy with the blond braids had caught their attention as an early hopeful. Despite being relatively slight of build and probably amongst the youngest of the warriors present, he moved with a delightful grace and ease, slipping past attacks and countering in the same movement. He had a strong, intuitive grasp of the way that the combat was unfolding, and was always to be found where the fighting was hardest and bloodiest.

'Is he a psyker, Prathios?' asked Gabriel, using the vox link inside their helmets.

'I cannot tell, Gabriel, but he does show evidence of foreknowledge – moving away from blows before they are landed, even when they are struck from behind or from blind spots. His awareness seems considerable,' mused the chaplain.

'And the others follow his lead. That is unusual charisma in one so young,' added Gabriel, impressed. There was something familiar about the boy's face, but he wasn't sure what it was.

'There are others who seem to have similar abilities today, including that one,' nodded Prathios, indicating the short man with the beard. 'If these aspirants do have latent psychic powers, then there would appear to be an unusually high number of them in this group. We will have to inform Jonas and Ikarus; a librarian must assess psychic potentials–'

Prathios broke off as Gabriel vaulted down from the pedestal and charged into the fray. He scanned the scene carefully, trying to work out what had triggered the action in his captain. For a horrifying moment, he feared that Gabriel had finally lost his sanity to bloodlust.

The aspirants were still fighting, hacking and swiping with their no-longer shining blades. But there was something different in the scene. If anything, more of the warriors were falling than before. Looking more closely, Prathios realised that some were collapsing to the ground even before they were struck down by fellow aspirants. Straining his eyes, Prathios saw a heavy-set, pale-skinned man suddenly drop to his knees, dropping his long, curving sword into the blood-drenched sand before him. As he fell onto his face, Prathios could see a spread of tiny exit wounds on the man's back.

Gabriel had his bolter drawn and was standing in the middle of the arena, on the edge of the deep, smoking ravine that bisected the amphitheatre. A circle of space had opened up around him as the aspirants fought to keep out of the Marine's way, while Gabriel tracked his gun through the crowd, searching for something.

After a few seconds, a slight figure came charging out of the crowd with a long-bladed dagger

brandished in his left hand. His blond braids
fluttered out behind him and his green eyes flashed
with intensity. Gabriel ignored the courageous boy as
he closed and then leapt forward, driving his dagger
into the armoured plate on the Marine's back. The
blade snapped like ice against the ancient armour
and, following through, the boy crashed into
Gabriel's legs. With an irritated backhand, Gabriel
swatted the boy across his face, knocking him
unconscious immediately. The captain made a brief
mental note to commend the boy's spirit.

Gradually, the rest of the battling aspirants stopped
fighting, turning to see what the Blood Ravens captain was doing in amongst them. He stood in a ring
of clarity with his bolter raised, sweeping it around
the perimeter of the arena, with the blond boy
unconscious at his feet. In the lull, Prathios jumped
down from the pedestal, his own bolter drawn in one
hand while the Crozius Arcanum was still held in the
other.

'What is it, captain?' he asked.

'They are here,' muttered Gabriel, his voice taut
with concentration.

'Who–' began Prathios, but he was cut off by an
abrupt burst of fire from Gabriel's bolter. The shells
flashed out to the edge of the arena and impacted
against the great stone walls, chipping out fragments
of masonry and causing the aspirants to scatter.

Prathios stared after the apparently arbitrary shots
and then turned to his captain, his voice rich with
concern: 'Gabriel, there is nothing there.'

'Blow the sulphur cloud,' said Gabriel, ignoring
Prathios's words.

As he spoke, a scream arose from the crowd of aspirants and then was cut off. Turning, Gabriel and
Prathios saw the short, bearded man slump forward
onto his face in the dirt, his back riddled with tiny
wounds.

'Prathios, do it now!' barked Gabriel.

The chaplain unclipped a grenade from his belt and
lobbed it into the smoking ravine behind them. It fell
only a few metres before the heat from the lava below
caused it to detonate. As it exploded, a great cloud of
sulphurous gas erupted from the crevice and wafted out
over the arena, rapidly filling the amphitheatre with
choking fumes. In a few seconds, most of the aspirants
had lost consciousness and collapsed to the ground.

Almost immediately, Gabriel opened fire with his
bolter, spraying shells out into the mist with unchecked
ferocity, dragging his fire around in a circle at about
chest height, now that the aspirants were all lying
down. Staring out into the sulphurous fog, Prathios
finally caught his first glimpse of Gabriel's targets –
slight, slender figures darting through the cloud, visible
only as distortions in the mist. Instantly, Prathios
opened up with his own bolter, tracking his fire in the
same direction as Gabriel, but facing in the opposite
direction.

The darting figures in the cloud started to flicker and
materialise more solidly, as though the noxious gas
was somehow degrading or interfering with their camouflage. As the targets crystallised, the two Marines
stopped their fire spray and placed their shots more
carefully, but by now the enemy was in retreat. The
fleet figures clearly had no intention of engaging in a
fire fight and they were dashing for the archway.

'Nobody leaves until the sun sets,' murmured Prathios, unleashing a volley of bolter fire in the wake of the retreating assailants. He clipped the leg of one of the figures, causing it to stumble and trip as its comrades rushed on without it.

Gabriel was already running, pounding across the arena towards the fleeing foes, clicking off rounds from his bolter as he ran. He reached the stumbling enemy just as it regained its balance and composure. Without breaking his stride, Gabriel launched himself into a dive, crashing into the back of the figure and flattening it to the ground, driving his combat knife down through the humanoid's shoulder, pinning it down.

You know not what you do, human. The thought jabbed into Gabriel's mind like a hot poker, making him snap his neck up and stare after the rest of the attackers. One of them had stopped running and turned to face him. A long, dirty cameleoline cloak billowed in the wisps of sulphur behind it, and the lower half of its face was covered by a tightly bound scarf, but its emerald eyes burned brightly, seeming to draw Gabriel towards them in hypnotic spirals.

Gabriel had heard those words before; the eldar witch on Tartarus had forced them into his head in an attempt to compromise his intent. He would not listen to them again.

A volley of bolter fire streaked past Gabriel's head as Prathios came pounding up behind him, and the eldar ranger finally broke eye contact and disappeared out of the archway, leaving Gabriel and Prathios with their wounded prisoner pressed into the blood-drenched sand.

CHAPTER SIX
PETRIFACTION

THE SLEEK SHAPE of the twin-finned Vampire Raider was bathed in red flames as it scythed its way through the upper atmosphere. Its broad, forward-sweeping wings sliced through the mesosphere and plunged into the gaseous resistance of the stratosphere, submerging the streaking vessel in furious waves of fire.

As the fireball burst through into the troposphere, revealing the slick black of the vessel's armour, a long hatch jettisoned from the underside of its fuselage and a slender missile-emplacement dropped into place. Immediately, the barrel flared and a rocket roared down towards the distant mountains below.

After a few seconds, the hypersonic missiles punched into the snowy peak of one of the largest mountains, instantly vaporising the ice and the glacial permafrost, sending avalanches of snow and abrupt waves of water crashing down the mountainside. The missiles drove their way down into the substance of the mountain, clearing a wide impact crater and blowing clouds of dust and debris into the air. Then, just as the avalanche seemed to stop and the dust started to settle, the warheads detonated in the molten core of the volcano.

The explosion caused the mountain to convulse, shrugging off its surface layer of snow and rocky debris. Then the peak trembled and cracked, as the pressure forced the molten lava out into streams that hissed and steamed through the icy heights, blending with the plumes of sulphurous gases into a towering cumulonimbus. Finally, the pressure was too great to be vented by the little lacerations in the mountainside and the whole peak blew clear of the mountain, blasting immense chunks of rock and spraying magma for kilometres in every direction.

Still descending rapidly towards the desert, the black Vampire Raider rolled in a tight corkscrew, signalling its success to the second Raider that was just emerging from the inferno of the lower atmosphere, its green and white colouring making it appear to shimmer amongst the flames.

The second Raider flicked its wings in acknowledgement as it burst out of the troposphere and dove down in pursuit of the first, spiralling gently as though indifferent to the intractable pull of gravity.

Strapped into the pilot's seat of the black Vampire Raider, Laeresh was confident that the eruption would cover their descent into the desert. He had very little faith in the efficacy of mon'keigh technology; the strike cruiser that he had almost crippled in orbit had merely served to confirm his preconceptions. A huge volcanic eruption would certainly register on the primitive instruments of the humans, but he was sure that the signal would swamp the fleet, delicate signatures of the two Vampires. The mon'keigh would simply assume that it was a natural event, or even that a freak meteor had struck the volcano. He knew that they had been confused by stories of natural disasters on that planet before.

He rolled the Vampire over and tipped its nose towards the desert, accelerating vertically through the sound barrier before pulling up less than a metre from the ground, hammering the sonic boom into the sand and blasting out an impact crater. He angled his bird out into the deep desert, leaving the mountains diminishing behind him. He loved to fly and he nearly always insisted that he should pilot his own craft, despite the fact that his Aspect Warriors would always try to insist that their exarch should remain secure in the transportation hold until touchdown.

In a manoeuvre that would have killed a mon'keigh in one of their primitive flyers, Laeresh hit the gravitic-repellers and brought the craft to a dead halt in less than a second. The extreme g-forces that should have instantly killed all of the eldar onboard were spontaneously nullified by the gravity stabilisers in the Vampire's occupied compartments. Laeresh had used this manoeuvre against the ignorant humans and retarded orks on many occasions, watching them overshoot his position by kilometres as their primitive craft struggled to decelerate slowly enough to keep their pilots alive. The eldar had been making use of anti-gravitic technologies for millennia and Laeresh was constantly shocked that the younger races had still not worked it out.

Slowly, Laeresh brought his stationary, hovering bird down onto the desert, resting it delicately on the blades of the wing-edges. The sand that blew through the air outside his cockpit was the product of a desert wind, or perhaps it was still the remnants of the sonic crater he had blown out of the ground, but it certainly had nothing to do with his landing – hardly a single grain of sand was disturbed as the elegant, black Vampire Raider touched down.

Popping the cockpit release, Laeresh vaulted out onto the fourth planet of the Lsathranil's Shield system for the first time.

'Exarch Laeresh, Dark Reaper, we have been expecting you,' intoned a quiet, patient voice almost immediately. As Laeresh turned, a cloaked and scarfed ranger stepped forward out of the mist and bowed deeply. Vaguely visible in the sand behind him, Laeresh could see the silhouettes of other figures.

The exarch nodded a greeting in return. He had fought with rangers before, but remained reluctant to trust anyone who would voluntarily banish themselves from the company of their own kin. He could understand the desire to be as far away from Uldreth as possible, but that was a different story. 'Ranger, do you have news?'

The ranger hesitated for a moment, as though unsure about whether to answer the Reaper's question. He gazed intently at the exarch's immaculate black visage, a feeling of slight repulsion welling in his stomach. Just before the hesitation itself became a statement, the second Vampire Raider dropped out of the clouds and touched down gently beside them. There was a barely audible hiss as the hatch on the transport compartment slid open and Macha walked warily down the exit ramp, flanked on both sides by her personal retinue of guardians; Druinir led a short column of warlocks behind them.

'Farseer,' breathed the ranger, turning away from the Dark Reaper and sweeping into an ostentatious bow before dropping to one knee.

Aldryan, please, there is no need for such formalities here, responded Macha, her thoughts still inconstant and weak. She glanced past the stooped figure and nodded her acknowledgement to the other rangers in the mist beyond. She knew them all, and trusted them well. *Aldryan,* she added, her thoughts suddenly full of concern. *Where is Flaetriu?*

Aldryan lowered his gaze to the ground hiding his eyes from the vision of the farseer, as they burned with humiliation and the passion for vengeance. 'He is alive. The mon'keigh took him.'

Macha was silent as she wrestled with her own emotions. She had known Flaetriu longer than any of the other rangers – longer than anyone else she knew. They had joined the Path of the Seer at the same time, in the company of Laeresh and Uldreth. However, whilst the exarchs had eventually ascended into a sacred state of forgetfulness regarding their pasts, Flaetriu had never forgotten, and Macha had often wondered whether it was his memories that had driven him from the embrace of Biel-Tan. No matter what his motivations, he was a trusted and valuable warrior and Macha needed him now, just as she had needed him on Tartarus.

'The mon'keigh are known to you, farseer. The captain from Tartarus is amongst them. It was he who captured Flaetriu,' confessed Aldryan, his eyes burrowing into the sand next to his knee, where he saw the ghost of the human's face as he pinned Flaetriu into the desert.

The Blood Ravens? wondered Macha. *Gabriel*? she realised, inhaling sharply as she saw the face of the Space Marine float back into her mind. It was not a face that she had expected to see again after he had sabotaged her plans on Tartarus. She had worked for millennia to prevent the release of the Chaos daemon on that planet, imprisoning it on that cursed rock, hiding it away. But then the clumsy mon'keigh had smashed the Maledictum stone and torn asunder the delicate barriers that she had erected between the immaterium and the material realm, ripping a gash through which the daemon could squirm into reality. Something in her soul told her that the captain had thought that he was doing the right thing, but his bumbling stupidity, so characteristic of all his race, had caused an incomparable disaster. She suspected that neither he nor his masters yet understood the true scale of their blunder. She had sworn that the next time they met she would kill him.

'You know these humans, farseer?' challenged Laeresh, clearly appalled. 'Why could you not see this before?'

Macha turned to face the fierce exarch, her eyes gentle with compassion. Her mind was still racing with images of Flaetriu and Gabriel, but Laeresh needed her reassurance now. *The Blood Ravens are on Tartarus, Laeresh. Their souls are not without merit, but their minds are weak and foolish.*

Weak and foolish minds are dangerous things, farseer, especially here, hissed Laeresh, demonstrating the strength of his with the force of his thoughts.

'If you already know these Blood Ravens, Macha, then why could you not see them before we arrived?' he repeated, noticing that Aldryan lifted his gaze slightly from the sand at the sound of the question.

I don't know, Laeresh. But I have never claimed to see everything, and Lsathranil's Shield is a murky place, where the tides of the past-future curdle and stir. That the mon'keigh are the Blood Ravens is of no matter – the aliens must be removed before things escalate further. This is an eldar world, and they have no place here. Macha knew that she hadn't answered Laeresh's question, and she realised that she didn't really know the answer herself. In truth, she could still see nothing of Gabriel in the eddying currents of future-time.

'We have begun the process of extermination, farseer. Principal targets have been identified, and we have made a number of successful incursions,' reported Aldryan, looking up at the pale beauty of the farseer as the desert wind whipped her emerald green cloak into a whirl behind her. 'We have been expecting your arrival, and have been anticipating the Bahzhakhain.'

'There will be no Swordwind, ranger,' stated Laeresh flatly, letting his bitterness about Uldreth's refusal to sanction it seep out through his words. 'The Dark Reapers are here; we will bring death to these mon'keigh and bring purity back to Lsathranil's Shield.'

KNEELING IN SILENCE at the altar of the Emperor in the very heart of the outpost-monastery, Gabriel's mind raced with questions. The captured eldar warrior had not said a word, not even uttered a sound since Prathios had thrown him carelessly into one of the cells that Jonas had moved from the dungeons up into the base of one of the great towers. The xenos wretch had simply crumpled into a heap, with apparently toxic blood hissing out of the gaping wound on its leg. It had not responded to any questions and had not even cried out when Prathios had attempted to administer some of his enhanced interrogation techniques. On his way to the chapel, Gabriel had looked in on the prisoner, only to find him sitting in the middle of his cell, legs crossed in front of him, eyes closed. The wound on his leg was apparently healed already.

The Blood Ravens captain searched his mind for any scrap of inspiration. He had been so certain about the presence of the eldar on Rahe's Paradise, certain enough to bring his Battle Company charging across the segmentum. In the voiceless depths of his mind, he had been sure that he was enacting the direction of the Astronomican itself, manifesting the very will of the Undying Emperor. However, now that he was there on the planet's surface with indisputable proof of the sustained involvement of the eldar, the guidance of the silver choir seemed to have deserted him. He had no idea how to proceed. It was as though something was interfering with his mind.

Immediately after he had returned to his cell, following the incident during the Blood Trials, Gabriel had received a communiqué from Sergeant Kohath, currently commanding the *Ravenous Spirit* in a low orbit around the planet. Kohath had reported a speedy and stealthy assault on the cruiser by an unknown assailant or assailants. Damage to the venerable vessel had been considerable, particularly in the control arrays, and the *Spirit* would have been unable to pursue the attackers even had their whereabouts been known. Kohath was not able to say where the assailants had gone, but Gabriel was certain that they were still in the system.

Opening his eyes and gazing up at the ancient iconography that illuminated the intricately carved wall behind the Emperor's altar, Gabriel sighed. There were dozens of images from the glorious history of the Blood Ravens, and dozens of others that might have been only legends. Elizur and Shedeur were there, planting the Blood Ravens' standard symbolically on a jagged mountain peak – they could have been on one of any number of planets, since the legendary missionary chaplains planted the seed of the Emperor's light on countless worlds, but convention and convenience dictated that they were held to be on Rahe's Paradise in that image.

The great librarian fathers, the Chapter Masters from the dim and distant past, including Great Father Azaraiah Vidya, the very first recorded librarian father in the uneven and broken annals of the Blood Ravens, stared down at the Commander of the Watch, their eyes fixed and unmoving, as though searching his soul for signs of weakness. At one time, Gabriel had seen nothing but pride in those eternal gazes, but the galaxy was no longer such a simple place for him. Now, he could hardly even look them in their eyes, and that filled him with a greater sense of shame than anything else he had done before.

'Captain,' said an urgent voice behind him.

Gabriel looked back over his shoulder, still kneeling in supplication, confused by the sudden voice and concerned that somebody could approach so closely without him noticing.

'Sergeant Corallis,' he replied, seeing the veteran scout standing in the doorway, clouds of red dust gusting from the recesses of his scarred armour.

'Gabriel,' said Corallis, dropping the formality and striding forward into the chapel, anxious resolve written on his face.

'What news, Corallis?' asked Gabriel, standing and turning to face his sergeant.

'As directed, together with Librarian Ikarus, I took a bike patrol out into the desert, reconnoitring the key points of strategic advantage and vulnerability around the monastery. The foothills and the mountains appear clean, but we encountered some resistance in the desert itself. We were ambushed by a group of what appeared to be eldar warriors, equipped with some kind of optical camouflage. I have reason to believe that these were the vanguard of a more substantial force, judging by their armament and actions,' reported Corallis, pulling himself up smartly as he reached his captain before the altar.

'Any casualties?' asked Gabriel, nodding without surprise at the revelations.

'Just one, captain. Librarian Ikarus fought valiantly and with courage. He died well.' Corallis hung his head as he reported the news, as though hiding a sense of his own responsibility for the loss. He had never taken the loss of his men well, which was at least partly why the Marines in his squads had such high morale.

Gabriel paused for a moment, and then turned away without a word. Staring back up at the icons of his forefathers, he shook his head. The constellation of eyes burned down at him like starbursts, riddling his mind with accusations that his subconscious was levelling at himself. He had hated Ikarus and had not given him a chance, condemning him of trying to step into the unfillable shoes of Isador. He had resented the librarian's competence – for he had been an outstanding warrior, and that was why he had been selected for promotion into the command squad – secretly accusing him of showboating in the wake of Isador's greatest failure. And, if Gabriel were honest with himself, he had feared Ikarus, feared that the young librarian would stumble just as the once magnificent Isador had done; if it could happen to Isador, it could happen to anyone.

Had he sent Ikarus to his death?

'Captain?' prompted Corallis, watching the back of Gabriel's head as he stared up at the glorious iconography.

'I will record his passing, Corallis. Thank you.' He didn't turn, and Corallis hesitated, unsure whether or not he had been dismissed. Out of the corner of his eye, he saw the heavy figure of Prathios, half hidden in the deep shadows behind the altar. The chaplain nodded silently, offering a moment of solidarity to the grieving Marine.

'There's something else, captain,' continued Corallis, spurred by the presence of Prathios, who stepped forward out of the shadows and into the dim light of the chapel. 'Despite our attempts to engage the aliens, they appeared unwilling to split their firepower.'

'What do you mean?' asked Gabriel, finally dropping his eyes from the sacred images, tilting the back of his head slightly in curiosity.

'They appeared to have targeted Ikarus specifically, captain, and their fire could not be drawn away from him to any of the others in the squad. Not even to myself,' added Corallis, his voice tinged with self-reproach.

Lifting his head briefly, Gabriel cast another glance up at the hallowed face of the Great Father Azaraiah, narrowing his eyes slightly as though trying to interrogate that inanimate stare. He turned, sharing a look with Prathios.

'We experienced a similar attack this afternoon, Corallis. A group of eldar warriors infiltrated the Blood Trials and started slaughtering the aspirants. They appeared to select those who showed the most psychic potential – eliminating the natural leaders, the charismatics, and those with unnaturally good reflexes,' explained Gabriel.

'Gabriel,' said Prathios calmly. 'The death of Ikarus means that our Company has only one sanctioned psyker at its disposal on Rahe's Paradise, until Ulantus arrives with the *Litany of Fury*.'

The captain nodded slowly, his mind still trying to piece together the events of the day: the attack against Kohath, the death of Ikarus, and the assault on the aspirant warriors. Characteristically, the Blood Ravens had a disproportionately large number of librarians in their ranks, many of whom were seconded to work in the Chapter's great librariums, the most senior being granted duties in the unparalleled Librarium Sanatorium aboard the magnificent battle barge *Omnis Arcanum* itself. The First Company, who were based on the *Omnis*, also had two entire combat squads of librarians – elite forces used to confront the most archaic or daemonic of threats to the Imperium. To have lost Isador on Tartarus was tragedy enough, but now to be reduced to a single, aging father librarian on Rahe's Paradise was potentially disastrous. The situation was now more serious than Gabriel's personal discomfort about Ikarus, and he knew it.

'Where is Father Jonas?' asked Gabriel. It was an order, not a query, and Prathios strode out of the chapel to find him.

'Sergeant,' said Gabriel, turning to Corallis. 'Find Tanthius and check on the defensive perimeter around the monastery. Make sure that there are no gaps, and warn him to expect action imminently. Inform him that the aliens are using cameleoline cloaks. The Biel-Tan are here, and we should expect war before dawn.'

JONAS DROPPED THROUGH the gap and then turned to help Meritia down into the dust-filled chamber below the main excavations. They had revealed a short vertical shaft under the stone casket in which they had found the wraithbone tablet. It seemed to provide access to a whole new layer of artefacts. A narrow beam of light shone down through the opening, casting a bright cone into the dim chamber below.

'What is this place?' asked Meritia as Jonas lowered her onto the rough, rocky ground. The floor had clearly been cut smooth a long time ago, but then worn by the passage of many feet and heavy equipment. It was scored through with gashes, as though damaged by sudden, sharp impacts.

'I'm not sure,' confessed Jonas, peering through the darkness and the dust towards the faintly visible walls of the chamber. 'There appear to be markings on the walls.'

Taking a couple of steps, Jonas brought his fingertips up against the finely textured walls, letting his eyes adjust to the scarcity of light. There were thin strips etched into the surface, reaching from the ceiling down to the floor, and the wall appeared to be made out of discrete, convex sections of about a metre in width.

Meritia pressed her hands against the surface, feeling the elongated cracks and scrapes under her skin. 'It feels like a tree, Jonas, like a petrified tree.'

'There's some kind of text here too,' nodded Jonas, agreeing. 'The script seems to alter as it moves down the trunks.' He pointed up towards the ceiling, squinting slightly into the darkness as his occulobe implant worked to enhance his sight. 'That looks like some form of High Gothic, albeit an archaic dialect. And that,' he continued, pointing down towards the floor, 'that looks like the runic script we saw on the wraithbone tablet.'

Bringing her face closer to the wall, Meritia traced her fingers around the bizarre-looking characters etched into the petrified walls at about head height. 'These characters are neither Gothic nor eldar runes,' she said, her voice full of intrigue. 'We should get some light down here, and make some copies of this text.'

The odd script looked like a bizarre synthesis of Gothic characters and eldar runes, all blended together. The achingly beautiful curves of the runes were twisted and contorted into familiar angles, giving the text an everyday banality that almost made Meritia cry; the odd hybrid language was like a perversion or a betrayal of the beauty of the alien script, and it was a sullied, polluted form of the Emperor's own tongue. Yet it was held in the fossilized trees, midway between the perfect runes at Meritia's feet and the austerity of the High Gothic by the ceiling, as though caught in a deliberate limbo between the two.

'Meritia,' called Jonas from over to one side of the chamber. 'You'll want to take a look at this.'

Reluctantly pulling herself away from the streams of fossilized text, Meritia hurried over to Jonas, who was stooped into the entrance of a narrow tunnel that led out of the once tree-lined chamber. It was inclined slightly, dropping further down under the foundations of the monastery. On the far side of the tunnel, Meritia could see the flickering of a dirty red light, sending tongues of brightness licking up towards her.

'Look at the walls,' directed Jonas, moving aside to permit Meritia into the tunnel.

'The light?' queried Meritia as she peered past the librarian.

'There must be a lava flow at the far end of the tunnel,' conjectured Jonas. 'The tectonic plates are riddled with magma streams under the mountains. We are just on the edge of Krax-7's tributary system here.'

At first glance, the walls of the tunnel appeared to have been constructed out of some kind of artificial substance, woven together in a giant weave. Threads protruded and interlaced themselves back into the walls. Others stuck out like barbs, jagged and complicated into the tunnel itself, like the ruins of a huge web.

Taking a tentative step forward, Meritia reached out and ran her hand along the interwoven tentacles. They were cold to the touch, like stone.

'The roots of the trees?' she suggested, glancing back towards Jonas for confirmation.

'Petrified, like the trees themselves,' agreed Jonas.

Meritia knelt smoothly, tracing her fingers along the length of one of the roots. She paused, retracing a section. 'There's a mark here,' she said, looking more closely. 'It's a rune.' Running her fingernail around the curves etched into the stone, she tried to recognise its shape in the near-darkness. It was familiar. 'Jain'zar,' she said, turning to face Jonas as she realised what that meant.

'There's another one further down,' replied Jonas, pointing towards another root a few metres further along the tunnel. 'And there, another.'

A sound in the chamber behind them made Jonas turn, only to see the lithe figure of Ptolemea rising to her feet in the cone of light that flooded down from the ceiling, from which she had just jumped.

'Sister Ptolemea,' said Jonas, bowing slightly in welcome. 'I am delighted that you could join us. We appear to have found something rather interesting.'

As he spoke, the librarian walked forward towards Ptolemea and thought he saw a look of discomfort cross her face. When he closed within a few strides, the Sister stepped deliberately out of the light, throwing her face into darkness.

'Is there something wrong, Sister?' asked Jonas, genuinely concerned.

'No, Father Jonas, everything is fine. Just a slight fever: probably the residual effect of the journey – I am not a well-seasoned space explorer. Most of my work keeps me enshrined in the sacred librariums of our convent, as you might imagine,' explained Ptolemea, keeping a distance between her and the librarian.

'I see,' replied Jonas evenly, watching the pale-skinned Sister edge her way deeper into the shadows, not entirely convinced by her story. The confidence and assertiveness of her previous demeanour had all but vanished. 'I trust that the effects will be temporary and painless.'

'Thank you, father,' she answered. 'Now, tell me about your latest finds.' She swept her arm around the unusual, subterranean chamber. 'What manner of place is this?'

'It appears to be the petrified remains of a ritual chamber of some kind – at one time it was constructed out of trees. You can see the fossilised trunks in the walls.'

Ptolemea was walking around the circumference of the room as she listened, dragging her fingers across the remains of the trees as she went.

'I wasn't aware that Rahe's Paradise was ever a densely wooded planet,' she said, pausing as the thought caught up with her.

'Yes. It was once a jungle-world, in the long distant past, before some form of natural disaster cracked the planet's crust and flooded the atmosphere with sulphur. The volcanoes and the desert were the results of that cataclysm. At one time, it would seem that Rahe's Paradise was a type of paradise after all,' smiled Jonas.

'How long ago?' asked Ptolemea, her face still turned to the wall as her fingers traced the shapes of some of the script cut into the stone tree trunks.

'Long ago. When the great missionary chaplains first arrived here, the jungles had already been gone for millennia. They found Rahe's Paradise more-or-less as it is today. Our monastery was built on barren land.' Jonas peered through the dusty shadows at the elegant back of Ptolemea, unsure why she made him feel uncomfortable. Something about her had changed. 'Is this information not available to your order on Bethle II?'

'I have no idea, father,' she replied, turning to face him at last. 'I had very little time to check our records before I came here.' She paused. 'Where is the Sister Senioris? There is something that I would like to discuss with her.'

'She is inspecting a tributary tunnel, which appears to be the entrance to a larger subterranean network of chambers and tunnels, running through the magma layer. She's…' His words trailed off as Ptolemea strode past him towards the mouth of the tunnel. Instead of turning after her, he stood for a moment, irritated at the abrupt return of the young Sister's brusque manner.

'Father!'

Jonas turned and rushed over to the tunnel's entrance, finding Ptolemea on her knees next to

Meritia's prone body, her hands clasped around the older woman's face. Taking in the scene in an instant, Jonas planted his hand onto Ptolemea's chest and pushed her away. He stooped down over the figure of Meritia, resting his scarred and rough cheek against her lips to feel for her breath. It was faint, but it was there. She had lost consciousness, but she was alive.

A COMPLICATED ARRAY of cables and tubes peppered Ckrius's head as he lay strapped to the adamantium tablet in the Implantation Chamber of the *Litany of Fury*. They covered his eyes, ears and nose, forcing his senses to remain active and jamming them full of new types of pain. The pipe that ran down his throat prevented him from making any noise, and the stimulants that were jetted into his ears and open eyes riddled his brain with suggestions of terror.

As the neophyte lay rigid with psychological horror, the apothecary worked feverishly in the massive cavity that it had opened up in his chest. The boy would have no idea about the violations that his body was suffering, since his brain was already overloaded with directly inserted agonies that would have been inconceivable to him only hours earlier, despite the unspeakable traumas of the last few days.

The apothecary had reopened the healed scar down Ckrius's chest and rebroken the ribs that had already knitted back together. The boy's entire sternum was cracked open and folded back while the shrouded figure of the apothecary inserted a series of new organs. The first, a large zygote that had to be inserted somewhere in the digestive tract, was the preomnor organ, which would act as a predigestive stomach for the Marine, bolstering his system against poisonous or indigestible materials so that he could extract maximum nutrition from them without suffering any ill-effects. It was an important organ for survival in some of the most inhospitable parts of the Imperium.

Whilst working on the digestive tract, the apothecary also inserted the complicated little omophagea implant in between the thoracic and cervical vertebrae. It would function in partnership with the preomnor organ, filtering out the essential genetic material from animals and organic substances that contained information about the survival mutations undergone by an organism to succeed in their particular climate. The Marine would eventually be able to verbalise these mutations, understanding them consciously after eating any part of a living creature.

From the smoke-filled darkness of the observation chamber, Captain Ulantus watched the implantations taking place. The *Litany of Fury* was already in orbit around Trontiux III, but he wanted to ensure that Ckrius survived the next round of zygote implantations before he took a landing party down to the planet's surface to start the Blood Trials. So far, the boy had responded remarkably well to the hideously accelerated process, and Ulantus was secretly full of admiration for his resilience.

It was not only Ckrius who was being rushed. Ulantus had received a constant stream of communications from the Imperial Guard regiment on the ice-planet of Lorn V. It seemed that the orks had received considerable reinforcements, and it now looked as though a full-scale invasion might be underway. Imperial Guard Captain Sturnn of the Cadians 412th had now made an official request for assistance from the Blood Ravens. He had intimated that there was more at stake there than the security of the local population – indeed, the Cadians were not local to the Lorn system and had been dispatched to Lorn V with their own agenda. Ulantus was concerned enough to send off a message to Captain Angelos, requesting that the Third Company might be able to depart Rahe's Paradise early and send assistance to Lorn. However, the astropathic communication had received no response from the Commander of the Watch. Not for the first time, Ulantus cursed the cavalier nature of the revered captain.

As Ulantus's head raced with thoughts, the apothecary lifted a large, tubular, bloody organ from a tray next to the neophyte. With two other hands, it pushed aside the already cramped organs in Ckrius's chest cavity, making space for the multi-lung just above the primary heart, where it would be inserted directly into the pulmonary system around the trachea. When this organ started to function, Ckrius would finally be freed from the nauseating effects of the toxic and poisonous gases that wafted around the Implantation Chamber, as the multi-lung would filter out the poisons for him.

With an abrupt movement, the apothecary snapped shut the gaping wound in Ckrius's chest, folding the ribs closed and pressing the sternum back together again, leaving a lead weight resting on the join to keep it pressed together. The cloaked figure then turned and nodded sharply at Ulantus, indicating that the procedure was now finished for the time being.

At once, Ulantus turned and strode out of the observation chamber, heading down to the launch bays of the *Litany of Fury*, where his Thunderhawk was already loaded and waiting for him to lead the landing party down onto Trontiux III. For a number of reasons, the Blood Trials would be particularly fast and efficient this time.

RUSHING THROUGH THE winding corridors of the monastery, Jonas held the slender, delicate arms of Ptolemea in one hand, almost dragging her along behind him as he searched for Gabriel. He barged past scurrying menials and bustling ciphers, as the human pledge-workers of the Blood Ravens on Rahe's Paradise went about their daily business, apparently unaware of the events that were unfolding around them.

Eventually, Jonas burst through into the librarium, shouldering open the great doors and ploughing forward in a eruption of dust and light as Gabriel turned to face him. The captain was standing at the ornate wooden desk under the stained-glass windows. He was leaning over a set of maps and blueprints, calculating his defensive strategy.

'Ah, Father Jonas,' began Gabriel. 'I assume that Prathios–'

'Captain, I have some unpleasant news,' interrupted Jonas, swinging the slight form of Ptolemea around from behind him and depositing her onto the floor between them. 'Sister Senioris Meritia has suffered some kind of attack and is presently in a coma. I have secured her in her chambers and posted guards on her door.'

'What kind of attack?' asked Gabriel. 'And where did it take place?' He was suddenly concerned that his plans to defend the monastery from the outside might already be obsolete.

'I am not sure what kind of attack it was,' confessed Jonas, glaring at Ptolemea on the floor. 'But, it took place in one of the new tunnels down in the dig. Ptolemea was the last person to see her, and they were alone when it happened.'

Gabriel nodded at Jonas and then turned his gaze on the young woman at his feet. 'What happened, Sister Ptolemea?'

'The Sister Senioris was already unconscious when I found her, captain,' said Ptolemea calmly, picking herself up and smoothing her body-glove over her hips. 'I'm afraid that I can tell you nothing about what happened. Father Jonas and Sister Meritia had been working in the excavation for a while before I got there.'

'I see,' said Gabriel, holding her dark eyes for a few seconds longer than necessary. Something about her seemed different; she was somehow less defiant than the last time they had met, despite the precariousness of her position now. There was something open and vulnerable in her gaze.

'And what were you working on, Jonas?' he asked, turning back to the librarian.

'We have found considerable evidence that the site was once occupied by eldar creatures, captain. The upper layers of the excavation are certainly human, and most of the artefacts appear to be directly related to the history of the Adeptus Astartes on Rahe's Paradise – albeit to a period before the arrival of Elizur and Shedeur. However, there is a lower level, where we found the tablet,' explained Jonas, indicating the wraithbone block on the table next to Gabriel's plans, 'which contains a mixture of the Imperial artefacts and those of the eldar. This presumably represents some form of transitional period in the history of the planet. The lower layers, to which we have just gained access, appear to be almost entirely composed of eldar findings. We have, literally, only just scratched the surface of that layer, captain.'

'Have you reached any conclusions about these findings, father?' asked Gabriel, wanting to hear the old librarian's opinions before sharing the recent events with him – they might colour his interpretation of the evidence. It was clear that Prathios had not found him.

'Nothing concrete, yet. As I said, we have only just uncovered the layer.'

'Hypothesise,' requested Gabriel, with an edge of urgency.

'Very well. I suspect that Rahe's Paradise was once an eldar colony – what is sometimes referred to as an Exodite World. It appears that something caused the eldar to leave the planet or to be wiped out. Without checking the dates in more detail, I cannot tell whether this event was a force of nature – such as the catastrophic climatic disaster that brought about the ruination of the jungles and pushed the volcanoes out of the planet's crust – or whether the event was linked to the arrival of the Imperium, perhaps even to the arrival of the very first detachments of Space Marines, who appear to have built their monastery in the remnants of the woods atop the remains of an eldar facility. As you are well aware, captain, we have no records concerning the actions or even the existence of the Marines who occupied the fortress that we uncovered in the foundations of our own. I assume that they were Blood Ravens, but there is little evidence to support such an assumption, one way or the other. It is conceivable that they were involved in purging the xenos taint from the surface of Rahe's Paradise.'

Gabriel nodded in admiration at the old scholar's logic, and he could see that the librarian's mind was at ease once more, having immersed itself in creative scholarship rather than bitter accusations towards Ptolemea.

'Your conclusions are apposite, Jonas,' said Gabriel, taking some satisfaction in the way that the archaeological record was now confirming the apparently groundless suspicions that he had voiced about Rahe's Paradise a few days earlier aboard the *Litany of Fury*. 'You may not yet be aware that this outpost has now been attacked several times by eldar forces. Your own Scout Sergeant Caleb was merely the first to suffer such an assault: Prathios and I witnessed an ambush against the aspirants during the Blood Trials; Corallis's sortie was attacked and Librarian Ikarus was killed by eldar warriors in the desert; and Sergeant Kohath has reported an attack against the *Ravenous Spirit*.'

'The Biel-Tan?' asked Jonas, apparently unwilling to reach the conclusion. 'Of course, the Biel-Tan. It makes perfect sense,' he explained, as though giving voice to his thought processes. 'From our previous encounters with these particular eldar, we know that they are unusually obsessed with trying to rebuild their lost, ancient empire. An old Exodite World like this one would be a logical choice for them, and I am sure that our presence here causes them much offence,' said Jonas, smiling with sudden satisfaction. 'I can remember reading...' he trailed off as Ptolemea caught his eye and he was suddenly unwilling to reveal the source of his knowledge. 'It is said that the name Biel-Tan might even mean "the resurrection of ancient days," because of their passion for this cause.'

'Doesn't it strike you as odd,' began Ptolemea, who was following the conversation carefully, 'that the Biel-Tan and the Blood Ravens would come into conflict on two separate planets, so far away from each other, but in such quick succession? Librarian Isador Akios informed me that your foes on Tartarus were also Biel-Tan – isn't that right?'

She stared at Gabriel, waiting for a response. But, just as the captain was about to speak, a huge explosion made the three of them turn and stare out of the intricately patterned stained-glass window. One of the largest volcanoes in the range around the monastery had suddenly blown its peak, jettisoning clouds of sulphurous gas, dust, and molten rock high up into the troposphere. Streams of lava were already cascading down the sides of the mountain, and the red sun was being rapidly obscured by the black, mushrooming cloud.

'It has begun,' said Gabriel, snatching up his plans and striding down the aisle towards the great doors.

* * *

WE ARE NOT *yet in range for an attack, but the Bahzhakhain is poised,* explained Taldeer, the projection of her face flickering slightly.

'I understand,' said Uldreth, pacing back and forth in front of the ghostly image of the farseer. He had remained on the craftworld and had watched as two separate fleets vanished off into the webway. He was resentful of his own position, and impatient for battle.

The mon'keigh will not succeed against the foul greenskins on Lorn. They have sent out a request for aid. Their nearest reinforcements are too far away, although the future indicates their presence in the present pathways.

'You are not there to assist the aliens, farseer, but rather to cleanse the planet. Do what you must, but do not trust the mon'keighs' will or their resolve,' warned Uldreth, his lip curling into a snarl at the thought of any form of alliance with the Imperium, even as a temporary expedient.

He paused, not wanting to ask the next question. 'And what of Macha? Do you have any news of her? She has not communicated with me since her departure.'

I cannot see her, confessed Taldeer, her face sad and forlorn.

'What do you mean?' demanded Uldreth, stopping pacing and staring into the apparition of Taldeer. 'She is our farseer and head of the Council of Seers! Your bond with her cannot be broken by space!'

It has not been broken by space, Uldreth Avenger, but it has been broken, nonetheless. I cannot see her, and I can see nothing of the future of Lsathranil's Shield. It is as though it has been erased from the future-past, hanging in the invisible limbo of the pure present.

'What does that mean!?' cried Uldreth, punching his fist into the wraithbone disc above which floated the image of Taldeer. 'Was she right? Are you saying that Macha was right about the danger?'

I cannot see any danger, replied Taldeer without any reassurance. *And I cannot see any safety. There is simply nothing to see there at all.*

'WE HAVE LOCATED the deposit, farseer, and excavations are almost complete,' explained Aldryan, leading Macha through the rangers' camp in the desert. 'The site was well hidden, and there is no evidence that it has been disturbed over the course of the millennia. The seals are still in place, and we are awaiting your word.'

Excellent, Aldryan, replied Macha, steadying herself by leaning on the ranger's shoulder as they walked through the soft sand; she was still weak from her ordeal with the runes. Laeresh strode easily alongside them, the heavily augmented psychoplastics of his leg-armour making the sand irrelevant to him.

So deep in the desert, there was a constant breeze of sand blowing across the dunes, wafting sheets and clouds of red like a pulsing mist. In her weakened state, Macha could hardly see ten metres in front of her, but in that fact there was some reassurance that the mon'keigh would not be able to see anything of their activity from the distant mountain range.

Walking another few steps, Macha's eyes widened suddenly as the extent of the rangers' work became evident. As she crested the dune, in the shadow of which nestled the makeshift camp, a huge quarry loomed into view before her. It must have been about a kilometre in diameter, and perhaps half that deep. In the bottom, she could just about make out the busy forms of rangers labouring at clearing away the sand. They had some kind of suction devices strapped to their backs which drew the sand off the ground and then blasted it into long, thin fountains in the air, sending it cascading over the lip of the quarry and mounding into the massive dunes that now completely surrounded the pit.

No wonder the air is full of sand, reflected Macha as she strained her eyes into the excavations, searching for some sign of the objectives. *How much longer?*

'We are already at depth, farseer. They are now merely working against the wind, keeping the site clear and at a consistent depth.'

'What are you waiting for, ranger?' asked Laeresh, his voice tinged with impatience and repressed violence. His distaste for the outcast was clear.

'We await the farseer's pleasure,' bowed Aldryan.

Macha looked again, but there was still nothing that she could see in the pit. *Let us descend.*

Before the words were even out of her mind, a film of sha'iel started to seep out of the farseer's skin, enveloping the three of them and lifting them gently off their feet. In a matter of seconds, they were already half-way down the steeply sloping sides of the quarry. By the time they reached the bottom, the shrouded figures of Druinir and the other warlocks were already there, formed into a ring around Macha as her feet touched down.

The base of the pit was hard, like stone, but it was run through with scratches and veins, as though water had once eroded little paths through the rock. In places,

Macha could see that the surface was uneven and cracked. Stooping and pressing her hand to the ground, the farseer saw that the lines in the stone were actually formed into patterns, some of them the natural signatures of fossils but others were artificial, inscribed like text into what may once have been a riverbed.

I see, thought Macha, letting the images of the jungle river flood into her mind from the point of contact with her fingers. The lines in the stone started to shimmer slightly and then move, swimming like eels or water snakes under the dusting of sand that blew constantly across the surface. The fossils seemed to come alive, sending the ghosts of long-extinct animals scurrying, charging and slithering across the quarry floor. And the artificial etchings began to hum, glowing with a purple heat that spoke of realms beyond the linear flow of time that had led to the eradication of life in the immense desert. The purple veins radiated out from Macha's touch, darting through the tiny scratches and scars that had been hacked into the stone plateau in the distant past. The eerie chant of the warlocks wafted into the wind.

After a matter of seconds, the whole of the quarry floor was awash with purple traces of sha'iel, like a small, shallow oasis of warp energy in the desert. With a sudden convulsion, the huge stone floor cracked in two, bifurcated by a faultlessly straight line. Then, very slowly, the two great slabs of rock started to move away from each other, as though receding back into the dunes that were mounded up on all sides, gradually revealing a dark, cavernous space below.

* * *

LOOKING DOWN INTO the exposed cavern below, Laeresh smiled. There, buried under the desert for millennia, waiting for the return of the Biel-Tan, was a pristine squadron of Wave Serpent transports and Falcon anti-grav tanks. What the mon'keigh called archaeology, he called sound strategic planning. A couple of the Falcons and two of the Serpents had already been painted in the featureless black of the Dark Reapers, and Laeresh vaulted down onto a black Falcon's roof instantly, while the rangers and the Guardians that had accompanied Macha and her warlocks as personal retinues jumped down to check on the other craft.

'Forward planning is the mark of a great farseer, farseer,' said Aldryan, permitting himself a faint smile at the sight of the ancient arsenal that Macha had just unlocked. Around the edge of the cavern, Aldryan could see massive, densely packed pillars, like primeval, fossilised trees, as though the battle squadron had once been secreted in a jungle-glade that had become petrified over the aeons.

Perhaps, replied Macha. *But planning for the future and realising those plans is not the same thing. Seeing what needs to be done is not the same as doing it. All that we have seen is that something is required – but it is not yet clear what. Yet, it is already the time for action, and there is nothing else to be seen.*

She watched the burst of activity in the cavern before her, weary with the effort of opening the ancient seal. But more than anything she was concerned that she had seen no visions since the ruination of her runes aboard the *Eternal Star*, and she had seen nothing of Gabriel's presence at all. All those millennia before, Farseer Lsathranil had used his foresight to provide these vessels for his kin in their time of need, but now Macha could not even see the sun going down at the end of the day.

CHAPTER SEVEN
JAIN'ZAR

THE ANTIGRAVITIC ENGINES made short work of the treacherous and inconstant dunes as the squadron of Falcon tanks whisked along in the front line of the eldar assault. In the centre of the line was the impeccable black of Laeresh's vehicle, now dusted with the red sand of the desert. Spread out to the sides were the white and emerald shades of the Biel-Tan force, sleek and deadly in the ruddy light. As the convoy had started to close on the edge of the desert and the fringe of the ring-mountains had become visible above the horizon, the exarch had climbed out of the gun-emplacement on top of the Falcon and stood on its roof, braced with his reaper launcher, eager for the battle to begin.

On either side of his Falcon there were two jet-black Wave Serpents, hovering smoothly over the sand and scything their dual-bladed prows through any errant dunes. Laeresh could feel the presence of his Aspect Warriors in their transports, and he could sense the faint, rhythmical chant of their battle chorus echoing through the ether as the vehicles slipped forward into their waiting destinies: war is our master, death our mistress.

As he stood expectantly atop the tank, there was a sudden and massive movement in the dunes ahead. His helmet twitched automatically, snapping the aim of his reaper launcher onto the point of movement as the weapon tracked the motion of his eyes. The mon'keigh monastery and the mountains were still over the horizon, so he was not yet expecting blood; his soul thrilled at the sudden promise.

The entire dune that the convoy was climbing began to shift, as though a gargantuan, slumbering, subterranean creature had suddenly awoken beneath it. The desert rolled and parted, opening up a series of chasms in the dune, into which poured waterfalls of sand from each side. As the sand crashed off the sudden peaks, large cylindrical structures started to become visible beneath the grainy torrent.

Laeresh stared at the odd structures for a moment, confused and disappointed, sensing no will or intention emanating from their apparently inanimate forms. They were still largely obscured beneath the sand when a bolt of energy flared near the top of one them and flashed down towards the convoy.

The bolt punched into one of the frontal wings of a Wave Serpent, but it bounced off the protective energy field, ricocheting wildly up into the air. Immediately, the other emergent gun towers erupted with fire, spraying laser bolts down on the eldar convoy and transforming the baking desert into an inferno.

The Falcons returned fire, their gun turrets rotating freely as the tanks wove with surprising elegance, taking evasive action under the unexpected onslaught. The starcannon on one of the Falcons convulsed and a lance of blinding light jabbed into one of the gun emplacements, severing the structure in two and setting off a chain reaction of explosions that strafed down the height of the base before the main power cell detonated and exploded in a ball of blue fire.

Meanwhile, Laeresh was instantly back in the gun turret on his own Falcon, his thoughts excited and his soul calling out for blood as he plotted the trajectory for his own attack. He counted under his breath, waiting for exactly the right moment, and then clenched his jaw. This was all that his customised vehicle needed from him, and three missiles roared out of the cluster launcher, spiralling around each other as they honed in on the heat source at the top of one of the mon'keigh gun towers. They all impacted at once, punching into the rockcrete structure and detonating inside, blowing a fountain of masonry and melting rock into air.

By now the atmosphere was thick with las-fire, rattling shurikens, and scything energy blasts, all shrouded in the blood-red mist of the desert wind. The automated defence guns of the mon'keigh had taken the eldar by surprise and they had been caught in the crossfire between two formations of gun towers: one directly in front of them and another that had risen out of the desert behind them, hemming them in like cattle.

Laeresh spun his turret, letting out a shrill battle cry and looking back towards the rear of the convoy to make sure that the farseer was unharmed. She was standing in a blaze of energy, surrounded by the coruscating forms of her warlocks, great lances of blue flame leaping out of her fingertips and crashing into the primitive mon'keigh emplacements. Her open-topped Serpent had been modified millennia ago to permit the farseer and her retinue to capitalise on their gifts during combat, and Laeresh was momentarily transfixed by the majesty of the scene.

Then a different sort of movement caught his eye and his gun turret spun once again. Blood. On the crest of the next dune, just outside the ring of death, Laeresh could see the glints of five small, red vehicles. They were stationary, as though simply observing the bloody scene that was unfolding before them. Angling his missile launcher with a grin, Laeresh punched the trigger, sending a stream of rockets flashing through a low curve towards the Blood Ravens scouts on the ridge. Just as the missiles were away, Laeresh looked up in time to see a rain of rockets dropping out of the sky from a steep parabola and he vaulted out of his cockpit, thrilled and cursing at the same time.

THE DISTANT THUNDER of ordnance rumbled through the ground, shaking the desert and sending streams of sand cascading down the dunes. The exchange was taking place just over the horizon, and even the superior augmetic vision of Corallis could not yet make out the number of foes. He stood on the roof of a modified Helios Pattern Land Raider, seemingly oblivious to the volleys of rockets that streaked out of the missile turret next to him. He watched the ballistics disappear over the horizon, nodding with satisfaction at the clouds of sand and smoke that plumed into the air after their invisible impacts. The Blood Ravens may not have a large force on Rahe's Paradise, but they could still pack a punch, even at this range.

Over the horizon in the desert, the monastery's automatic defence cannons had been activated while Tanthius and Corallis were still seeing to the last-minute preparations around the base of the towering, black edifice itself. The desert gun emplacements had laid dormant for centuries, since they were set to respond only to a serious threat – a band of pirates or even a small ork war party would not be enough to trigger them. Whatever was coming over the horizon towards the monastery had set them off, so it was a force worthy of the new defences being hastily erected by the Blood Ravens.

A cloud of dust appeared on the featureless and barren horizon as a single vehicle crested a large dune. It was a burst of blood red against the dull monotony of the sand, shrouded in frenetic dust. The bike tore through the dunes, the roar of its engine now vaguely audible under the constant concussions that were thudding through the air. It bounced and swerved, traversing the passes in the undulating and ever-shifting ground, ploughing straight through the smaller dunes and blasting their sand into sprays and fountains.

The sound of this proximal vehicle made Tanthius pause and turn to face the desert. To him the shape was still blurred and distant.

'Corallis?' He knew that the elevated eyes of the sergeant would be more reliable than his own.

'It's Caleb.'

'Just Caleb?' asked Tanthius, staring out into the swirling cloud that engulfed the speeding figure.

'Just Caleb,' confirmed Corallis, sharing the concern of the massive Terminator Marine.

Eager to impress the famed Captain Angelos and the officers of the Third Company, Caleb had taken four of his trainee scouts out into the desert to check on the form and number of the enemy.

Tanthius nodded and turned back to his work, organising the defensive perimeter around the monastery-outpost. Whatever was coming, it was coming now; this was no time for sentimentality.

He had already deployed the magnificence of his own Terminator squad in the centre of the arc, between the hulking forms of the two Land Raider tanks. Without much effort, they had pushed back the sands of the desert, creating a giant, artificial dune behind which they would be granted some measure of cover. More importantly, this close to the mountains, which towered up behind the monastery, the sand layer was shallow, and by excavating a trench the Terminators had found solid rock on which to plant their heavy boots.

Four Marines in shimmering power-armour stood to attention, waiting for directions from Tanthius – Gabriel had delegated authority to the Terminator sergeant while he saw to matters inside the monastery itself. 'Hilkiah, take your Devastators and form a line on the north of the second Land Raider. Necho, fall in behind Hilkiah with your Assault squadron to provide aerial support when needed. Topheth, organise the assault bikes in a detachment to the west and be ready to sweep round and flank the enemy from the south. Asherah, take the Razor-back and fall in behind Topheth's bikes.'

The four Marines snapped crisp nods and strode off to ensure that Tanthius's instructions were carried out.

Turning to the west, Tanthius noted with satisfaction that Sergeant Gaal had already dug his Tactical squad in on the other side of Corallis's tank. The line was almost complete and, despite the limitations of the hardware and numbers available, Tanthius was confident that they would be able to hold it.

By now the rider had closed and, with a roar, Caleb's bike skidded to a halt behind Tanthius. He cut the engine just as Corallis crunched into the ground next to him, having vaulted down from his vantage point on top of the Land Raider to debrief the scout.

The young scout swung himself off the bike and drew himself up to attention before the senior Marines. Despite his best efforts to conceal it, the pain that wracked his body flickered across his face. He had not felt pain like that in years, not since the completion of the Implantation process – it was as though something had deliberately reactivated his pain receptors.

'Sergeant Corallis. Sergeant Tanthius,' he bowed to the Terminator as the imposing figure turned to face him. 'There are jetbikes and a squadron of Falcon tanks. At least three Wave Serpent transports, and an open-topped vehicle that I do not recognise – it appears to contain a group of psykers of some kind. They will break the horizon in a matter of minutes.'

'Understood,' replied Tanthius briskly. 'Thank you, Scout Caleb,' he added, seeing the passion burning in the pale, grimy face in front of him. 'This is valuable information. Your brothers did not die for nothing.'

'Caleb, are you damaged?' asked Corallis, as Tanthius turned away to continue with the preparations, striding away into the midst of the line of Terminators.

'No. No, sergeant,' He didn't seem sure. 'I don't think so,' he added, his face still creased with concealed agony.

Corallis inspected the scout but could see no sign of damage on his armour. 'But you are in pain?'

'Yes,' replied Caleb reluctantly. 'A little. But it is nothing, probably just a temporary imbalance in my pain receptors. I have been having some minor problems with a couple of my implants… I was awaiting your apothecary.'

Corallis looked at the scout with concern, but at that precise moment a tremendous roar erupted from the Terminator line behind him as they unleashed the first volley of hellfire shells at the eldar force as it crested the horizon, a billowing cloud of silence, sand and shimmering lethality. The automatic defences had failed to hold them, so now it was time for war.

THE DARKNESS INSIDE the chapel seemed to enshroud the kneeling figure of Gabriel before the faintly lit altar. His head was angled up and his blue eyes were wide, staring at the images of his forefathers and the Emperor himself. Even from the corridor outside, Prathios could see the sweat on his captain's brow as he struggled to put his soul at ease before the battle to come. Despite himself, Prathios had to concede that Gabriel was getting worse.

Quietly, the chaplain pulled the great doors closed, squeezing out the last of the light. As he did so, the sound of footsteps heading towards him from down the corridor made him turn. The light in the passageway grew increasingly dim and shadowy as it approached the chapel, but the far end was brightly lit, as sunlight streamed in from the huge windows set high up in the fresco-strewn walls. And in the flood of pristine light at that end marched five glorious figures of imperial virtue.

At the front of the group was the delicate, shapely and lithe figure of Ptolemea, moving easily and confidently in her asphalt and red body-glove, a scarf tied carefully around her hairless head and her limbs speckled with holsters and straps. Flanking her on both sides, marching magnificently in her wake, were the breathtaking Celestians of the Order of Golden Light, their polished armour shining brilliantly in the startling beams of light.

'Chaplain Prathios,' said Ptolemea formally as the glittering group stepped out of the light and into the shadows before the great doors to the chapel. 'We desire to speak with the captain.'

'He is indisposed at present,' replied Prathios, resolutely not looking back over his shoulder in the direction of Gabriel. 'He is administering to his armour and preparing for battle.'

Ptolemea stared at Prathios for a moment, holding his even gaze with her fierce dark eyes. Her pale jaw clenched slightly and then her eyes flicked towards the closed doors. In fact, they were not fully closed. A crack of darkness seeped out of the middle, where the doors had not been pulled properly shut. In the interior beyond, a single javelin of light from the crack caught the kneeling figure of Gabriel at the altar, holding him in a weak spotlight as he appealed to the icons above the altarpiece.

In the dark depths of Ptolemea's eyes, Prathios saw the reflected figure of his captain kneeling in supplication, held there as though contained as much in Ptolemea's thoughts as in the chapel behind him. He took a step to the side, blocking Ptolemea's view and watching the image of Gabriel blink out of her eyes. 'I am sure that he will be pleased to receive you, if you would have the grace to be patient.'

'I understand that the battle has already begun,' replied Ptolemea, tilting her head slightly and looking deeply into the chaplain's face. There was a challenge written somewhere in her thoughts. As though to underline her point, a loud explosion resounded in the distance. It was followed by a series of smaller detonations and the commencement of the general, muffled rattle of distant combat. In their pristine, golden helmets, the Celestians behind her turned their heads as one, instinctively turning to face the sounds of war outside the walls of the monastery.

'Indeed it has,' said Gabriel, pulling open the doors and stepping out from behind Prathios. 'We have no time to lose. How may I assist you, Sister Ptolemea?'

'Captain Angelos,' bowed Ptolemea, her manner changing completely. 'As you know, the Order of the Lost Rosetta is non-militant, but the Celestian Sisters of the Golden Light wish to fight at your side.'

Gabriel looked down at the top of Ptolemea's bowed head for a couple of seconds; something had definitely changed in her manner towards him. She did not look up until he lifted his own gaze to the Battle Sisters behind her.

'Battle Sisters,' said Gabriel, looking from one to the other since he could find no indication or markings that might differentiate their ranks on their armour. 'You do the Blood Ravens a great honour.'

The four Celestians bowed efficiently, and for a moment there was silence.

'They will not speak, captain,' explained Ptolemea. 'The Order of Golden Light requires a vow of silence from their Celestians – in honour of their lost and fallen brethren.' She met his eyes, finally.

Gabriel nodded. He had heard of the ferocious piety of the order, but had never encountered any of their elite Celestian warriors before. He understood that they used no insignia to stipulate their ranks and provided nobody with their names – believing that all the Sisterhood was equal before the Emperor, equally devoted and utterly selfless. For such devout servants, there was no need for the differentiations of name and rank. They did not care for personal identities, but thought only of in whose name they would die.

'This is no time for talk,' smiled Gabriel, nodding a bow to the Celestians. 'It is time for death.'

* * *

THE ELDAR LINE burst through the immense dune that obscured the horizon, leaving the wreckage of the automatic gun emplacements out of sight in their wake. Columns of smoke and jets of flame that aspired towards the sun from the blindside of the dune lay testament to the ruined defences and to the few eldar craft that had fallen.

The bladed prows of the Wave Serpents cut through the base of the dune and punched out onto the smoother stretch of desert that approached the foothills and the imposing form of the Blood Ravens monastery. Huge clouds of sand were thrown up into the air, temporarily hiding the speeding, alien vehicles as they pressed on towards the waiting Marines. It was as though the desert itself was rising against them.

As soon as the first vehicle broke the dune, a volley of fire erupted from the line of Terminator Marines dug into the sand between the two Land Raiders that held the most advanced position in the Blood Ravens' defensive arc. A torrent of hellfire shells lashed through the sand-riddled air before exploding into lethal shards of shrapnel as they impacted against the armour on the front of the eldar vehicles.

Only a fraction of a second later, the Land Raiders themselves opened up with the twin-linked lascannons housed in each of their side sponsons, streaking the dusky air with strips of brilliance. The Wave Serpents returned fire with a constant spray of tiny black shuriken, visible only because of the incredible numbers being unleashed – like clouds of night whining towards the Marines, blackening the sandstorms into a lethal menace.

As the impacts thudded into the sleek form of the eldar craft, they seemed to slow and pitch forward, driving their dual-pronged prows into the sand and half burying themselves, like a row of gravestones in the desert. The twin barrels mounted on their roofs pitched upwards, counterbalancing the unusual angle of the transporters themselves, and permitting them to continue firing relentlessly.

'Topheth,' said Tanthius, the vox bead in his ear whistling with feedback. 'Get your bikes round behind them – they're digging in.'

'Understood,' hissed the reply through the vox, but it was almost drowned out by the blast of sound that erupted as the attack bikes roared forward of the line and prowled out into the desert, curving round to the southeast.

'Necho. Let's see what a little height will do,' suggested Tanthius, his storm bolter beginning to smoke from the constant stream of shells that was ripping out of it. He looked along the line of his battle-brothers in the Terminator squadron and he nodded to himself with pride – a relentless and formidable sheet of hellfire was ploughing out towards the aliens, like the Emperor's fury made manifest. Not even the slippery and treacherous eldar could stand against the righteous ferocity of Blood Ravens Terminators.

This time there was no verbal response from the sergeant, but his reaction was rapid, obvious and dramatic. The roar of engines from the north reassured Tanthius and made him grin as he imagined the Assault squadron lifting majestically into the air from behind the furious line of Hilkiah's Devastators, which was alive with the discharge of heavy weapons, filling the rapidly shortening killing zone with gouts of flame, pulses of melta and streaks of bolter shells.

'Your strategy seems sound, sergeant,' said Gabriel, striding up to the Terminator's shoulder from the direction of the monastery behind the line. 'I approve.' He nodded his helmet, communicating his admiration efficiently.

'Thank you, captain.' Tanthius turned to greet his captain, finding him at the head of a startling group of Battle Sisters, accompanied by Prathios and Father Jonas, all in full combat armour – a glorious and inspiring sight, even for a Terminator Marine. 'The theatre is yours.' He bowed crisply.

Gabriel stood for a moment, staring over the rim of the long sand bunker that Tanthius had constructed in a crescent around the monastery. It wasn't rock-crete and it certainly wasn't an adamantium barrier, but it would serve its purpose. The eldar assault appeared to have stalled, and their transports had pitched themselves into the ground. From the north and south of the Blood Ravens tanks, vicious and relentless salvoes of fire lashed against the downed vehicles from the Devastator and Tactical squads, chipping away at their armour and blowing great eruptions of sand out of the desert around them. The gun turrets on the roofs of the Serpents were still active, but the clouds of monomolecular projectiles being released were largely being absorbed by the sand banks around the Marines.

'Is this it?' asked Gabriel, disappointed. He had come to expect more from the eldar; they didn't appear to be trying. 'Where is the witch?'

As he spoke, the sand in the bunker wall started to tremble and shiver, as though something vast and heavy were approaching from the distance. Fine cascades began to slide and shift down the bank, drawing Gabriel's attention from the eldar force in the desert. Gradually, the shuffling sands started to crackle with friction, sending little sparks of static arcing between the grains. After a few moments, the sparks had begun to coalesce and merge into pools of flickering energy, dark and shimmering. As Gabriel watched, the pools were drawn into streams running up the bank against gravity, merging and blending with others to form rivers and veins of pulsing darkness, spidering out across the desert towards the eldar like a great web.

Looking out into the desert, Gabriel could see that similar tendrils were being emitted from the eldar barricades, pulsing out towards the centre of the battlefield.

Suddenly, the sky seemed to crack and open out into space, as though some terrible god had reached down and ripped a gash into the planet's atmosphere. A great javelin of darkness spiked into the contested desert between the Marines and the eldar, merging with the black lattice of tendrils in the sand, superheating and crystallising it instantly, rending the shifting tides suddenly solid and impenetrable.

As one, the Blood Ravens and the eldar stopped firing, all eyes turning up to the heavens to find the source of the unearthly blast. High up in the mesosphere there was a small, black starburst, like a jagged hole in the atmosphere itself. Beyond it seemed to glimmer an impossibly distant light, as though it were a window to the stars themselves.

When Gabriel looked down from the mysterious phenomenon, he saw dozens of eldar warriors emerging from behind the barricades of their pitched Wave Serpents, as though responding to this incredible signal. A stream of jetbikes hissed off towards the south, heading to intercept Topheth's column of attack bikes, while neat formations of green and white troops went sprinting over the suddenly glassy, rocky ground, heading directly towards the Blood Ravens. In the centre of the vanguard was an elegant, female form that Gabriel found instantly familiar, surrounded by a coruscating sphere of blue energy that seemed to encompass the dark, shrouded figures at her side.

'For the Great Father and the Emperor!' yelled Gabriel, striding past Tanthius and vaulting up onto the crest of the artificial sandbank as he drew his chainsword.

A volley of fire rippled out of the Blood Ravens' line, tearing into the advancing eldar forces, before the Marines clambered up out of their trenches with a resonating war-cry and charged forward in support of their captain – the golden Celestians storming forward with them like brilliant jewels in a wave of blood.

At exactly that moment, two jet-black vehicles slid into view on either side of the green and white wall of pitched Wave Serpents, spilling scores of shimmering black-armoured warriors into the desert, who immediately braced their long, heavy weapons and loosed a hail of projectiles into the charging line of Marines. Simultaneously, the strangely elongated gun turrets on the vehicles themselves erupted with light, sending spikes of brilliance searing through the gathering fury of battle, punching into the sheer, black walls of the Blood Ravens monastery itself. As the pulses of light faded, a glittering and magnificent eldar warrior appeared in the smoke on the roof of one of the Wave Serpents. He was taller than all the others and his armour shone with an eerie light as the elaborate crests around his ornate death mask fluttered in the desert winds. He braced a cannon in his hands and threw back his head, letting out a dark wail.

'This is more like it!' yelled Gabriel, rattling off bolter shells as he pounded across the desert.

'Yes,' agreed Tanthius, spying the magnificent foe on the distant dune. 'This is much more like it.'

HER EYES WERE twitching, flickering erratically under her eyelids as though trying to trace the movement of a dream. The skin of her face was slick with perspiration, but it was cold as Ptolemea pressed her fingers against the older Sister's cheek. Her loose, grey hair was matted and clumps clung to her forehead, soaked in the exertions of her nightmares.

'Meritia,' whispered Ptolemea, leaning her face down towards the Sister Senioris and pressing her lips against her ear, breathing her words against the clammy skin. 'Meritia – what do you see?'

There was no response. The older woman's arms lay limp by her sides, and her legs were stretched straight out on the tablet, unmoving. There was the faintest trace of breath, as though she were lost in a deep meditation.

Straightening up, Ptolemea looked away from her unconscious Sister, inspecting the little cell that had

been her home for the last few years. It was neatly
kept, as she had expected, with tightly packed shelves
full of manuscripts, books and scrolls.

On the small desk, bathed in the light reflected
from the mirror on the back of the chamber's door,
was a crisp adamantium tube with its seal broken
and its lid discarded casually. Next to the tube was a
rolled manuscript, clearly ancient but exceedingly
well preserved. Meritia had apparently been consult-
ing it recently, and Ptolemea unfurled a short section
with mild curiosity. The script was cursive and elegant – some form of archaic High Gothic – and it
appeared to be a folk tale of some kind.

Ptolemea unrolled a little more of the story, reading the unusual yet familiar script with ease. She
nodded, accepting that this was exactly the kind of
artefact that she should have expected to find in
Meritia's chambers, given that the older woman was
charged with co-operating in the Blood Ravens'
investigation into their shadowy history. She lifted
her hand from the desk and let the scroll roll back
into a tube as she looked around the rest of the
room.

To her mild surprise, Ptolemea found a weapon
rack in an alcove cut into the window nook. It contained a pair of ornate bolt pistols with elaborately
decorated handles, each inscribed with the chalice
and starburst insignia of the now disbanded Order of
Lost Light. The alcove was covered by a rough, dis-
coloured tapestry bearing the image of Canoness
Silentia – one of the founding mothers of the Order
of Lost Light – kneeling in supplication before the
Golden Throne of the Emperor of Man.

Holding the tapestry back like a curtain, Ptolemea looked back over at Meritia and smiled slightly, silently impressed by this unexpected twist in her older Sister's personality. There were agents back on Bethle II that would consider such a tapestry heretical on a number of different grounds: firstly, the canoness appears in the company of the Emperor himself, which was almost certainly an apocrypha, or at the very least a blasphemous crisis of narcissism; and secondly, the Order of Lost Light was disbanded and split into the non-militant Lost Rosetta and militant Golden Light for a good reason – any allegiance to such an unsanctioned institution would be frowned upon by the Ordo Hereticus, no matter how romantic the stories about it might be. And to possess artefacts from that organisation, particularly in the form of weapons, would certainly not be condoned; whilst the tapestry might conceivably be part of a research project, the ancient bolt pistols would be much harder to justify.

Perhaps I have underestimated the venerable Meritia, thought Ptolemea, intrigued. She made a mental note to report the pistols on her return to Bethle II, and then walked back over to the unconscious body of her Sister, stretched out on the stone tablet against the far wall. Gazing down at her face once more, she watched her hidden eyes twitch and flutter blindly. For a moment, she wondered whether the older woman's nightmares would be anything like her own – they did seem to have more in common than she had thought.

As she turned to leave, pushing open the door and striding out of the chamber, heading down towards the dig in the foundations, an abrupt impact rocked the tower, knocking her off her feet and sending her stumbling against the cold, stone wall.

THE ELDAR WITCH was alive with furious power, streaks of purple and blue flame pouring out of her fingertips. Surrounding her were a clutch of other psykers, bedecked in sinister black robes that fell in heavy folds, billowing as their smooth movements turned the cloaks into whirls. Flanking the psychic inferno were loose squadrons of warriors, each armoured in the familiar white and green of the Biel-Tan. Gabriel had seen those colours so recently, and his soul thrilled and shuddered simultaneously to see them again so soon after Tartarus. He had known that the farseer was there.

The fleet-footed eldar had rapidly closed the gap on the Blood Ravens' line and engaged them at close range, capitalising on whatever distraction had suddenly rent the sky and petrified the ground. But the Marines had risen to the challenge, charging out of their positions with bolters blazing and their chainswords spluttering with thirst. Before long, the charge had splintered and fragmented, and Gabriel had found himself in the middle of a frenetic battlefield, surrounded by a crescendo of blades as the eldar and the Marines met each other in intimate ferocity.

Meanwhile, Topheth's attack bikes were struggling to outflank the eldar jetbikes to the south, attempting to get around behind the killing zone to take on the pitch-black Wave Serpents and the sinister dark warriors that continued to blast away at the monstrous walls of the Blood Ravens monastery, firing salvo after salvo of thunderous light. But the jetbikes were too fast, and Topheth had been forced to change tactics and attempt a frontal assault.

Sergeant Necho had also identified the threat posed by the heavy weapons, and he too had angled his squad towards the jet-black eldar craft. His Assault Marines were already airborne, and they were striving to engage the Serpents from the north, spraying hails of bolter shells and capturing the enemy vehicles in a lethal rain of grenades. But they were being held at bay by the macabre-looking, black-armoured warriors that had spilled out of the transports, who had set up tiers of firing lines and were returning the fierce brutality of the Marines shot for shot, unleashing banks of projectiles from their unusual weapons. The magnificent warrior that had appeared on top of one of the Wave Serpents – presumably the leader of this dark force – had vaulted down from the vehicle and was running forward into the heart of the fray, howling with what might have been pleasure.

As Gabriel's spluttering blade jammed in the stomach of an eldar warrior and he fired off a staccato of bolter shells straight into the alien's face, cleaning the foul xenos creature off his blessed chainsword, he looked up in time to see a gout of flame erupt from the jump-pack of one of Necho's Assault Marines. It spluttered and coughed, and Gabriel knew what was about to happen; he kept his attention fixed on the doomed Marine whilst parrying a force-sword with his own blade and snapping off a couple of shots with his bolter, each finding its target in alien flesh.

With a blinding blast of red light, the Assault Marine's jump-pack went critical and its fuel cells detonated, firing him down towards the ground like a giant bolter shell. Even from where he was standing, Gabriel could see the Marine working to release the grenades that were clipped around his belt, flinging them down into the formation of eldar below him even as he rocketed down towards them. The disciplined aliens seemed unphased for a fraction of a second, holding their firing vectors until they realised what was about to happen. Then, as the xenos creatures began to scatter away from the Wave Serpents, the string of grenades smacked into the ground and detonated all at once, blowing a huge crater into the desert and rocking the nearest Wave Serpent. In an instant, the Marine's jump-pack roared down towards the vehicle, spiralling on its axis now that it had been jettisoned by the Marine himself, until it punched heavily into the gunnery cockpit on top of the Wave Serpent, blowing it clean off the vehicle and engulfing the whole thing in a giant red fireball. The Marine himself ploughed down into the desert nearby.

With a roar, Gabriel snatched his attention away from the heroics of his Marine and spun on his heel, always inspired by the exploits of his men. Bringing his chainsword around in a wild and wide arc, he expected to feel the thick resistance of alien flesh at any moment. As he turned, he could see the glorious figure of Jonas in the melee around him, ablaze in warp-fire, lashing out against the fury of the eldar warlocks with bolts of energy from his force staff. In the blur of reds, greens and whites that cycled past his eyes, Gabriel also caught bursts of shimmering gold as the Celestian Sisters unleashed their righteous wrath against the tainted xenos creatures that seemed to dance and leap with intricate and terrible splendour. If the Imperium had any troops to match the exquisite grace of the eldar warriors, they were the Celestian Battle Sisters. And he could see the glorious form of Tanthius storming through the mire in his ancient Terminator armour, his attention fixed on the magnificent eldar warrior that ploughed through the theatre towards him. The battlefield was roiling with combat, as though the eldar and the Marines were involved in their own grandiose version of the Blood Trials.

Completing his turn, Gabriel's blade slowed to a halt as though losing its momentum, coming to rest only millimetres from the neck of the eldar farseer. For a long second, the Blood Ravens captain stared at the breathtaking alien before him, shocked to see her there but falling into her deep emerald eyes as though momentarily mesmerised. His chainsword still whirred with hunger, but something stayed Gabriel's hand or his intent.

Gabriel.

He had felt that thought before and it sent a thrill tingling along his spine, as though icy fingernails were caressing his neck. But a fraction of a second later he slammed shut his mind, smashing the corrupted thought that violated his Emperor-given soul. As he regained his senses, a huge roaring weight crashed into his back, flattening him to the ground in a thud of armoured plates and battle cries.

When he looked up, Gabriel saw Prathios standing in his place, his Crozius Arcanum blazing with purity and purpose as he brought it round in powerful strikes at the farseer. But Macha just seemed to melt around the attacks, flowing around each thrust and sweep, almost taunting the heroism of the magnificent chaplain who had thrown himself into the defence of his captain.

Then, without warning, everything went black, even more dramatically and completely than before, as though the local star had been suddenly extinguished. It was a brilliant and startling flash of darkness, more blinding than any explosion of light.

For a moment combat ceased, as though held in suspension by the abrupt loss of the sun. But as the light returned, as suddenly as it had been lost, battle was joined once again. This time, however, the eldar were suddenly in retreat, fighting their way back to their makeshift barricades, which started to rise back up out of the sand and resume their function as transports. Once again they appeared to be responding to the dramatic signal. Macha had vanished inexplicably and Gabriel clambered to his feet next to Prathios, resting his gauntleted hand on his old friend's shoulder in a gesture of gratitude and confusion.

'What in the Emperor's name is going on?'

HAVING MADE HER way down into the dig, winding through the shaking corridors of Meritia's tower, Ptolemea crouched down to the ground, pressing her fingers against the ancient inscriptions that adorned the ruined foundations of what once must have been a great fortress monastery on Rahe's Paradise. She traced the shapes of the unusual script and lingered on the decorative pictures that had been carved directly into the stonework. There were definitely Space Marines in the time-worn images, although it was impossible to differentiate any particular features or individual characters; the detailing had been lost to the weather and to history ages before. She stared at them, bringing her face so close to the relief that her pale nose almost touched the stone: there was something disturbing about the images, but it remained just out of reach of her thoughts. She had never heard of Blood Ravens artefacts dating from more than four or five millennia before, and this lost monastery must have been considerably older than that.

She took another look at the Marines in the fresco, touching her skin against the texture of their armour, trying to feel whether there was still some trace of their Chapter insignia. In the back of her mind, she wondered whether they were not Blood Ravens at all. Then she shook her head, trying to clear it of these extraneous thoughts, and she pulled back from the stone images: she was not here to help Jonas with his research, she had an investigation of her own to conduct. It did occur to her, however, that Meritia's condition and her own lapses might both be connected to something on Rahe's Paradise – the commonality might well turn out to be Captain Angelos himself, which would not surprise her given the information that had been supplied by Librarian Isador Akios before he mysteriously died on Tartarus, but it might also have something to do with the history of the planet itself.

Taking another quick look around the excavation site, Ptolemea strode over to the hole that dropped down to the next level. At some point in the past it had clearly been covered by a large, heavy, rectangular block – presumably some kind of hatchway or door. The ground on each side of the indentation around the hole was riddled with tiny tracks and carved lines, like veins in the rock. They interlaced and crisscrossed in complicated webs, but it was clear that their patterns would have continued across the surface of the missing slab, since a number of veins were terminated abruptly at the lips of the indentation. At first, Ptolemea thought that the little channels had been cut by water trickling through the rock, or perhaps that insects had trawled their way through the earth long ago, leaving their trails carved into the stone as their only legacy. However, as she looked more carefully, it became clear that the lines had been cut by hand, deliberately etched into the rock in this specific pattern, although the significance of the pattern was beyond her.

Sitting onto the rocky lip, Ptolemea swung her legs down into the hole and then dropped through into the chamber below, finding herself surrounded by the petrified trees once more. Jonas had set up a few light-orbs on the floor up against the trunks of the trees at regular intervals around the curving, circular wall, filling the eerie chamber with a dim glow and making the rocky ground shimmer as though it were wet.

To Ptolemea, this chamber seemed to represent a wholly separate archaeological layer, clearly distinguished from the ruined foundations of the Adeptus Astartes facility above. It seemed to her that the Marines had deliberately built on this site – the gradual transition of eldar runes into High Gothic script etched into the trunks of the fossilised trees suggested that there was a self-conscious plan at work in the location of the later buildings. This bizarre chamber was almost a liminal point, a ritualisation of a chamber acting as some kind of bridge between eras that were otherwise unconnected. What was the connection?

The narrow, angled tunnel in which Meritia had collapsed was still shrouded in darkness, although the dull-burnished radiance of the lava-flow at the far end gave it a gentle ruddiness. Ptolemea took a few experimental steps down the inclined passageway and then stopped. If the peculiar chamber behind her really represented an intermediate historical stage between the forgotten presence of a Space Marine Chapter on Rahe's Paradise and the even earlier presence of something else, presumably a settlement of eldar, then this tunnel had to lead down further into that alien past. She paused, gathering her resolve against what she might find.

Standing almost exactly on the spot where she had previously found Meritia, Ptolemea looked down at the intricate webwork of petrified roots and vines that interwove to form the walls of the passageway.

'Jain'zar,' she muttered to herself, spotting the eldar rune etched into the rocky roots near her feet and stooping to inspect it more closely. As she ducked down, the ferrous red light burst delicately off a mark on the opposite wall.

'Nrulhinus,' hissed Ptolemea, vocalising the syllables of the alien language with practiced elegance.
'The banshee cries.'

A flash of movement made the Sister Dialogous
start, snapping her head around to face down the
tentacle-draped tunnel. Her dark eyes dilated in sudden and inexplicable terror as a gust of shapeless
darkness rushed up the passageway, consuming the
ruddy hints of volcanic light as though sucking them
out of existence as it swept towards her.

She had time to open her mouth, but no time to
scream.

IN THE MIDDLE distance, Gabriel could still see the
report of weapons discharge from the shimmering,
golden figures of the Celestian Battle Sisters. They
were not willing to let the eldar retreat so cheaply,
and they had pursued the xenos creatures almost to
the point where they had rapidly dismantled their
barricades. Above the battle-sisters, resting on miniature infernos of flame, Necho's Assault Marines were
still pouring fire down from the sky, filling the wake
of the fleeing eldar with a purifying blaze. And from
the south came Topheth's squadron of attack bikes,
falling into pursuit and opening up with their heavy
bolters.

'Tanthius!' called Gabriel over the tumult, pulling
off his helmet and staring after the fleeing eldar. His
face was still creased with confusion and concern.

'Captain?' replied the huge Terminator Marine, his
feet planted firmly against the rocky ground and his
storm bolter still trained on the rapidly vanishing
foe, which were now almost out of range. He had

been cheated of his duel with the magnificent alien, and he was exorcising his frustrations with his bolter.

'This is unexpected,' confessed Gabriel, still gazing towards the horizon where the last silhouette of a Wave Serpent finally vanished from view, chased by a line of explosions as Necho's squad strafed the ground with grenades. 'But we must not be thrown off our guard. Regroup the Marines back behind the sand bunkers. Ensure that they are ready for an imminent counter-attack. The eldar are devious and snide creatures – they would not retreat unless it was to their advantage to do so. Make sure Necho and Topheth are recalled – we will not be pursuing the Biel-Tan today. If their intention is to divide our forces and lure us into a trap, they will not succeed.'

Tanthius hesitated for a moment, wanting to ask Gabriel about the incredible blasts of darkness that had transformed the battlefield.

'We must consider this new alien weapon,' continued Gabriel, as though sensing the concerns of the sergeant. 'When preparations here are complete, we will meet in the librarium,' he added. Then he turned and strode back towards the sheer, black walls of the monastery, leaving Tanthius and Corallis to organise the defences once again.

'WE SHOULD NOT have run from the mon'keigh, farseer. It dishonours us.' Laeresh's voice was rich with anger and his mind emanated a field of barely suppressed rage as he spoke – he had been forced to withdraw from the field just as he was about to engage one of the giant mon'keigh machine-warriors. He drew one of the Dark Reaper

Wave Serpents up in front of Macha's transport platform, cutting off her route and forcing the retreating convoy to a halt.

Macha did not answer immediately. Instead she turned to look back towards the Blood Ravens' monastery, the tops of its towers still visible above the horizon, with the immense form of Krax-7 looming up behind it. Thin wisps of smoke still wafted through the air, acting as an ephemeral and transient legacy of the abortive battle. She sighed, letting her soul calm.

'Farseer!' Laeresh was on the verge of shouting, forcing his voice through clenched teeth in an effort to control himself, as he stood in fierce determination on top of the transporter.

Seeing the simmering fury of the exarch, Druinir stepped in front of Macha, cutting off Laeresh's line of sight. The warlock dropped his hood and revealed his long, wizened face. He was old, even by eldar standards, and his skin was beginning to become dry and cracked. But his eyes shone like distant stars, profound and brilliant, as though confining incredible power within those tiny orbs. He didn't have to say anything.

Laeresh bit down on his lip, sinking a curving incisor down into his flesh and drawing a bead of blood into his mouth. The pain stabbed at his thoughts, contesting with his anger, and his rage cleared a little.

'My apologies, farseer,' he said tensely, as though forcing the words out against his will. 'It is not my place to question your judgment.' His eyes flashed, betraying his true emotions.

You are wrong, Laeresh, Dark Reaper. To question is exactly your role. As the thoughts pushed their way into his mind, Macha turned to face him and Druinir slipped back to her side.

We are not running from the humans, exarch. Did you not feel the movement of the Yngir? Did you not hear the howling of the banshees? You witnessed their call, and it turned the desert to stone. It is as we have feared, as we fear now and as we will fear again before the ending of days. The mon'keigh know not what they do as they stand on the glory and ineffable power of Lsathranil's Shield. We must bring about their end, but this is not the way. We must restore Lsathranil's legacy to its rightful place.

The exarch was breathing deeply, holding his rage in check. With his mind he knew that the farseer was right; he had complete and utter faith in her judgement – that was why he was there, after all. But his soul rebelled against the humiliation of retreat, no matter what the reasons. He was the exarch of the Dark Reapers; if he did not bow to the Court of the Young King, he was not about to kowtow to the stupidity of the mon'keigh. The image of the massive crimson Terminator Marine charging towards him flashed back into his mind, and he cursed inwardly about the lost opportunity for battle.

'I understand, farseer,' he sighed heavily, bowing curtly and then turning away.

Macha watched his vehicle bank and then speed off through the desert with the exarch still standing dramatically on its roof, his cloak washing out behind him like a jet-stream. He was heading back to the rendezvous point with the rangers. She shook her head silently, wondering what his role would be in the events yet to come. The Dark Reapers were clearly meant to be there – Lsathranil himself had provided for them – but their future was shadowy and vague, hidden behind heavy shadows of the past and run through with the burning passions of the present. She could not see the currents of history on which Laeresh sailed; something seemed to be blurring her vision.

Gabriel, she thought, only half to herself.

CHAPTER EIGHT
YNGIR

THE HIGHEST ROOMS in the towers of the monastery were the smallest, built into the tapering shape of the great spires, and Meritia's chamber was near the top of one of them. She had chosen it because of its seclusion from the rest of the edifice, which bustled with menials, curators, servants and pledge workers during the waking hours. When she had first arrived on Rahe's Paradise, Jonas had found her yearning for solitude rather strange, thinking that being light-years away from Bethle II and the rest of her order should seem secluded enough for his guest. He was wrong.

As Gabriel paced up the stairs of the tower, taking three steps at a time without giving it any thought, his mind raced with the events of the brief battle with the eldar. It had been the same farseer that they had encountered on Tartarus, and she had recognised him. She had waited for him in the middle of the theatre and had just stared at him, as though searching his soul for something hidden deep within it. If he closed his eyes, Gabriel could still see those glittering emerald eyes radiating something unspeakable and alien into his being. If Prathios hadn't pushed him aside, he had no idea what would have happened, and he shuddered at the realisation that he could have cut her down in an instant, but that he hadn't done so. He hadn't even tried.

And then there had been the bizarre cracks of darkness that had flashed through the combat zone, presumably superheating and condensing the sand under their feet into mica glass and rock. He had never seen anything like it before, and his intuition told him that it must have something to do with the odd xenos artefacts that Meritia and Jonas had unearthed under the monastery. But intuition was not good enough for a Blood Raven – he needed some evidence. Perhaps this old Exodite world was hiding an ancient eldar weapon in its depths – something that the farseer could use to shift the terrain of a battle into her favour? Whatever it was, Gabriel needed to know about it – knowledge is power, as the Great Father had said to the earliest recorded Blood Ravens, so we must guard it well.

'Sister Meritia,' he called, drawing to a standstill outside the door to her chamber. If she had regained consciousness, he needed to consult the Sister about her thoughts concerning the mysterious wraithbone tablet and the tunnel network that seemed to run underneath the monastery itself. Jonas was already on his way down into the site, a new sense of urgency driving his scholarship.

There was no answer.

'Sister Senioris,' repeated Gabriel, rapping on the door.

Still no answer.

Pushing open the door and preparing an apology in his mind should he find Meritia in the room and conscious, Gabriel stepped into the small cell. It was neat and orderly, as he would have expected. The shelves supported a well-organised collection of tomes, together with tablets and scrolls. On the little desk, Gabriel could see an open adamantium scroll tube and the ancient document that it had once contained – clearly Sister Meritia had been working on it before her incident.

Meritia herself was still lying on the tablet against the wall where Jonas had put her so carefully. She was perfectly still and utterly silent, one arm hanging casually down to the ground; for a moment Gabriel thought that she was dead. He had no idea what had happened in the tunnels under the monastery, but it was clear that Meritia was suffering. Jonas had voiced his suspicions about Ptolemea, but there would be little evidence until the Sister Senioris regained consciousness and could tell them what happened.

Taking a couple of strides towards the Sister, a fluttering motion caught Gabriel's eye and he turned to see a hanging tapestry flapping in the draft from the open doorway. Even from the centre of the room, Gabriel could see that there was an antique pistol hidden in a shallow alcove behind it, and he nodded to himself, silently approving of the Sister Senioris's preparedness. Even the Ordo Dialogous should be able to enforce the Emperor's will if necessary. Gabriel was aware that the Order of the Lost Rosetta had not always been so puritanical about being non-militant.

He took another step and his boot crunched down on something on the floor; he felt its resistance collapse under the considerable weight of a Space Marine's foot. Lifting his leg he saw the crumbled and powdery outline of what must have once been a pistol. Instantly, his head snapped back to the tapestry on the opposite wall. As it billowed out from the alcove, Gabriel could clearly see that the pistol hidden behind it was the pair of the one he had just crushed underfoot.

'Sister Meritia,' he said for a third time, but now with more urgency.

There was still no response from the unconscious Sister Seniors, but as Gabriel loomed over her he noticed a trickle of red running over her neck. He reached down and turned her face away from the wall, bringing it square with his own. Her thick, muddled, grey hair was matted in liquid and stuck haphazardly all over the side of her face, and there was the faint, ferrous smell of blood in the air. Pushing the hair away with his fingers, Gabriel saw the neat, cauterised entry wound that had punched through Meritia's temple, killing her instantly. The grey and red liquid in her hair had gradually seeped out of the hole in her skull under gravity, as her head had slumped over to the side. The book on which she had rested her head as a pillow was soaked through.

* * *

As HE DESCENDED down towards the foundations of
the monastery, the shadows seemed to grow longer
and heavier until the corners of the corridors were all
but invisible. Instinctively, Jonas whispered something inaudible and his force staff flared with light,
pushing back the darkness as he rushed through the
winding and labyrinthine passageways. Gabriel had
been adamant that there was some kind of connection between the bizarre happenings on the
battlefield and the unusual finds in Jonas's dig. And
Jonas had to concede that the appearance of ancient
eldar artefacts under the monastery did not bode
well. It was entirely conceivable that the conniving
aliens could exploit some long-dormant technology
as a weapon in the battles to come; it did not befit a
Blood Ravens librarian to be ignorant of such risks.
Knowledge is power.

After a few moments lost in his thoughts, Jonas
realised that the shadows in the old, vaulted corridor
remained heavy and impenetrable despite the light
spilling out of his staff. He paused, stopping in the
middle of a long, high-ceilinged corridor, its walls
punctuated with tall alcoves in which loomed the
menacing visages of fallen Blood Ravens, their like-
nesses carved into the strange igneous rock so
prevalent on Rahe's Paradise.

It was always dark this far down in the monastery
– there was no natural light and the passageways
down there were hardly ever used, especially since
the dungeons had been moved to higher ground. The
main route down into the foundations was elsewhere, but this was the most direct path from the
desert entrance into the monastery. The Chapter's

menials performed maintenance sweeps only twice a month, which was enough to keep the unfrequented passages respectable, but not enough to keep them shimmering and clean like the rest of the monastery. Nonetheless, there was no reason at all why the shadows themselves should be indelible marks against the floor and walls. They glinted faintly, as though they were merely mica glass.

Jonas surveyed the corridor from the centre of the sphere of light that emanated from his staff. When he quietened his mind, he thought that he could hear the suggestion of whispers from the shadows, although he wasn't sure whether the breathy, aspirated sounds were actually coming from inside his own head.

There was something in the shadows at the feet of the statue of legendary Third Company Captain Trythos, further down the corridor, just beyond the reach of his staff's radiance. Jonas held his staff in both hands, diagonally across his body, and took a couple of strides forward, watching the edge of the sphere of light gradually creep nearer to the shape. After a few steps, the mound on the floor resolved itself into the slumped figure of a menial. He was crumpled into a heap and clearly dead. Jonas knelt briefly, rolling the man onto his back with a touch of his staff; his eyes were wide open and bulging, but their irises had turned completely white. His mouth was open and a look of utter terror was etched across his features. It was as though he had been drained of his very life force. In some inexplicable way, the shadow in which he was laying did not vanish under the glare of the psychic light from Jonas's staff. He was bathed in death.

Rising back to his feet, Jonas jogged down the corridor towards the last flight of stairs that would lead him down into the excavation site. He vaulted the staircase in one bound, tucking in his legs and barrelling through the air like a cannon ball, flipping slowly through a single revolution. At the last moment, he untucked his legs and whipped his force staff into a whirl above his head, landing solidly in a crouch with his weapon poised and coruscating with blue energy.

The excavation site was a mess. The carefully extracted Imperium artefacts had been smashed and scattered across the ground, and the painstakingly excavated features in the ground had been compressed and ruined by some form of pounding weight. Here and there, where Jonas and Meritia had uncovered eldar artefacts, the site was bathed in the bizarre, indelible, glassy shadows that Jonas had seen in the corridors of the lower monastery. The eldar items themselves appeared to have been incinerated and burnt beyond salvation, and the sandy ground around them had been rendered mica by the incredible heat. The effect appeared similar to what Jonas had seen outside on the battlefield.

Jonas took it all in instantly as he strode through the site towards the hole that dropped down into the lower level of the dig. Without pausing at the edge, he brought his staff up vertically in front of him and dropped straight down into the chamber of petrified trees below, landing with a crunch on the stone floor, with his staff ablaze with light once again.

The subterranean chamber seemed unchanged. It was shrouded in the same heavy darkness as before, but seemed to shimmer slightly, as though the darkness itself were a form of light. Over to one side, the faint, ruddy glow of Krax-7's lava-flows edged its way into the chamber from the narrow tunnel in which Meritia had collapsed. The dim light was distorted and spiked with the shadows of the petrified roots that crisscrossed the tunnel itself, but Jonas also noticed that a more substantial, humanoid shadow was cast into the tree-lined chamber in which he stood.

Swirling his staff and sending little shards of radiant blue sparking through the gloom, Jonas strode down into the tunnel and brought the dazzling light into focus in front of him. About halfway along the tunnel, collapsed onto the floor, lay the lissom body of Ptolemea, face down on the rock. Without emotion, Jonas paused briefly, checking her body for breath, then stepped over her and increased the intensity of the light that now poured from his staff. He strode purposefully to the end of the tunnel and emerged into a wide underground cavern, run through with veins of molten lava. The walls were studded with caves and tunnels, too many for the librarian to investigate on his own.

Turning on his heel decisively, Jonas strode back towards Ptolemea and picked her up, swinging her body over his shoulder easily and stalking back up into the foundations of the Blood Ravens' monastery. Captain Angelos would want to deal with Ptolemea immediately, then he would return to the explore the caves.

THE ARMOURED DOORS to the Implantation Chamber hissed open smoothly, sucking a gust of fumes and smoke out into the corridor. The mist was heavy and pungent, tinted green with noxious chemicals, but it was carried out of the ceremonial chamber on a choral wave of harmonies, as the Chapter priests of the Third and Ninth Companies chanted litanies of purification.

Captain Ulantus strode into the ritually cleansed space, his polished armour glinting with its own purity seals. The Blood Trials on Trontiux III had been conducted with more haste than he would have liked; he had condensed the week into only two days. The landing party had returned with three successful aspirants, all of them strong and resilient, all of them slightly too old to be ideal. The course of the trials had made Ulantus even more conscious of the importance of Ckrius – not only as an individual neophyte undergoing the sacred transformation, but also as a test case for the ascension of older aspirants. It was never something that a Space Marine Chapter liked to do – the results could be unreliable, unpredictable and occasionally abhorrent – but in times of need even the most pristine of the Emperor's servants had to compromise. Above all other things, the Chapter's gene-seed had to survive. If Ckrius's travails were to fail, Ulantus would not hold out much hope for the others.

While he had been down on the planet's surface, Ulantus had received another message from Imperial Guard Captain Sturnn of the Cadians 412th on Lorn V, reiterating his request for assistance from the Blood Ravens. It seemed that the situation on the iceworld was becoming desperate, and Sturnn was not confident that he would be able to hold off the ork

warhost for much longer. The relay stations around
the Lorn system were also reporting signs of an
approaching alien fleet. The signatures of the vessels
did not support the conclusion that they were reinforcements for the orks, and tentative intelligence
suggested that it may be an eldar force en route to
Lorn V. Sturnn had been reluctant to hypothesise
about why the eldar and the orks might both be
interested in that particular planet, but it was clear
that he knew more about it than he was admitting.
The Cadians were not local to Lorn, and they must
have been briefed on the situation before they were
dispatched. Whatever the case, Ulantus was fully
aware of his duty – if the aliens were threatening an
outpost of the Imperium and if the Emperor's Imperial Guard required the support of the Adeptus
Astartes, then he would do everything he could, short
of jeopardising the survival of the gene-seed of the
Chapter by failing to recruit more aspirants. His
compromise seemed reasonable: finish the Blood
Trials on Trontiux III, but finish them quickly. He
hoped that Gabriel would be willing to make a similar compromise on Rahe's Paradise, since the *Litany
of Fury* was greatly weakened by the absence of its
main Battle Company and its venerable captain.
However, there was still no word from the Commander of the Watch, despite numerous attempts to raise
him. Ulantus was considering dispatching Saulh in
the *Rage of Erudition* to take the message to Gabriel
personally.

As the *Litany of Fury* cruised through the outer
reaches of the Trontiux system, leaving the third
planet as a rapidly diminishing dot on the rear

view screens, Ulantus had returned to the Implantation Chamber to check on the progress of Ckrius. It would not be long before the *Litany* would have to make the transition into the warp, and the captain wanted to ensure that Ckrius was as stable as possible before that happened. Although the geller-field around the *Litany* was powerful, it had been breached before, and a neophyte in Ckrius's weakened and susceptible condition would be even more vulnerable to the whispered temptations of the daemonic host in the warp than the rest of the human crew. It would be wholly unacceptable if Ulantus had to execute the young neophyte because of any suspected corruption during the journey through the warp, especially after all the time and effort that had been expended on him already.

Ckrius was still laying on the tablet in the middle of the chamber with his limbs bound under adamantium shackles. The egregious wounds that had been hacked into his chest had healed completely over the last couple of days, leaving long ugly scars running down his sternum – his Larraman's organ was clearly functioning efficiently.

Stepping into the chamber to permit the great doors to hiss and clunk sealed behind him, Ulantus watched the apothecary manoeuvring a large, hemispherical device into place above Ckrius's face. The inside of the machine was bristling with projections, syringes and blades. They were focussed into bunches that approximately coincided with the positions of the neophyte's eyes and ears as he lay on the tablet beneath it.

Even from his position next to the doors, Ulantus could see the settled horror on the youth's face as he realised what was about to happen to him. For a fraction of a second, Ulantus felt a surge of sympathy for the boy, wondering whether it might not be more humane to perform some of these operations whilst the aspirants were unconscious. Immediately, he threw the thought aside, berating himself for his own weakness in the face of pain. Without pain the Adeptus Astartes would be nothing – how could they prove their worthiness of the Emperor's blessing? The wash of sympathy was instantly replaced by a wall of resentment: pandering to this youth was delaying the insertion of the *Litany* into the warp and jeopardising the Blood Ravens' capacity to fulfil its duty.

His resentment was misplaced, and Ulantus regretted it almost as soon as he felt it. Ckrius and others like him were the future of the Blood Ravens. Without him there would be nobody left to fulfil the duties of the Chapter. As his mind calmed again, Ulantus realised that the real source of his resentment was Gabriel and his apparently cavalier disregard for both Ckrius, the Blood Trials and now the developing crisis on Lorn V. It was not his place to question the dignity of the Commander of the Watch, but Ulantus was concerned and infuriated by his recent conduct – he seemed obsessed by the eldar and by that cursed, manipulative farseer.

As the thoughts raced through Ulantus's mind, the apothecary slowly lowered the machine over Ckrius's head, obscuring his horrified features inside the dome. A series of whirring noises and cracking sounds told Ulantus that the boy's ears and eyes were being removed by the device so that the occulobe and Lyman's ear implants could be inserted into the brain stems behind them. After a few minutes, the dome stopped clucking and lifted clear of Ckrius's head, leaving him blinking with sustained trauma, terror and awe at the new world which was suddenly revealed around him, through his now highly enhanced senses.

HER FACE WAS pressed against cold, moist stone floor and her head was aching. It was as though she had fallen and knocked herself out. For a few moments, there was only darkness as her eyelids refused to respond to the nerve impulses that commanded them to open. There was a dull, unspecific pain all over her body, making her muscles rebel against her will as she tried to move them. She lay motionless, her back twisted against a rough wall behind her, with her neck angled uncomfortably around to the other side. In the featureless black before her eyes, Ptolemea struggled to remember what had happened.

She remembered colours more than anything else. Lush and vibrant greens riddled her memory, swamping specific shapes with the overwhelming presence of generalised, verdant life. Her eyes flicked back and forth, as though her brain had not yet properly registered that she was gazing at images in her memory. As her eyes twitched, the green wash started to resolve itself into distinct shapes. Here and there she could see the outlines of trees, dozens of trees, hundreds of trees, trees beyond counting stretching out into the furthest reaches of her mind. It was an epic jungle, covering the surface of an entire planet, swamping it in life and fecundity.

But just as the green resolved itself into a world-wide canopy, a burst of fiery orange erupted near the equator, like a flaming hurricane. The patch of dazzling colour flared and whirled like a maelstrom, eating into the jungle that surrounded it on all sides. And as it gyred and spun, the firestorm seemed to burn itself out – it became speckled with flecks of black, like moments of darkness in the inferno. Soon, before the raging torrent of fire could spread out into the forests, the moments of darkness expanded and commingled, consuming the radiant, orange flames in a wash of black. And the darkness continued to expand, overflowing the perimeter of the maelstrom and spilling out into the jungles, where its growth accelerated and proliferated, rushing around the entire planet in little more than an instant, until there was not a shred of green left to be seen.

As she watched, the darkness seemed to sense her presence and turn towards her, as though the newly engulfed planet was a single, giant eye. Slowly at first, but gathering speed all the time, it rushed towards her, and she had nowhere to turn. Her mind thrashed about, frantically searching for a place to hide; something, somewhere, anything. But there was nothingness all around and the darkness pressed in rapidly and inexorably.

Screaming, Ptolemea forced open her eyes at last. For a few seconds she was completely disorientated and wracked with pain, as she stared fixedly down into the wet, rough-cut rock on the floor. Slowly, movement returned to her limbs and she pushed her face away from the ground, feeling the blood drip from the abrasions on her cheek where the rock had cut into her skin.

Her cramped surroundings surprised her, but she wasn't really sure why. Then gradually her memory started to come back: she had been down in the excavation site. She remembered something about dropping down into that odd, tree-lined subterranean chamber. That's right – she had gone to investigate the site where Meritia had fallen previously. But then what had happened? She couldn't remember.

Looking around, Ptolemea realised that she was probably in one of the makeshift prison-cells that Jonas had constructed around the base of one of the main towers. The little room was dark, cramped and damp, and the only source of light was a small, barred gap in the wall, high up next to ceiling. The heavy adamantium door beneath it was sealed so perfectly that not even a crack of light pushed in around the edges of it.

Wincing with the pain that suddenly shot through her muscles, Ptolemea struggled to her feet and reached her hand up towards the light. She could not even get her fingers into the beam, so high up was the window and so shallow was the angle of the light-source outside. Judging by the red hue, the light was the sun itself.

Why was she there? Her mind raced with possibilities. Immediately, her brain pursued its first instincts and lurched into suspicion. She wondered whether Gabriel had discovered that she was there to investigate reports that he was having unsanctioned psychic visions of the Astronomican. She knew that the Adeptus Astartes operated at a complicated symbolic distance from the Ecclesiarchy and even, at times, from the Inquisition, and she didn't find it inconceivable that a Space Marine captain would resort to incarcerating an agent of either body if he felt that she was threatening his reputation or that of his Chapter.

But there was no way that Gabriel could know why she was there. She had told nobody, not even Sister Senioris Meritia, although the older woman must have had her suspicions. After all, this was why the Bethle sub-sector of the Ordo Hereticus had sent Ptolemea to perform the investigation and not a fully ordained inquisitor: the Blood Ravens on Rahe's Paradise had a long history of cooperation with the Order of the Lost Rosetta, and the arrival of an extra Sister Dialogous should have caused very little concern, despite the happy coincidence of her arrival at the same time as Captain Angelos.

The only person who could have told Gabriel anything was Isador Akios himself, and even he could not have known exactly what course of action the Ordo Hereticus would pursue after receiving the unusual reports that he had filed about his captain from Tartarus. The Inquisitor Lords of Bethle sub-sector were impressed by the librarian's piety and devotion to the Emperor's purity, but Ptolemea had been shocked that a Space Marine would betray the confidence of his captain in this way. She had certainly never heard of anything like that happening before. Whatever had happened on Tartarus had clearly had a profound effect on Isador too, before he died.

After prosecution, Ptolemea's mind raced to a defensive standpoint. If she could discount the idea that Gabriel had locked her up because of the threat he thought that she posed to him, it was conceivable that he had thrown her into the cell because of the danger that she herself appeared to be in. Again, the pivot here was Meritia – if the elder Sister's coma was accompanied by the kind of visions that had been plaguing Ptolemea since her arrival in the local system, it was not incredible to believe that she had suffered similar visions before, and that she could have told Gabriel that she suspected Ptolemea of having succumbed to some kind of taint, resulting in her experiencing unsanctioned visions.

Cycling her mind back through her memories of recent events, Ptolemea saw once again the look of empathy and understanding on Meritia's face when the Sister Senioris had awoken her from the cold sweat that had accompanied her first vision of the eldar in the jungle. In hindsight, it certainly seemed possible that Meritia's empathy was sympathy for the afflicted. All of the Sisters of the Lost Rosetta had seen the gradual, subtle and insidious effects of taint in the past, and Meritia would have recognised the signs at once. And unlike the Adeptus Astartes, the Sisters of the Order of the Lost Rosetta were certainly not above stabbing each other in the back when it came to suspicions of heresy – a long history of intimate relations with the Ordo Hereticus had made the order suspicious and highly political by nature.

At least Meritia was in no state to say anything at the moment, reflected Ptolemea with relief.

Ptolemea laughed painfully – she would have turned in Meritia, if she had found evidence of taint in the Sister Senioris, even while she was unconscious and helpless. She should expect no different treatment for herself. If she had any courage at all, she would already have turned herself in or killed herself – she wasn't sure that her visions were anything more than dreams, but uncertainty is so often the midwife of damnation.

She laughed again, coughing and convulsing as her ribs spasmed in pain. The irony of her situation struck her with full force: she had come to investigate the possible taint of a Space Marine captain and now found herself in one of his holding cells on suspicion of taint herself. Even worse, she was fairly sure that he was right to have locked her up. If he warranted an investigation by the Ordo Hereticus, then she certainly did.

A scratching noise on the wall made her swallow her shallow, aching laughter. She gulped and cackled slightly, trying to calm her nerves, fearful of hysteria: she was a Sister of the Order of the Lost Rosetta, not a battle-sister of the Golden Light – she was not psychologically prepared for the situation in which she now found herself. But she was also a faithful servant of the Emperor, no matter what her own suspicions were about herself, and she retained her faith that her purpose was pure and unsullied. For a moment she wondered whether there might be acceptable degrees of taint or heresy, whether psychological defects might be excusable if one's soul was pure. She was clutching at straws, perhaps, which, she suddenly realised, is what all of the people she had ever interrogated back in the cells on Bethle II had done.

The scratching returned, louder this time and more rhythmical, as though someone was trying to tap out a message. Ptolemea listened carefully, holding her breath, her eyes wide and wild as she realised that the strangely musical scraping was probably the eldar prisoner in the next cell trying to communicate with her.

'THEORISE,' PROMPTED GABRIEL, staring at the Marines of his command squad, his back to them as he faced out of the elaborate stained-glass window at the back of the librarium. An aura of red light seemed to surround him, giving his presence a touch of the divine.

'Such events have never been recorded before,' responded Prathios, stating the crux of the problem plainly.

'Whatever power it was,' offered Corallis, 'it was clearly unleashed at the call of the eldar farseer.'

'It did not damage us,' added Tanthius, trying to isolate the most important features of the unusual phenomenon as a weapon. 'It appeared to be extremely powerful, but its influence was limited to the silicon in the sand itself. It's not clear that it had impact on any organic matter.'

'Tanthius is right,' confirmed Prathios. 'Its effect on our Marines was mostly psychological or perhaps psychical; it brought them all to a standstill.'

'But not just our Marines, chaplain,' interjected Gabriel, still gazing out towards the volcanoes in the distance. 'The eldar were also taken by surprise, it seems.'

'Perhaps,' replied Prathios, 'but we must be careful not to interpret the actions of the aliens as though they were human. We can see that the blast gave them pause, but we do not know why – no action is transparent, captain, and the actions of the eldar might well contain a thousand different meanings.'

'You are suggesting that the eldar's response does not contradict the idea that it was an eldar device?' asked Tanthius.

'I am suggesting that we would be foolish to leap to conclusions about the deceitful xenos creatures – for all we know their withdrawal was designed with some tactical advantage in mind. The blast may have been a signal for them.'

'Prathios is right,' concluded Gabriel, turning to face the Marines. 'Until we have evidence to the contrary, we must assume that the eldar were behind the phenomenon. If nothing else, the very fact that it happened during the course of the battle must lend support to this interpretation.'

'Does Father Jonas have an opinion on this matter?' asked Corallis, aware that his former mentor had been based on Rahe's Paradise for many years. 'Has he ever seen anything similar?'

'He is as uncertain as we are,' replied Gabriel. 'But the father librarian is also exploring a hypothesis of his own. His theory rests on some of the finds that he and Sister Senioris Meritia made in the excavation below this monastery. As you know, it seems likely that Rahe's Paradise was an Exodite colony at some point in the past – probably before the destruction of the forests. Jonas seems to believe that the Blood Ravens cleansed the system during a righteous purity sweep of the sector, eradicating the eldar colonists and establishing an outpost on Rahe's Paradise. There is evidence to support the hypothesis that the eldar did not surrender the planet completely, but that they left a system of traps and automated defences that could be activated when the Biel-Tan returned to reclaim the planet – foresight being one of the eldar's greatest assets.'

'You believe that this weapon has laid dormant until now, waiting for the arrival of the alien witch to reactivate it?' asked Tanthius, sceptical.

'It is not a matter of belief, Tanthius,' stated Gabriel flatly. 'It is a matter of history. We are Blood Ravens, and we must not ignore the evidence before us. Whilst the eldar have the advantage of farsight, we must combat it with scholarship. Father Jonas is confident that this weapon is only the first of a series that we might expect – he calls it the Cry of the Banshee, after a phrase on this tablet.'

Gabriel turned away from the Marines and looked down at the wraithbone tablet that still lay on the old, wooden table under the gloriously coloured windows. 'This tablet appears to hold the keys to unlock the secrets of the eldar weapons here. It talks of the Cry of the Banshee at the start, and intimates that there are other things waiting in the depths of the desert and volcanoes. We must be vigilant while Jonas tries to decipher the rest of the alien text.'

'What about Sister Meritia?' asked Prathios, aware of the linguistic skills of the Order of the Lost Rosetta. 'What does she make of this tablet?'

'She is dead.'

There was a considered silence.

'I found her in her chamber. She was shot through the head,' explained Gabriel.

'And the young Sister Ptolemea?' pressed Prathios, concerned about the implications of murder within the Blood Ravens' monastery, but more concerned about the urgency of the matter at hand. 'Can she not translate this tablet?'

'She is presently in a detention cell,' said Gabriel, turning once again to face the chaplain. 'We suspect that it was she who killed Meritia.'

THE RED SAND swirled around the rangers' camp in the desert, cloaking the makeshift structures in a veil of dust that rendered the emplacement all but invisible. In the very centre of the camp, an elegant and deceptively fragile structure had been erected. It appeared to be little more than a tent, with a length of fabric stretched over the black, shiny frame in place of a roof. There were no walls. The material and the struts were covered in tiny, silver runes, each of which glowed with an imperceptible hint of power. And the desert sand was not able to penetrate the space within despite the apparently open sides.

Macha sat in the heart of the gazebo, her legs folded perfectly beneath her and her cloak falling into even folds from her shoulders. Behind her were arranged the warlocks from her retinue, each sitting in mirror-images of their farseer, with their faces lowered to the ground and their lips working silently at a gentle psychic chant.

In front of her, Macha had laid out a set of rune stones, placed carefully onto the shimmering surface of a disc of wraithbone. Her glittering green eyes were burning faintly, as the waves of power that were circulating around the pagoda washed through her mind and touched her soul. She was perfectly motionless, and the rune stones lay utterly still.

Laeresh stood in the corner of the ritual space, his arms folded across his chest and his thoughts set defiantly. He was flanked on both sides by two darkly coloured Aspect Warriors from his temple. The three of them stood without moving, staring down at the farseer before them, breathing an aura of resentment into the atmosphere of the purified space.

'Well?' prompted the exarch, his impatience finally overcoming his reverence.

For a moment there was silence, and then Macha slowly lifted her sparkling gaze from the runes, gazing directly over into Laeresh's soul.

There is nothing, she conceded. *I can see nothing, and the runes are deaf to my calls.*

'Your uncertainty is not helpful, farseer,' hissed Laeresh.

I have never claimed to be certain, Laeresh. It was you who found certainty in my visions, not me. We are here in the wake of your great passion. Decision and guidance are often separate callings, but wisdom is found in the synthesis of both.

'No more riddles, Macha. We have heard the banshee cry, and we must act now.' Laeresh unfolded his arms and stepped forward, crouching down towards the suddenly fragile figure of the farseer. 'We must attack the mon'keigh and drive them from this world. That is why we have come. It is why we are here – you have protected them for long enough – your precious Captain Angelos is an ignorant fool.

Even Uldreth Avenger would support me in this, farseer. Even that bloated, vainglorious courtier would support me, so why should I expect less from you? Where is your guidance now, farseer?'

As he spoke, Laeresh reached his arms forward, beseeching the farseer to condone his thoughts. His hands gripped her slender shoulders, as though he believed that he could convince her of his will through the physical strength of his arms. Immediately, the warlocks broke their silent chant and sprang to their feet. Druinir was first, sliding to the farseer's side with preternatural speed, as though slipping through space without encountering the resistance of physical laws.

The warlock touched his fingers against Laeresh's outstretched arm and a flash of energy lurched into the exarch's flesh, making him recoil, snapping back his arms and staggering back away from the unmoving figure of the farseer. As their exarch shrunk back, the two Aspect Warriors behind him stepped forward to his side, shrugging their reaper launchers out of the holsters on their backs and clasping them diagonally across their chests.

No. The thought was calm, even and utterly incontrovertible. The warlocks arrayed behind Macha and the Dark Reapers who were staring menacingly into their burning eyes all stalled. Druinir and Laeresh exchanged a look of understanding, and then the warlock stepped aside as Laeresh knelt down in front of the still-sitting farseer.

I have never commanded you, Laeresh, and I do not seek to control your destiny. I am merely a farseer of Biel-Tan. Your path is your own, Reaper exarch. Your presence here is your own doing, although I can see the echoes of your intent even in the dimness of the past – you were always bound to be here. Lsathranil himself must have seen this. I cannot see the future in this present – the runes will no longer respond to my touch – but the ripples of the past are clear enough in the present. You must act on them as you deem appropriate. That is your path; it is the way of the Dark Reapers.

'No, farseer. I am here because of your vision.' Laeresh was adamant.

No, exarch. We are both here because of your faith in my vision, not because of the vision itself. Uldreth also knew what I saw, but he interpreted it differently. He is not here. The Bahzhakhain is not here to reclaim this world for the Biel-Tan. We are here because of you, Laeresh, Dark Reaper.

'I don't understand,' conceded Laeresh, the passion gradually seeping from his manner as confusion washed through his mind.

Neither do I, Laeresh. Farsight does not make the future more simple, but rather explodes it into myriad possibilities. We must each choose our path – that is the Way of the Eldar, after all.

'Is it also our way to flee from battle? I cannot believe that Lsathranil intended the warriors of Biel-Tan to show their tails to the mon'keigh,' hissed Laeresh, his anger rising once more at the memory of their retreat, his soul raging at the taunts of the huge crimson machine-warrior. 'Did you not hear the banshee?'

Yes, I saw the signs. Macha's thoughts were weary.

'Then we must attack!' snapped Laeresh, jumping to his feet and staring down at Macha. 'If you will not condone the honour of the Dark Reapers, then we will act without your sanction, farseer of Biel-Tan. I do not require your permission, and I will not stand by and watch the filthy humans pollute this world further. We must annihilate them before their stench ruins this once magnificent planet forever.'

With that, Laeresh swept his cloak around in a whirl and strode out of the gazebo with his Aspect Warriors in tow, vanishing almost immediately into the eddying sand storms that raged outside.

Macha watched the impassioned exarch leave and then sighed deeply, nodding a signal to Druinir. *You were right, old friend. Laeresh is a prisoner of his passions. We must take the fight inside the Blood Ravens' fortress. Laeresh will provide the perfect distraction – although his passion may do more harm than good. We must be fast and we must be stealthy. Tell Aldryan to prepare the rangers.*

JONAS TRACED THE runes down through the passageway in which both Meritia and Ptolemea had fallen. The script appeared to be identical to that on the first page of the Ascension tablet that he had found blocking the mouth of the entrance to the bizarre, tree-lined chamber.

He read them off as he walked down the tunnel, using his force staff to support his weight as he leaned down to read each one in turn: The banshee's call shall wake the dead when dark portents wax nigh. Heed them as the counsel of a seer, or a father.

The final rune was carved into the last fossilized root, just before the tunnel opened out into the wide underground cavern, from which a blast of heat pushed up into the passageway. The subterranean cave must have been more than a hundred metres in diameter, and it was riddled with heavy shade and lines of darkness that seemed to pulse through cracks in the floor and the walls. The strange, glossy, indelible shadows that Jonas had seen in the corridors above were also in evidence down there, as though the outline of vaguely humanoid corpses had been burnt into the rock after a catastrophic explosion.

The scene was thrown into an eerie and bloody red by the light of the lava flows that coursed through deep channels in the ground, giving off jets of sulphurous smoke and hisses of steam at occasional intervals. The streams of molten rock turned, twisted, and meandered through the cavern, sweeping through intricate and intermingled patterns, as though designed by an artist with incredible understanding of tectonic currents and the geological movements of rock over impossible stretches of time.

With his glimmering force staff planted between his feet, Jonas swept his eyes over the incredible scene and his mind worked to draw connections between it, the eldar text on the walls, and the wraithbone tablet that they had unearthed in the foundations of an ancient, lost fortress monastery. For the moment, his concern for the bizarre explosion of darkness in the desert was forgotten in the scholar's excitement over his new find.

Eventually, his eyes picked out some new details in the rough-cut walls. He wasn't sure whether his eyes had become accustomed to the unusually shifting light in the cavern or whether the icons had just swum to the surface of the stone. Either way, the long curving wall was now clearly decorated with faintly glowing icons and runes, interspersed between the entranceways to subsidiary caves and small tributary tunnels. His intuition told him that these symbols had appeared in order to be read – much like the text on the wraithbone tablet.

Starting on the right hand side of the tunnel through which he had just descended, Jonas walked slowly around the perimeter of the cavern, studying each of the symbols in turn. Almost at once he realised that this was the same text as was inscribed on the second page of the Ascension tablet, and he was suddenly conscious that he was actually walking through the narrative told by the ancient eldar on this world.

By the time he had patrolled the entire circumference, Jonas had collected together a constellation of fragmentary meanings from the text that had been inscribed into the walls. There was something about the Chaos powers. There was talk of a thirst for warmth. And there appeared to be a reference to some kind of tomb. However, no matter how Jonas juggled the words, he could not find a grammatical subject. All of the phrases appeared to lack a subject, as though it were merely implied or assumed in the centre of them all. He got the distinct impression that the author of the text had presupposed a knowledge of the subject before any reader would have progressed this far.

Jonas retreated away from the walls, picking his way towards the centre of the cavern, stepping over streams of molten rock and jumping lava-filled cracks in the ground. Then, standing in the very centre of the chamber, balanced on an island of rock surrounded by the flow of lava, Jonas turned slowly on the spot, looking from one rune to the next, checking to see that he had not missed anything. As he turned, he was struck by a sudden realisation – the grammatical subject was implied at the centre of each phrase.

With a burst of light and power from his staff, Jonas pushed himself up off the ground, his feet lifting slowly as the bulk of the Space Marine librarian began to levitate up towards the stalactite ridden ceiling. He was a radiant, blue star in the dim, ruddiness of the subterranean cavern.

Looking down from his new vantage point, Jonas smiled as the text was revealed to him in its full glory. The wide, circular stone floor of the cavern was run through with lines and cracks, each flooded with streams and rivers of glowing, molten rock. But these were no random or naturally occurring lines – they were the product of incredible artifice, carved into the very crust of the planet many millennia before. Hanging in a sphere of psychic brilliance, Jonas stared down at the exquisite splendour of the giant rune that was cut into the cavern's floor. It was simply breathtaking in its beauty: the gentle curves of its cursive strokes were accentuated by the steady, graceful flow of the lava; where angles cracked and jutted through the pattern, the lava roiled and broke in thick waves, giving the sharpness a real air of violence and power. The runic character seemed to live in the very bowels of the planet, giving expression to something ancient and forgotten in the geological past.

Yngir, thought Jonas, unsure of the correct sounding.

'Yngir,' he whispered, trying out the unfamiliar syllables while his mind raced to put a meaning to the sounds. As he spoke, the ground started to tremble and shudder. The movements were slight at first, but they rapidly gathered momentum, shaking the entire cavern in growing violence. The stalactites above him juddered and then cracked, crashing down against his armour and then spiking down into the molten inferno below. At the same time, the runnels in the ground started to glow with spluttering energy, and pulses of blue light coruscated over the floor.

A thunderous crack shot through the chamber, suddenly rending the floor in two, splitting the huge rune in the middle. As the two sides of the floor started to crumble, collapse and to retreat back into the walls around the perimeter of the chamber, the streams of lava broke over the edges and started to cascade down into the widening chasm like burning, molten waterfalls.

After a few seconds, a wide space had opened up in the middle of the cavern, flanked on two sides by rains of lava that tumbled and flowed down into it, pooling into shallow reservoirs of fire and molten stone. In between the flaming pools, at the bottom of the abrupt chasm, Jonas could see the shimmering shape of a radiant black pyramid. On each of its four faces, it was covered in webs of tiny silver hieroglyphs, the like of which Jonas had never seen before.

Slowly, and with a considerable effort of will, Jonas lowered himself down into the chasm, his force staff pouring power out beneath him to support his substantial weight. He landed firmly on the freshly exposed floor of the cavern, and immediately he stooped down to inspect the new artefact that had been uncovered.

Despite himself, Jonas gasped in awe as he stared into the spiralling infinities that seemed to open up within the shimmering blackness of the waist-high pyramid. It was like nothing he had ever seen before. Even wraithbone seemed pallid and dull in comparison with the unearthly effervescence and profound lustre of this material. It seemed to contain an entire universe of its own. And the little silver hieroglyphs were alien beyond his experience – little more than bizarre pictograms, illuminated with a complicated array of boxes, circles and painstakingly constructed curves. It was like nothing he had ever seen before, and he was certain that this object was beyond even the artifice of the ancient eldar.

CHAPTER NINE
CONSECRATION

THE DOOR JOLTED and a crack of light seeped in around the edges, making Ptolemea squint as her eyes adjusted to the sudden brightness. There was a pause and then the door was pushed open, silhouetting the massive form of a Space Marine in the dazzling light. Curled into the corner of the cell, Ptolemea turned her face away from the light, holding her hand out in front of her as a shield.

'Sister Ptolemea of the Order of the Lost Rosetta, I have come to hear your confession,' said Prathios, stooping under the lintel and entering the little chamber. He looked around the small room, absorbing the dark, damp, cramped squalor of it; Jonas had done a good job of replicating the conditions of an underground dungeon – even the narrow slit of a window near the ceiling gave the impression that the rest of the cell was below water-level.

As the door clanged shut behind the chaplain, closing out the brightness, Ptolemea looked up at his imposing shape – he nearly filled the cell all by himself.

'Confession?' she smiled, feeling a slight pulse of hysteria in her voice. In truth, she had resolved to confess everything. Sitting there alone in the dark, listening to the rhythmical scraping of the eldar in the adjoining cell, watching the flickering images of trees, jungles and death spiral through her mind, she had been determined to cleanse her soul by confessing her taint to the authorities. She had thought ahead to her eventual execution as wistfully as one anticipates the return of a lost lover.

'Confession of what, Marine?' she asked, her delicate lips pursed. Almost as soon as Prathios had opened the door, she had changed her mind about confessing to anything. There was still a chance, a slim and almost invisible chance, that the Blood Ravens were not aware of her visions. Although she realised that this was a virtually impossible hope, she also realised that when faced with the prospect of her death she would clutch at any flickering hope of life, even if that meant denying her own nature. She was no warrior, and she mocked herself for trying to behave like one.

'We are the Adeptus Astartes, Sister,' began Prathios, misunderstanding her resistance. 'And this is a time of war. We have no need for the Adeptus Arbites here, and there is no call for the Inquisition – we may dispense our own justice.'

Ptolemea wrapped her arms around her knees and looked up at the chaplain, studying his proud gait and his earnest manner. 'I do not question your authority, Blood Raven. I question your judgment. To what do you expect me to confess? I have heard no charges against me – can you not do even this courtesy to a fellow servant of the Emperor?'

'Your crimes are written in your soul, Sister,' said Prathios. 'There should be no need for you to hear them with your ears as well.'

'Indulge me,' whispered Ptolemea, leaning forward over her knees and breathing the words with an amused smile. She was not going to give anything away without at least the show of a fight – she may be insane, but she wasn't an idiot.

'You are charged with the assassination of a loyal and devoted servant of the Imperium and with the attempt to disrupt the execution of a Blood Ravens mission on Rahe's Paradise. We have been unable to raise Bethle II to confirm the real reasons for your presence here, but we suspect that you are acting for personal reasons, and we are sure that, whether this is true or not, it would be confirmed by your convent.' Prathios stared down at the young woman in the cell and watched her eyes widen in shock as he spoke. She seemed to be relieved.

'I'm afraid that I cannot confess to these charges, chaplain,' she said, leaning back against the wall. 'I have done no such thing. I would be more than willing to confess to something that was true. To confess to anything else would simply be a lie – and that too would be a crime.' She smiled again, a relaxed and satisfied smile that made Prathios uneasy.

'Do you not wish to know who it was that you are charged with killing?' asked Prathios carefully, watching the pale, beautiful face of Ptolemea as she closed her dark eyes with a new calm.

'Very well, tell me.'

'Sister Senioris Meritia, of the Order of the Lost Rosetta,' said Prathios with slow deliberation.

Ptolemea's eyes flashed open immediately. 'What?' she said, scrambling to her feet. 'What? But I just saw her in her chamber. She was still unconscious...' her voice trailed off as her mind raced back to the scene. She could still see the flickering eye movements of the older Sister, and could clearly remember the dawning of solidarity that had accompanied her suspicions that the older woman was suffering from the same dreams as her. Despite all the suspicions about Meritia's betrayal that had cycled through her mind since being thrown into that cell, Ptolemea felt the loss of her Sister.

Chaplain Prathios watched the complicated emotions dance over Ptolemea's elegant features. She looked genuinely surprised to hear the news. 'What were you doing in her chamber?'

Snapping out of her reverie, Ptolemea's eyes fixed on those of Prathios. 'I was checking to see that she was alright. I was... worried about her.' She paused, unsure about whether to go on. 'We... we seemed to have more in common than I realised.'

Prathios said nothing, sensing that there was something further that the young Sister wanted to say.

'She killed herself,' stated Ptolemea, vocalising her conclusion but not her chain of thought. Her certainty was written clearly on her face as she stared into space.

'Why should I believe that?' asked Prathios reasonably, although his intuition told him that she was telling the truth.

'Because it is the only possible answer,' replied Ptolemea, meeting his eyes once again.

'Why would she kill herself, Sister?' paraphrased Prathios, needing something more.

'Why would I kill her?'

'You tell me.'

'You don't understand: Meritia was suffering. She was afflicted by... she was suffering from nightmares.'

'What sort of nightmares?' prompted Prathios, wanting to keep the momentum going.

'Dangerous nightmares. Like visions. They racked her with pain and with guilt, making her wake in cold sweats, screaming. They literally turned her grey,' realised Ptolemea as she spoke. 'I... she didn't understand them, and thought that they were signs of taint.'

'And were they?'

'No! No, don't you see? She killed herself out of fear. She was scared that she was becoming something hideous and monstrous. She was afraid that something had got inside her soul and ruined her purity. But she killed herself!' Ptolemea was almost shouting now, as though carried along by the impassioned logic of her thoughts. 'She killed herself and that proves that she was still pure! She killed herself to save her soul for the Emperor – she killed herself because she thought that she was becoming everything she despised... she killed herself because she was still a pristine servant of the Emperor.'

'Why should I believe this?' asked Prathios, impressed by Ptolemea's passion but aware of his responsibility to discover evidence and truth. 'How do I know that you didn't kill her because you suspected her of taint?'

'You're right,' answered Ptolemea, her self-knowledge falling into place. 'I would have killed her. I even thought about it. I did. I thought about turning her over to the Sisterhood on Bethle II, or even to the inquisitors of the Ordo Hereticus. But I didn't do it. I couldn't. And in the end she saved me the trouble and killed herself – don't you see?'

'You do not persuade, Sister,' countered Prathios. The story was plausible, but she had given him no reason to believe her. Passion is not an argument in itself. 'Give me a reason to believe you.'

Ptolemea sighed and looked up into the chaplain's eyes, holding his gaze calmly. 'It seems that I must give you my confession after all,' she said. 'I know of what I speak because... I have been suffering these same visions since I arrived on Rahe's Paradise.'

Prathios said nothing. After a few seconds he nodded and turned away, pulling open the cell door and leaving without a word. He believed her. If there was a charge more serious than murdering a fellow servant of the Emperor, it was that of being tainted by the unclean and treacherous powers of daemons or aliens. Ptolemea's confession made no sense unless it was true. Whether or not her visions were actually signs of taint was an entirely different question, and it was not something that a Space Marine chaplain was able to judge by himself, although his intuition told him that her unforced confession was in itself evidence that her soul was pure.

GABRIEL GAZED AROUND the stiflingly hot and impressively wide, subterranean cavern, amazed by what Jonas had uncovered beneath the foundations of the lost monastery. The walls were aglow with eldar runes, which he could not read, and riddled with the entrances to tunnels and caves. There must be an entire network of tunnels reaching out into the desert and up into the mountains. He had thought that the only navigable route was between the great amphitheatre and the Blood Ravens' monastery. It was now clear that he was wrong.

There was a narrow ridge running all the way around the edge of the cavern, providing a ledge from which there was access to each of the tributary tunnels. In the centre, the floor just dropped away down into a sheer and wide pit. The walls were covered in cascades of molten rock, which fell from runnels and cracks in the ridge on which Gabriel stood, collecting into pools of burning light down in the pit.

Looking down towards the base of the pit, Gabriel could see the shimmering, angular form of a black pyramid in the centre. Next to it, slumped on the ground, was the shape of a fallen Marine, face down on the stone floor.

'Jonas!' cried Gabriel, realising immediately who it must be. He launched himself off the ridge in front of the bizarre, root-entangled tunnel that led down from the monastery, vaulting down into the pit and thumping into the rocky ground, landing into an alert crouch.

Rising to his feet, Gabriel surveyed his surroundings, conscious that Jonas must have suffered from some kind of attack and aware that his assailants may still be around. The walls of the pit were bathed in fire and trickles of lava, and Gabriel could not see what was hidden in the recesses beyond. It seemed logical to him that there would be caves and tunnels down there, just as there were around the ridge above, but he could see no sign of them through the molten waterfalls.

Cautiously, he stepped over towards Jonas, taking note of the mysterious, alien-looking pyramid-artefact that the librarian must have been examining. Jonas was lying on his front, with his force staff still clutched in one hand. He was unconscious, but he was breathing.

The sound of a tumbling rock made Gabriel look up, snatching his bolter out of its holster. He scanned the perimeter of fire with the barrel of his gun, looking for signs of the movement that he had heard. But there was nothing.

'Gabriel!' called a familiar voice, making the captain look up. Prathios bowed slightly from the ridge. 'We need to talk about Ptolemea.'

Gabriel nodded briskly, still uncertain that the noise he had heard had come from such a high elevation. He pointed to his eyes and then gestured to the circumference of the pit, indicating to Prathios that he thought there was a threat nearby.

Spotting the fallen form of Jonas behind his captain, Prathios nodded in understanding and drew his weapon, springing down into the pit to join Gabriel. As soon as he hit the ground, all hell broke loose.

A sleet of projectiles hissed out from behind a molten cascade of lava, slicing easily through the heavy, sulphurous air like burning shards through flesh. The two Marines saw the rampaging cloud just in time, and they dived for the ground, rolling neatly before coming back up into a crouch, their bolters levelled and coughing towards the source of the attack.

The explosive shells detonated as they penetrated the screen of lava, spluttering the cascades into bubbling partitions of fire, but Gabriel couldn't tell whether they were having any impact on the assailants beyond.

After a couple of seconds, the two Marines stopped firing and there was silence in the underground pit, broken only by the distant echoes of their shots as the sound bounced and ricocheted through the maze of tunnels that fed into the wider cavern. They glanced at each other and then stood to their feet next to the bizarre alien pyramid, turning back to back as they swept their weapons around the perimeter of the pit.

The silence was compromised by the grating of sand and gravel under the weight of their heavy boots, and by the spluttering hiss of molten rock falling into the burning pools on the ground.

Gabriel paused, concentrating his gaze into the sheets of lava that pulsed down the walls of the pit. They were not uniform or even, and there were occasional gaps in the flow, as though the volume of lava was not quite enough to cover the walls properly. The captain focussed carefully, holding his eyes on the slits of clarity torn into the molten flows, watching the red and orange light from the cascades spark and reflect off the slick surface of the rock beyond.

There! Gabriel squeezed a couple of shells out of his bolter and watched the little contrails that poured out behind them, as though in slow motion. They spun through the thick, gaseous air and then slipped through a gap in the lava flow, punching into the kaleidoscope of reflections beyond. There was a dull thud, but no explosion against the rock.

He had hit something.

Pulling his chainsword from its holster, Gabriel stalked forward, keeping his eyes fixed on the little slit of clarity in the wall of fire and molten rock. The quality of the reflected light next to the floor was slightly different from that in the middle of the wall, as though the surface was bulging or uneven. Gabriel held his chainsword out in front of him as he advanced, pointing it at the misshapen reflections, while he held his bolter in his other hand, pointing out at right angles to his side.

It looked like a camouflaged body. A cloaked eldar ranger, thought Gabriel.

Just as he reached the wall of lava, a series of explosions and a cry made Gabriel spin on his heel. He left the tip of his chainsword pointing down at the prone body of the eldar warrior behind the screen of molten rock, but he turned his head and snapped his bolter around.

Behind him, in the middle of the pit, stood Prathios, his glittering Crozius held high in one hand while his bolter barked repeatedly in the other. In front of the chaplain were three eldar warriors, each brandishing long, elegant blades that seemed to coruscate with suggestions of purple flames. They were prowling around the chaplain in a complicated pattern that meant he could only ever see two of them clearly – the third was always at least partly hidden behind one or both of the other two. With rhythmic but syncopated regularity, the eldar lurched forward at Prathios, sometimes one by one, sometimes two at a time, and sometimes all at once.

The Blood Ravens chaplain parried and hacked with the sizzling power of his Crozius, meeting the coruscating blades of the aliens with thunderous strikes of his own. Meanwhile, he rattled off shots with his bolter, spraying shells almost randomly as he had no time to take even the most casual aim. The eldar seemed to slip around his shots without concern, and without breaking the rhythm of their dance.

Immediately, Gabriel's bolter spat a volley of shells towards the alien assailants, but the hail of bullets didn't even seem to break the pattern of their movements, as though their dance-like performance had somehow pre-empted his shots. They continued to lurch and swipe at Prathios, their blades flashing radiantly in the dim light of the subterranean pit as the chaplain swept his Crozius in powerful arcs, somehow managing to parry every strike.

Checking back towards the slumped body at the tip of his own blade, Gabriel made up his mind at once. Firing off a constant tirade of shells, he charged back across the pit, spinning his chainsword in eager preparation for combat.

After only a couple of strides, a strip of explosions ripped up the ground in front of him, making him slide to a halt and dive to the side. As he hit the ground he rolled, angling his bolter up towards the ledge around the top of the pit and sending off a salvo of fire. Chunks of rock and spurts of lava erupted as the bolter shells punched into the lip of the ledge. The four eldar marksmen who had taken up the elevated position scattered away from the fire, rolling away from the suddenly unstable ledge. As he skidded along the ground, Gabriel yanked a frag grenade off the clip on his belt and instinctively thumbed the timer down to two seconds. From the prone position on the floor, he lobbed the grenade up towards the eldar snipers. It arced steeply, reaching its peak just over the heads of the aliens when the timer blipped and the grenade detonated into a brilliant, shrapnel-filled fireball.

Three of the aliens dived flat against the ledge, disappearing from view, but the fourth staggered back in the sudden blast of pressure and heat, losing his footing in a flail of limbs and falling head over heels off the ledge. Gabriel watched the hapless creature, ripped through by the shrapnel from the frag grenade, as it splashed down into one of the pools of magma, sending up a thick, viscous fountain of molten rock and then a cloud of steam as the body vaporised in the intense heat.

By the time the other eldar on the ledge had regained their firing solutions, Gabriel was already back on his feet and pounding over towards his embattled chaplain.

IMAGES OF DEATH cycled through Laeresh's mind: *war is my master, death my mistress*. The chant filled his soul with power and longing as the Dark Reapers swept through the desert towards the Blood Ravens' monastery. The jet-black Wave Serpents were flanked by the greens and whites of the Biel-Tan vehicles that had accompanied the exarch, deferring to his authority in the theatre of battle. He was an Exarch of Khaine, the Bloody-Handed God, and war flowed through his veins, rendering him into the best and the worst of his kind. In a time of war, there was no figure more inspirational for the warriors of Biel-Tan than an exarch at the head of a battle-force. Besides, Macha had made no attempt to stop Laeresh mustering his army. She had not interfered when he had clambered up on top of his Wave Serpent with his reaper launcher held into the air like a standard and led the eldar force out of the rangers' camp and into the wind-racked desert. She had simply sat silently in her gazebo, flanked by her retinue of warlocks, waiting for Aldryan to muster the rangers for her own more stealthy purpose.

As the convoy crested a high dune, the heavy black of the mon'keigh monastery loomed into view, breaking the dull, rusty monotony of the desert and marking the beginning of the mountain range beyond.

Laeresh stamped his foot against the roof of the transporter and his vehicle slowed to a halt. The bone-white plumes around his death mask fluttered and whirled in the dusty wind. The other Wave Serpents spread out into a line next to him, running along the apex of the dune with their gun barrels bristling out towards the enemy. The red sun glinted against their armoured plates in little bursts of colour.

Staring out across the desert towards the heavy and ugly edifice that had been constructed by the clumsy, dirty humans, Laeresh rolled his top lip back into a snarl of disgust. He couldn't believe that Macha had been willing to retreat from the pathetic mon'keigh. The cry of the banshees may have pierced her confidence, but it would not shake his own resolve. The vile aliens had to be removed from the surface of this once pure and verdant world – Lsathranil's Shield must be made clean again.

War is my master, bellowed the exarch, forcing his thoughts out through the desert wind, running them through the armoured sides of the Wave Serpent transports and into the minds of the eldar warriors within. His words dripped with hatred and disgust, filling his warriors with an unspeakable, primal passion for death.

Death is my mistress, came the response, as though shouted out from a thousand voices all at once. Laeresh felt the resolve of his Aspect Warriors and the Guardians of Biel-Tan buoy his soul, lifting his resolve and fixing his spirit on the battle to come. He stared across at the solid blackness of the monastery walls, and he visualised them cracking and crumbling under the furious assault of the eldar. Even he could see the end of the mon'keigh there; he didn't need Macha to foresee his victory. It was clear and obvious. The bumbling humans were no match for the timeless wrath of the exarch of the Dark Reapers.

He stamped down once more, this time triggering a stream of light from the gun-turret next to him on the Wave Serpent's roof. The lance of brightness seared out across the desert, flashing in perfect straightness until it smashed against the huge walls of the monastery in the distance. Following the lead of their exarch, the other Dark Reaper Wave Serpent also unleashed strips of lightning through the desert air, crunching its beams into the massive shape of the mon'keigh structure. From a distance, there were few forces in the galaxy that could match the Dark Reapers.

As the pulses of lance fire streaked out of the line that ran along the crest of the dune, the green and white Wave Serpents of the Biel-Tan Guardians lurched forward, skating down the face of the dune and racing forward towards the monastery, leaving clouds of sand in their wake as they accelerated to attack speed. After a few seconds, the flashing reports of weapons fire could be seen around the base of the monastery, and ordnance started to rain down on the speeding eldar vehicles. Shells punched into the desert on all sides of the Wave Serpents, exploding into huge craters and sending great plumes of sand billowing up into the air.

THE EXPLOSIONS SHOOK the cavern, breaking stalactites from the high ceiling and sending them darting down towards the ground like stone spears. They splashed and sizzled into the pools of lava around the edge of the pit, or crashed into splinters as they struck the hard rocky ground. Concussive clouds of smoke, fire and shrapnel billowed out around the ledge, blasting heat and pressure waves out through the tributary tunnels, chasing in the wake of the fleeing eldar rangers.

Gabriel had launched the grenade cluster into the air on a tight timer and then thrown himself flat over

the top of the prone figure of Father Jonas, shielding
the unconscious librarian from the force of the blast
and absorbing the impacts of the falling masonry
against the thick armour on his own back. As the rain
of debris lightened, Gabriel sprang back to his feet
and ran over to where Prathios had fallen.

The chaplain was collapsed on the ground between
the corpses of three eldar rangers; their blades, shattered and broken, lay in ruins across the floor.
Prathios had confronted their force-swords with his
Crozius and wrecked them all, ploughing through
the alien technology with the power of his faith. His
bolter had punched holes through the psycho-plastic
armour of the eldar warriors, leaving seeping wounds
in their limbs and abdomens, from which hissing,
toxic blood poured into little pools around the dead.

But he had suffered terrible wounds. The snipers
on the ledge had almost ignored Gabriel, seeking
merely to prevent the captain from assisting his
chaplain, while raining gouts of shuriken down at
the embattled Prathios.

He had fought valiantly and with passion, but the
odds had been stacked impossibly against him. He
had parried and struck with his Crozius, snapping off
shots with his bolter, fighting three eldar warriors at
close range and trying to contend with four more at
distance. Not even the magisterial might of a Blood
Ravens chaplain could stand against such terrible
force.

At the last, as his body was ripped through by
streams of tiny projectiles from the rifles of the
snipers, Prathios had let out a great roar of defiance that echoed powerfully around the cavern

and out into the surrounding tunnels. He had lashed out with his Crozius for a final time, smashing through the lancing blades of his attackers and splintering them into shards. Even as his ruined legs collapsed under his weight and he started to fall, he had tracked his bolter around the cavern, placing his last shells precisely into the flesh of the aliens around him. By the time he hit the ground, his three assailants were broken, wretched, and dying.

'Prathios,' said Gabriel, kneeling at the side of his old friend. 'Prathios, can you hear me?'

There was no reply. The chaplain lay face down on the ground with his powerful legs buckled underneath him; the thick armour around his knees had been perforated by shuriken fire and his lower legs almost severed. His ornate and ancient death mask was twisted around to one side, suggesting that his neck may have broken, and his arms were stretched out in front of him, as though reaching for the weapons that were still clutched in his hands. His arms were riddled with tiny holes where the monomolecular projectiles of the eldar snipers had ripped through his armour, flesh and bones.

'Prathios,' repeated Gabriel, refusing to believe that even such egregious wounds could bring an end to such a great warrior. He released the clasps on his own helmet and pulled it off, dropping it onto the ground next to the chaplain. Then he carefully removed Prathios's revered death mask, lifting it gently and placing it next to the fallen Marine. It was clear that the chaplain's neck was twisted at an unnatural angle, but his eyes were half open and Gabriel could see the irises jittering. He was still alive.

With anger rising in his body, Gabriel stood up and looked around the cavern, absorbing the turmoil of the scene – the ruined cavern, the smashed stalactites, the eldar corpses, the rains of lava, the unconscious figure of Jonas and the ruined body of Prathios. And there, in the middle of it all, still glinting with a distant and ineffable darkness, was the shimmering black pyramid, sparkling with pristine silver hieroglyphs.

Throwing his head back and his arms out to his side, Gabriel let out a cry, drawing it up from the pit of his stomach and yelling it out into the subterranean world as a threat, a promise, and an impassioned defiance. The sound was amplified and echoed around the cavern and out into the labyrinth of tunnels.

After a few seconds, silence fell and Gabriel stood motionless, his arms still held out, as though beseeching the Emperor himself for some sign. Then, so quiet as to be almost inaudible, a single voice seemed to reply. It was a soprano, high and clear like crystal, singing directly into Gabriel's mind. The note soared into heaven, and then was joined by others, more and more of them until there was a silvering chorus of voices. They seemed to be singing into his soul, drawing his purpose towards the Astronomican itself. He had heard these voices before, but never had they been as clear, as pristine or as beautiful as now.

* * *

'ON THE HORIZON!' called Corallis as he stared out across the sand. He was standing up on the roof of one of the Land Raiders, keeping watch for the return of the eldar forces while Tanthius organised the Blood Ravens' defences.

The huge Terminator Marine stopped what he was doing and turned to follow Corallis's line of sight. Arrayed along the crest of a dune on the horizon, he could clearly see a line of eldar vehicles glinting in the red sun as clouds of sand gusted past them. They appeared to have stopped moving, as though they were waiting to be seen before they launched their attack. On the roof of one of the Wave Serpents, Tanthius could just about make out the distinctively tall form of the crested, ornate warrior-leader. He had heard that such magnificent figures were known as exarchs, and he thrilled in anticipation of the battle to come.

'Prepare for battle,' said Tanthius calmly, his vox bead hissing and crackling with interference from all the heavy machinery. The rest of the Blood Ravens sounded in around him, confirming their readiness to defend the monastery-outpost from the xenos assault. 'Our guests have returned,' he murmured under his breath, inspecting the distant prospect of the exarch.

'For the Great Father and the Emperor!' The voices rang out in the desert air, unassisted by the vox units and amplifier arrays, as the Blood Ravens shouted their resolve all along the defensive line. Tanthius nodded with satisfaction.

A burst of brightness flashed on the horizon and a strip of brilliance lanced over Corallis's head, punching into the walls of the monastery behind him. After a second, another beam of energy followed the first, burning through the dusty air and smashing into the towering edifice at the backs of the Marines. In rapid succession, another flurry of beams pulsed into the wall, this time launched from multiple locations on the horizon. The walls shook under the onslaught and rains of debris fell, but the structure was sound – the Blood Ravens knew how to construct fortifications.

Under cover of the lance fire that lashed out of a few of the Wave Serpents on the horizon, Corallis and Tanthius could see the rest of the eldar convoy lurch forward, rushing down the face of the dune as it began the charge across the open desert towards the glassy and rocky ground in front of the Blood Ravens' defences.

'And so it begins again,' muttered Tanthius, signalling to the gunners in the Land Raiders to start their bombardments and bracing his own weapons ready for the combat to come.

THE ELDAR RANGER was sitting silently in the cell. Its legs were crossed and it was sitting on its heels. Its eyes were closed and its lips were working silently, as though muttering silent prayers to some unspeakable eldar god. The silence was abruptly shattered as the door to the cell burst open, smashing back against the wall with violent force, leaving the shape of Gabriel filling the doorway.

'Get up!' snapped Gabriel, taking a step into the tiny chamber.

The alien did not move. It didn't even open its eyes.

'Get up!' shouted Gabriel, his eyes burning with anger at the indefatigable composure and quiet of the creature.

Still no response.

'Get up, now!' yelled Gabriel, his fists clenching automatically as his anger started to boil. Taking another step forward, he swung a thunderous punch against the eldar's face, striking it against the side of its head and knocking it sprawling onto the ground.

'I know you can understand me, ranger,' he whispered, stooping down and lifting the alien off the ground by the collar of his cloak. 'I have spoken to your kind before. I know that you can understand me.'

Gabriel straightened his arm and slammed the eldar back against the wall of the cell, pushing his hand around the creature's neck and holding him off the ground, half-choking the infuriatingly calm alien. 'You will help us, or you will die. It is that simple,' explained Gabriel, glaring into the smooth, unwrinkled face. 'Do you understand? Do you understand!'

The alien opened its eyes and looked down at Gabriel, letting an aura of sadness wisp out through its gaze.

'I'll take that as a yes,' stated Gabriel, ignoring the melancholy eyes of the creature in his grasp. He withdrew his hand and let the eldar slump down the wall into a heap on the ground. Then he snatched at the creature's slender wrists, clamping them into the vice-like grip of his own hand, before turning and dragging the alien out of the cell, towing it behind him like a dead weight.

After nearly a kilometre of winding passageways, Gabriel kicked open the huge, heavy doors of the librarium and dragged the limp, unresisting eldar inside, striding up the central aisle towards the magnificent stained-glass windows at the far end.

With a swing of his arm, Gabriel dumped the alien into an unceremonious pile on the floor next to the old wooden table under the window.

'What does that say?' he snapped, pointing at the wraithbone tablet on the tabletop.

The eldar didn't even sit up.

'What is that?' demanded Gabriel. 'This is not a game, eldar. We have no time for your tricks or your games – we are not your toys. People are dying because of this. What is it?'

The ranger stirred, propping himself up on his arms and looking up at Gabriel. The ranger's emerald eyes glowed with complicated depths, but he said nothing.

At the limit of his patience, Gabriel reached down and grasped the alien's long hair, lifting it off the ground by its scalp and thrusting its head towards the tablet, pushing its face right up against the shimmering wraithbone.

'What does it say?'

For the first time, the ranger offered some resistance, struggling against Gabriel's grip and recoiling from the tablet, pushing against the edge of the table with its arms. It shook its head, and its eyes blazed with sudden awareness and shock.

'What does it say?' demanded Gabriel, holding the creature firmly in place, ignoring its flailing attempts to get away. 'Tell me, and I'll put you back in your cell.'

The eldar thrashed impotently, rising urgency written across its face.

Ishandruir! Yngir Ishandruir!

CHAPTER TEN
COLLABORATION

'It was no eldar,' said Jonas, sitting up with his legs thrown over the side of the medicae-tablet in the monastery's apothecarion. He looked older and more tired than usual, as though part of his life-force had been drained out of him by his recent traumas. In the background, he could hear the dull thuds of impacts against the walls of the monastery.

In the temporary absence of an apothecary on Rahe's Paradise, Techmarine Ephraim of the Ninth Company was administering to the damaged librarian. He could do little more than check the integrity of the ancient armour's seals and ensure that its more mechanical features were functioning properly. Jonas had regained consciousness by himself, once he had been carried to the apothecarion and deposited on the adamantium tablet. He didn't appear to have suffered any physical wounds that his own enhanced physiology could not deal with on its own.

'You're certain?' pressed Gabriel, momentarily concerned that the great scholar's memory might be playing tricks on him: there had certainly been eldar down in the excavation, as he and Prathios knew to their cost.

'I am certain, captain,' replied Jonas, pushing himself off the edge of the tablet and trying his weight on his feet. He shook slightly with the effort, as though it took more of his strength than he anticipated to keep himself upright.

'Then what was it?' asked Gabriel, sidelining his scepticism for the time being and instinctively reaching forward to help steady the father librarian. He was certain that the eldar were at the centre of it, even if it had not been the eldar themselves that had attacked Jonas.

'I cannot say,' replied Jonas, leaning back against the heavy tablet for support but lifting his eyes to meet Gabriel's. 'But I am sure that it was no eldar trickery. I was inspecting the new find – that fascinating black pyramid – I assume that you saw it? There was nothing around. No footfalls and not even the hint of a psychic presence – the eldar give off such a psychic stench that it is almost impossible for them to take a Blood Ravens librarian by surprise. There was nothing...'

Gabriel waited as Jonas lapsed into his memories. He could see the librarian's eyes lose their focus as he stared into his own past, replaying the events of earlier that day in his mind.

'It was a shadow. Just the suggestion of a figure or a form, like the wraiths found in the ancient legends of this world. It was as though it was something not quite real, not quite alive, not quite… there at all.'

The librarian sounded wistful, as though genuinely amazed by what he had seen. Gabriel watched him carefully, unused to this kind of sentimentality from one of the Blood Ravens.

'I don't know how to describe it, Gabriel. It rushed at me, as though from everywhere at once, engulfing me in its darkness. Then it vanished, as suddenly and inexplicably as it had appeared, leaving me drained and semi-conscious on the ground.' Jonas paused, recalling something else. 'It vanished when the eldar arrived,' he realised. 'They came before you and it fled from them, as though recoiling at their stench as it flowed into the cavern.'

Gabriel nodded carefully, unsure what to make of Jonas's account. He looked over towards Ephraim, looking for some kind of sign, but the techmarine just shrugged, unable to judge whether the librarian had suffered any psychological trauma.

'Rest easy, Jonas,' said Gabriel at last, placing his hand on the librarian's shoulder. 'We will have need for your skills before this affair is finished, I am sure.' Jonas was now the only sanctioned psyker on the planet, which did not bode well for a conflict with the eldar. Even Chaplain Prathios, with his finely tuned psychic sympathies and sensitivities, had been put out of action. It was as though the eldar were systematically removing the Blood Ravens' ability to manipulate warp energy. Thinking back to the Blood Trials, Gabriel realised suddenly that the rangers had focussed their attacks on those aspirants that Prathios had suspected were psykers, including that green-eyed boy with the blond braids who kept appearing in Gabriel's mind.

Turning away from Jonas with a comradely smile, Gabriel strode over to the other side of the apothecarion, where Prathios was laying in an elaborate, ceremonial sarcophagus. His limbs had been shattered beyond the skill of anyone on Rahe's Paradise and his neck was broken. His eyes were wide and wild, although they seemed blind. The Third Company's apothecary was still light-years away aboard the *Litany of Fury*. Despite a number of attempts, Gabriel had not been able to get a message to the battle barge to try and encourage them to hurry through the Blood Trials on Trontiux III. The apothecary was needed badly, not least to tend to the grievously wounded Prathios, but also to maintain the recently erratic implants of a number of the scouts based on Rahe's Paradise, including Caleb.

In the absence of the apothecary, Gabriel had no choice other than to seal Prathios in one of the ancient sarcophagi that were kept in the walls of the monastery's chapel. He had no idea how the archaic and revered cabinets worked, but there was a legend in the pantheon of the Blood Ravens that told how the Great Father Azaraiah Vidya himself had been mortally wounded in a terrible battle against the unclean powers and then enshrined into the hallowed confines of such a device. It is recorded in the *Apocrypha Azaraiah: Travails of Vidya* that the Great Father floated freely through space for many decades, encased in the ceremonial purity of his sarcophagus, until he was finally recovered by the *Ravenous Spirit*, which was the strike cruiser of the Commander of the Watch even then.

If it had worked for the Great Father, it should work for Chaplain Prathios, thought Gabriel, holding fast to his faith as he closed the heavy lid over the face of his oldest friend.

'This is not the end, Prathios, chaplain of the Blood Ravens' Third. We will see each other again, Emperor willing,' muttered the captain in tones that only Prathios would have heard, had he been able to hear anything at all. 'The Emperor protects.'

The lid clunked shut heavily; jets of steam hissed out from around the seam as the interior of the carved and illuminated sarcophagus pressurised, sealing the chaplain in until such a time as expert help arrived.

THE CORRIDORS WERE silent. Nothing seemed to move as the row of Devastator Marines stood sentinel around the entrance to the Implantation Chamber – it was an entire squad. Their armour glinted crisply, and they held their weapons ready across their chests in pristine and perfect attention. The Ninth Company had three librarians and they were all there, standing side-by-side directly in front of the huge armoured doors with the other Marines spreading out on either side of them. The Implantation Chamber had its own separate protective field, which activated automatically when even the tiniest glitch appeared in the *Litany of Fury*'s own warp shields. The Chapter Priests within worked hardest of all when the *Litany* slipped into the warp. Within that chamber was the future of the Chapter itself: not only the half-finished form of the neophyte still strapped to the ceremonial tablet, but also one of the armoured repositories of the Blood Ravens' gene-seed itself.

The *Litany* had dropped into the warp about half an hour before, heading for the Lorn system, just after Ulantus had finally dispatched Sergeant Saulh with the *Rage of Erudition* to inform Gabriel of the recent developments and to request his aid on Lorn.

Captain Ulantus had waited for as long as he could before dropping into the warp, conscious that the young Ckrius was at a very vulnerable stage of his implantation. His concern was only partly for the youth himself, since he would be unusually vulnerable to the curdling insanities of the warp that engulfed the vessel, but it was mostly for the integrity of the *Litany of Fury*. Although the ancient battle barge had sailed its way through countless warp storms throughout the course of its long and venerable existence, it was never wise to be complacent about the unearthly and incomprehensible forces that swam through the empyrean, stirring time and space themselves as though they were merely water. The unspeakable powers would not be unaware of the presence of a vulnerable soul in the bowels of the *Litany*, even though it would be shielded behind the massive geller-field of the ship itself and then behind the psychic walls that were maintained around the Implantation Chamber at all times.

Ulantus had been right to be cautious. For a short time, the journey had seemed to be progressing smoothly, but, after only a few minutes in the warp, one of the *Litany*'s Astropaths had collapsed, flinging itself out of its station with blood pouring out of its eyes, dead. Something had slipped through a phase variance in the ship's shield and emerged into the open and sensitive mind of the astropath. However, even the disciplined, trained, controlled mind of the astropath had been unable to contain the presence, and it had ripped itself clear of the organic container, shredding the astropath's mind, brain and eyes.

Immediately, the Implantation Chamber had locked itself down, sealing the priests, the Apothecary and the neophyte inside. But Ulantus was not about to take any chances: he dispatched the Ninth Company's librarians and a detachment of Devastator Marines to stand guard over the vital chamber. He could not afford to take the *Litany* out of the warp until it had reached its designated extraction point – there was no telling where it might emerge, and the imperative of reaching Lorn before the suspected eldar fleet drove him on.

The lights in the brightly lit corridor flickered slightly, as though a power surge threatened to overload the glow-orbs in the ceiling. In the failing light, a faint purple light shimmered out from the walls themselves, as though weak veins of power coursed through the structure of the corridors.

'Prepare yourselves,' murmured Librarian Korinth, planting the tip of his force staff onto the deck between his feet. A crackle of blue flame sparked at the gentle impact. 'It approaches.'

The librarian stood in the very centre of the line, with the imposing figures of his librarian brothers Zhaphel and Rhamah on either side of him. Unlike the majority of other Space Marine Chapters, it was not unusual for a Blood Ravens Company to have a number of librarians in it, and they were quite accustomed to fighting alongside each other.

As Korinth spoke, the Devastator Marines braced their weapons, hefting chainswords and levelling flamers along the corridor in front of them. Zhaphel took a step forward from the line, swinging his force-axe in an arc around his shoulders, loosening his muscles in anticipation of the conflict to come. Meanwhile, Rhamah remained completely motionless; he had an ornate force-sword bound into a custom-holster on his back, but he made no attempt to reach for it. Instead, the librarian stood with his arms folded defiantly across his massive chest, with tendrils of warp-fire playing around the contacts that protruded from the psychic hood which obscured much of his face. Inside the hood, his eyes burned with a startling blue.

The lights flickered again, more violently than before. At the far end of the corridor, one of the glow-orbs overloaded and exploded, shattering glass down onto the metallic floor. The rest of the lights continued to flicker and pulse, throwing the passageway into a fit of strobe-lighting. Then another orb blew, and another, raining shards of glass down into the corridor.

The Marines remained motionless, with their feet planted firmly and their resolve undaunted. They were simply waiting for something to appear that they could kill.

The flashing of the lights grew faster and faster, and the frequency of exploding orbs accelerated as they drew closer to the Marines and the Implantation

Chamber. After a few seconds, the line of exploding glow-orbs became a strafing run, ploughing along the ceiling and racing towards the Blood Ravens, scattering glass like shrapnel. Keeping pace with the vicious rain was a ring of purple flame that looped around the floor, walls and ceiling, burning forward towards the Marines in a crackling halo of fire.

Korinth struck his staff against the deck, sending out jabs of energy through the metal panels, making the floor buckle and buck. As the boltss of energy from his staff met the advancing halo of fire, there was an abrupt, cackling shriek, like a thousand voices raised in agony.

The walls trembled and appeared to melt as the inferno intensified and tendrils of dripping energy started to reach out into the corridor. The screams of pain echoed along the passageway, bouncing from wall to wall and crashing against the staunch Marines that stood against the wave, even as the wailing scraped and grated against their minds.

For the merest fraction of a second, the Blood Ravens awaited direction, but then Zhaphel launched himself forward, spinning his force-axe in great sweeps around his head, hacking it through the daemonic tentacles and releasing spurts of phosphorescence from the severed protrusions.

Nothing shall pass! His voice echoed into the minds of the Marines around him, filling them with resolve and certainty.

Rhamah stayed planted before the great doors, but brilliant cracks of energy flashed out from his fingertips and from around the amplifier modules in his hood, lashing out against the daemonic incursion

and bringing it to a standstill. At the same time, the
Devastator squad stormed forward through plumes
of their own flames, brandishing chainswords and
powerfists, meeting the warp-daemon with the righteous fury of the Blood Ravens.

'For the Great Father and the Emperor!' they yelled
as they charged forward into the fray.

SINCE PRATHIOS HAD left the little cell, Ptolemea had
simply settled back onto the floor, drawing herself up
against the back wall and pulling her chin down to
her knees. Her mind raced through the implications
of what she had said to the Blood Raven, wondering
whether he had passed her confession along to
Gabriel. Her thoughts spiralled in confusion as she
tried to keep track of moral correctness: it seemed to
slip and slide through her grasp even as she
attempted to focus on it. Nothing would settle. Her
thoughts floated freely, as though no longer even
constrained by her mind. It seemed that she had lost
the ability to stand in judgement over her own
thoughts.

She tried to rehearse the scenario in her head: she
had been sent to Rahe's Paradise on orders from the
Bethle sub-sector of the Ordo Hereticus, charged
with investigating allegations that Captain Angelos
had been tainted and was consequently suffering
unsanctioned visions; since arriving, she herself had
started to suffer from dreams that may themselves
constitute visions; assuming that Sister Senioris Meritia had suffered the same visions, she had found
them so unbearable that she had been forced to kill
herself in order to escape the possibility that her soul

was tainted; rather than killing herself, however, or even permitting herself to be wrongfully executed for killing Meritia, Ptolemea had confessed her suspicions of her own taint to the chaplain of Captain Angelos himself. Perhaps her confession had been a subconscious plea for execution? Rather than being the righteous investigator of Gabriel's alleged taint, she was now at his mercy, apparently sharing with him the affliction of which he stands charged. Even if he were guilty of all the things Isador accused him of, would this really make him any more tainted than her?

Ptolemea didn't feel tainted, just confused.

As she sat feverishly against the wall of her cell, muttering to herself and struggling to find order in her thoughts, the door creaked and then crashed open, smashing back against the interior wall. In the flood of light that suddenly poured into the dark, little cell, Ptolemea saw the outline of a Marine. He was carrying a large block under one arm and clutched an elegant, slender, struggling figure in the other.

With a brisk movement, Gabriel tossed the eldar ranger into the cell. The alien smashed into the wall above Ptolemea's head and then slumped down into a heap next to her. She recoiled instinctively, scrambling away from the creature and pressing herself up against the sidewall.

'You will translate this, now,' asserted Gabriel, ignoring the Ptolemea's panic and holding forward the tablet that he had brought with him.

Ptolemea's face twitched back and forth between Gabriel and the eldar that still lay crumpled on the floor of the cell. She had no idea how to respond.

Although she had been expecting to see Gabriel soon, she had thought that he would have arrived to tell her his judgement on her confession. She had assumed that his arrival would have meant her death. Instead, she found herself confined in a cell with an alien creature, with her only way out blocked by a Space Marine captain wielding an alien artefact. A sudden revulsion gripped her soul as she realised that Gabriel was demanding that she should co-operate with the alien.

'But, Captain Angelos–'

'No buts, Sister Ptolemea. There is no time for buts. Just do it, now,' said Gabriel, turning his back and striding out of the cell, letting the door slam closed behind him, leaving Ptolemea alone with the alien and the tablet in the dim, half-light of the cramped chamber.

VARJAK POKED HIS head out of the sand, surveying the scene around the submerged exit of the tunnel. His people had known about these tunnels for decades; they often used them to spring ambushes on neighbouring warbands that strayed too close to his village. He had been part of such killing parties more than once already, despite his youth.

In the sand and the dull, yellowing sun, Varjak's dirty blond braids acted as a kind of camouflage. As he pushed his head up into the desert, he was confident that nobody would be able to see him, unless they were right above him at exactly the wrong moment.

Looking over towards the massive, black structure of the Sky Angels' fortress, Varjak could see the battle

unfolding. The huge, red and gold forms of the Sky
Angels themselves were meeting the sinister, slippery
aliens one to one in mortal combat. It was a breathtaking and glorious sight, and Varjak's brilliant green
eyes flashed with excitement as he pulled himself out
of the mouth of the tunnel and lay flat against the
sandy ground.

He had never seen the magnificent, godly warriors
fight before. He had heard the legends, of course. As
a small boy his father had recounted the legends of
the Sky Angels to him, telling him that one day he
might become strong enough to join their ranks if
only he trained hard enough, and lived long enough.

In one of the very oldest stories of his people, it
was reputed that the heavenly warriors had actually
brought light into the darkness of the world. In the
form of huge, winged birds, they had stolen the light
from the gods of night and returned the sun to Rahe's
Paradise. But that was long ago.

The eldest members of his village could remember the Sky Angels in combat, or so they claimed.
They told of them meeting an invasion of grotesque
green-skinned beasts with massive and undeniable
force, crushing them like the galactic vermin that
they were. But Varjak had always suspected that
these stories were exaggerated by the decrepitude of
old age. There were inconsistencies in the stories –
sometimes the accounts even described the Sky
Angels wearing armour of different colours. In any
case, he did not believe that even the Sky Angels,
who had built the massive fortress on the edge of
the desert and who dropped down out of the heavens once or twice in every generation, could

command such power as was attributed to them in
the stories.

Had he believed the stories, he may not have
charged in to attack one of them during the Trials a
couple of days earlier. He had simply assumed that
the huge, warrior-god's presence in the arena was
another part of the test, and he had launched himself
at the glorious figure without a second thought. In
truth, he couldn't really remember what happened
after that. He could recall seeing a clear line of attack
– the god's back was to him and it was preoccupied
with something else. He remembered diving forward
with his blade drawn. And then he remembered waking up again on the floor of the arena, surrounded by
dead and bleeding bodies. The Trials appeared to be
over; the other surviving aspirants and the Sky Angels
themselves had all vanished.

The side of his face was still raw and bruised, and
he suspected that his cheek-bone was cracked, so he
assumed that he had been struck unconscious by the
warrior-god. This was Varjak's first hint that the legends may be rooted in fact.

His second hint was taking shape right in front of his
eyes. Over towards the edge of the desert, in the shadow
of the immense fortress, the Sky Angels were a blaze of
power, charging out to meet the advancing alien threat
and loosing innumerable volleys of fire from their
thunderous weapons. The air itself seemed to burn, as
though their combat unleashed fragments of the volcanic wrath that Varjak had seen so many times before
in the mountains of Rahe's Paradise. It was as though
the gods themselves had descended onto the surface of
the planet to unleash an inferno on the world.

Leaning back into the mouth of the tunnel behind him, Varjak beckoned to the others to come out. Slowly and hesitantly, a small band of fellow aspirants from the Blood Trials clambered out of the tunnel into the fading desert sun. They were the warriors that had grouped around Varjak during the trials, recognising his skills and his power on an intuitive level, knowing that he would be on the victorious side. Although they were not all from his village, they had returned to the arena after it had been evacuated and had recovered the semi-conscious form of Varjak, not wanting his prone body to be mistaken for a corpse and fed into the flames of Krax-7. For his part, Varjak had accused them of stupidity: had their positions been reversed, he assured them, then he would have left them to burn, knowing that they would no longer be competition in the Blood Trials.

The ad hoc band of warriors lay pressed against the sand, letting the gusts of wind sprinkle them with desert dust and blur them into the landscape. They had been fighting in the desert all their lives, and they knew how to pass unseen.

After watching the spectacular battle for a while, a horrifying realisation began to dawn on Varjak: the Sky Angels were not winning this fight.

Despite the awesome firepower of the warrior-gods and their inspiring valour in combat, the Sky Angels had not managed to break the back of the alien advance. The bizarrely elongated and strangely elegant aliens seemed to dance and flash around the battle-field, slipping around and through assaults that should have devastated them. Whilst their odd-looking weapons made very little noise in comparison with the great war engines of the Sky Angels, they more than compensated in terms of accuracy and efficiency of fire.

In a moment of clarity, Varjak realised that the battle was a stalemate. And in that moment, his impressions about the warrior-gods that had made a home on his planet since before the time of memories came full circle. He had disbelieved the stories of their divine infallibility and incredible power, and then he had seemed to witness it firsthand. Now, he realised, it didn't matter how powerful a warrior might be, there would always be a foe worthy of him. It seemed that these extraordinary aliens could neutralise the advantage of the Sky Angels' firepower.

The battle unfolding before him was of proportions of which Varjak had never before dreamed. It was awe-inspiring, thunderous, and titanic in its scope and drama. And yet, watching the once-invincible Sky Angels struggling against the beautiful, deceitful and devious aliens, he saw them simply as warriors once again – heroic warriors like those from his own village, pitting themselves against a foe that was at least their equal, fighting with passion, faith, and desperation.

'We have to help them,' hissed Varjak, letting his whispered voice carry on the desert wind. 'We can use the tunnels.'

There was not even a murmur of dissent from his comrades and, as Varjak turned to observe their faces, he saw that they too had realised that there was more at stake in this battle than a spectacular show. The unspoken bond of a shared destiny seemed to tie Varjak and the other aspirants to the fate of the Sky Angels.

As they watched their gods do battle against the foul
and incomprehensible forces of the treacherous and
breathtaking aliens, they began to identify them as
brothers in arms, as battle-brothers of Rahe's Paradise.

THE MON'KEIGH woman stunk of fear and stupidity as
she cowered in the corner of the little cell. He could
smell her and it repulsed him. It was insulting
enough to have been captured by one of the cumbersome humans and to have been thrown into one
of their primitive cells, but to have been dumped in
with a feeble mon'keigh female was the utmost
humiliation. It was as though the humans were
taunting him, daring him to take her life, throwing
him easy prey in the hope that he would bite. Did
they really think so little of him? Could they really be
so conceited that they believed he would find this
pathetic specimen worth his time?

He twisted his body and brought himself upright,
propping his back against the wall. Staring at the
female, he spat, watching the viscous globule of
saliva splatter against the woman's cheek, hissing
with delicate toxicity.

Her eyes darted to his, meeting them with an intensity that surprised him. She hated him. He could see
it clearly in her dark eyes – a hidden and concentrated fire of hatred. But it was not just hatred, he
realised slowly, gazing into those surprisingly interesting eyes. There was something else, something
more subtle than hate. Contempt? No, it was something else: pity.

With a slow and deliberate movement, the human
female wiped his saliva from her face, leaving a raw

blemish of red on her otherwise porcelain skin. She had pressed her body against the other wall, keeping it as far away from Flaetriu as she could manage. But it was not out of fear, he realised, or at least not just out of fear. She did fear him – he could smell it. He could feel the fear oozing out of her thoughts. And he had been led to expect fear from the mon'keigh, fear and hate. But he had not expected to be an object of disgust – how could these stinking, festering mon'keigh be disgusted by him? It was absurd. And he had certainly not expected pity. Of all the emotions that he had expected to sense from a degenerate primitive, pity was the very last one on the list. On what grounds could she possibly pity a superior species of life?

The woman held his gaze for a few seconds, and then he was struck by the notion that she might actually be able to see something of his own confusion in his eyes and he looked away. He regretted it immediately, cursing himself for the apparent show of weakness – he was sure that the primitive female animal would see the aversion of his eyes as a capitulation. Animals have simple and direct minds. However, when he snapped his eyes back up to confront hers again, she had already looked away. He had lost his chance to impose himself and he was angered by it. He had been tricked by the relatively interesting eyes of the human woman – they were not as ugly or as crude as he had been expecting – and he had read too much insight into them.

And what did she think she was doing now? The stupid woman was staring down at Lsathranil's tablet, which the Blood Ravens captain had dropped so disrespectfully onto the floor. She was gazing at it and prodding it with her fingers, as though pretending to be following along with the flow of the runes – like a baby learning to read. Her face was contorted and ugly with concentration.

Flaetriu laughed, amused by the pathetic scene and the ridiculousness of the female's pretence. It was his turn to feel pity, and this time it was entirely justified.

'What?' demanded Ptolemea, snapping her round and glowering at him. 'What's so funny, outcast?' Her voice dripped with aggression and contempt, as though lashing him with torrential rain.

Flaetriu's eyes flashed and narrowed. The mon'keigh had struck out at him in his own tongue. Of course, the language was slightly confused, the grammar was bad and the pronunciation was appalling, but the sense of it was clear enough. He had never heard of such a thing in his entire life. He stopped laughing.

'You know my tongue, human?' he asked, redundantly.

'It hurts my head, but I know enough,' she replied, having already turned her face back down to the tablet. It was as though she didn't care that he was there. Or, perhaps, she simply wished that he wasn't there at all.

Flaetriu's mind flickered between abject revulsion at this living monstrosity before him and utter fascination that he seemed to have found a human female of such unusual depth. How typical, he reasoned, that the other mon'keigh had thrown this creature into their dungeons. He was sure that they would have no hope of understanding her.

'What are you hoping to do with that?' asked Flaetriu, pointing at the tablet in front of Ptolemea.

'I am hoping to translate it,' she replied, mimicking his sentence structure like a student.

Flaetriu laughed again. Did she really think that Lsathranil's tablet could be captured in the dull, clumsy, blunt language of the mon'keigh? Had she no idea what it meant to write using the ancient and unspeakable powers of the runes?

'It is not easy,' she conceded, apparently choosing not to be offended by his scepticism. 'But our need is great.'

'Yes, the need is great,' concurred Flaetriu, nodding his assent. She was right. He wondered whether her mind could really comprehend how great the need really was. Perhaps if she knew what the tablet said, then she would be on the right path?

He suddenly remembered that Macha had once counselled him to take the mon'keigh seriously. She had even suggested that they might serve as useful allies in times of great need or terrible crisis. She had cautioned him that 'their motives can be pure, but their souls are full of shadows that none can recognise. They are haunted by themselves, and not one of them will ever face up to himself.' But she had insisted that their motives could be pure, and that they could be guided towards the light. She had even claimed that the light might rid them of the shadows in their hearts.

'Let me help you,' said Flaetriu, the words grating even as he spoke them. This was not something that he had ever expected to say to a human and it caused him real physical pain to utter the request. Pride was not something that the eldar swallowed easily, but Flaetriu was certain that Macha would approve of his choice, even if the exarch Laeresh would not; there are some things more important than pride and more important than scouring the human stench off the planet, and Lsathranil's Shield was certainly one of those things.

The woman looked over at him, her upper lip curled into a snarl of repugnance and disbelief. If he was expecting her to say thank you, he had another thing coming.

The banshee's call *shall wake the dead when dark portents wax nigh,*
   Heed them as the counsel of a seer, or a father.
   The Yngir, who have slept since the very birth of Chaos,
   Shall crawl once more from their tombs, thirsting for warmth.
   The war in heaven shall be as nothing to their vengeance,
   For the sons of Asuryan, few in number, cannot stand against them.

And the Eye *of Isha shall dim, closing for all eternity;*
   Such a gentle goddess cannot witness the atrocities they will wreak.
   The soulless ones shall be the harbingers of the dark fate,
   And then shall come the living dead, the progeny,
   The thirsting ones, the forever damned,
   And the galaxy shall run red as the blood of Eldanesh.

   Ishandruir, pages 1-2 of 3, Farseer Lsathranil,
Ulthwé

* * *

'There is more,' explained Ptolemea, her exhausted features running with perspiration as she looked up at Gabriel, framed in the cell's doorway once again. 'We have not yet had time to tackle the last page.'

'This is more than enough, Sister Ptolemea,' said Gabriel, nodding gravely. 'We must take this information to Father Jonas, and see what he makes of it.'

He held out his hand towards Ptolemea, who reached up to take it, letting the strength of the Space Marine pull her to her feet at last. She held the tablet tightly under her other arm, as though clinging to a baby.

Weakened and dazed by her spell of detention and intense concentration, Ptolemea was unsteady on her feet in the flood of light, and Gabriel supported much of her weight against his arm. As they stood uneasily in the doorway, Flaetriu jumped up and dashed towards the exit. In stark contrast to the gingerly, fragile motion of Ptolemea, his sudden movements were smooth and fleet, and he took them both by surprise.

Gabriel was his match. In a flash of glittering red, the captain's powerful arm shot out to the side, punching his fist into the stone doorframe and blocking the eldar's escape route. His other arm still supported the swaying figure of Ptolemea.

Flaetriu slid, changing his pace and ducking down, trying to slide his slim figure under the sudden barrier, but Gabriel dropped his fist, bringing his arm crashing down on the eldar's head as the ranger tried to slip underneath it.

'I don't think so,' he said, as Flaetriu slumped to the ground under the blow.

With his other arm still holding Ptolemea, Gabriel reached down and wrapped his hand in the dazed creature's long, thick hair. He tugged the ranger into the air, holding it suspended from its scalp. Then, without regard or effort, he flung the creature back into the cell, watching it smack into the back wall and bounce off onto the floor, where it lay motionless and dejected.

'Thank you for your help,' said Gabriel dryly, and then he slammed shut the heavy door to the tiny, dark chamber.

'He did help,' muttered Ptolemea faintly, looking up into the fierce face of Gabriel. 'I could not have translated the text without him...' Her voice trailed off, uncertain about the wisdom of continuing her confession, and quite certain that she should not make an appeal to a Space Marine captain on behalf of an alien. As far as she was aware, Prathios had already shared her earlier confession with his captain.

'Then it is fortunate that he was here,' replied Gabriel curtly, his expression belying his words. He had no interest in Ptolemea's sensibilities at the moment; the ruined figure of Prathios burned in his mind's eye. 'The eldar are attacking,' he added bluntly.

Ptolemea nodded meekly. She could see the passion in Gabriel's glittering eyes and she thought that she understood it better than he might imagine. He was releasing her from the cell, which meant that either Prathios had not yet passed on her confession or that Gabriel was unconcerned by it. Either way, Ptolemea realised that they were more alike than she had wanted to admit when she first arrived on Rahe's Paradise – they both had secrets, both had communed with the eldar, but neither of them would be swayed from their duty to the Emperor. Their souls were pure, no matter what fate and aliens threw at them.

CHAPTER ELEVEN
SENTINEL

THE THUNDER OF impacts outside pulsed through the ground, resonating through the stone floors of the librarium and making the book stacks tremble. The sounds of battle raging in the desert added a sense of urgency as Gabriel and Jonas poured over the wraithbone tablet on the ancient wooden table under the stained-glass windows. It went against part of their natures to be sheltered away when their battle-brothers were fighting so valiantly outside. But, nowhere was the dual nature of the Blood Ravens captured more vividly than in the image of Gabriel and Jonas, bathed in the red sunlight that streamed down through the hallowed Chapter emblem that was emblazoned into the stained-glass, studying the archaic script of an alien eldar tongue while all hell was loosed around them. It was not for nothing that the Blood Ravens were famed as

scholar-warriors, and never had living up to that reputation been more important than now.

'But, what does it mean, Jonas?' asked Gabriel.
Impatience was rarely a virtue, but sometimes it was
necessary. If they could make no sense of the tablet,
then he was determined to get outside to support
Tanthius and his Marines.

'This is the same rune that I saw in the cavern
under the foundations: Yngir,' explained Jonas,
pointing deliberately. 'I'm not sure what it means,
but it appears to refer to a threat. Perhaps something
buried within Rahe's Paradise itself.'

'And the great blast of darkness that transformed
the desert into mica glass, should we assume that was
the "banshee's call"?' asked Gabriel. 'Did it awaken
these Yngir, or perhaps mark their awakening in
some way?'

'It is possible, Gabriel,' mused Jonas, submerged in
his thoughts and less aware of the battle that roared
and thudded outside. 'It is this line here that
intrigues me,' he continued thoughtfully. 'It says that
we should heed this call as though it were the counsel of a seer or a father.'

'Yes?' queried Gabriel, looking distractedly back
over his shoulder towards the doors to the librarium
as they swung open. For a moment, he could see
nothing in the burst of light, but then five figures
strode into the central aisle. In the middle, in the
lead, was the lithe and lissom shape of Ptolemea.
Her body-glove had been cleaned and repaired, and
her limbs were covered with straps and holsters.
Looking more closely, Gabriel could see that she had
equipped herself with an array of bladed weapons,

each bound to her body glove in a manner that he had never seen before, vaguely reminiscent of the techniques used by some of the assassins in the employ of the Ordo Hereticus. On her right thigh was a more substantial holster, and Gabriel immediately recognised the antique pistol from the alcove in Meritia's chamber. Tied around her hairless head, in place of her customary red headscarf, Ptolemea had wrapped the worn and atrophied tapestry that had covered the little alcove – the emblem of the chalice and starburst centred on her forehead. Bound to her shoulders, abdomen and legs were precisely sculpted plates of armour, which must have been designed specifically to wear within the fabric of a body-glove without much external sign.

Behind Ptolemea strode the magnificent Celestian warriors of the Order of Golden Light, their armour polished and sparkling as their name deserved.

'It is strange,' continued Jonas without looking round. He hardly seemed to have noticed the dramatic and unexpected entrance behind them. 'But this appears to be an appeal to us as well as to the eldar.'

'What?' asked Gabriel, dragging his eyes away from the majesty of the approaching women and turning back to Jonas and the tablet. 'What do you mean?'

'Look here,' said Jonas, pointing. 'It says to heed the banshee's call as the counsel of a seer or a father. I know of no records that speak of the eldar revering a rank known as a "father." Given where we found the tablet, it does not seem incredible that this phrase was designed to act as an imperative for us – it is the Blood Ravens who place our faith in the Great Father.'

Gabriel stared at the tablet, unable to decipher the runes but trusting in Father Jonas's interpretation. His mind raced to unravel the implications of this reading as Ptolemea and the nameless Celestians arrived at the table behind him.

'Captain Angelos. We place ourselves at your disposal in this time of need,' said Ptolemea formally, sweeping into a low bow as she spoke.

'Thank you, Sister Ptolemea. You are most welcome here, and your timing is impeccable,' replied Gabriel, turning to greet her properly and returning the bow. Despite himself, he was impressed by the determined and battle-ready Sister of the Lost Rosetta. They may not be a militant order, but it seemed clear that Ptolemea was not merely a bureaucrat. She was quite transformed from the arrogant and officious young Sister who had arrived only a few days before. 'We were just discussing the inscription that you kindly translated for us. It seems that there is more to this affair than the eldar, and it also seems that–'

'Captain,' interrupted Jonas earnestly. 'If this tablet was really written by a source that was aware it would be read by the Blood Ravens, this suggests that the mixture of Adeptus Astartes and eldar artefacts in the foundations of this monastery indicate more than simply a transitional period in the history of Rahe's Paradise.'

'You're suggesting that there was some kind of collusion?' challenged Gabriel, his soul repulsed and certain all at once.

'Perhaps,' replied Jonas, nodding slowly as a theory started to unfold in his mind.

'The author was Farseer Lsathranil of Craftworld Ulthwé,' said Ptolemea, stepping up to the table to converse with Jonas.

'Who? How do you know?' asked the librarian, startled by the interruption.

'The eldar prisoner told me,' she answered matter-of-factly. 'Lsathranil knew that the Blood Ravens would be here when the tablet was uncovered. It says nothing about the conditions under which it was written, only about the foresight of the author himself. He knew that you would be here now, which doesn't mean that you were there then.'

'I see,' replied Jonas, staring at the Sister for a moment, wondering what to make of the source. He still distrusted the young Sister, and still suspected that she had something to do with the death of his friend Meritia. And, on top of that, she was claiming to have received the information from the most devious of all possible sources, an imprisoned eldar ranger. Then he realised that there was no time for scepticism and his brow furrowed as he tried to fit the new knowledge into his evolving model.

'Collusion is not finally the issue,' interjected Gabriel, cutting through the historical theorising. 'The real issue concerns the nature of the threat: these Yngir, whatever they are, must constitute a serious danger if the ancient eldar spoke of them in such terms.'

'And if they deigned to send a warning even to us,' continued Ptolemea, remembering the contempt with which Flaetriu had viewed her and all of humanity.

'We can worry about our history later, old friend,' said Gabriel, placing his hand onto the old librarian's shoulder. 'Right now we have to get down into the foundations of this site and see what these Yngir really are. The "Sons of Asuryan" may not be able to stand against them, but the Emperor's Blood Ravens will not be so easily cowed.'

Outside, a tremendous impact rocked the librarium itself, causing tomes from the top of the stacks to fall, thudding into the ground like dead birds. Faintly audible through the great walls, Gabriel could hear his Marines rally and let out a cry, followed by a blaze of noise as they threw their fury back into the faces of the eldar assailants. His heart swelled with pride even as it was flooded with frustration at being away from the action outside.

'If the message on the tablet was really meant for us both, then it seems to make little sense that the aliens are so set on annihilating us now,' muttered Gabriel as he strode past Ptolemea, heading for the doors. 'But then, sense is not something that I have come to expect from the eldar.'

'WE NEED TO close the distance on those eldar craft,' said Tanthius as javelins of light seared over his head and punched into the walls of the monastery behind him. The air was dark with constant clouds of shuriken projectiles that bounced and ricocheted off the thick armour of the Terminator squad that spearheaded the Blood Ravens' charge. Tanthius had abandoned his trench long ago, and was now standing defiantly in the very centre of the mica glass battlefield, thrashing his powerfist through the enemy at close range and letting his storm bolter spit death freely. He was searching for the exarch.

There was a deafening screech of feedback through the vox-bead, but Tanthius could not make out a voice. 'Necho?' barked the Terminator sergeant, as though trying to force his words through the intense interference with the power of volume. 'Necho, get your assault team out to those troop carriers – they're doing too much damage. Close them down.'

The vox signal hissed, whined and then cut out automatically, as though overloaded. Tanthius cursed and scanned the fray for signs that the sergeant had heard his orders. He could see the Assault squad over to one side of the battlefield, raining fire and grenades down onto a clutch of weapon batteries that the eldar had dug into the sand where the petrification ended. The batteries themselves were pulsing with emissions, as though firing waves of disruptive energy through the battlefield, and two knots of eldar warriors stood guard over them, angling their long-barrelled weapons up into the sky to confront the Marines. Necho showed no signs of moving out.

'Topheth!' yelled Tanthius, feeling the cold incision of a blade slide in between the armoured plates around his knee. Letting out a thunderous cry, the Terminator Marine thrashed out with his powerfist, spinning his upper body around to confront whatever had dared to penetrate his defences. His fist flew only millimetres above the ducking head of a darting eldar warrior, clad in the green and white armour of Biel-Tan. The creature dropped elegantly, spinning with practiced ease and letting its blade lash around in a perfect circle, bringing its crackling edge back towards Tanthius's knee once again.

Tanthius stepped aside with an agility belied by his massive stature, and he punched his fist down like a hammer, driving it into the top of the eldar's head. He didn't even feel the creature's neck snap, but he saw its head crumple down through its shoulders and bury itself in the alien's own chest cavity.

'Topheth!' he yelled again, scanning the vista for signs of the attack bikes. Then he saw them, out on the perimeter of the battle. They were bouncing and sliding over the dunes, their heavy bolters spluttering with continuous fire as they twisted and manoeuvred in pursuit of the eldar jetbikes that were skimming over the desert like flecks of emerald lightning. Asherah's Razorback had been defeated by the terrain and had been left behind; his squad had spilt out into the desert and were in the midst of a staunch defence of the venerable vehicle. Meanwhile, the eldar jetbikes seemed to be defending a couple of larger weapon platforms, which were ploughing onwards towards the core of the battle, bringing their heavier weapons into play against the Blood Ravens on the ground.

'Emperor damn it!' bellowed Tanthius, reaching forward and grasping the head of an alien fighter as it tried to dash past him, lifting it off its feet and then shredding it with a flurry of shells from his storm bolter. The vox was clearly not functioning.

From behind him came the roaring hiss of ordnance being launched, and he turned to see Corallis directing the rockets from the Land Raiders that remained nestled in the shadow of the monastery.

The missiles raked overhead, howling out towards the Wave Serpents on the horizon in shallow parabolas. But the eldar vehicles were too fast, sliding over the dunes and shifting position before the rockets could reach them. The shells ploughed into the sand left vacant by the slippery eldar, exploding into craters and great plumes of sand.

Almost instantly, brilliant strobes of lance fire flashed out of the Wave Serpents. It was as though they were mocking the powerful, explosive impotence of the Land Raiders, as the javelins of energy punched into the black towers of the monastery once again.

Straining his eyes out to the horizon, Tanthius saw one of the jet-black Wave Serpents pitch and twist suddenly, as though it had collided with something or was under attack. Instinctively, he snapped his head back round to check on the location of Necho's squad, but they were still entrenched in their own fire fight. Topheth was on the other side of the combat zone. Hilkiah's Devastators were a blaze of fire around the northern side of the defensive arc, holding off a frenzied attack by a host of alien creatures. Not even Gaal's Tactical squad had managed to push so far forward through the enemy lines, they were caught in the very heart of the battle, each Marine matched against two or three of the eldar warriors.

So, what was attacking the eldar vehicle? Tanthius sprayed off a volley of hellfire shells from his storm bolter, clearing a space around him so that he could look more carefully.

There seemed to be a small gang of human warriors clambering over the armoured panels of the

Wave Serpent. They appeared to be armed only with blades and blunt clubbing weapons, but they were using them well, jamming them into the barrels of the vehicle's guns and attacking anything that stuck its head out of any of the hatches. Some of them looked very young and one, with long, dirty blond braids, seemed hardly more than a boy, but he appeared to be the leader, and the others followed his example with devotion and bravery.

Were they the locals? wondered Tanthius, sidestepping a lunging force-sword and clutching its blade into the irresistible grip of his powerfist, crushing it into splintered shards before sweeping his back-fist into the face of the alien swordsman. Where they the aspirants from the Blood Trials?

'Caleb!' he called, spotting the scout sergeant as he skidded his bike to a halt next to the Terminator, its twin-linked bolters ripping up the ground in front of it. The remnants of the scout squadron were churning through the solidified desert in a loose formation around him, spraying bolter fire in undisciplined volleys.

'Caleb – get over to that Wave Serpent and give those locals some help. They've got the right idea!' As he spoke, Tanthius saw the incredible visage of the plumed eldar exarch stride into view as it crested a glassy dune. 'Yes,' he said under his breath. 'At last.'

THE LAVA BUBBLED and roiled even more violently than usual, as though reacting to the dramatic events that were unfolding around it. Ptolemea moved cautiously behind the two Space Marines, with the Celestian Sisters at her back. She had not made it this far down through the tunnels before – something had stolen her sight and her consciousness last time she had made these steps, and she was left with only the vaguest memories of something dark and terrible in the shadows. Unlike the armoured warriors around her, she was ill-protected from the tremendous, stifling heat of the volcanic world; for a while she felt feverish and nauseous, fearing that she would collapse once again.

The group arrayed themselves along the narrow ledge that ran around the circumference of the wide cavern. The pit in the middle remained ringed with fire and cascades of molten rock, and in its centre glistened the pristine and implacable black pyramid. Other than the persistent sizzles and hisses of the lava and the distant thunder of war out in the desert above, the scene was enshrouded in silence.

'The Yngir rune was etched in the ground itself,' explained Jonas, addressing his remarks to Sister Ptolemea with an air of professionalism. 'It was comprised of veins of lava. When I read its name, the ground parted and revealed this pit...' His voice trailed off almost dreamily. 'And that pyramid,' he said finally, fascinated and troubled by the fact that he couldn't really remember what had happened to him after he had descended into the pit.

Ptolemea nodded her understanding, her face fixing into an expression of determination as she stood there flanked by the superhuman figures of the Adeptus Astartes and Sororitas. Without waiting for their lead, Ptolemea took a couple of rapid steps forward and then launched herself out over the pit, as though diving into water. As she dived forward towards the

ground, she pulled her feet down into a pike and
turned a gentle half-rotation over her back. By the
time she hit the ground, her legs had spun round
perfectly, and she landed so lightly that she made
almost no sound at all. She was determined to over-
come her human frailties in the stifling heat, even if
only through the strength of her will. In an instant,
the slight figure of Ptolemea was flanked by the glittering golden armour of the Celestians – the
battle-sisters landing only slightly heavier than her.

Gabriel and Jonas shared a glance, silently
impressed and surprised by the dangerous and composed grace of the Sister of the Lost Rosetta. Gabriel
smiled and then vaulted down into the pit to join the
group, leaving Jonas standing on his own for a
moment, looking down at the unusual assortment of
Imperial servants collected into his excavation. He
couldn't shake the feeling that something wasn't
quite right. It could have been residual concerns
about his last experience down in the pit, especially
since he still couldn't quite remember what had happened, but there was something in the air that made
him feel uncomfortable. It was a smell. It was the
faint stench of–

'Gabriel!' Jonas launched himself forward as his
staff burst into life, sending a crackling blast of blue
fire flashing down against the lava flow on the far
wall. The lightning strike blew clear through the
molten cascade and punched into the rock behind it,
sending showers of stone and lava spraying over the
floor.

As the librarian landed in the pit, he broke into a
run, pounding across towards the point of impact

with a continuous stream of energy pouring out of his staff and crashing into the far wall. Meanwhile, the rest of the group had already started firing, filling the confined space of the pit with volleys of bolter shells. But they were all firing in different directions, as though tracking separate targets around behind the veils of fire.

All at once, great streams of warp energy lashed out from behind the molten cascades, flaring from different points around the circular wall, arcing and cracking through the sulphurous air in the pit, converging on the group in its centre like jagged spokes in a giant wheel.

Gabriel threw himself against Ptolemea, pushing her to the ground as a sheet of raw energy flashed over her head. He saw the Celestians diving for cover, striving to avoid contact with the treacherous energies of the warp. Only Jonas stood firm, slicing his force staff through the streams of power and disrupting their flow, redirecting them and parrying them off into the boiling lava.

After a second, a number of shrouded figures stepped out of their hiding places behind the cascades of molten rock, walking slowly through the sheets of falling lava as though they were little more than waterfalls. All the time, huge pulses of warp fire lashed out of their finger tips, stabbing out towards the besieged figures in the centre of the pit, as Jonas strove to protect them all. From their positions on the ground, Gabriel and the Celestians snapped off volleys of bolter fire at the advancing warlocks, but their shells just seemed to bounce off the energy fields that surrounded the cloaked eldar.

'For the Great Father and the Emperor!' yelled
Jonas, spinning his staff above his head and letting
intense shards of power spiral off around the chamber.

Then everything started to spin. The shards of light
from Jonas's staff seemed to be caught into a kind of
vortex, and they began to whirl around the perimeter of the pit. For a moment, Gabriel wondered
whether this was Jonas's intention, but then he saw
the librarian lowering his staff in disbelief. At the
same time, the channels of warp-fire that were flooding out of the fingers of the eldar warlocks started to
twist and spiral, as though curdling into a
whirlpool. Very quickly, the alien psykers stopped
their attacks, watching in amazement as the prod-
ucts of their passion were whipped into a spiralling
gyre.

After a couple of seconds, the flecks and lines of
energy that whirled around the room started to draw
in towards the centre, as though sucked into the
heart of a vortex. It was only then that Gabriel
realised what was at the heart of this: the mysterious
black pyramid was drawing in all the loose warp
energy in the pit, drinking it in as though thirsty for
the power.

In a blinding flash of darkness, the last remnants of
the energy trails vanished, sucked into the pyramid
like matter into a vacuum, leaving the Marines, the
Sisters of Battle and the eldar standing motionless
and silent.

Stop. The command was firm, reaching directly into
all their minds.

* * *

HE COULDN'T BELIEVE that it was really her. Despite their encounter on the battlefield in the desert, Gabriel had still been reluctant to believe that Macha had followed him to Rahe's Paradise. Hell has no fury like a scorned eldar witch, it seemed, and he had certainly scorned her back on Tartarus.

The slender, elegant figure of the female farseer emerged from the veils of lava and flame, pushing them apart as though they were curtains and stepping out into the bottom of the pit. She did not look around the scene, but instead she focussed her unmoving, sparkling, eyes only on Gabriel as she walked towards him.

Gabriel. The name pushed through his head, gently working its way into his mind. *Gabriel – I know that you understand me.*

The warlocks had fallen back, regrouping behind the farseer like an organic and lethal wake. Meanwhile, the Marines and Sisters were back on their feet with their weapons primed and ready. Gabriel stepped forward, aiming to intercede in the farseer's advance towards the group, letting the others fall in behind him. He could sense Jonas's unrest at the sudden ceasefire, and he could hear the weapons of the Celestian Sisters snapping back and forth as they held targeting beads on each of the warlocks. But nobody fired.

'What are you doing here, farseer?' asked Gabriel, his hands twitching distrustfully over the bolter in his holster.

I might ask you the same question, Gabriel, replied Macha, using his name like an old friend.

'You might, but you won't and you don't need to,' snapped Gabriel, aware that his companions could hear his voice but not the focussed thoughts of the eldar witch.

Yes, I do know what you are doing, human. It is you who seems oblivious to the consequences of your actions. There was something self-satisfied and smug in the tone of the thoughts, leaving Gabriel's mind slightly nauseated by the sickly intrusion.

Gabriel stared at her, unsure of how to proceed. He had trusted her once before, during the battle for Tartarus. He had trusted her enough to place his soul on the line at the feet of the Inquisition and the daemons of Khorne. But he knew that trusting an eldar once did not mean that he should trust her twice, especially since it was he who had betrayed that trust last time. Gazing into her complicated and fathomless emerald eyes, he wondered whether she would hold a grudge.

'Do not play with me, Macha,' he said, speaking her name. Behind him, he heard the disturbed and uncertain movements of Ptolemea. 'You know what your secrets did to the galaxy last time.' There was no reason why he had to stay on the defensive.

There was a moment of silence, but Gabriel couldn't tell whether it was caused by exasperation or amusement.

Secrets are never a problem, and they are never kept. They are always revealed to those who are in a position to know them. This is the nature of knowledge, Gabriel, as you, of all people, should know well. The problem lies in the choices made by those without knowledge and, even worse, in those made by those for whom there are no secrets at all. Knowledge and understanding are seldom the same.

'What does that mean?' asked Gabriel, his face contorted in failed resistance as the thoughts curdled through his brain.

It means that you should leave before you do anything stupid, Blood Raven. Before you do anything more stupid than you and your kind have done already. Macha's tone had changed. She was no longer playing. It was as though she were shouting into his mind, filling it with carefully restrained and controlled violence. If she were to raise the volume any further, she might kill him in an instant.

'We will not be leaving, farseer,' replied Gabriel. forcing a calmness into his voice. 'This world is part of the Imperium of Man and it is a home for the Blood Ravens. If you want it back, then you will have to take it from us.'

As he spoke, the Celestian Sisters racked their weapons and stepped up alongside him. Jonas strode forward and planted his staff between his feet. Only Ptolemea was left behind Gabriel.

You think that we want this planet for ourselves? There was some amusement in the thought.

'Was Rahe's Paradise not an Exodite world, before it was cleansed of the stench of the eldar by the righteous fury of the Blood Ravens?' challenged Gabriel, sensing the desire of his comrades to do battle there and then. He may as well test a theory.

Then Macha laughed. She actually laughed out loud. It was a gesture that made her look even more alien, if only because it was such a human action.

Yes, the eldar were here once, and now you are here, Gabriel. Things change – such is the nature of time. Now the eldar have returned, so we are here together, again.

Gabriel was confused – did she want to reclaim this planet for the lost eldar empire or not?

This was once a beautiful planet, Gabriel, cloaked in jungles and forests. The eldar used to protect its beauty. Now look at it. It is ruined, and the Blood Ravens are here. We were only ever guardians, standing sentinel over the Yngir, keeping the planet free of the taint of unclean or uncontrolled minds. Now such minds are everywhere – although we have done our best to remove them.

Macha's mind seemed to direct Gabriel towards images of Ikarus and Prathios, conjuring up memories of the suspected psykers amongst the aspirants in the Blood Trials – the green-eyed youth with blond braids. Involuntarily, he turned and glanced at the defiant figure of Jonas by his side, and Ptolemea shuffled uneasily behind him.

Yet you persisted. We gave you this planet, Gabriel. We gave it to the Marines who came here ten millennia ago. After our own defeat, we left it in trust. There was a war, the skies were shattered and the heavens fell, leaving the sons of Asuryan broken and too weak to stand vigil over this world. So we left. But the echoes of that time live on, resonating in the sensitive and undisciplined minds of the more receptive of your kind, where they incubate, breed, and amplify.

'The Blood Ravens were here ten millennia ago?' asked Gabriel, trying to make sense of the farseer's story. It seemed incredible.

She laughed again. *The Adeptus Astartes were here. They came and built a monstrous fortress – your little monastery is but a pale imitation of that ugly edifice. It was destroyed before you were born, when the forests were burnt and the desert emerged from the ground, but you were destined to be here even then. It was to them that we left this world in trust – but your memories are short, it seems.*

'But, were they Blood Ravens?' persisted Gabriel, his mind racing off on a tangent, suddenly intrigued by the chance of discovering something new about his mysterious Chapter. He had never even heard legends that placed the Blood Ravens so far back in history.

Macha looked at him, her eyes suddenly flickering with doubt. *Blood Ravens.* She paused. *This is the name of your Marines?* She paused again, as though realising something. *There are many types of Adeptus Astartes?*

'Yes, many.'

I did not know that – you all seem the same to me.

'THE DECISION IS yours, captain. We will follow you,' stated Jonas firmly, although he lifted his gaze to check on what the eldar were doing on the other side of the pit. He didn't trust them. Just because they had agreed a temporary truce so that Gabriel could explain the situation, it didn't mean that he believed they wouldn't attack. As it was, they were standing exactly where they had been for the last half an hour – the warlocks arrayed behind the farseer in a perfect V, utterly motionless.

The Celestian Sisters stood in a line between the two Marines and Ptolemea, and the eldar, forming a glittering human shield. They would not contribute to the discussion, and had signalled their willingness to follow Ptolemea's lead.

'I do not think that it would be wise to trust the aliens,' continued Jonas, almost contradicting himself. 'But the decision is yours.'

'I have trusted Macha before,' murmured Gabriel, thinking out loud and avoiding Ptolemea's eyes. 'If she is right about this, then we have no choice. We must work with them to prevent the ascension of these Yngir, or to confront them if they are awake already.'

'But it told you that it was responsible for the deaths of Ikarus and the aspirants. And you yourself saw what they did to Prathios. Is not vengeance a more suitable response than trust?' queried Jonas.

Gabriel was silent. 'Perhaps, Jonas. Perhaps. I do wish that Prathios were here. His guidance would be invaluable. But he is not, and we must act in a manner worthy of his memory.'

'Why did she claim that the death of your librarian was necessary?' asked Ptolemea. Her thoughts were all over the place. Before he had died, Librarian Isador Akios had warned the Ordo Hereticus that Gabriel had been consorting with the eldar farseer on Tartarus – it had been one of the most damning piece of evidence that had convinced the authorities on Bethle II to dispatch Ptolemea to investigate him. They had hypothesised that his unusual visions might be linked to his odd relationship with the farseer. Now, however, having collaborated with an eldar ranger to translate an ancient artefact and having suffered what may well have been visions herself, Ptolemea's righteous certainty was dwindling. She felt that her soul and Gabriel's travelled a similar road, and she still clung to the hope that it was not the road to damnation.

'Ten millennia ago, the eldar left a device on this planet that regulated the psychic field around its surface,' explained Gabriel. 'The device was designed by a powerful farseer, who understood that the Yngir would sleep for as long as they believed that the eldar still dominated the stars. The psychic field synthesised the presence of the eldar on this planet, even after they left. It seems that the excavations of Father Jonas disturbed the device causing it to malfunction. The result was an emission of the psychic echoes of the original battles between the eldar and the Yngir on this planet, which would be picked up and amplified by receptive minds on the planet's surface–'

'–minds like those of a librarian?' asked Jonas, finishing the thought.

'Exactly, but not only librarians. Other people with latent psychic potentials or sensitivities might also be affected. People like the local aspirants in the Blood Trials, or…' Gabriel trailed off, not wanted to finish the thought out loud in front of Ptolemea and the Battle Sisters. However, Ptolemea nodded slowly, as though expressing an unspoken solidarity, as the images of eldar fighting in a jungle swam back into her mind.

'The eldar had to remove those minds lest they disturb the slumber of the Yngir?' concluded Ptolemea, realising that the explanation fitted exactly with her own experiences.

'How could it be that the Blood Ravens have been here all this time and not realised what was under our own monastery?' asked Jonas, still reluctant to be persuaded by the alien's story.

'We have not been here all this time, Jonas,' said Gabriel, knowing that it would come as a shock to the old scholar. 'The fortress on whose remains we built our outpost was not a Blood Ravens facility. Another Chapter was here before us – a Chapter that seems to have made some kind of pact with the eldar to stand guard over the slumbering evil under the planet's crust. But the fortress was destroyed or abandoned, perhaps at the time when the forests were scoured from the face of this world. Whatever Chapter was here, it left the planet to die. But it did not die, and the Blood Ravens discovered it, making it our own, ignorant of the promises made by the servants of the Emperor before our arrival, and ignorant of what lay beneath the tectonic plates of this ruinous world.'

'Knowledge is power,' muttered Jonas, bitterly reciting the motto of the Chapter. 'The eldar farseer knew that we would be here,' he realised, 'even after all this time – it knew that it would be the Blood Ravens, not any other Chapter – the wraithbone tablet was written with us in mind… We must make amends for our ignorance.'

'And we must stand by the word of the Adeptus Astartes, in the name of the Emperor of Man,' concluded Gabriel.

CHAPTER TWELVE
CATACOMBS

'WHAT IS IT, Loren?' asked Kohath. After the unfortunate incident with Reuben, the Blood Ravens sergeant had been forced to learn the name of another serf, and he was trying to use it whenever possible. The crew on the command deck had been on edge since the still-untraced attack shortly after Captain Angelos and the others made landfall. Using their names seemed to settle their nerves.

They had been watching the faint signature flicker on the edge of the *Ravenous Spirit*'s scopes for the last few minutes, since it had emerged from the warp and entered the edge of the system. It was moving fast, and seemed to be heading directly towards Rahe's Paradise.

'I'm not sure, sergeant,' replied the serf without lifting his head from the screen on his console. 'It will be within range of the resolution sensors in a few minutes, then we will be able to get a better fix on its signature.'

Despite the fact that Loren was not looking at him, Kohath nodded his response and didn't say a word. The silence was shattered almost immediately by the sound of a warning claxon.

It was a proximity alert.

Kohath spun and punched one of the controls on the main view screen. The image on the screen spun, leaving the dull red of Rahe's Paradise and wheeling through space, dragging the stars into parallaxes of motion. But he couldn't see anything that might have triggered the alarm.

'What in the Emperor's name was that?' barked Kohath, turning back to his command crew. The claxon was still sounding, and a ruddy red light was pulsing on the deck.

Nobody replied, as all heads bowed earnestly over their terminals, frantically searching for some sign of a vessel that had managed to slip past all of the *Ravenous Spirit*'s long range sensors.

'I have nothing,' responded Loren at last, looking up from the glowing screen on his terminal with an expression of consternation on his face. 'There's nothing there,' he paraphrased, as though repeating it would make it seem more plausible.

'Of course there's something there!' bellowed Kohath. 'Look harder! You–' He pointed at one of the other serfs, sitting just beyond Loren at one of the terminals that had just been repaired. There was still the faint stain of blood on the floor around his seat.

'Me, sergeant?'

'Yes, you. What's your name?'

'Krayem, sergeant.'

'Very well, Krayem, what do you have for me?'

The helmsman looked down at the green, glowing screen in front of him and then back up at the Marine. 'There is something. Little more than a light distortion, but its path appears to taken it directly past our starboard side.'

'Can you track it, Krayem?' asked Kohath, repeating the name to imprint it in his brain. Loren had turned out to be useless.

'I think so, sergeant,' replied Krayem, glancing back down at the tiny shimmer on the screen. 'But it is moving very fast. Very fast.'

'Don't make excuses, just do it,' said Kohath, bringing his view screen round to match the orientation of Krayem's terminal. Sure enough, there was something there – as though a ghost-ship were skirting along the edge of reality.

'Is this the same vessel that attacked us before?' asked Kohath, squinting his eyes into the darkness, his voice grating with aggression.

'I don't think so, sergeant.' It was a nameless serf. 'The sensor signatures are different. This one is getting stronger all the time, as though it were moving towards us.'

Kohath stared at the screen without acknowledging the new intelligence. Whatever it was, it was moving away from the *Ravenous Spirit*, not towards it. But something was happening – it was as though it were gradually taking shape in front of his eyes. It was becoming less intangible and less ghostly. It looked for all the world like it was being born into the vacuum of space for the first time, as though gradually emerging from a different dimension. As it started to take on a more substantial form, it seemed to slow down, giving the impression that it could not sustain its incredible speed in the universe of the here and now.

'By the Father, what is that thing?' asked Kohath, staring as though transfixed as the elegant craft gradually resolved into its final form – a long, slender vessel with massive, swooping star-sails along three axes. At its prow, a graceful command deck protruded in the form of a crescent, with massive cannons mounted on each forward-facing point.

'Sergeant, we are being hailed by Sergeant Saulh from the *Rage of Erudition*,' chirped Loren, reluctant to interrupt the present drama but pleased to have a simple function to fulfil.

'What? Saulh? Where is he?' snapped Kohath, dragging his eyes away from the miraculous birth outside.

'The other signature, Sergeant Kohath. The one on the edge of the system – it is Sergeant Saulh aboard the strike cruiser *Rage of Erudition*.'

For a moment Kohath paused. He had received no word from Captain Ulantus that a Ninth Company strike cruiser was en route. In fact, he had received no communiqués from the *Litany of Fury* since they had entered orbit around Rahe's Paradise. It was well-known that the space in that sector made astropathic communication particularly difficult, and the distant position of the planet made conventional modes of communication so slow as to be almost worthless. It was often quicker to take the message yourself.

As he was pondering the arrival of Saulh, Kohath saw a school of fighter-drones pour out of the newly born vessel off his starboard side. They teemed out into space and banked around in a giant shoal, bringing their weapons to bear against the *Ravenous Spirit*. At the same time, sheets of las-fire erupted from the gun batteries that ran along the side of the long, elegant ship itself. No sooner had it opened fire than its fighters also opened up, spraying the shields of the *Ravenous Spirit* with a tirade of las-bolts. As all this happened, the mother vessel itself started to bank around, presumably to bring its main frontal cannons into play.

'Emperor damn it!' yelled Kohath, barking orders off to the command crew, demanding evasive manoeuvres, increased shielding, return fire, and the launch of the Cobra gunships. 'Tell Saulh he is most welcome. Then tell him to haul his guns over here right now!'

THE ENTITY THAT *attacked your psyker was but a wraith, a shadow of the Yngir, Gabriel. He spoke their name. And the blast in the desert was merely a warning. You must not underestimate this enemy. Our needs bring us together once again.*

Gabriel tried to ignore the persistent whisperings in his mind as the group pressed on through one of the tunnels that dropped down away from the lava-encircled pit in the foundations of the monastery. In places the passageway narrowed so much that the group was forced to press into single file, and it was in such places that the lack of trust between them became evident. Nobody wanted to permit the others to walk behind them, but nobody wanted to let the other lead the way. In the end, Gabriel and

Macha took the lead, walking close on each others heels. Then came Jonas and Druinir, with the others falling in behind. It was an unquiet company.

We must be careful with the psykers, Gabriel, for the Yngir will sense their movements and feel their presence. They will recoil from the fragrance of the warp, but in recoiling they will wake. And when they wake they will hunger and thirst for the warmth of the lives that woke them. But our lives will not be enough, and the Sons of Asuryan are no longer numerous enough to hold them at bay. They are the Great Enemy: we will cease to ever have been as the universe becomes severed from its own memories – so it has been written.

'Quiet,' snapped Gabriel, glaring at Macha and making the others start. Everyone thought that they were already walking in silence.

The winding tunnels were shrouded in shadows, but a faint red light seeped into them from veins of lava that flowed through the walls. The temperature was hot and the confines of the narrow spaces were stuffy with sulphur dioxide and wisps of methane. The passageways appeared to have been cut by machines in places, where they were perfectly tubular. But elsewhere they were little more than cracks and crevices in the planet's crust. From time to time the group encountered great, gaping cracks in the floor, where the rock had shifted over the millennia and rent the passageways into fractions. Through the cracks poured clouds of noxious gases, and molten rock bubbled audibly down below.

They had seen a couple more black pyramids like the one it the lava-pit, and Macha had explained that they were markers, defining the perimeter of the

Yngir catacombs. The sentinel eldar had fashioned them out of the Yngir's own thirsting materials and technologies, rendering them into conductors of psychic energy, which absorbed any unusual warp discharge in their vicinity, acting to further insulate the slumbering creatures within from any fluctuations in the warp signature around the planet.

There had been other artefacts too. Some control terminals had been dug into the concave walls, forming little alcoves and side chambers off the main route. The dials and readouts had ceased functioning centuries before, perhaps even millennia before. Some of them lay half-melted and half-buried beneath solidified lava flows, as though they had grown into the walls and become fused with the inorganic structure of the catacombs themselves. Most of these devices bore the eerie imprint of eldar design, but some of them seemed almost familiar to the Blood Ravens.

Macha and her warlocks had taken it all in their stride, as though they were expecting to find the tunnel network exactly as it was. For Gabriel, however, everything was alien and almost impossibly ancient; he was unnerved by the casual disregard of the farseer towards these relics from a forgotten past. It was as though the eldar saw such things every day. Jonas was wide-eyed at the extent of the labyrinth that had been uncovered below his excavations, and amazed by the artefacts that they were studiously ignoring.

Taking another couple of steps, Gabriel emerged first into a cavernously wide chamber. Stairs had been cut into the uneven floor, and the expanse of the cavern was on a number of different levels. Flights of stone steps led up to little platforms, each of which ringed and overlooked a central pedestal. The light was faint and red, just as it was in the tunnels, but here it glowed down from the high-domed ceiling in a constant and even ruddiness. Looking up as the rest of the group pushed past him into the cavern, Gabriel saw that the entire ceiling was laced with veins of flowing lava, as though they were running over an impossibly resilient glass roof.

'Gabriel, you should take a look at this,' called Jonas from the bottom of the nearest flight of stairs.

Striding to the top of the steps, Gabriel peered down at Jonas's find. It was a body. A long, elegant humanoid body, still sealed into its jet-black suit of body armour. Indeed, it may have been only the armour.

Leave it alone, human. The voice was powerful and deep, blunt and forceful in a way that Macha's was not. Druinir had drawn up next to Gabriel and was staring down at Jonas with his burning eyes only partly concealed below his hood. *You will not sully our dead with your stench.*

'Here's another one,' called Ptolemea. She was crouching to her knees next to a different flight of steps, having dropped down to the lowest level. Apparently she was making her way towards the centre of the cavern. The Celestians had deployed themselves around her position, securing it silently.

There will be many bodies, Gabriel. But they are not your concern. Macha had descended to the lowest level of the cavern and made her way over to its centre where she was already striding up a narrow staircase towards one of the precarious little viewing platforms that overlooked the elevated pedestal in the heart of the chamber. She did not turn to face the Blood Raven, and she showed no signs of having seen what the others had found, but her thoughts pressed firmly into Gabriel's mind.

'Leave them,' said Gabriel, slowly and deliberately, directing his remarks to both Jonas and Ptolemea. 'Secure the chamber.'

Even as his words were still echoing around the cavern, a shrill cry made everyone turn, searching for the source. It didn't take long to identify it.

Up on one of the balconies on the far side of the cavern, one of the eldar warlocks was emitting a hideous, keening scream. He was surrounded by a cackling blue energy field, which was spitting and sparking as though short-circuiting, and he seemed to be levitating a few metres above the ledge. For a couple of seconds, nobody could understand what was happening. But then there was a shimmer, like a phase shift, and a grotesque floating form appeared behind the eldar. It had an elongated spinal column that whipped up into a spiny, dragon-like tail, and its skull-like face leered down over the warlock, which now appeared skewered on two long, barbed spikes that seemed to protrude like arms from the beast's wide, skeletal shoulders.

Wraith. The thought was solid, definite, and tinged with urgency.

As one, the Celestian Sisters opened up with their bolters, sending a unified salvo smashing into the location of the hideous creature. At the same time, Druinir launched himself off the ledge next to

Gabriel, and started to sprint across the wide floor of the chamber, bursts of crackling warp-fire lashing out of his fingertips towards his hapless brethren.

But the wraith just seemed to fade away, as though drifting out of phase once again. The Celestians' bolter shells tore through its shadow and impacted against the wall behind it, exploding into showers of shrapnel that ricocheted back into the thrashing warlock.

A second later and it reappeared, still clutching at the eldar psyker with the blades and scalpels that constituted its arms. But this time Druinir was ready for it, vaulting up onto the balcony and thrusting his hand through the semi-material substance of the beast's spine. There was a deafening shriek as the wraith threw back its head and brayed, dropping the warlock from its metallic talons. Then the beast simply exploded, as though it could not bear to be touched by Druinir. Vast streams of energy poured down the warlock's arm, filling the apparitional form of the wraith with dazzling warp energy until it could hold no more. Then it exploded into a rain of light, showering down from the balcony like a waterfall.

Druinir stooped down to the broken form of the other warlock, checking his vital signs. An instant later, he stood up and made a signal to Macha in the centre of the room, drawing his finger across his throat to indicate that the warlock was dead.

CALEB'S BIKE SKIDDED and bounced over the sand dunes, weaving in and out between sleets of shuriken fire and exploding craters. As he closed on the jet-black Wave Serpent, he could see the valiant efforts of the local fighters as they clambered all over the nearly impregnable armour of the eldar transporter, clattering against it with their dulling blades.

A bolt of energy slammed into the front of his bike as he crested the last dune. It shattered the front weapons and lifted the wheel clear off the ground, throwing Caleb back. The rear wheel spun as it dug down into the sand, suddenly bearing the entire weight of the bike and Marine. Then it gripped abruptly, pushing the rear of the bike forward and under the front, turning the bike over in a flurry of sand. Caleb fell back off the saddle and then rolled clear as the bike came crashing down.

Scrambling to his feet, the scout checked behind him and realised for the first time that he was the only member of his squad to have made it this far. The main battle was still raging behind him, and he could see clearly see the inferno of destruction that ringed Tanthius and his Terminator squadron in the heart of the theatre.

Tugging his bolter out of its holster, Caleb started down the other side of the dune, snapping off shots against the Wave Serpent as he went, being careful not to hit the other human warriors that were swarming all over the vehicle.

'For the Great Father,' he muttered under his breath.

As the Wave Serpent pitched violently to one side, trying to find an angle for another blast at the monastery, a hatch opened up at the back, folding down onto the ground, and a squad of black-clad eldar warriors came storming out. They didn't even pause to take aim, but instantly turned and started

spraying the outside of the Wave Serpent with projectiles from their reaper launchers.

Before Caleb could do anything, two or three of the
local warriors were already dead. They lost their grip
on the transporter as their limbs were lacerated by
fire from the Dark Reapers, falling helplessly into the
sand where they were crushed under the antigravitic
field of the vehicle itself.

Caleb loosed a volley from his bolter, and watched
one of the eldar warriors stumble and fall as the shell
punched through the armour on his leg. Immediately, a youth with blond braids saw his chance and
leapt off the roof of the Wave Serpent, crashing down
onto the wounded eldar and driving his blade down
through the hairline seal at the base of the alien's
helmet.

But this was not a battle that the primitive human
warriors could win, and Caleb was fully aware that
he could not hold off a squadron of Aspect Warriors
all by himself.

As though triggered by a sudden and secret signal,
the locals leapt clear of the eldar vehicle and ran.
They scattered in all directions, leaving the eldar
unsure about which way to fire. And, by the time the
Dark Reapers had organised themselves, the local
warriors had vanished.

Caleb shared the eldar's amazement as he scanned
the desert for some sign of the human fighters. One
moment they had been running through the sand,
and the next they had gone, as though swallowed up
by the desert itself.

After a couple of seconds, Caleb's amazement was
replaced by resolve as he realised that he was now the

only fighter left to confront the eldar squadron and the Wave Serpent. One by one, the Aspect Warriors turned to face him, as they too realised that he was their last target. Even the secondary gun turrets on the transporter tracked round to his position.

'For the Great Father and the Emperor!' he yelled, stepping forward and letting loose with his bolter. If this was going to be his end, he would make it something worthy of the Blood Ravens.

The last thing he saw was the report of nine reaper launchers as their muzzles flashed with discharge. Then everything went black.

MACHA PAUSED, LOOKING down from her elevated position, half way up one of the staircases in the centre of the chamber, and an aura of tension and trepidation seemed to emanate from her. It was as though she were holding her breath. Druinir's poise matched that of the farseer. They were waiting for something.

No more. Macha was decisive. She could feel something shifting in the atmosphere of the catacombs. *No more warp casting, Druinir. We cannot risk waking more of the Yngir. Lsathranil's Shield cannot nullify our presence within the catacombs themselves – assuming that it is still functioning, at least partially.*

I understand, farseer.

Gabriel. Inform your librarian not to use his staff. His clumsiness may cause more damage than good.

The captain looked up at Macha, fixing her with his narrowed eyes. Did she really think that she could talk to him like that? He was not her lackey, and he would not stand for the dispersions that she cast on

Jonas. In the entire Blood Ravens Chapter, there were only a handful of librarians more experienced than Jonas Urelie.

As he glowered up towards the farseer, she simply turned away from him and continued to make her way up the stone steps towards one of the elevated platforms. Either she was unaware of the offence that her arrogance was causing the Blood Ravens, or she didn't care. Whatever the case, Gabriel grated his teeth in annoyance as he realised that he had little choice but to listen to the alien witch – neither he nor Jonas understood the nature of the enemy that they faced. Having followed the eldar farseer this far, it would be irrational to doubt her instruction now. Despite the logic of the situation, Gabriel hated his conclusion.

'Jonas. We must not disturb the slumbering enemy – stow your staff.' He called the request down to the floor of the cavern, making the librarian look up.

'As you command, captain,' replied Jonas, nodding smartly and making it clear that he was obeying Gabriel rather than anyone else. 'But you had better tell those warlocks to do the sa–'

Before he could finish, a stutter of bolter fire erupted from the knot of Battle Sisters that had collected around Ptolemea. The little golden group was flanked on both sides by huge arachnoid creatures that scuttled in aggressive agitation, twitching their long, flexible metallic limbs and stabbing forward with their front legs, lancing them towards the Sisters of Battle like spears. Under their dark hooded carapaces, hundreds of tiny, glittering eyes shone out in dizzying patterns.

As Gabriel vaulted down from his ledge and charged across towards the fray, he realised that the tomb spyders had emerged from previously hidden alcoves cut into the stonework around the central pedestal in the cavern. It was as though they were guarding it.

The Celestian Sisters were ablaze with fire as Gabriel arrived, each parrying the thrashing arachnid legs with their blades and lashing back at the spidery forms with volleys of bolter fire, which seemed to bounce harmlessly off the hardened carapaces. Ptolemea was also alive with action, leaping and flipping away from the metallic limbs, and hacking into them with her own blades.

With an abrupt crunch, one of the arachnid legs punctured the stomach of a Golden Sister, lifting her off her feet and into the air. The Celestian did not cry out or yell as the cold, alien talon skewered her abdomen: all that Gabriel could hear was a sharp intake of breath. She didn't even break the rhythm of her fire, as her bolter continued to cough and splutter against the armoured shell of the creature. Her Sisters turned their weapons onto the offending spyder, momentarily ignoring the other one – leaving it to Gabriel and Jonas, who had just come storming in with his bolter flaring.

As the spyder's legs thrashed and interlaced, Ptolemea saw her chance and sprung forward, grasping hold of one of its legs and flinging herself up onto the back of the giant insectoid. Once there, she instantly unclasped one of the long blades that was strapped to her thigh and drove it down into the creature's carapace, cracking it open with sheer will power. Using the blade's hilt as a piton, she then threw herself around in front of the ghastly arachnid, swinging from one arm only a metre away from the hundreds of eyes that were hidden under its armoured hood. With her other arm, she unholstered the antique pistol that she had taken from Meritia's chamber and levelled it into the spyder's reeling eyes.

'For the Order and the Emperor,' she whispered, squeezing the trigger and watching the explosive shells punch directly into the creature's face.

The impacts made the giant spyder shudder and twitch, staggering back under the point-blank onslaught. It thrashed its legs wildly, casting the skewered Battle Sister off one of its talons and sending her skidding to the ground. Then a series of little explosions strafed along under its carapace, as though Ptolemea had started a chain-reaction. After a couple of seconds, a tremendous keening erupted from the beast and its power-core detonated, blowing the grotesque spyder into lethal metallic shards.

As Ptolemea pulled herself back onto her feet, she saw the ruined remains of the creature spread out over the ground. The second spyder was still twitching with the last remnants of its life, but its legs were all shattered and its belly was pressed helplessly into the dirt. Father Jonas was standing on its back with his force staff plunged deeply into its innards. He muttered a few words and a brilliant light pulsed for a fraction of second, then the beast exploded into a metallic rain.

Looking up, Ptolemea could see the figure of Gabriel already striding up the steps towards the eldar farseer, who was nearly at the platform at the top of stairs. Propped up against the bottom steps, Ptolemea could see the heroic Celestian Sister with blood coursed out of the gaping wound in her stomach. Dropping down onto her knees in front of her, Ptolemea checked the Battle Sister for signs of life, but she was dead.

'Sister Ptolemea,' said Jonas, striding over towards her, as though taking her into his confidence. 'These spiders – I have heard stories of them before.'

Ptolemea stood to her feet and bowed silently to the dead Celestian before turning to face the librarian. 'Yes,' she agreed. 'They are described in the *Apocrypha of the Nightbringer*. It is a forbidden text,' she continued, eying the librarian with a mixture of distrust and confession.

'Are they not described as tomb spyders, as guardians of their master's tombs?' asked Jonas.

'Yes, they are thought to protect the enshrined remains of unspeakably ancient lords – a lost species known as the necron. I have never heard of anyone actually confronting a living example,' said Ptolemea, looking around the chamber for signs of further threats. Something told her that there would be more than two of these things. As though to confirm her suspicions, she saw the two remaining warlocks patrolling the perimeter.

'Necron. Yngir?' wondered Jonas out loud. 'Do you suppose that the ancient eldar buried a necron lord in these catacombs?' he asked, drawing the evidence together into an exciting conclusion.

As one, Ptolemea and Jonas looked up towards the figure of Macha as she approached the platform at

the top of the long flight of steps. Gabriel was nearly
running now, trying to catch up with her.

BETWEEN THEM, THE two Blood Ravens strike cruisers
easily outclassed the single Dragon-class eldar
cruiser. Their heavy weapons batteries were pounding at the alien's armoured shielding, and the fleet of
Cobra gunships that had emptied out of the launch
bays of both the *Ravenous Spirit* and the *Rage of Erudition* were engaging the Shadowhunter escorts two
to one.

'Sergeant Kohath?' crackled a voice over the vox
link, as the image of a Blood Raven sergeant flickered
onto the view screen.

'Ah yes, Sergeant Saulh. Good of you to join us,'
replied Kohath calmly. His confidence had returned
as the tide of the battle had tipped clearly in his
favour. He was not fond of space battles – like most
Space Marines, he preferred to meet the Emperor's
enemies with his feet on the ground and a bolter in
his hands – but victory always had a sweet taste.

'It seems that Captain Angelos was correct about
the eldar, sergeant,' said Saulh, a look of earnest concern darkening his features.

'Of course,' replied Kohath simply. Taking note of
the other's expression, he continued. 'Were you not
sent to offer assistance in the battle on the surface,
sergeant?'

'No, Kohath. I was sent to request the assistance of
the Third Company in the Lorn system. Captain Ulantus is en route as we speak, but the *Litany of Fury* is
experiencing some problems in the warp. He sent me
to request that Captain Angelos cut short the trials on

Rahe's Paradise and make speed to Lorn V. The green-skins are already on the ground, and it appears that an eldar fleet will arrive shortly.'

More eldar? The significance of the coincidence struggled to resolve itself in Kohath's mind.

'As you can see, Saulh, we have our hands full here at the moment. I don't think that the captain will be sending any assistance today. Besides,' added Kohath, faintly amused by the request after Ulantus had been so disparaging about Gabriel's departure for Rahe's Paradise, 'I have not been able to make any contact with the captain for several hours. Something is interfering with our signals down to the planet.'

Saulh nodded. 'Yes, we were also unable to make contact with you after you entered this system. Hence my presence now.'

'What is your complement of Marines, sergeant?' asked Kohath, aware that he was basically on his own aboard the *Ravenous Spirit*.

'Just one squad. The rest of the Ninth are still aboard the *Litany*, en route to Lorn V.'

'Understood. After we have dispatched these aliens, perhaps you would be kind enough to send a landing party down to the surface to inform Captain Angelos of the situati–'

'Sergeant!,' yelled Loren, cutting him off. 'Incoming!'

Kohath punched the controls of the view screen, vaporising the image of Saulh and replacing it with an external view. He could see that the *Rage of Erudition* had seen the new arrivals already. The cruiser was pitching around to face the two charging vessels, and a flurry of torpedoes had already been loosed from its frontal batteries. But the alien vessels were faster, and flashes of las-fire were already streaking towards the two Blood Ravens vessels. At the same time, shoals of little fighters were pouring out of the two new vessels, filling the surrounding space with darting flecks of light.

'Return fire!' commanded Kohath. 'And brace for impact,' he added, making sure that his priorities were correct.

One of the las-bolts struck the *Ravenous Spirit* square on its nose, rocking the command deck and reigniting the fires that been extinguished only hours before. But the torpedoes were away, and Kohath saw them punch into the side of the jet-black eldar cruiser as it banked and started to pull away from the combat zone, presumably preparing for another attack run. The other newcomer was ablaze with light already, as though made out of pure energy. It swooped and fluttered like a giant phoenix, spitting out gouts of warp fire into the gyring confusion of the dogfights that now raged all around.

'Tell me that these were the signatures that we saw before!' yelled Kohath, without turning to the nameless serf. This was already more than he had bargained for, and the possibility that there was another eldar cruiser out there in the darkness filled him with trepidation.

'One of them is, yes sergeant,' came the reply. 'The other one doesn't seem to have a signature at all.'

'Great,' muttered Kohath as the *Ravenous Spirit* came about, and the starboard weapons batteries opened up once again, shredding the surrounding space with explosive shells and sheets of las-fire.

On the view screen, Kohath could see that the *Rage of Erudition* had evaded the first attack from the incoming eldar, and it was charging off in the wake of the jet-black Void Dragon that Kohath had hit, spraying its hide with las-fire and sending volleys of torpedoes chasing in its wake.

Meanwhile, the *Ravenous Spirit* was caught in between the two other cruisers and the fighter swarms were massing around it.

'Damn it,' snapped Kohath, as he started to wish he was on the ground with a bolter once again. 'I guess that Lorn will have to wait a bit longer.'

WATCHING THE VIEW screen without satisfaction, Uldreth, Exarch of the Dire Avengers, glowered. He felt as though he had been tricked into coming to Lsathranil's Shield. He had not forbidden Macha to leave – and would not have been able to even had he desired to do so. And he had not been able to prevent that untrustworthy Dark Reaper from escorting the farseer. But he had been adamant that the resources of the Bahzhakhain would not be misdirected on this futile flight of fantasy. The rest of the Seer Council had been clear about the threat posed in the Lorn system. That was the location of greatest need.

He had been adamant, but never certain. Passion and truth make uncomfortable partners in the eldar mind.

Having watched Macha and Laeresh vanish into the webway, and then seeing Taldeer take the Bahzhakhain in the opposite direction towards Lorn, Uldreth had cursed himself. He had cursed his decisions. He had cursed his indecisiveness. He had cursed the fact that it

was down to him to make these decisions, but cursed
even more the idea that somebody else might have
done better.

Finally, alone in meditation in his private chambers, high up in one of the aspiring spires of Biel-Tan
itself, Uldreth had cursed himself for being so passionate and so blind. No matter what the history was
between himself and Macha, he should not let it
interfere with the security of Biel-Tan or with the
responsibilities handed down through the Court of
the Young King. If he were honest with himself, he
could not even remember the source of the tension
between the three of them – his passions raged in a
rootless and dangerous way. He just knew that
Laeresh and Macha drove him to distraction.

So, Uldreth had organised a force from his own
Aspect Temple and set out in the wake of Macha and
Laeresh, guiding his Ghost Dragon cruiser through
the labyrinthine webways himself. If there was even
the slightest chance that Macha's visions foreshad-
owed the future, then he had no choice but to act on
them. That is what it meant to be the future. He muttered and grumbled all the way, realising that it took
a separation of days and light-years for him to deign
to agree with Laeresh on that point.

When he had entered the system and seen the
mon'keigh strike cruiser unchallenged in orbit around
the key planet, his rage had been heightened once
again. He reasoned that it could mean only one of two
things: either the mon'keigh had destroyed Macha and
Laeresh, which meant that he had let them go to their
deaths; or the unpredictable farseer had come to
Lsathranil's shield precisely to rendezvous with her pet

mon'keigh, which meant that Uldreth had been foolish to follow her after all.

Unable to raise Macha with any type of communication, he had charged into battle immediately,
calculating that destroying the mon'keigh cruiser
would resolve his problem either way. In his rage, he
hadn't even noticed the arrival of the second pedestrian vessel on the edge of system.

Finally, when he was beginning to realise that even
his *Avenging Sword* could not stand against two
mon'keigh strike cruisers simultaneously, the *Eternal
Star* and the *Reaper's Blade* had emerged from the
dark side of the planet and engaged the enemy, turning the tide of the battle once again. To his disgust,
however, this meant that they had been in orbit the
whole time, and that they had suffered the aliens to
live. He discovered from their pilots that Macha herself had ordered them not to attack the humans until
they received further word from her. But they had
heard nothing since she had descended to the
planet's surface, and they could not stand by and
watch an eldar Ghost Dragon struggling for its life.

Uldreth cursed again – things didn't appear to have
become any simpler since his arrival. As usual, proximity to the farseer made everything seem very
complicated. As the space battle raged around him,
Uldreth's mind raged with unquiet thoughts: the old
Fire Dragon, Draconir, had been right after all –
Macha's vision had been realised despite the decision
of the Court to ignore it – Uldreth had lost his wager
with the fiery exarch, and now he must win the war
against these filthy mon'keigh.

* * *

TANTHIUS STOPPED. DESPITE the jumble of combat in between them, he could see the grotesquely beautiful eldar exarch clearly, its bone-white plumes fluttering dramatically in the desert wind. The two massive warriors glared at each other across the fray, unperturbed by the rest of the battle, focussing their intent on each other. The other combatants seemed to steer clear of them, leaving little pockets of clarity in the sand and glass around each of them, as though the rest of the combatants knew that these warriors were destined for each other.

For a moment they were motionless, as though preparing themselves for what was to come. Then, with movements meant to be so imperceptible that the other would not really be able to discern them, they both nodded fractionally – conceding these hints of respect for the finest warrior on each side of the conflict.

Tanthius grinned, unaware of the sickly smile that creased the face of his opponent at the same time.

'For the Great Father and the Emperor,' he murmured under his breath, still not moving.

As Laeresh watched the mon'keigh machine-warrior, he could not help but be impressed by its composure. It was certainly a magnificent sight, ablaze in the reds and golds of its kind, towering out of the frenzy of combat like a beacon in a tumultuous sea. A worthy opponent – even Macha could not deny him this battle. He lived for moments like this, but they came so very infrequently. The last time that he could remember the thrill of not knowing whether he would prevail in battle he was facing a daemon prince of Slaanesh – against whom there was much more at stake than merely victory or defeat. Today, facing the undeniable might of a Blood Ravens Terminator, Laeresh once again felt the keening of war in his soul. Once again, he could hear the whispered words of Maugan Ra, the Harvester of Souls – *war is my master, death my mistress*. For the first time in decades, those words resounded through his being, as though filling him with the power of the Phoenix Lord himself.

The decadent courtier Uldreth Avenger was not his master, and the beautiful Macha was not his mistress. He was Laeresh, exarch of the Dark Reapers, and he answered to nobody but fate itself.

'War is my master,' he murmured, bringing his reaper cannon into both hands, his incisors stabbing down into his smiling lower lip and drawing trickles of blood down his chin. 'Death is my mistress,' he hissed, squeezing the trigger at exactly the same moment as he saw the flashing report of the storm bolter in the Terminator's hand.

IT WAS CLEAR that the alien witch knew what she was doing. She had made her way up the stone steps towards that platform as soon as she had entered the cavern, and Gabriel was not about to let her get away with any kind of trickery. He may have agreed to co-operate for the purposes of this sortie into the catacombs, but that did not mean that he trusted her. Even as the last of the tomb spyders were dying on the cavern floor, Gabriel was running up the steps towards Macha.

When he was halfway up, a call from Jonas made him pause and turn. The old librarian had left the remains of the arachnids and was patrolling the floor; he had found something. He was squatting down on the ground behind a bank of machines, inspecting something laid out on the floor. From where he was, Gabriel could just about make out a pair of dirty red boots sticking out the side of the bank. He activated the vox-bead, but a rush a static squealed into his ear and he snapped it off again. With his hand, he signalled to Jonas that he would be back shortly, and then he turned to continue his way up the steps. As he climbed, he couldn't shake the thought that there did seem to be something unusual about those boots.

To his surprise, he was caught by the athletic, sprinting figure of Ptolemea before he reached the top. They shared a silent glance and the two of them approached Macha together.

The farseer was inspecting an ancient and arcane control panel that protruded from the stone in the floor of the platform. It still appeared to have power, and the dials glowed with a faint light. A series of switches were blinking, but they were marked with runes that Gabriel could not read.

Macha clicked the switches, and a hum started up in the distance, like a generator coming on line. Gradually, the lights under the control dials grew brighter, until they shed light up into the farseer's alien beauty. Then the chamber itself started to grow lighter, as though artificial lights that had been fixed into the walls at some forgotten time in the past were being revived.

The device has been dormant for centuries, whispered Macha's thoughts. *Without maintenance work, it failed ages ago. You should have taken better care of it, Gabriel. Its protective field – this psychic prison – has been gradually decaying all this time. It is a wonder that the Yngir did not ascend centuries ago.*

She clicked a few more switches and the cavern burst into brightness. In the distance, all around, the hum of power coursing through ancient circuits could be heard.

I pray that we are not too late.

As the light flooded around the cavern, the pedestal in the middle of the room started to rise up towards the three figures on the platform. It spiralled gently as it rose, as though unscrewing itself from the ground. For the first time, Gabriel noticed that a large, black sarcophagus was resting in the middle of it, shimmering with an ineffable light. It was longer than a man or an eldar, but otherwise seemed to be shaped for a vaguely human occupant.

After a few seconds, the sarcophagus reached the same height as the platform, and Macha stepped forward onto the stone pedestal that supported it. She stooped over the glimmering sarcophagus, running her fingers gingerly over its surface as though checking it for breaches, cracks or blemishes. It was perfectly smooth, without any ornamentation of any kind on its surface. There was not a single mark, rune or hieroglyph. It was the simplest, purest and least ornamented object that they had seen in the entire complex. But under the surface, swimming like fish in the depths of a black ocean, runes and purity seals flashed and curdled, flowing around the casket like streams of other-worldly power.

Macha rose and turned back to the other two, her face calm with relief.

He is yet undisturbed.

As her thoughts slipped into their minds, the new light in the cavern suddenly dimmed. At the same time, a javelin of blue flashed out of Macha's eyes and plunged into Gabriel's face, making him stagger back in shock. The stream pulsed continuously, holding Gabriel upright and binding him to the farseer. Almost at once, the beam split and a pulse shot into Ptolemea's eyes, uniting the three of them into a single pulsing triangle. For a few seconds, the triangle was unbroken, and a flood of images coursed around it, filling their heads with dying stars, vortexes of darkness, and screams from the dying in an epic space battle: a darkly glittering humanoid figure hovered momentarily in front of the sun.

Then the triangle of energy fizzled out and the three slumped to the ground, dazed and confused; not even Macha seemed to know what had happened. After a few more seconds, the lights went up again in the cavern and everything seemed stable.

Gabriel climbed to his feet, shaking his head to clear his thoughts and to ensure his balance. Ptolemea had lost consciousness at his feet, and Macha seemed weakened by the unexpected ordeal. With an unanticipated feeling of compassion, Gabriel reached down and helped Macha to her feet. Then he picked Ptolemea up with his other arm, and the three of them set off down the long, narrow staircase.

When they reached the bottom, Jonas was waiting. 'Captain, before we leave, I really think that you should look at this,' he said, his face animated and excited.

'What is it, Jonas? We really must leave now,' said Gabriel wearily. Although he could not explain why, his soul was tired. And he was certain that they needed to get off Rahe's Paradise before any more damage was done.

Macha said nothing as Druinir took her off Gabriel's arm. She looked gaunt and weak, and she hung off the warlock like a dead weight.

'It's a suit of armour,' explained Jonas, indicating the figure that he had found behind the bank of machines. 'It was a Space Marine.'

CHAPTER THIRTEEN
REAPER

'Is HE ALRIGHT?' The voice was faint – not distant, just whispered in the darkness.

'I'm not sure. How can you tell?' The reply was closer.

There were at least two people in the darkness around him, but Caleb felt sure that he could sense the presence of a larger number. For some reason, his occulobe was malfunctioning again, and he could not make out any shapes in the poor light. He could only just see the narrow confines of the curving walls that reached around him. He was lying on the ground, but did not quite fit in the width of the space, so he was partly propped up against one of the sloping walls. Where in the Father's name was he? For the time being, he decided not to move.

'Does he have a pulse?'

'I can't feel one. He seems to be made out of some kind of metal.'

Small hands were wrapped around his right wrist, as though searching for a pulse in his armoured gauntlet. After a moment or two, the hands started to move towards his bolter, which he could still feel clenched into his fist.

'I don't think so,' snapped Caleb, forcing himself upright and snatching his weapon across to where he imagined the face of his captor to be.

To his surprise, Caleb caught a faint glimpse of a young face in the shadows as a beam of light reflected off his bolter. It quickly recoiled away from him, vanishing into the darkness, but it left a vivid impression in his mind: it was one of the youths that had been attacking the Wave Serpent – the one with the blond braids who had finished off one of the Aspect Warriors with a dagger.

'Where am I?' asked Caleb, looking about blindly, hoping that the boy would recognise him as an ally. He lowered his bolter to the ground and tried to stand, but the ceiling of the confined tunnel was too low and he ended up stooped over into an uncomfortable hunch.

'You're under the desert, Sky Angel,' came the faceless reply from the darkness. 'In one of the old tunnels.'

Caleb looked around him, his eyes still not adjusting to the dark. Nonetheless, he could see the truth of it. Holding out his arms to his sides, he could feel the curving walls of the narrow, tubular tunnel. Judging by the sound of his voice, the local warrior-boy was crouched in the shadows just south of him. With a sudden motion, Caleb shot out his left hand and caught the boy by his neck, lifting him off his feet and bringing him closer to his own face.

'How did I get here?' he asked, almost whispering.

'You fell, Sky Angel,' answered the youth, his wide green eyes flashing with excitement, not fear. 'You fell into one of the access shoots.'

Of course, he had been on the cusp of death, facing a squad of Aspect Warriors in the desert; he had taken a bounding step towards his foe and then fallen straight down into the desert. Thinking back, Caleb remembered that the local warriors themselves had vanished mysteriously shortly before, presumably by making use of similar tunnels under the desert.

The scout sergeant nodded. 'What's your name, boy?'

'I am called Varjak, Sky Angel,' replied the youth, still dangling from Caleb's fist. 'These are my battle-brothers,' he added, gesturing behind him with his arm.

'I am Scout Sergeant Caleb of the Blood Ravens, Varjak,' said Caleb, placing the youth back on the ground. 'I should thank you for your assistance in this battle, but I must ask you for more help. Tell me, how extensive are these tunnels under the desert?'

TANTHIUS TWISTED TO the side and arched his back down towards the ground, letting the sleet of projectiles hiss past him. They scraped across the armoured plates on his chest, sizzling with toxic heat and inscribing gashes through the embossed raven's wings. He dropped his left hand to the ground behind him and caught his weight before he over-balanced, bringing his storm bolter around in his right hand at the same time and loosing an explosive response.

Pushing himself back up to his feet, Tanthius saw the exarch flip backwards as the volley of hellfire shells closed. The timing was immaculate: the darkly armoured eldar warrior leant back as the shells reached its chest, dropping its head and hands down to the ground behind it and letting the explosive rounds skim over its chest armour and slide just over its neck as it leant its head back. An instant later and its legs cycled over its handstand, bringing it back up onto its feet with its reaper cannon ready in its hands once again. Immediately, another burst of monomolecular projectiles lashed out of its weapon towards Tanthius.

The Terminator sergeant was getting frustrated by this ostentatious exchange, impressive though the alien was proving to be. They could exchange long-range fire like this all day; he had to find some way of closing the distance.

As he sidestepped the eldar hail, he squeezed off another volley from his storm bolter and broke into a run, trying to rein in the slippery exarch. But for every step forward taken by Tanthius, the eldar took one back, turning flips and summersaults to main-tain a constant distance. It seemed determined to conduct this fight at a range of a hundred metres, as though this was the only kind of combat it was com-fortable with. If the alien really wanted to keep the range constant so badly, then Tanthius was all the more determined to shorten it.

Storming forwards, Tanthius detached a clutch of grenades from his belt and lobbed them into a high curve, letting them pitch up over the eldar warrior as it flipped and turned underneath them, somehow slipping around every hellfire shell that whined past it. But Tanthius wasn't expecting to hit the alien with those shots.

As the grenades dropped down behind the tumbling exarch, the hellfire rounds that had slid past it stabbed into them, detonating them into a huge burst of flame and shrapnel, blasting a concussive wave into the charging figure of the Terminator and sending the incredibly elegant alien stumbling to a halt.

Taking his chance, Tanthius crashed forward through the other combatants in the field, wading through them with single-minded determination, ploughing on towards the temporarily stunned exarch, scattering eldar warriors as he went. With each stride he fired off volleys of shells from his bolter, trying to keep the alien tied down as he closed the range.

With about twenty metres still to go, the exarch finally recovered its composure and started to return fire. It was moving less smoothly than before, as though suffering some kind of concussion from the unexpected explosion, but it was still a match for the screeching ballistics of Tanthius.

The distance had closed, but Tanthius was still too far away to bring his powerfist into play or to make the most of his brute power. If anything, the situation was now worse for the huge Terminator, since he had reduced his own margin for error. The eldar exarch was a slender and dextrous creature, and the closer range did not prevent it from responding quickly enough to his fire. But Tanthius was heavy and even cumbersome in his Terminator suit; the reduced range made it almost impossible for him to move quickly enough to avoid the rapid fire of the alien. He had to close the final distance to capitalise on his strengths.

Suddenly dropping to its knees, the exarch levelled its reaper cannon and took careful aim. Seizing his opportunity, Tanthius charged forward, letting his bolter spit freely in barely controlled blasts as he stormed towards the stationary exarch. Twenty metres were rapidly reduced to ten, then five – and Tanthius primed his powerfist in anticipation – then the spray of projectiles from the alien's weapon slammed into his chest, arresting his forward motion and racking him with shards of agony.

For a second, Tanthius's vision blurred, as though the impacts had somehow interfered with the visual systems in his helmet. He stopped charging and lunged to the side, trying to throw off the alien's aim while he waited for his sight to return. Another constellation of burning shards slid through the flesh in his leg, passing through the ancient armour with incredible ease.

Thrashing out instinctively, Tanthius caught hold of a slender arm in the grip of his powerfist and yanked it into the air. Turning his bolter, he blasted into the suspended body, spending twenty explosive rounds into its abdomen before his helmet's vision finally crackled and settled back into place.

In an instant, he realised that the bloody stump of an eldar arm in his hand was not that of the exarch, and he cast it into the sea of battle with disgust. Another rain of toxic shards made him turn as they sunk into his ribcage. He brought his storm bolter around and returned fire instantly, without taking the time to aim precisely or even to check the line of sight – he simply refused to let the alien take unanswered shots at a Blood Ravens Terminator. The exarch was back on one knee with its weapon braced securely, but now it was nearly fifty metres away again.

Tanthius growled and then roared in defiance. He would not be outgunned by a slippery alien wretch – not even by a eldar exarch. Clicking his storm bolter onto full-manual, he took careful aim and squeezed off three shots, one to the creature's right, one directly at it, and the other just to its left. The staggered timing caught the exarch just as he had hoped: as the first shot sizzled past its face, the second made it twitch to its left, where the third punched straight into its shoulder, digging down into the psychoplastic armour and detonating into a cluster of vicious shards which shredded the alien's muscle.

'Game on,' grinned Tanthius, striding forward to close the gap once again, keeping his storm bolter trained on the creature and placing occasional shots to keep it out of its comfort zone.

THE SHADOWHUNTER ESCORT ships rolled and dived in breathtaking shoals, shimmering like tropical fish as they flicked through sunbeams and darted in between lances of las-fire. The Cobra gunboats that spiralled after them were no match for their speed or agility, and they were also outnumbered by the f. eet alien ships.

Through the view screen on the command deck of the *Ravenous Spirit*, Kohath watched the dogfights develop into a mist around his cruiser. Not for the first time, he wished that Gabriel had taken him down to the planet's surface with the landing party – space battles were not the perfect domain for the Adeptus Astartes, and he was not wholly comfortable. The *Spirit*'s Cobras were performing well, and their kill-rate appeared to be slightly better than that of the eldar; the sergeant was silently impressed at the abilities of the Third Company's pilot-serfs – desperation could make geniuses of anyone. However, the eldar would not be held off for long, and eventually their superior numbers and technology would prove decisive: something had to be done now.

The *Ravenous Spirit* was taking heavy punishment, trapped in between the firing solutions of two of the eldar cruisers. The command deck was already bathed in flames as a number of the control terminals burned. But Kohath had faith in the ancient machine spirit of his vessel – he knew that it would hold together long enough to take at least one of these xenos aberrations down with it. He was virtually the only Marine onboard, so even if he had to scuttle the venerable cruiser and ram it into one of the eldar boats, it would only cost the Chapter the gene-seed of a single Marine. For the first time, he was grateful that Gabriel had taken all the others down to the surface – their absence widened his tactical options in the last resort.

The ship was trembling and convulsing with constant fire, taking impacts on both sides and loosing torpedoes and las-fire in equal measure. The *Ravenous*

Spirit had been involved in innumerable battles in its time, and it had not survived this long by being fragile; its weapons batteries were ablaze like infernos along the length of either side, dousing the enemy cruisers with unrelenting tirades of violence. At the same time, Kohath was swinging the venerable vessel around in tight arcs, striving to bring its main frontal cannons into play, and hoping that the movement would throw off the targeting of the eldar weapons.

In the distance, through the quagmire of circling dogfights that surrounded the *Spirit* like a shroud, the sergeant could see the streaking shape of the *Rage of Erudition* still in pursuit of the jet-black alien cruiser, which appeared to have lost some power to its engines after Kohath had landed his torpedoes into its flank. Saulh was closing on it gradually, prowling after it like a lion stalking wounded prey.

As he watched, Kohath saw the black, eldar Dragon bank around and head back in towards the main combat zone, accelerating slightly as though starting an attack run. It seemed to be ignoring the *Rage of Erudition* completely, shrugging off its attacks as though they were merely petty annoyances, making no attempt to engage the hunter that stalked after it.

The intention of the eldar pilot was clear, and, on the bridge of the *Spirit*, Kohath nodded to himself in understanding. The wounded Dragon was doing exactly the same thing that Kohath himself had just been contemplating: assuming that its most valuable crew had already been dispatched down to the surface, the wounded, sleek vessel was offering and expecting no quarter. If it had to sacrifice itself to

destroy the humans and save its brethren, then it
would be done.

Nonetheless, Kohath was not about to let his own
vessel become the victim of such desperate but honourable tactics. It was already taking more damage
than it could possibly sustain and a full frontal
assault from the third cruiser might be the end of it
– its prow armour was already in shreds after the first
attacks by that same cruiser.

'Loren. Turn us ninety degrees to the port – let's see
what damage we can do to one of these other cruisers with our frontal arrays,' said Kohath slowly,
realising that the *Spirit* would not survive the attack
run from the closing Dragon cruiser, and deciding to
see what damage could be done to one of the others
before it arrived.

As the view screen pitched around, Kohath could
just about make out the report of las-fire lashing
out from the *Rage of Erudition* as it charged into pursuit of the black Dragon once again, spraying its
engine vents with lance beams and torpedoes, striving to hobble it before it could reach the *Spirit*. Both
vessels were charging in towards the *Spirit* at incredible speeds, and Kohath realised that the black
Dragon would be unable to avoid ploughing into
the *Spirit* if both vessels were still in one piece when
it arrived.

'May the Father and the Emperor give you speed,
Saulh,' muttered Kohath, permitting himself the slim
hope that the *Rage of Erudition* would catch the
speeding alien cruiser. Then the image slid off the
edge of the screen and the radiant glow of the
wraithship emerged onto the other side. Streams of

crackling lightning were arcing out of its strangely fluid form, like tendrils of the warp itself.

'Krayem – check that the geller-field is operational and reinforce its phase variance over the prow,' snapped the sergeant, wondering whether the unusual enemy was really using pulses of the warp as weapons.

'Give me torpedoes. Give me all the torpedoes!' he yelled.

THE CORRIDOR IN front of the Implantation Chamber was alive with purple fire and the crackling energy discharge that lashed out of the librarians. Zhapel was an inferno of motion, sweeping his force-axe into spins and arcs, slicing through the reaching tentacles of warp that quested for purchase around his limbs. Meanwhile, Korinth spun his staff above his head, spilling gouts of flame and power through the corridor like a critical centrifuge – where the shards of loose energy sunk into the warp tendrils, they shrivelled and withdrew back into the walls. And Rhamah remained implacable in front of the heavy, armoured doors to the chamber itself, blue fire dancing across the nodules in his psychic hood and lashes of flame leaping from his fingertips.

The daemonic energies in the walls were struggling to reach resolution, aspiring into congealed pools in the metal structure of the passageway, screaming and cackling with the frustrated desire to find birth in the material confines of the *Litany of Fury*. But the librarians shattered and dispersed the energies, ruining their patterns before they could resolve themselves properly. Ghostly shapes reached into the corridor, covering the walls in the suggestions of faces and limbs, as though daemonic souls were fighting each other for a place in the light.

Nothing shall pass! Yelled the voice of Zhaphel, directly into the minds of the Marines as the Devastator squad took up firing positions along the middle of the corridor itself, facing the walls on both sides and dousing them with flames.

As they fought, tendrils of power started to course through the floor, like burning, purple veins. They flowed down the passageway under the boots of the Marines, heading for the doors at the end of the corridor, before which stood the magnificent figure of Rhamah, alive with psychic power of his own.

By the time the Devastators noticed the daemonic flow under their feet, the veins had already started to wrap and mesh around their boots, rooting them into the deck. Meanwhile, great sheets of energy poured out of Rhamah's psychic hood and his fingertips, gushing down onto the floor and forming a pool of power that checked the advance of the daemonic flows, flooding the end of the corridor with his own energy.

After a few seconds, Korinth and Zhaphel realised that the tendrils in the middle of the corridor were getting weaker and fewer, as though their power was being drained by efforts elsewhere. Looking back down the passageway, they saw the veins coruscating through the floor, enwrapping the feet of the Devastators and questing forward towards Rhamah and the Implantation Chamber beyond. In an instant they understood what was happening, and they broke into a run, storming back down the corridor towards their librarian brother, hacking and slicing through the tendrils that dragged at their armour, seeking to slow their progress.

But the pool of warp energy that was collecting in front of Rhamah was already too big. It was drawing in all the tendrils from the corridor, concentrating them and mixing them into a single, nauseating reservoir of warp. It was flooding out over the floor, sheening like an oil slick, and from its heart there reached arms and talons, as though it were a doorway into the warp itself.

Like an inevitable tide, the waves of the pool lapped out towards the feet of Rhamah, who still stood unmoving on its coast, a breakwater barring its progress towards the Implantation Chamber, psychic lashes flashing out from the amplifier arrays in his hood, holding back the waves with sheer will power. But the pool was growing and edging closer with each second.

By now, the Devastator squad had also realised that their enemy was slipping away from them, oozing along the floor under their feet. As Korinth and Zhaphel stormed past them, they turned together and saw what was happening at the end of the corridor: Rhamah was ablaze with psychic brilliance, like a human angel standing guardian before the great doors of the Implantation Chamber. His arms were held out to his sides and his eyes burned with unearthly power, as blinding blue energy flowed out of his embrace, crashing down into the daemonic pool at his feet. As far as they could tell, the librarian had still not moved his boots.

Just as the eyes of the entire squad fell on him, Rhamah looked up to check on the proximity of his librarian-brothers, the burning light in his eyes flickering for a moment; they were charging towards him, but were still a few seconds away. As though making up his mind in that instant, Rhamah lowered his left hand and pointed a great blast of energy down into the pool. At the same time, he lifted his right arm above his head and grasped the hilt of his ornate force-sword, lifting it slowly and deliberately out of its holster on his back. He flipped it in his hand until its point faced vertically down in front of him.

'No!' yelled the storming figure of Zhaphel as he saw what Rhamah was about to do.

With a flicker, the enormous power of Rhamah's psychic onslaught faltered and blinked out, as he clasped the hilt of his force-sword into both hands. Immediately, the waves of warp from the pool at his feet started to wash forwards, lapping at the toes of his boots.

'No!' cried Korinth as he charged forwards, knowing that he could not reach his battle-brother in time.

With a flash and a cry, Rhamah drove his blade down into the deck in front of him, pushing it through the pool of warp energy and plunging its length into the metal panels below.

A tremendous, blinding explosion of light blasted through the corridor, knocking Korinth and Zhaphel off their feet as they ran, and forcing the Devastators to lean into the torrent. Then, as the light faded, they saw the radiant figure of Rhamah on one knee, his hands still clasped around the hilt of his sword, the end of which was still submerged in the deck. The daemonic pool raged and bubbled around him, spitting fragments of purple fire into the air as grotesque arms reached out and grasped at the librarian's limbs.

The daemonic forces keened and shrieked in a final effort, flinging tentacles and tendrils around the dramatic form of Rhamah, enveloping him in lashes of purple flame. Finally, he stood to his feet and pulled his sword clear of the pool, holding it up in front of him, touching its blade to his forehead in a salute to his battle-brothers. Then he vanished, yanked down through the pool-portal itself, dragging the tendrils and reaching limbs of the daemonic forces with him. As he disappeared from view, the warp pool and the veins of power seemed to be sucked after him, like matter into a vacuum, leaving the corridor suddenly quiet and immaculately clean once again.

Korinth and Zhaphel climbed back to their feet and stared at the last few metres that separated them from the doors to the Implantation Chamber. The space was completely empty, and they bowed their heads in despair and pride as an awed silence coursed through the passageway.

PAIN SPIKED THROUGH his shoulder as he reeled backwards. The mon'keigh's weapon was clumsy and slow, but it packed a real punch, realised Laeresh, as he let the force of the impact turn him and knock him off his feet. There was no point in trying to resist such force: he dropped his other shoulder and rolled with the blast.

As he returned to his feet, Laeresh caught a glimpse of red out of the corner of his eye and he dived

instantly into another roll, tugging his power-sword
out of its holster as he turned head over heels. The
instant his feet hit the ground, he pivoted on the
spot, spinning with his sword held out horizontally,
defining an elegant killing zone around him. But the
sword found no target.

The huge shape of the Blood Ravens Terminator
stood just out of range of his sword, its spluttering
gun held forward in an approximate aim. As he
watched, Laeresh saw the pistol cough and a single
shell flash out of its barrel towards him. Instinctively,
the exarch twitched his shoulder to twist his body
aside and to bring his own reaper cannon back into
play, but a sharp pain reminded him that his shoulder was already shredded. As he winced, the shell
punched into the body of his own weapon, detonating against the metallic material of his cannon and
shattering it into a spray of black shards. The impact
knocked him back, pushing him off balance and
sending him crashing to the ground on his back.

Rolling backwards, Laeresh pushed his legs over his
head and flipped back up onto his feet, his blade
held out in front of him to keep the massive Terminator at bay. But the huge, human machine-warrior
was already charging forward. It stepped inside
Laeresh's killing zone and swatted his blade aside
with a crackling powerfist, snatching its gun-barrel
up into Laeresh's face and squeezing the trigger from
point-blank rage.

But Laeresh was not finished yet. Rather than
retreating under the onslaught, the exarch dropped
and dived forward, letting the bolter shell sizzle over
his head as he lanced his sword into the heavily

armoured leg of the Terminator. The blade dragged over the surface of the armour, scoring through the outer layers but failing to dig in. Nonetheless, the diving weight of Laeresh's body smashed into the mon'keigh's knees and knocked its legs out from beneath it.

Both warriors crashed to the ground, stunned by the impacts and by the sudden change in the duel's range. Laeresh was first back on his feet, but his poise was off and his shredded shoulder had been completely ruined by the impact against the Terminator's legs. He held his sword out in one hand, pointing its blade at the struggling form of the massive machine-warrior that was trying to clamber back onto its feet. Its huge bulk was to its detriment in the soft sand.

This is no time for pity, realised Laeresh as he watched the travails of his worthy opponent. 'War is my master,' he hissed, staggering forward towards the vulnerable mon'keigh. 'Death is my mistress,' he cried, raising his sword above his head for the death-blow.

His elevated blade glinted with a burst of crimson as it caught the desert sun, just before it flashed down towards the neck of the struggling human warrior, leaving an arc of red light in its wake.

As the blade dropped, Laeresh grinned, turning his top lip into a snarl. Perhaps this mon'keigh monstrosity was not such a threat to him after all: *death is my mistress.*

The blade bit down into the Terminator's armour, sparking and spitting with power. But it did not cut through the ancient panels. At the same time, the human warrior abandoned his fight to stand up and let himself fall back into the sand, turning over onto its back as it fell. In one smooth movement, he reached up with its powerfist and grasped Laeresh's blade, tugging him down towards the ground. Simultaneously, it brought up its gun, pushing it into Laeresh's face and clicking the tigger.

As his eyes opened wide and flashed with glorious defeat, the last thing that Laeresh heard was the war-cry of his human foe: 'For the Great Father and the Emperor!'

THE ASTARTES CRUISER had pitched away from the *Avenging Sword*, presumably to bring its frontal arrays to bear against the wraithship, *Eternal Star*, which pulsed and flowed with energy on the other side of the human vessel. Uldreth had been confident that they had caught the mon'keigh in their crossfire, and for a few moments he struggled to understand the purpose of the alien cruiser's manoeuvre. Then he saw the swooping shape of the Dark Reaper Void Dragon speeding in from out of the sun, and he understood: the humans were resigned to their deaths, and they were determined to take as many sacred eldar souls with them as they could.

Despite his revulsion at the thought of losing precious waystones at the hands of the mon'keigh, Uldreth felt a tinge of admiration for the valour of the human fighters. He stamped it out quickly, as though it were a naked flame in the dark and dry forests of his soul.

Lasfire poured out of the frontal lances of the *Avenging Sword*, now bursting into explosions and punching into the armour around the engine vents at the rear of the Astartes cruiser. All he had to do was wait for the *Reaper's Blade* to scythe into the side of the human vessel, and that would mean the end of both the strike cruiser and the irritating Dark Reaper Void Dragon. Uldreth smiled uneasily at the prospect of ending so many problems so efficiently.

As he watched, he saw the side batteries of the Space Marine cruiser open up against the sleek, incoming shape of the *Reaper's Blade*, loosing torrents of torpedoes and las-fire directly into the speeding Dragon's path, even as its frontal arrays unleashed an inferno of fire against the *Eternal Star*. At exactly the same moment, he saw the image of the second Astartes cruiser leering into view behind the *Blade*, spraying its engines with fire and strafing lines of explosions.

The already-wounded black Dragon was slowing rapidly, as though its engines had virtually failed, and the second mon'keigh vessel was closing on it quickly. From his vantage point, Uldreth could see a line of explosions racing through the rear of the Dark Reapers' ancient ship, and he suddenly realised that its death-charge might not reach the trapped mon'keigh cruiser.

Checking the status of the *Eternal Star* one last time, Uldreth cursed the Dark Reapers and tore his own *Avenging Sword* away from the confrontation with the rear of the Space Marine cruiser. He had to shake the second vessel off the tail of the *Reaper's Blade* so that its sacrifice would not be in vain – it had to be given the chance to charge into glorious death against the side of the mon'keigh warship.

'Death is their mistress,' he muttered cynically as the *Avenging Sword* banked round and flashed off to intercept the predator on the *Blade*'s tail.

No sooner had Uldreth pulled away than a cold wind blew through his soul, whispering faint agonies into his mind: *death is my mistress*. At first he thought it was merely a consequence of his own words. He had taken the sacred words of Maugan Ra in vain. But then he realised that the psychic voice was not his. Yet is was familiar to him, as though it spoke to something deep within his being, something lost, forgotten or misremembered.

It was Laeresh. His cry resounded and echoed around Uldreth's head, touching something profound and beautiful in his soul, sparking recollections of the times they had shared before they had ascended into the glorious visages of exarchs of Khaine. Before he could rationalise the unexpected wash of thoughts, Uldreth felt tears seeping out of his eyes. The Dark Reaper was dead. Somewhere down on the planet's surface, Laeresh lay slain in the desert.

As though sensing the abrupt flood of tragedy that pulsed out from the planet, the *Reaper's Blade* seemed to slow even more, gradually falling to a stop, hanging in space between the frontal lances of the predator behind it and the side batteries of its own prey in front of it. The mon'keigh vessels, finding the dark Dragon unexpectedly prone and caught in their crossfire, loosed everything they had at the ancient and beautiful Void Dragon.

No! thundered Uldreth's thoughts. *No! You know not what you do, humans!*

All at once, the shielding around the *Blade* collapsed, and the mon'keigh torpedoes tore into its hull, drilling their way in towards the power core. A series of smaller explosions shook the ship, sending plates of armour spiralling out into space. And then a colossal detonation blew the *Reaper's Blade* in two, cracking it through the middle and breaking it like the branch of a tree.

The physical explosion was immense, sending rings of shock waves and flame searing out through the star system. But the proportions of the psychic blast were incomparably terrible. The spirit pool of the ancient vessel contained the souls of thousands of eldar warriors, stored there in the hope that they would one day be reunited with their brethren in the infinity circuit of the lost craftworld of Altansar. Not for millennia had the Dark Reapers given their dark souls over to Biel-Tan, and for all those thousands of years they had collected themselves into their own spirit pool.

Now those pristine souls were sent screaming out into the vacuum of space, skirting the abyss of the immaterium, clawing at the ledge of the material realm, desperately striving to keep themselves from the salivating jaws of the warp daemons that lay in wait on the other side, circling like sharks around a droplet of blood. The immense wave of shrieking and wailing souls crashed out of the wrecked ship and smashed across the planet below, smothering the atmosphere in psychic radiance, making the planet itself seem to shudder in horror.

* * *

GABRIEL LEANT INTO the boulder that blocked the tunnel and pushed it out into the sunlight beyond. It rolled freely for a few metres, dropping away down the slight incline that led into the arena of the grand Blood Ravens amphitheatre. The remaining members of the party squinted into the sudden flood of light as they walked out of the subterranean network at last.

The Yngir lord is sleeping still, Gabriel, but we must all leave this place. Any further psychic disturbances may occasion their ascension, and we are no longer in a position to protect the galaxy from their icy wrath.

The Blood Ravens captain turned to face the unspeakable, fragile beauty of the farseer once again. He looked into her eyes and saw the emerald fires burning with deep, passionate certainty. Ptolemea was by his side, and Jonas had already taken a few steps out into the arena. The surviving Celestians were glittering in glorious golds in the sunlight, one of them carrying their fallen Sister over her shoulder.

Macha was weak and broken, slumped against the shoulder of one of her warlocks. Only one other warlock remained from her party, and Gabriel was fully aware of the favourable mathematics of the situation. If he wanted to, he could kill the aliens there and then, and Macha knew it. Was that why she now thought in such conciliatory tones? Was her present vulnerability the source of her apparent willingness to make an equal deal with the humans that she professed to despise? If she had really reset the psychic prison around the planet, why did they need to leave now? Gabriel's mind raced with questions and suspicions, but he saw only sincerity and certainty in the farseer's breathtaking eyes.

As Gabriel considered his response, a flurry of movement in the rocks around the tunnel exit made him lift his bolter instinctively. Standing out of the rubble, partly concealed under the flickering camouflage of his cameleoline cloak, was the eldar ranger that Gabriel had captured last time he had been in the arena. He looked bruised and wounded, his armour was dirty and scratched and his cloak was ragged.

For a moment, Gabriel froze with his bolter aimed directly at the alien's head. He fought against his instincts to pull the trigger, realising that there might still be more at stake on Rahe's Paradise than the Imperium's command to suffer not the alien to live. Glancing to the side, he was relieved to see that the Celestian Sisters had responded in exactly the same way.

Pausing for a moment, as though merely to test Gabriel's resolve, Flaetriu stepped forward and approached Macha, kneeling on the ground in front of her and speaking in a tongue that Gabriel could not understand. He could see that the farseer was pleased to see this ranger, and for some reason that made him a little uneasy.

A small group of other rangers stepped out of their hiding places in the rocks, and presented themselves to the farseer, using low, sweeping bows.

'Flaetriu is explaining that you treated him poorly,' whispered Ptolemea, pressing herself against Gabriel in order to talk without being overheard. 'He said that he tried to warn us about the shield. The other rangers – one is called Aldryan, I think – they rescued him from the monastery while the battle raged in the desert.'

Gabriel nodded his understanding but kept his gaze on Macha, watching the expression in her eyes change. He was fully aware that the mathematical advantage had now swayed away from him again, and that it would be hard to maintain this truce amidst charges of mistreatment and with a battle still raging between the two sides on the far side of the monastery.

After a few seconds, Macha turned her gaze back on Gabriel, the emerald fires within burning with a different sort of passion.

It seems that I have overestimated you again, Gabriel, but the battle is not your doing, just as it is not mine. The Reapers were destined to fight you, and thus you fight them. We must bring this to an end, now, before it gets even more out of hand–

A piercing scream stabbed into Gabriel's head, making him throw his hands up to his ears in an effort to shut out the agonising noise. His eyes closed in a reflex reaction as his mind strove to battle the intrusion, but he forced them open again in order to return the gaze of his attacker – he would not be cowed by the farseer, not after everything they had already been through.

To his astonishment, he saw that the eldar were all in the same position, each clutching at their heads as though being tortured from within. Macha had slumped to the ground as her warlock had released his arm, clutching at his own head in obvious pain, and she was writhing.

It was not her; something else was happening.

At his side, Ptolemea was clearly suffering the same thing. Gabriel closed his eyes and concentrated on the scream. He let it echo and ricochet around his mind, trying to catch glimpses of it, but it was like nothing he had ever felt before. It was a death-knell of some kind, but in a language that was utterly alien to him, even the gentlest tones of which wracked him with pain. Then he saw it, just a couple of words flickering on the very edge of his comprehension: death my mistress.

As suddenly as it had started, the psychic death cry ceased, leaving a backwash of silence flooding into their minds as everyone climbed back to their feet.

But then a real explosion shook the amphitheatre, and the group turned to see one of the majestic towers of the Blood Ravens monastery explode into a rain of rubble, as though blasted by a constant tirade of rockets that had finally broken through the heavy stone armour.

At the same time, high up in the atmosphere, another explosion flashed brilliantly, like a dying star. Tiny fragments of wreckage started falling through the stratosphere, streaking the sky with burning meteor trails. And then a wave of coruscating blue energy washed over the heavens, pulsing across from one side to the other, like a terrible aurora. Little flecks of the startling blue fell down into the atmosphere, sizzling and shrieking as they flashed and jigged like dying fairies. In the aftermath of the explosion, a hideous background of screaming voices whirled around the planet, as though the atmosphere had suddenly been riddled with tortured souls.

As he looked down from the incredible sky, Gabriel saw Macha's face only centimetres from his own, her eyes flaring with hatred and anger.

What have you done, human!? What have you done? The souls of the Dark Reapers will damn us all, you fool. The only way to trust you is to kill you – something that I should have done on Tartarus.

Macha lifted her hands and clasped them around Gabriel's face, holding him as though about to kiss him, but wracking his head with agony as streams of sha'iel flooded through her arms into his brain.

Immediately, the Celestian Sisters opened up with their bolters, snapping off shells at the rangers that quickly scattered back into the cover of the fallen rocks. Jonas lashed out with his staff, sending gouts of burning energy crashing into the remaining warlocks.

Ptolemea stood for a moment, watching the short-lived alliance collapse around her. She saw the alien farseer and Gabriel locked in a lethal embrace and she realised that she could not let the captain die. She may have come to Rahe's Paradise to investigate allegations of his taint, but now she felt as though the fate of her own soul was tied inextricably to his. She could not let him die like this; it would be like condemning herself to a life of deceit and dishonesty.

Diving forward, Ptolemea crashed into Macha and pushed her away from the stunned figure of Gabriel, letting her momentum carry them both down into a heap on the ground. Landing on top of the farseer, Ptolemea whipped a slender dagger out of a holster along her shoulder-blade and plunged it down into the alien's chest. It sunk in down to its hilt, and Macha screamed with the shock. Her reflex reaction was to fire out her hand into the other woman's face, planting her open palm over her beautiful, porcelain features.

Muttering something inaudible, Macha's eyes squinted and a pulse of emerald fire flashed up through her arm, smashing Ptolemea in the face and throwing her up into the air. Continuing to mutter her words of power, Macha remained laying on the ground and the dagger slowly withdrew out of her flesh. In less than a second, the blade flipped round and shot upwards, plunging deeply into Ptolemea's heart as she fell back down towards the ground. Her dark eyes bulged and her mouth opened as she slumped down on top of the farseer once again, dead.

CHAPTER FOURTEEN
PYROCLASM

As THE CHAOS of battle persisted in the desert in front of the crumbling Blood Ravens monastery, a deep rumbling sound pulsed through the ground and the mountainous form of Krax-7 behind the edifice trembled visibly. The sand in the desert started to shift and the dunes began to collapse. The mica glass that still sheened under much of the battlefield cracked and splintered, unable to shift with the waves of subterranean movement that shunted under the ground.

Corallis turned from his vantage point on the roof of his Land Raider and glanced at the unstable volcano behind the monastery. He could see rocks and boulders cascading down its sides, and avalanches beginning to grip the lower reaches of the great mountain. He had seen enough volcanoes on Rahe's Paradise to know what was about to happen.

Turning back to the battlefield, he could see the distant figure of Tanthius struggling to his feet. The huge Terminator sergeant was limping slightly as he started to make his way back towards the main battle; he had overshot the centre of the conflict during his pursuit of the magnificent, plumed eldar warrior, which now lay dead on the ground behind the hulking figure of Tanthius.

The other eldar fighting in the field seemed to have fallen into a slump following Tanthius's victory, and their numbers were beginning to dwindle as the Blood Ravens rallied, capitalising on the opportunity. Even the destruction of one of the monastery towers did not seem to raise the aliens' spirits. Corallis had heard that they were an emotional species, and this behaviour seemed to confirm the rumours.

Only a couple of minutes earlier, Corallis had seen strange streaks of blue light flash through the upper atmosphere, and he wondered whether Kohath was engaged in a fight that mirrored this one on the ground. He smiled slightly at the thought of the sergeant cursing the serfs on the command deck and wishing that he was down on the planet's surface with a bolter in his hand. Despite his protestations, however, Kohath was a fine ship's commander, and Gabriel had left him in charge of the *Ravenous Spirit* for a reason. Corallis had faith that the *Spirit* would put up a valiant fight, no matter what the odds.

Finally, Krax-7 convulsed and blew its top, spitting great chunks of rock up into the sky, splintering hundreds of tonnes of mountain-top as effortlessly as casting grains of sand. The huge tumbling boulders flew out in all directions, some of them looping out over the monastery and smashing down into the field of battle, as though the planet itself were launching ordnance in retaliation to the violence being done to it. The stone ballistics crunched down against the mica glass, pounding out craters and spraying the battlefield with lethal, black shards of glass, shredding the armour of Blood Ravens and eldar alike – the volcano showed no discrimination.

As the masonry rained down, a huge superheated mushroom of smoke, ash and debris plumed up from the peak, rapidly expanding to obscure the sky and blot out the light of the red sun. Even as he watched, Corallis could see the pyroclastic flow surging down the sides of the volcano, engulfing everything in its path. He could even hear it as it shunted the air along before it, driving it at speeds greater than sound. In a matter of seconds it rolled over the towering monastery, swamping it like a tsumani and then driving on into the desert beyond, blasting chunks of masonry off the once-impregnable towers and throwing them like primitive projectiles.

There was nothing that he could do other than brace himself against the Land Raider as the super-sonic surge of heat and ash ploughed on into the desert, rolling over the combatants and submerging them into volcanic darkness. The battlefield simply vanished from view, and even the keen eyes of Corallis could see little further than the end of his own arm. He couldn't even see the great, burning rivers of lava that were streaming down the sides of Krax-7.

* * *

THE TUNNEL SHOOK and debris fell from the ceiling, raining down onto the stooped figure of Caleb as he tried to keep pace with the local warriors that jogged along in front of him, their smaller bodies easily fitting through the confined and twisting spaces. They ran with practiced ease, always knowing the right turn when a junction was reached, always knowing where to put their feet when the ground grew treacherous.

The thunderous impacts of combat above made the tunnels unstable, but something had changed. No longer were the passageways trembling with persistent dull shocks, but abrupt and powerfully violent movements wracked the ground, twisting it and running it through with giant fault lines, cracking the tunnels into fragments. Something other than war was threatening the integrity of the desert.

A huge and sudden quake cracked through the ground, throwing the local warriors off their feet and causing Caleb to stumble. Cracks and faults appeared in the ceiling of the tunnel, small at first but rapidly expanding and dashing along its length.

'Move!' yelled Caleb, reaching down and grasping hold of two fallen warriors, hefting them under his arms and charging along the passageway. 'Cave-in!'

The other warriors were back on their feet and running, this time chasing after the pounding shape of the Blood Ravens scout, who barrelled along through the confined space as it shook, debris crashing down against his armour in ever-increasing quantities.

Another massive explosion rocked the tunnel and large sections of the roof collapsed all at once. Caleb took another couple of giant strides and then dived forward, launching himself headlong through the last few metres, tumbling out into a wider, rocky chamber at the end of the passage, throwing the two warriors out from under his arms as he flew.

A suddenly muffled scream made Caleb turn as he pushed himself up off the ground in the cavern, showers of sand cascading down his armour. Looking back into the tunnel from which the group had just emerged, he could see the outstretched hand of one of the local warriors, reaching out of a wall of fallen sand and rock. The hand was tense and, for a couple of seconds, its fingers twitched. A few of the other locals ran back to the tunnel and started to scrape and scratch at the landslide that had swamped their comrade, but then the reaching fingers fell limp and they stopped digging, collapsing in exhaustion against the fatal wall of sand.

The sound of falling rock and sand gradually subsided, leaving the group struggling for breath in the underground cavern.

'What was that, Sky Angel?' asked Varjak, walking over to Caleb. 'I've never seen the tunnels behave like that before.'

'I'm not sure, Varjak. But I don't think that it was a weapon. It might have been a volcanic eruption – perhaps even Krax-7 itself, judging by the proximity. We need to get above ground,' replied Caleb, his eyes already scanning the perimeter of the cave for exit tunnels.

The fine, granular sound of falling debris was beginning to fade, and it seemed that whatever had caused the cave-in had subsided for the time being. But then a new sound started to hum through the

subterranean network. At first it sounded like
another rockslide, or perhaps a series of them in far-
off tunnels, but then it grew louder, as though
drawing closer. After a few seconds, it began to
resolve itself from a dull clattering into a higher
pitched hum, almost an insect-like buzz.

'What's that noise?' asked Caleb, scanning the
heavy shadows that riddled the various cave-mouths
and tunnels that peppered the perimeter of the cavern. He dropped his eyes to meet the sparkling greens
of Varjak's, hoping that the local boy would be familiar with the odd sound.

'I don't know, Sky Angel,' replied the youth, turning
away from Caleb and trying to locate the direction
from which the noise was emanating. The bizarre,
metallic hum seemed to come from everywhere at
once as it echoed and bounced around the complicated and restricted acoustic space. 'I've never heard
it before.'

The scraping buzz grew louder and more intense,
drawing in around them from the darkness of the
surrounding tunnels. The dull, rattling hum started
to develop a metallic edge, as though hundreds of
delicate sheets of metal were rubbing against one
another.

A faint shimmer caught Caleb's keen eyes and he
strained his vision into the shadows beyond the
mouth of one of the widest passageways. The darkness seemed to move, as though it were composed of
thousands of tiny little flecks of shadow. But he
couldn't see anything decisive, even as the hum grew
louder and began to make the unprotected ears of
the locals ache.

'We should leave,' said Caleb, still not understanding what was happening but deciding that ignorance and curiosity should not always be identical. 'Varjak – which way to the surface?'

The boy pointed to one of the smaller tunnels set into the far wall, and Caleb strode over towards it immediately. Peering up through the narrow, tubular passageway, he could see the faint red light of the local sun seeping down, and he nodded decisively. 'Everyone out!'

As he spoke, there was a sudden shift in the quality of the background noise, as though whatever was generating it had broken through a barrier and had emerged into an area with open acoustics. Turning on his heel, Caleb heard a scream and saw a roiling cloud of black flecks emerging out of the wide tunnel mouth on the other side of the chamber. The cloud was swarming around one of the locals, and he was screaming. Even as he watched, Caleb could see the boy's flesh vanishing before his eyes: little spots of blood appeared on his skin, rapidly stretching out into cuts and gashes, then into open wounds. Eventually, parts of the screaming youth's skull and skeleton became visible, glinting with specks of white in amongst the teeming and glittering shadows that swarmed around him. The other locals just stared in disbelief.

Breaking the transfixed horror of the scene, Varjak dashed forward and took a swing with his long-bladed dagger, sweeping it through the cloud of little scarab beetles and driving into the neck of his doomed comrade. The insects parted around the plunging blade, letting it slip through between then as though offering no resistance at all. The screaming stopped instantly as the boy's head crashed down into the sand – his body slumping into a heap next to it.

As the beetles swarmed around the fallen corpse and feasted on its flesh, consuming it in a matter of seconds, the warriors turned and dashed up into the exit tunnel. Caleb paused for a moment at the mouth of the passage, watching the little metallic insects work their way through the flesh of the fallen warrior. It was disgusting, but his mind was plagued by questions and doubts. What in the name of the Great Father was going on? He had never heard of anything like these shimmering, black beetle-like scarabs. They appeared to be made of metal, as though they were artificial constructions, like tiny insectoid robots, and there were hundreds of them, perhaps thousands in the swarm.

As he watched, the rustle of carapace on carapace grew even louder as more of the beetles flooded into the cavern. They started to pour out of the tunnels all around, coating the walls, the ceiling and the floor, pluming out into the middle of the space as though riding the wave of an explosion further under the ground.

Caleb had seen enough and he turned again, dashing up through the exit tunnel in pursuit of the local warriors, questing for the sun. Behind him, he could hear the deafening rattle and rustle of carapaces flooding into the narrow passageway.

As KRAX-7 BLEW, Tanthius looked back towards the magnificent black walls of the Blood Ravens' monastery. One of its towers had been destroyed by the continuous fire from the Wave Serpents in the desert, but the eldar transports were now under siege from squads of Marines, and they no longer had any time for long range assaults on the huge edifice. Necho's Assault squad was pestering one of them from the sky, dousing it with fire, and Topheth's attack bikes were engaging the other, whilst fending off the counter-attacks of the alien jetbikes. The battle appeared to have swung in favour of the Blood Ravens since Tanthius himself had defeated the exarch.

The pyroclastic flow surged down the face of Krax-7, enveloping the towering shape of the monastery in voluminous clouds of ash in a matter of seconds. Tanthius paused, balancing his weight carefully on the damaged mechanical sinews of his armoured legs. As the cloud billowed out in the desert, finally swallowing the monastery and then the first lines of the Blood Ravens' defences, including the figure of Corallis on the roof of one of the Land Raiders, Tanthius scanned the battlefield quickly, trying to assess what needed to be done before the visibility vanished.

Then the superheated cloud of ash and debris blasted through the theatre, lifting huge gusts of sand and blasting them out into the desert. For a few seconds, the whole scene went black, lost in the smoke and volcanic dust.

Even when the strong desert winds finally blew the ash away, thinning it into a fine mist, the battlefield was still cast in semi-darkness. The ash was caught in the atmosphere itself, obscuring the sun and rendering the planet's surface an unearthly grey. But Tanthius could see the monastery once again, and beyond it he could clearly make out the streams of lava that poured down the sides of Krax-7.

The ground trembled with an aftershock, and Tanthius started to make his way back towards the last vestiges of the battle, half-dragging his damaged limbs as he went.

The ground bucked again, and the sand started to subside, slipping down into itself as though the desert were caving into some lost underground chambers. Tanthius swayed with the motion, pausing as huge cracks appeared in the mica glass up ahead of him. The whole scene seemed to shake and vibrate. Even the towering form of the monastery trembled, as though the entire tectonic plate was shifting.

Through the ashen atmosphere, Tanthius could see patches of intense, black smoke wafting up into the air, seeping out of cracks in the ground and then billowing out across the battlefield. As he watched one them drift slowly over towards the ruined Razorback and the Tactical Marines of Sergeant Asherah, who were engaged in the final stages of a fire-fight with a dwindling contingent of eldar Aspect Warriors, an odd humming noise struck up in his ears.

Assuming that the noise was being generated by parts damaged during the fight with the exarch, Tanthius punched the side of his helmet to try and clear the interference. It made no difference and, after a moment, the noise grew louder.

As the smoke cloud approached his position, Tanthius could see that Asherah turned to face it, breaking off his fight with the eldar and turning his flamer against the cloud itself. One by one, the other Marines in his squad did the same thing, turning their backs on the eldar and spraying fire into the advancing cloud. For a few seconds, the eldar lowered their weapons and watched the Blood Ravens' behaviour, but then they rapidly raised their guns again and opened fire. Although they were firing towards Asherah's squad, Tanthius realised that they were not firing at them – hails of shuriken projectiles hissed past the sergeant's position and zipped into the growing, dark cloud, sending up little sparks as the monomolecular projectiles struck pieces of flying metal.

The hum grew louder and more of the dark clouds seeped up from the desert as cracks started to appear all over the ground. Tanthius swept his eyes across the dim, misty battlefield and noticed that wherever the clouds appeared the Marines and eldar stopped fighting each other and turned their weapons on the clouds together. What was going on? He wasn't close enough to see.

Even as he watched, he saw the cloud near Asherah billow and shift under the tirade of fire, but then it morphed around the impacts and reached out towards the sergeant, touching him with a shadowy tendril. The Marine flinched away from its touch, as though stung, but the tentacle of darkness followed after his movements as though attached to his gauntlet. And the tendril grew thicker, pulsing with darkness as more of the cloud flowed along its line and started to engulf Asherah's hand, then his arm.

The Tactical squad hesitated, unwilling to fire on their sergeant, and in the lull the cloud engulfed him completely. The eldar were not so reticent, and they continued to unleash shuriken into the obscure form, forcing a couple of Marines to turn and threaten them with their bolters. For a few seconds, the armoured shape of the Marine thrashed against the cloud, lashing out with his weapons in almost random abandon. Then, quite suddenly, the thrashing stopped and Asherah slumped to the ground. A couple of moments later and his armour was rent asunder, and pieces of it went scurrying off across the sand before vanishing down into newly opened crevices. After little more than ten seconds, there was no trace of the sergeant left at all, and the cloud of tiny black fragments billowed up once again, heading for the other Marines in his squad.

Turning in confusion, Tanthius could see similar scenes unfolding all over the battlefield. Blood Ravens and eldar were both being picked apart by these dark, buzzing clouds of what now appeared to be insects of some kind.

As Krax-7 continued to erupt, the ground continued to shake, and more and more of these swarms were emerging from the cracks and crevices that were opening up all over the battlefield, darkening the already ashen sky. But there were other shapes emerging from the ground now – humanoid shapes clambering out of holes and pulling each other up out of weeping gashes in the sand. In the dim, foggy light, it took Tanthius a couple of seconds to recognise the profile of Caleb emerging from the ground in the middle of the battlefield, surrounded by a small group of human warriors.

However, Caleb's warband was not the only group of figures emerging from the depths. Here and there, as lava began to bubble up through the gashes in the earth, Tanthius could make out odd, inhuman, skeletal figures rising out of the sand, climbing out of the streams of molten rock as through they were water. The sinister creatures carried long barrelled weapons, the likes of which Tanthius had never seen before.

The eldar in the field seemed to recognise the dark, sinister warriors immediately, and they all turned their weapons on the newcomers, leaving the Blood Ravens to deal with the swarms of scarab beetles that still drifted through the air. But the eldar shurikens just bounced harmlessly off the mysterious warriors, ricocheting in little metallic sparks, as though their skeletal forms were composed entirely of some kind of metal.

Slowly and deliberately, one of the metal skeletons lifted its own weapon and pointed it at a white and emerald eldar Guardian. A stream of glittering darkness flashed out of the barrel and crashed into the elegant alien as it struggled to move aside, catching it in its ribs. The stream instantly spread out, creeping and flowing all over the eldar warrior, coating it completely in a shimmering, silver darkness in less than a second. A fraction of a second later, the darkness blinked and evaporated into the air, leaving the flickering image of an atrophied and decomposed eldar where the Guardian had been. The image flickered and then vanished, leaving nothing of the alien at all.

Tanthius lumbered into a run, dragging his damaged limbs across the trembling, lava-riddled, smoke-enshrouded battlefield. In the distance, he could see the Blood Ravens' monastery rocking and cracking as the movements in the ground became more violent. He wasn't sure what was going on, but he was certain that the Blood Ravens should get off Rahe's Paradise as quickly as possible. He had never before seen warriors that could climb imperviously out of magma and resist eldar fire as though it were nothing, and he had certainly never seen weapons that could vaporise an eldar Guardian in less than a second. Whatever was ascending out of the bowels of the planet, Tanthius had a very bad feeling about it.

DESPITE HIS NATURAL instincts and his horror, Gabriel knelt down at Macha's side. The wound in the farseer's abdomen was bleeding copiously, and it looked as though she would die from loss of blood. All around him, Gabriel could hear the fury of the fire-fight between the Celestian Sisters, Jonas and the eldar, but he paid it no mind. The ground was trembling violently and great wafts of sulphurous gas were billowing out of the huge fissure that rent the arena in two. Lava was beginning to bubble to the surface, and very soon the amphitheatre would be little more than a pool of molten rock.

Gabriel. The thought was weak and tremulous. Gabriel could sense the effort being put into formulating thoughts that he could understand.

Gabriel, it is shifting. The Yngir lord is awaking. Can you not feel it? Look at the signs, Gabriel, look at the progeny. The living dead, the thirsting ones, the forever

*damned are walking in the desert once more. You have…
we have failed, Gabriel.*

The thoughts faded into silence, and Gabriel looked deeply into the wounded farseer's eyes, seeing the emerald flames flicker on the point of extinction. His own eyes flicked to the pale, beautiful face of Ptolemea, who was laying in the sand next to Macha, her own dagger still protruding from her chest. There was a confused sadness in his heart – he had not trusted the young Sister of the Lost Rosetta, but he had become sure that they understood each other. As for Macha, Gabriel was neither sure that he understood her nor that he ever could.

The souls of the Reapers, Gabriel. Thousands of them. They have breached Lsathranil's Shield and the Yngir will ascend to consume us. You have released them. They shall be the harbingers of the dark fate, and the galaxy shall run red as the blood of Eldanesh.

'What must we do?' asked Gabriel, whispering his heretical thoughts in to the beautiful farseer's ear. As he spoke, a thunderous crack split the arena along a new axis and a burst of red lava spurted out of the ground like a fountain. At the same time, a river of molten rock flowing down from the peak of Krax-7 breached the wall of the amphitheatre and spilt into the arena.

'We must leave this place,' he said, scooping the farseer into his arms and turning to face Jonas.

'Jonas, we must leave. Sisters – stand down. I know that you can understand me,' he continued, turning to the warlocks from Macha's retinue – they had stopped fighting as soon as Gabriel had picked up their farseer. 'And you know that I am right. We must leave this place, now.'

Druinir glared at Gabriel, his eyes burning with revulsion and hatred and his fingers still crackling with blue light. As he stared, the looming monastery behind them shuddered and then the second tower collapsed. The ground started to buckle and shake as though something massive were pushing up from underneath. Lava burst out from new cracks and holes that opened up all over the arena.

The warlock nodded, and the other eldar lowered their weapons.

Gabriel returned the nod then turned sharply to his librarian. 'Jonas – which is the quickest way to the Thunderhawks? We need to get off the planet and deal with it from space. Sound the retreat.' As he spoke, Gabriel watched the remaining Celestians gather up the body of Ptolemea.

When he turned back to the eldar, he found Druinir standing directly behind him, staring fiercely into his face. *I will take the farseer.* There was a hostile pause. *Thank you, Blood Raven.*

'WHAT IN THE name of the Great Father was that?' bellowed Kohath, turning rapidly away from the main view screen and shouting his demand to his command crew. 'Well? What the hell was it?'

Together with the charging *Rage of Erudition*, the *Ravenous Spirit* had destroyed the jet-black eldar cruiser, but it had exploded in a completely unexpected way, sending rings of warp energy lashing out through the system and raining down into the atmosphere of Rahe's Paradise. Immediately afterwards, the shimmering wraithship onto which Kohath had turned all of his guns had suddenly flickered and then

flashed away, darting through the neighbouring space
like an agile bird of prey, avoiding an entire salvo of
torpedoes from the *Spirit*. Simultaneously, the Ghost
Dragon that had been inflicting such heavy damage
on the engine blocks at the rear of the *Spirit* suddenly
disengaged.

For a moment, everything was quiet.

'Sergeant Kohath – what in the Emperor's name is
going on?' The face of Saulh resolved itself onto the
view screen as the *Rage of Erudition* pulled into formation next to the *Spirit*.

'I have no idea, Saulh, but we're working on it,' said
Kohath gruffly, surveying his crew expectantly. 'Well?'
he prompted. 'Anyone?'

There was no reply. Loren and Krayem exchanged
glances with each other and then looked down at
their terminals.

'Sergeant–' began the familiar but still nameless
serf. 'I think that you should take a look at the
planet.'

'Bring it up,' sighed Kohath, shaking his head in
disappointment and turning back to the view screen.
Saulh's face rippled and then vanished, to be
replaced by the ruddy image of Rahe's Paradise. It
filled the screen with a deep, blood red. A plume of
black had erupted around a constellation of volcanoes on the equator, but it looked like little more
than a normal, albeit rather large eruption.

'Well?' challenged Kohath, unimpressed. 'What am
I supposed to be looking at?'

The image on the screen chimed, shifted and
zoomed, as though pulling a section of the planet
closer to the *Ravenous Spirit*. It showed a close-up of

the quadrant near the foothills of the volcanic mountains, where the Blood Ravens' monastery was based.
He waited for the image-systems to filter out the ash-
clouds in the atmosphere. For a moment, Kohath
thought that the sensors were malfunctioning and he
impatiently made some manual adjustments to
resolve the clouds and interference patterns. But then
it gradually dawned on him that the clouds were
what he was supposed to be looking at.

'By the throne...' he murmured, watching the
shimmering shadows spill out over the landscape
around the location of the monastery. It was certainly
true that Krax-7 was the volcano that had erupted,
but he had never seen anything like this before.

'Saulh, are you getting this?'

'Yes, sergeant. What's going on down there?' crackled the voice of Saulh over the vox.

'Sergeant Kohath,' said Loren, reluctant to interrupt
but sure that he had some important news.

'Yes?' snapped Kohath, pulling his eyes away from
the mysterious events on the planet.

'There appear to be some vessels launching from
the surface.'

'What sort of vessels?' asked Kohath, suspicious.

There was a pause. 'All sorts of vessels, sergeant.
Captain Angelos's Thunderhawk appears to be
amongst them, but there are also some eldar signatures – perhaps Vampire Raiders – and there are
also...' he trailed off.

'Yes?'

'There are also some signatures that I have never
seen before. They are moving faster than any of ours.
Faster even than the eldar Vampires.'

'Where?' demanded Kohath. 'Where are these vessels launching?'

'That's just it, sergeant, they're everywhere. It's as though they're spilling out of the planet itself. Some of them are already breaking out of the atmosphere.'

The image on the view screen snowed into nonsense and then resolved itself again, showing a section of the upper atmosphere. The eldar wraithship and the Ghost Dragon were just visible on the edge of the screen, and they were streaking towards its centre with their remaining Shadowhunter escorts in tow. Little bursts of light started to spark in the atmosphere as lightning-fast vessels burst out of it. No sooner were they birthed into space than the eldar opened fire at them, lashing out with tirades of torpedoes and las-fire, dousing the planet's atmosphere in flames. But the little silvery-black gunships flashed through the fire as though impermeable to it. Then, after only a few seconds, they returned fire.

'By the throne...' gasped Kohath as he saw the kind of damage that the little ships could do.

FROM THE CONTROL room of his Thunderhawk, Gabriel watched the sleek shape of the eldar Vampire Raider bank and then flash up into the atmosphere. It was out of sight in a matter of seconds, carrying Macha and her warlocks back up to their cruiser in orbit.

'Kohath. Sergeant Kohath,' repeated Gabriel, punching his fist down into the terminal next to the vox-array. 'Emperor damn it, Kohath. Where the hell are you?'

'Perhaps the vox will work when we break the cloud layer?' offered Corallis.

'Perhaps,' replied Gabriel, unconvinced. He strained his eyes back down to the surface of the planet. All of the surviving Blood Ravens had been brought on board the Thunderhawks and now there was little trace of their presence on the surface of the planet at all. Instead, the desert was awash with lava, sulphurous gases and rolling pyroclastic surges. Partially hidden in the smoky darkness were swarms of little scarab beetles, which seemed intent on dismantling any mechanical device that they came across, be it of Imperial or eldar origin. The mysterious, metallic, skeletal warriors stalked the desert like the undead, but all of their prey was dead or gone already.

'And we thought that it was a meteor strike that wiped out the forests,' murmured Jonas, shaking his head in disbelief. 'All this time, a necron catacomb was hidden under our very noses. How could we have been so blind, Gabriel?'

As the librarian spoke, a thunderous noise cracked through the atmosphere, pulling everyone's attention down to the diminishing form of the crumbling monastery-outpost. As they watched, the monastery itself seemed to heave and lift. The ground around it cracked and splintered, and the once-magnificent black edifice lurched up into the air, sending huge chunks of masonry and sections of towers scattering out into the desert. Then a great explosion of darkness erupted in the heart of the monastery, blasting its remaining walls into streams of vapour as a shimmering black shape emerged from within.

The levitating craft was shaped like a crescent, with a series of little pyramidal structures running around its rim. In the very centre was a larger pyramid – presumably housing the control decks. It eased slowly into the air, as debris rained down from its edges, crashing back into the craterous ruins of the Blood Ravens' facility and into the desert.

'Get us back to the *Ravenous Spirit*,' said Gabriel calmly. 'We are going to need some bigger guns than we have here.'

With that, the Thunderhawk angled steeply and then roared up into the stratosphere, tracing the wispy contrail left by the speedy exit of the Vampire Raider.

CHAPTER FIFTEEN
ASCENSION

As the Thunderhawk blasted out of the atmosphere, Gabriel's eyes widened at the scene that greeted them in orbit. The vacuum was riddled with las-fire and spiralling dogfights. Torpedoes flashed through the combat zone, exploding into brilliant stars. It was a mire of space combat, the like of which Gabriel had not seen for decades.

'Captain Angelos,' crackled an unknown voice through the vox. 'We are here to escort you back to the *Ravenous Spirit*.'

Gabriel clicked the view screen to a portside orientation and saw a detachment of Cobra gunships drop into formation alongside his Thunderhawk. The Thunderhawk may pack a considerable punch as a planetary assault craft, but it was slow and cumbersome in space – little more than a sitting duck.

'My thanks, pilot,' replied Gabriel.

Clicking the view screen back to a forward view, Gabriel watched the battle unfolding. There were dozens of fleet eldar Shadowhunters, flashing and rolling in elegant formations, unleashing las-fire and torpedoes in vast numbers. He had seen such craft in action before, and he knew that they were easily a match for anything that the Imperial Navy could field against them. Just off to the side of the main battle, Gabriel could see the glorious, glowing shape of a wraithship, its cannons flaring and pulses of warp energy flaring from its beautifully curving wingtips. There was also a second eldar cruiser – part of the so-called Dragon-class, thought Gabriel. It was slightly withdrawn from the battle, but its weapons were working hard in support of its smaller escorts.

For a moment, Gabriel was struck by a sudden horror that there were so few Cobra gunships in the fray. It looked as though the eldar were winning. But then the glorious shape of the *Ravenous Spirit* loomed into view, with an almost complete complement of Cobras hanging in space off its starboard side. They appeared to be utterly uninvolved in the fight.

Gabriel affected a double-take, looking back into the quagmire of combat and trying to resolve his confusion. If the eldar were not fighting the Blood Ravens, who were they fighting? He could hardly make out an enemy at all, although it was clear that something was moving through the void at incredible speeds, making even the Shadowhunters look pedestrian. Whatever they were, they were small, manoeuvrable and extremely fast, flashing through the mire like shimmering flecks of shadow.

'What are those things?' asked Gabriel, vocalising his question without thinking about it as he squinted into the light-flecked darkness.

'I do not know their name or class, captain,' said Jonas, standing beside Gabriel at the view screen. 'But the Imperium has confronted them before, though only rarely, and never with much success. They are necron vessels, Gabriel,' he added, as though sharing a secret.

'That's not very reassuring, Jonas,' replied Gabriel dryly.

'Sergeant Kohath,' said Gabriel, clicking the channel on the vox. 'Sergeant Kohath – why are you not assisting the eldar in this fight?'

There was a long hiss of static and then silence. For a moment Gabriel wondered whether the vox was still not operating properly, but then a reply came.

'Captain Angelos – good to hear your voice again.' It was Kohath. 'We have only just disengaged from battle with the eldar, captain. I had not anticipated your preference to join them at this time.' There was a note of scepticism in his voice. 'Sergeant Saulh of the Ninth is here with the *Rage of Erudition*, captain. He came with a request from Captain Ulantus that we should make speed for the Lorn system – it seems that the green-skins have invaded. I thought that we might make our way there now that the eldar are otherwise engaged, captain.'

Gabriel smiled. He liked Kohath – he was a straightforward military man and always spoke his mind. Saulh was a different matter, but his opinion was of no concern to the Commander of the Watch. 'We will not be going to Lorn just yet, sergeant,' he replied. 'And I will receive your report on the fight with the eldar later. For now, you will direct your Cobra gunships to assist in the battle against the necron. Do you understand me, sergeant?'

There was another cackle of hesitation. 'Necron, captain?' Kohath's voice betrayed his surprise.

'Do you understand me, sergeant?' repeated Gabriel.

'Yes, captain. It will be done. Preparations are already underway for your return aboard the *Ravenous Spirit.*'

'Very good, sergeant,' replied Gabriel, clicking off the vox and turning back to the battle outside. As he watched, a line of Cobra gunships streamed into the fray, engaging the impossibly rapid Dirge Raiders as best they could.

STRIDING BACK ONTO the command deck of his strike cruiser, Gabriel surveyed the mess that Kohath had left him with. A number of the terminals were shattered and burnt out. There were stains of dried blood on the deck and at least three of the crew were missing.

'I see that you have been busy in my absence, sergeant,' said Gabriel, nodding his greeting to Kohath as the sergeant turned from the main view screen.

'It has not been uneventful, captain,' conceded Kohath, bowing efficiently.

Outside, the spiralling gyre of the space battle was still raging. No matter how many of the Dirge Raiders that the Shadowhunters and Cobras destroyed, dozens more flashed out of the planet's ever-darkening atmosphere to replace them. It was as though there was an entire fleet hidden in the bowels of the planet, waiting to be born into the cold abyss of space.

The Blood Ravens Cobras were suffering more casualties than the eldar Shadowhunters; they were only just fast enough to deal with the eldar vessels, and these necron fighters put the other aliens' vessels to shame.

'Loren, take us closer to the action,' snapped Gabriel. 'And Krayem, tell the gunners to provide fire in support of our Cobras.' Gabriel paused for a moment. 'Where's Reuben?' he asked.

IN THE SHADOWS of his command deck, Uldreth watched the Vampire Raiders flash out of the planet's atmosphere and head directly for the effervescent form of the *Eternal Star*, skirting the edge of the combat with elegant accomplishment. He knew that Macha was on board one of them, and his soul was a curdling mix of relief and anger. He was naturally relieved that Biel-Tan's farseer was still alive, but he could not dampen his resentment about his own conduct in this increasingly messy affair. Macha had been right from the start. Laeresh had been right. Even the old Fire Dragon, Draconir, had been right. The space battle at Lsanthranil's Shield was here and now, in the present, where it had always been – waiting for the past to catch up with it.

A little while later, Uldreth also watched the ugly shapes of the Blood Ravens Thunderhawks roar out into orbit, ploughing their way clumsily into the midst of the battle on their way back to one of the strike cruisers that had ended the *Reaper's Blade* and spilled its spirit pool into the atmosphere of the tomb world.

His lips curled into a snarl. The mon'keigh had always been thorns in the bubbles of space-time, ruining the perfect futures that the farseers had tried to sculpt for the sons of Asuryan. He hissed involuntarily, venting his disgust in a physical form as it boiled out of his mind: *how could the farseer believe that these ignorant, clumsy fools could do anything other than harm? Disaster followed them like diseased rats.*

A sudden convulsion pulsed through orbit, rippling out from the planet as another vessel started to push its way slowly out of the atmosphere. A tiny point of shimmering black was the first thing to break the atmosphere, like the tip of an iceberg. It grew slowly, with the atmosphere bursting into flames on all sides of it as the pyramid pushed out into space. A moment later, and the broad, crescent-shaped hull of the Shroud Cruiser pressed up into the troposphere, highlighted in an aura of burning ozone.

Macha! Uldreth's thoughts were urgent and precisely directed. *Macha! He has ascended!*

The *Avenging Sword* disengaged its cannons from its support role in the dogfights and redirected them down towards the emerging Shroud Cruiser, knowing that the Yngir lord was encased within it. At exactly the same time, the weapons of the *Eternal Star* also turned down to atmosphere, pounding it with tirades of violence.

Even as the Shroud pulled clear of the planet and into orbit, with lashes of fire and torpedoes bouncing off its hull, entire squadrons of Dirge Raiders zipped out of the atmosphere in its wake, flashing straight into the mire of combat with the Shadowhunters and the lumbering mon'keigh gunships.

Starting slowly the Shroud quickly gathered pace as it accelerated off towards the sun, apparently ignoring the continuous bombardment to which it was being subjected by the eldar cruisers.

'SERGEANT SAULH – HOLD this position and provide assistance to the Cobras,' said Gabriel. 'I assume that the Exterminatus array is still functioning aboard the *Rage of Erudition*, sergeant?'

'Yes, captain. It remains undamaged,' replied Saulh, his image crackling and snowing on the view screen.

'You are to fire on Rahe's Paradise when you are ready,' directed Gabriel firmly. This was not the first time that he had ordered the destruction of a planet, but perhaps that was why it felt like such a weight of responsibility. 'We can no longer leave it intact – its labyrinthine structure is riddled with slumbering necron. It must be destroyed.'

'But captain…' Saulh's voice faded out, as though he wasn't quite sure what to say. 'Captain Angelos, what evidence do we have of contamination on such a scale? We cannot just exterminate entire planets, Gabriel.'

Gabriel sighed, looking out through another view screen at the tumbling, curdling space battle developing outside. 'There is evidence enough, sergeant. And I myself am certain. The responsibility is mine,' he said. Just as is was on Cyrene, he added in his mind. 'And you are quite wrong, Saulh. We can exterminate entire planets. It is the righteous wrath of the Emperor himself that we bring to bear against Rahe's Paradise – and it is in his honour that we must do what we were pledged to do many millennia ago.'

'As you say, captain,' replied Saulh, not convinced but duty-bound to obey. 'It will be done.'

'You are sure about this, Gabriel?' asked Jonas, standing at his captain's shoulder. 'The eldar witch is not to be trusted.'

'Can you doubt your own eyes, Jonas? Look out there! I am not doing this because Macha told me to, I am doing it because it is right! Look at the floods of Dirges. Even if we stop their reinforcements, the destruction of the planet will have been justified.'

Gabriel clicked the main view screen back to the scene of battle and watched the necron cruiser accelerating off towards the sun with the two eldar cruisers in pursuit. 'We must assist her,' he said. 'Loren – take us into the sun.'

THE SHROUD CRUISER closed on the star as hostile fire rained onto it from its eldar hunters. It was beginning to suffer under the onslaught and it started to rotate to face them. Even as he watched, Uldreth could see dark sunspots appearing on the red star behind the Shroud and thin solar flares lashing out from its burning surface like massive storms. He knew what was coming.

The sunspots grew and darkened as the solar flares lengthened and strengthened, reaching out towards the Shroud as it pitched up vertically in front of the star. Then in an incredible burst of power, a searing flare exploded out from the sun striking the central pyramidal structure on the Shroud, from where it was refracted into a constellation of beams that flashed through the other pyramid-prisms on its hull, lighting the vessel like a brilliant, geometric star of its own. Then, the beams reconverged on the central pyramid and combined into a single bolt, lashing out at the *Eternal Star* as a blinding lightning-arc.

The wraithship quaked under the impact, spiralling backwards, out of control.

No! yelled Uldreth into the warp, watching Macha's cruiser tumbling uncontrollably through space.

Just as he screamed, his own vessel returned fire, throwing everything it had into the side of the Shroud.

At the same time, a flood of fire lashed into the Yngir cruiser from another side, and Uldreth snatched his head around to see the roaring engines of a Blood Ravens strike cruiser blasting into the blind side of the Shroud, throwing las-fire and torpedoes at the nearly impregnable hull. It was also firing some kind of bombardment cannon that was probably designed for planetary assaults, but its shells were punching into the armoured plates of the Shroud and detonating inside.

In a matter of seconds, part of the central pyramid on the Yngir cruiser exploded and cracked off, sending the concentrated beams of solar power crackling for uncontrolled targets. The lightning arcs lashed out into space, striking the *Avenging Sword* with a wild and crackling whip of power, but then turning back on themselves and engulfing the Shroud itself.

The vessel convulsed and shook, throbbing with an overload of power, and then detonated right in its core. The silvery black Shroud Cruiser erupted into flames of darkness and then blew apart, sending lethal shards and shadows hurtling out through the system. For a moment, silhouetted against the dying sun, where the Shroud had once been, there was the shimmering figure of a glorious humanoid – like a star god caught in his own inferno. And then it was gone.

THE LAST OF the Dirge Raiders spiralled down into the atmosphere of Rahe's Paradise, flames pouring from its engine vents and armoured plates free falling from its hull. Beneath its fall, the planet's surface was vaguely visible beneath the clouds of toxic smoke and viral contagions that roiled around in the atmosphere. The Exterminatus arrays had caused all of the volcanoes around the equator to erupt at once, spilling the planet's core out onto its surface and effectively turning the entire world inside out. For good measure, the epic bombardment had continued, throwing viral and bacterial agents down into the mix to ensure that nothing could survive, even if it could swim in molten rock and breath sulphur. In a matter of minutes, the atmosphere had been completely eaten away and then, in less than an hour, the planet's structural integrity collapsed and it simply fell apart, scattering itself into asteroids and meteorites.

Gabriel watched the planet die with confidence. This time he knew that he had done the right thing. It would, in any case, be only a matter of days before the local star would collapse in on itself and turn supernova. The necron lord had destabilised it enough, even in that short period of exposure. Emperor only knows what harm it could have done had it escaped the system.

Clicking the view screen, Gabriel watched the speeding form of the eldar Ghost Dragon flash after the tumbling wraithship. It had departed without a word only an instant after Gabriel had destroyed the necron cruiser. Not a single word, and certainly no thanks.

THE *Litany of Fury* lurched out of the warp on the edge of the Lorn system, and its corridors fell into sudden silence. Ulantus punched the release on the great doors of the Implantation Chamber and stepped inside, letting gusts of noxious gases flood out into the pristine, brightly lit passageway outside.

Laying on the ceremonial tablet in the middle of the chamber, with the apothecary fussing around him with dull, dirty surgical instruments, struggled the scarred and horrified figure of Ckrius. He had survived the warp jump, it seemed. Walking around to the side of the adamantium table, Ulantus saw that the boy's head had been cut open from ear to ear in order to expose the upper half of his brain.

The apothecary bowed slightly to the captain as he lay the flat, circular sus-an membrane into the neophyte's skull, and Ulantus smiled at the irony. In a few years time, that membrane would enable Ckrius to drop into a state of suspended animation in the event of extreme physical trauma. It was the same technology as was used in stasis sarcophagi for

Marines irredeemably injured in the course of duty –
they could be kept alive almost indefinitely, until a
dreadnought shell became available and they could
be transplanted into a new, entirely mechanical
body. For a moment, Ulantus wondered whether
Ckrius might enjoy the irony of the trauma he was
experiencing in order to enable him to survive even
more trauma later on.

'Captain, we are entering the Lorn system now,'
reported Korinth, bowing as he entered the sacred
space of the Implantation Chamber. 'You are needed
on the command deck.'

'Of course,' replied Ulantus, nodding and following the librarian out.

As he walked onto the command deck, Captain
Ulantus cursed the Commander of the Watch once
again. There was no sign of the *Ravenous Spirit* any-
where the in system. Not even Saulh was there in the
Rage of Erudition. Gabriel had probably roped him in
to some kind of fanciful scheme on Rahe's Paradise.

But the system was far from empty. There was space
trash and debris drifting all over the outer reaches of
the system – sure signs that the foul green-skins had
passed this way – and the fifth planet was a veritable
blaze of activity. The Imperial Navy had vessels in
orbit, where they had already engaged the ork fleet.

'Captain Ulantus,' reported a serf on the command
deck. 'There are incoming vessels.'

'Show me,' snapped Ulantus, flicking the view
screen.

He watched the eldar fleet slip gracefully into real
space and then accelerate towards him. If Gabriel
had really wanted to confront the eldar, he should

have come to Lorn where he's needed, thought Ulantus bitterly, instead of running off to Rahe's Paradise on some fanciful errand. Not for the first time, Ulantus cursed the cavalier Commander of the Watch.

'Prepare for battle,' he said calmly. 'It seems that we must do battle with Gabriel's eldar after all,' he added quietly, although not quite to himself.

'IT WAS NOT a complete loss, captain,' said Tanthius, as Techmarine Ephraim tended to his damaged armour. 'We did come away with a number of very able aspirants. Caleb managed to save a group of six local warriors, including a young psyker called Varjak, whom Jonas feels will make a fine librarian one day.'

'That is just as well, old friend. Our visit to Rahe's Paradise was more expensive than I anticipated. We can afford no more losses on this scale. The Third Company is skating perilously close to the line,' replied Gabriel thoughtfully. The fact that Rahe's Paradise was the third recruitment planet in a row that had cost more Blood Ravens than it had recruited was not lost on him.

'We will survive,' said Tanthius evenly. 'It is to our credit that we fight to the brink of our own annihilation,' he added with pride. 'There are not many others who could claim the same.'

'No, there are not many – and that may well be the point, Tanthius,' said Gabriel, smiling weakly. 'Rest well, old friend,' he said, turning and walking out of the apothecarion.

Pushing open the great doors to the *Ravenous Spirit*'s chapel, Gabriel strode down the central aisle.

On the altar at the front was the ornate sarcophagus in which Chaplain Prathios had been laid to rest. This would be his place of honour until such as time as he was called again from his sleep.

'My old friend,' said Gabriel, kneeling before the altar to the Emperor but addressing his words to the entombed husk of Prathios. 'We need your guidance now, more than ever. Our numbers are diminishing, and yet I led our Company into this battle. Somehow I knew that it was waiting for us, and I brought us here...' he trailed off, not wanting to finish his thoughts.

Closing his eyes, Gabriel tried to let his mind relax. He tried to fill his soul with light. He waited for the first hints of the Astronomican once again, but there was nothing.

Gabriel. Gabriel, I know that you can hear me. We have little choice when the future is laid out in the past. But decisions are not always about casting into this pre-emptive future-space. Your decisions are your own, Gabriel, even if your choices can never be.

Gabriel's eyes snapped open. For a moment he had caught sight of Macha, sitting cross-legged in the darkness of a small circular chamber. Her dazzling emerald eyes were shaded behind long, elegant lashes, and her lips had been working silently – or perhaps forming words different from those that appeared in his head. So, she had survived the necron's lightning arc and the assault of Ptolemea. Despite himself, Gabriel was pleased by the thought.

Closing his eyes once again, a single silver voice struck a note in his head. It was high and majestic, glorious like a solo soprano, soaring and perfect. After a few seconds, a second voice joined it, even higher and more crisp. Then a third and a fourth, deepening the harmony into something profound and resonant, putting his soul at ease once again.

A great crash broke his reverie and Gabriel turned his head to see the silhouette of Corallis in the wide open doorway at the other end of the aisle. 'I am sorry to disturb you captain,' he bowed. 'But Captain Ulantus is insisting that we make haste for Lorn V immediately. It seems that he is under attack, captain.'

'Understood,' replied Gabriel, climbing to his feet and striding back towards Corallis. 'The orks?'

'No, captain. The eldar.'

ABOUT THE AUTHOR

C S Goto has published short fiction in
Inferno! and elsewhere. His previous
novels for the Black Library include the
Necromunda novel *Salvation* and the
Warhammer 40,000 epic *Dawn of War*.

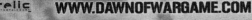